ᵀᴴᴱ BLACK MADONNA

BOOK THREE
THE MYSTIQUE TRILOGY

TRACI HARDING

HARPER
Voyager

Harper*Voyager*
An imprint of HarperCollins*Publishers*

First published in Australia in 2008
by HarperCollins*Publishers* Australia Pty Limited
ABN 36 009 913 517
harpercollins.com.au

HarperCollins*Publishers*
25 Ryde Road, Pymble, Sydney, NSW 2073, Australia
31 View Road, Glenfield, Auckland 0627, New Zealand
A 53, Sector 57, Noida, UP, India
77–85 Fulham Palace Road, London, W6 8JB, United Kingdom
2 Bloor Street East, 20th floor, Toronto, Ontario M4W 1A8, Canada
10 East 53rd Street, New York NY 10022, USA

National Library of Australia Cataloguing-in-Publication data:

Author: Harding, Traci.
Title: The black madonna / author, Traci Harding.
Publisher: Pymble, N.S.W. : HarperCollins, 2008.
ISBN: 978 0 7322 8114 4 (pbk.).
Series: Harding, Traci. Mystique trilogy 3.
Dewey Number: A823.3

Cover design by Jenny Grigg
Cover and author photograph by Montalbetti+Campbell
Hair and makeup by Zenga Butler
Photographed at Baltronic Studios, Artarmon, Australia
Typeset in Goudy 11/15pt by Helen Beard, ECJ Australia Pty Limited

To Chez,
Thanks for providing a sanctuary
for my well-being and creativity.
I could never have completed this trilogy
without you.

ACKNOWLEDGEMENTS

Those close to me know that, due to some life challenges over the past few years, this hasn't been an easy trilogy for me to write. But through it all I have had many shining stars that kept me going, and none have shone quite so brightly as my daughter, Sarah, who has been so very helpful at home with her little brother that I feel she really deserves to take out line honours in the 'thank you' stakes for this book. So thank you, Sarah, for being so very patient, loving and helpful, and for excelling at school and making me so proud of you in every aspect of our lives together. Thanks too to my husband, David, for giving me time away from my family duties to go away and finish this book. And thanks to you too, John, my lad, for *trying* to be good *most* of the time.

Cheryl Hesketh, whom most of my avid readers will know better as Chez, I had to dedicate this book to you as I would never have finished it — or the previous book, for that matter — without the retreat you provided me to write in. You are a rock, a legend and a true friend.

Speaking of true friends, thanks to Sue Moran for doing yet another rush edit over the Christmas and New Year period so I could make a deadline. As always, I am so very grateful for your time, input, encouragement and support.

My very sincere thanks to everyone at HarperCollins, especially Stephanie and Linda, who have been so very patient and supportive whilst I finished this epic trilogy. I thank my agent, Selwa, for her guidance and wisdom, and all my family and friends for putting up with my hectic life and working around it in order to see me.

To all my readers, thanks again for waiting a little longer for this one, but the wait is over now, so ... ENJOY!

CONTENTS

LIST OF CHARACTERS

The Staff of Amenti
DEXTER aka Taylor
VESPERA aka Ajalae Koriche
ARCTURUS aka Albray Devere
MERIDAN aka Mia Devere (Montrose)
POLARIS aka Captain Sinclair; Earnest Devere
SOLARIAN aka Ashlee Granville-Devere
LEVI aka Levi Granville-Devere
THANA aka Lillet du Lac
CASTOR aka King Arthur; James Devere
TALORI aka Susan Devere
ZALMAN aka Akbar
DENERA aka Lillith; Lady Charlotte Cavandish
KALI aka Tamar Devere
MATHU aka Thoth; Hermes

The Nefilim
ILL aka Enlil — Lord of the Nefilim
ERRAGAL aka Jeb Savage — Lord of the Underworld
NAMTAR aka Morell Labontè — Viceroy of the Underworld
ERESHKIGAL aka Co-co Yamamoto — Queen of the Underworld
ISHTAR aka Sabine Labontè — Goddess of Desire
ISHKUR aka 'Wildcat' Steve Marx — Storm God
The Smiter

The Anu
Lugh Lamhfada
Ki aka En Ki, the Sanat Kumara
Sud aka Ninlil

The Dracon
Taejax
Pax
Jinx
Rattus
Ruffinnic
Jezabel
Angelica

Site Crew — Montségur
André Pierre, site chief
Dr Colin Rich, project anthropologist
Emmett Rich, Dr Rich's son
Killian Labontè, project benefactor

The Guardians of the Seven Gates of Hell
Shock
Denial
Anger
Unfinished Business
Depression
Acceptance
Death

Additional Character
Sharon, Killian's assistant

A NOTE FROM THE AUTHOR, MIA MONTROSE

Time has no meaning for me any more. I have been backwards and forwards through history so often that past and future have melded into an all-consuming now.

The time lines of the physical world are precarious and liable to change at the slightest provocation. We, the staff of Amenti — designers of Earth's evolutionary scheme — knew this before we agreed to take part in the Amenti Project. What we did not anticipate was this: that our antagonists here on Earth would devise their own means to move through time and alter history.

Hence, the staff of Amenti have become humanity's mercenaries in the resulting inter-time war. Ancient time zones, and those in the distant future, are no longer accessible to us or to our adversaries, as time is collapsing from both the alpha and omega ends of its flimsy existence.

A crisis point will be reached at midnight on 21 December of this year, 2017 — the moment of judgement that psychics and prophets have been predicting for aeons. For the majority of people living on this planet, it will pass unnoticed. It will not be marked by fire and brimstone falling from the sky, or plagues, or the hand of God crushing us all from on high — all that will come, but later.

That crisis point moment is humanity's last chance to open the gateway home to the multi-dimensional universe from whence we originally came and were so unfairly torn. The fate of all rests upon the vibrational frequency of humanity's combined consciousness at this time and, despite our ignorance, we will be judged.

Our Earth is dying. It is being murdered by the hidden enemies of humanity who hope to enslave us. All they have to do is keep us preoccupied, greedy and self-obsessed until the current Stellar Activation Cycle ends. This Stellar Activation Cycle (SAC), which began on 21 December 2012 — the end of the Mayan calendar — is when Earth aligns with its higher planetary bodies in the harmonic universes and the stargates to these universes open. It is an ascension event that only happens for five years in every twenty-five thousand. If we do not succeed in opening the Halls of Amenti then, our last chance to escape this dying planet will be lost. All life on Earth — including those of us who volunteered to be guardians of this project — shall perish.

With only eight months remaining, the staff of Amenti have several concerns, but none so pressing as the full reactivation of all twelve stations in the Earth's Signet Grid. It is hoped that the combined energy and inspiration of the fully functional Signet Grid will be enough to raise the planetary consciousness of the Earth to a level where it might again host the Sphere of Amenti.

All but one of the fourteen soul minds of Amenti's staff are now fully aware and have taken up their positions on the Amenti Project. Naturally the disappearance of one of our staff members, Mathu, is another grave concern. For without all fourteen members of our team there shall be no going home for any of us.

The thirteen souls with whom I share my destiny — Polaris and Solarian, Talori and Castor, Vespera and Dexter, Levi and Thana, Denera and Zalman, Kali and Mathu, and my partner, Arcturus — have been my dearest friends, my family, my lovers and children throughout every major incarnation I have endured in Earth's evolutionary scheme.

It is no accident that I am the sixth and last of the Dragon Queens to have been born, or that it has fallen to me to compile and record our secret history. For I am the key-holder to Signet Station Twelve, named Triogenes, which resonates with the frequency of 'the storyteller'.

Due to the constant time-hopping activities of my fellow Amenti members and myself, it will be near impossible to form a straight time line of events. But I shall endeavour to do so with a little help from my daughter, Tamar, now better known to the staff of Amenti as Kali, and my sisters: Solarian, the once prolific Ashlee Granville-Devere; and Talori, who has also contributed to our family histories in her lifetime as Lady Susan Devere.

Since taking up my position on the staff of Amenti, I have been telepathically linked to the other six females on the staff, known in legend as the Dragon Queens. And so it is that my Dragon sisters can lend to me their perspective of events so that I may set pen to paper again to record this final chapter in the history of the Grail bloodline.

PART 1

THE ABSENT PRINCE

CHAPTER 1

TRIOGENES —
MONTSÉGUR

In cycles the legends come forth,
each with its own cast of characters,
incorporated into a work without beginning or end,
but forever perpetuating new stories.

In myth, they are the keys to the creation process,
to the great mysteries of creation and humanity.
Imagination flows from the Triogenes,
not bound by space or time,
to be entered as desired
by any soul mind with the patience to listen
to the flow of creation.

For in truth,
all is myth,
myth is all.

I was lost in contemplation out the window of the private aircraft that was carrying me towards my Signet station at Montségur.

It felt rather surreal to be embarking on my first official mission as an Amenti staff member, along with my husband, Albray — Amenti code name Arcturus — and our thirteen-year-old daughter, Tamar. Our task was to secure and open my Signet station, for an archaeological excavation had broken through to its outer labyrinth and, although there was no chance of anyone finding the station hidden within, we did not wish to attract any attention to the area. It was our job to keep any discoveries made beneath Montségur under wraps.

As fate would have it, the head excavator at Montségur, André Pierre, was an old friend and admirer of my translation skills of ancient languages. So when the project leaders broke through to the labyrinth and discovered ancient text therein, their first call was to me, to assist with translation. The excavation project had found symbols associated with the Knights Templar, side by side with well-known emblems of the Cathars — much like those found nearby in the grottoes of Sabarthez. Hence my husband had also been invited to join the excavation project due to his expertise on the period that had seen the demise of the Cathars. Of course, the fact that Albray had actually been there to witness the burning fields of Montségur in the thirteenth century had a bit to do with his knowledge.

Dangerous circumstances lay ahead of us, hardly the kind of situation that most parents would choose to lead their teenage daughter into — but then Tamar was no ordinary teenager.

On Tamar's thirteenth birthday, her biological clock triggered the integration of her consciousness with the advanced extraterrestrial soul mind of the

Anunnaki Queen Kali, who had been lying dormant in our daughter's non-coding DNA since her conception. In less than a week Tamar developed into a mature woman, more beautiful, more intelligent and infinitely more powerful than any other being on Earth.

This would have been truly horrifying for me to witness had a prophetess not given me prior warning of the event, and still I was finding the adjustment far more difficult than my daughter was. The part of me that was Mia Devere, Tamar's human biological mother, was compelled to question, challenge and teach her. The part of me that was my higher self, Meridan, mistrusted the Anunnaki race, of which Kali was queen, for their offences against humanity both in this universal dimension and the next.

Few traces of my little girl were still apparent in the woman I now saw when I looked at Tamar. Her long, straight, near-black hair she had inherited from her father, but her once brown eyes had now turned a deep shade of violet and her skin was darker, more akin to the Anunnaki. Her tall, slender form made her appear a little fragile, and her outer beauty stopped traffic, yet she had the psychic power and physical capability to destroy the most hardened and skilled warriors.

Our fellow staff members suspected that the Montségur project was being secretly backed by our foe, the Nefilim, or their Illuminati operatives, and Tamar's purpose on this mission was to sniff out any Nefilim involvement. Albray and I had been given very strict instructions to give her a free rein; despite any parental instinct we might feel, we were not to question her methods.

I was a little perturbed about the black mini-dress and high heels Tamar had decided to wear today — André Pierre was a renowned womaniser, and the outfit made her look as if she'd just stepped off a catwalk in Milan. When I mentioned this, Tamar only grinned.

'All the easier for me to siphon information from him. The majority of human males are easily manipulated by their desires, and this is doubly true of Nefilim males,' she said.

'Am I supposed to find that reassuring?' Albray lowered his paper to have a quiet word. 'This body is my daughter's temple, so do try to be a little selective about who worships it. Please, Kali,' he added, realising that she was no longer bound to listen to him or follow his advice.

'As there is only one being in this entire evolutionary scheme that I hold the slightest desire for, you need have no fear on that count,' Tamar assured him. 'You must trust that I know what I'm doing. No one knows the Nefilim like I do.'

I sensed my husband felt a little silly at having pulled her up.

'In that case ... go get 'em, sweetheart,' he said. 'Let me know if you need a hand at any time.'

'I will,' she promised, with a huge adoring smile, and Albray returned to his reading and I turned my gaze back out the window to the runway below.

André Pierre met us at Toulouse airport in the project chopper. He was the best excavation manager in the business — if he couldn't unearth an archaeological find intact, then no one could.

My French friend removed his sunglasses when he saw my daughter coming. 'Who is this beauty?'

he said with a smile, then recognised Tamar and burst out laughing. 'Tamar! Could it have been so long? I thought you were still a ...' he searched for the word, 'adolescent. You look *fantastique*!'

He kissed both her cheeks and held her closer than usual.

'Just celebrated her thirteenth birthday a couple of weeks ago,' my husband informed him, and the embrace abruptly ended.

'How cruel life is.' André turned down the charm a little, but desire was in his eyes. He greeted Albray briefly before turning his attention my way.

'Mia, my goddess, you look beyond *fantastique*.' He held both my shoulders, kissed each of my cheeks in turn and then held me at arm's length to admire my form. 'I swear you look younger every time I see you.'

I was perpetually thirty since I had walked the Halls of Amenti thirteen years ago; thus I appeared barely older than my rapidly maturing daughter.

'And you are more in need of a wife every time I see you, *mon ami*.' I held André's face between my hands and shook it. 'You look a mess.'

I was referring to his unshaven, unkempt appearance. Tamar and Albray had a quiet chuckle at how quickly I'd brought André's amorous advances under control.

'I've been down a hole for weeks,' he said defensively, backing away. He ran one hand over his unpressed clothes, and with the other combed his shoulder-length, unwashed, mousy-brown hair behind his ears.

'You're not eating properly either.' My mothering tone served to remind the Frenchman that I was married with a child, whilst assuring him that I did still care about his welfare.

'I've been busy.' He smiled. 'You know how it is. I get distracted.'

'It must be exciting for you to be working in France for a change.' I began fishing for information as we waited for our baggage to be loaded on board the chopper by the ground crew. 'Is the project funded by the French as well?'

'This project was the brainchild of a man by the name of Labontè,' André said. 'You may have heard of —'

'The mining and media magnate Morell Labontè?' I queried. I'd never heard anything about the wealthy tycoon's interest in archaeology; goldmining was what he was known for.

'No,' André corrected, 'his son, Killian —'

'The thrill-seeking, socialite playboy?' Tamar butted in, having read about Killian Labontè's exploits in teen mags.

'*En effet*,' André confirmed. 'He has a very keen interest in the occult and in the Holy Grail in particular.'

'He's following Otto Rahn's theory that the Grail was hidden beneath Montségur by the Cathars,' I guessed, and glanced at Albray. He looked amused, for he had been the knight who had helped in sneaking Montségur's sacred treasures from the mount.

'The Grail itself may not be hidden beneath the mount of Montségur,' André said, 'but it is certainly an area where the Grail legends converge and our employer is paying us to discover why.'

'Hey, if there's a good pay cheque in it ...' My husband shrugged, playing up his scepticism.

'Labontè's hunches have proven excellent so far,' André said, suggesting we not pass judgement until we had seen the find for ourselves.

The excavation site was rather larger than I had expected. Labontè's team had unearthed the remains of a thirteenth-century village at the base of the mountain and re-opened a secret cave, the entrance to which had collapsed centuries ago.

'The cave contains a passage leading up inside the mountain. We suspect it was used by the Cathars to get supplies into their besieged fortress and their treasures out,' André told us as we flew around the mount, past the tunnel excavation and towards the remains of the medieval village, alongside which the site house and helipad were located.

'I suspect you may be right,' Albray agreed, with a knowing grin in my direction.

'Is that the hole you've been working in?' Tamar referred to the newly exposed cave.

'Ah, no ...' André was amused. 'We have discovered a much larger cavity to get lost in.'

The helipad was on high ground and gave an excellent view of the camp site and dig beyond.

'In the village we discovered an ancient labyrinth of tunnels, accessed via the basement of one of the previously buried structures,' André informed us as we descended the stairs towards the camp. 'We'll just drop off your bags and I'll take you straight down.'

The site comprised several large structures that accommodated a canteen, preservation rooms, a large office and an amenities block. There were smaller individual units that served as sleeping quarters. Tamar had been given her own living module next to ours.

'Are you coming, Tamar?' I asked as André set off towards the excavation.

'You go ahead.' She waved me on. 'I'm going to check out the camp facilities … maybe find some lunch?'

I knew the last thing on her mind was food.

'Be good,' I cautioned, then my husband and I followed André towards the dig that led to the unearthed labyrinth.

CHAPTER 2

KALI'S MISSION

TAMAR DEVERE — KALI

I did look a little out of place wandering through the camp dressed as I was, but apart from a few friendly hellos from passing males and some repressed smiles of envious approval from females, no one was confident enough to try and engage my attention for long. The kind of souls I was seeking would always be attracted to a thing of beauty and would never doubt their ability to acquire it for themselves.

'Are you lost?'

The accent was American. The query came from the site office and I turned to find a young fellow standing at the door. He struck me as the studious, intellectual type, no doubt due to the heavy dark-rimmed glasses he wore.

'Never,' I replied, heading over to introduce myself.

My psychic impression was of a good and helpful soul. His straight dark-blond hair was neatly trimmed and he was shorter than your average human male, but perhaps he would grow taller as he was still young. His youth was emphasised by his college-style shirt, trousers and sweater-vest.

'Do you need a jacket or something, Miss —'

'Tamar Devere.' I held out my slender, perfectly manicured hand.

He shook it very briefly, a little flustered by my attention. 'You're Mia Devere's little girl?' He was stunned, as he'd obviously been told how old I was.

'We mature fast in my family.'

I eased past him to enter the office, finding it all but deserted. 'And you are?'

'Emmett, Dr Rich's son,' he said. I was none the wiser so he explained further. 'Dr Colin Rich, the anthropologist who's project manager here.'

'Ah. Do you work for your father?'

'I work with him sometimes, yeah.' Emmett returned to his desk. 'I'm still a student, but I run the site office while Dad is down the hole.'

He took a seat, and became immediately engrossed in what he was reading on his computer. Either he was overwhelmed by my beauty and very shy, or he did not find me the slightest bit attractive.

'Are you gay?'

Emmett nearly choked on the drink he was slurping through a straw. 'What? No ... no.'

'How old are you?' My guess was around sixteen.

'Do you always ask such personal questions of perfect strangers?' he said indignantly.

'I was just wondering why you don't find me attractive.'

He looked back to his computer, which annoyed me. 'Legally, I'm not permitted to find you attractive for at least another three years.'

Since my merger with Kali, I was used to bowling people over, inspiring awe and desire. What could he be reading that was so all-absorbing? I strolled behind him to find out.

It was an article titled 'The Circles of Power Behind UFO Secrecy', written by the founder of CSETI — the Center for the Study of Extraterrestrial Intelligence.

'So you're a believer?' I said.

He jumped, clearly oblivious to the fact that I had moved. 'Absolutely,' he said, his eyes still pinned to the screen. 'I'm a regular A to Z directory on anything remotely relating to a cover-up.'

'Have you been abducted?' I asked directly.

'Not that I recall. I'm just a good researcher.' His tone implied I was being predictable. 'You're a sceptic, I take it?'

'Not at all. I know quite a bit about the Old World Order . . . or the New World Order as it's now known.' I'd finally secured his attention. 'Why so surprised?'

'Why am I surprised that a girl like you would spare a thought for conspiracy theories?' Emmett thought the answer was obvious. 'Hell, I'm surprised you even read!'

I took offence. 'Excuse me! I've just co-authored a book, so I write as well.'

'Good for you.' He seemed more interested in his article. 'What's your book about?'

'The Grail bloodline,' I said, and his attention shot back to me. 'It's just a fantasy story.'

Disappointed, he went back to his screen. 'Then you should have a lot in common with our sponsor, Mr La-bent . . . most of the time,' he said sarcastically. 'Otherwise known as "I have the money and can afford to have an eccentric interest in digging up half the country while chasing an ancient myth".'

Emmett's resentful humour amused me. 'You mean the myth that the Grail is buried beneath this mountain?'

He arrowed down the page on his screen. 'My personal opinion is that the Grail hunt is just a smokescreen for what La-bent is truly seeking down there.'

How interesting, I thought. 'And what might that be?'

He shook his head and chuckled quietly. 'I'm not going to tell you, in case what I heard is a fabrication and I look a fool for repeating it. But fear not, I'm sure he'll confide in you presently.'

'Really. Why?'

He laughed again. 'He is going to love you. Legal constraints have never been a major concern of the rich and shameless.'

A tall fellow came into the site office, his dark hair flowing in the breeze. He strode towards one of the private offices, engrossed in a conversation he was having on his remote headset.

'Speak of the devil,' said Emmett without looking up.

Killian Labontè was wearing a filthy pair of shredded jeans and a T-shirt so soiled its true colour was no longer determinable; it was difficult to recognise him from the celebrity pictures I'd seen of him. He sounded American rather than French, but I'd read that he'd spent most of his youth in the US and had been educated there.

'It speaks of the location of the lance,' he said, then frowned as he entered the largest of the offices. 'Of course I'm fucking sure!' The door slammed closed.

'Lovely,' I commented, referring to Killian's

phone manner rather than his person. I looked at Emmett. 'What lance does he mean?'

'The all-powerful lance, staff, rod, sword that appears over and over again in Arthurian legends, and is supposedly the weapon that pierced the side of Christ at the crucifixion, yadda, yadda, blah, blah.' Emmett sounded terribly bored as he rattled off the theory.

'You think otherwise?'

'The lance, or rather, the rod of ancient myth, didn't make its first appearance at the crucifixion of Christ. Moses, the Levites and Solomon all had possession of the Rod and Ring of Power. It took an adept soul to wield either treasure, and they were creative tools more than implements of destruction. I believe that together the ring and rod might have formed a key.'

I smiled. Emmett was right on the money. 'A key to what?'

'No one knows.'

I knew. The rod and ring in question, when united by the Black Madonna, formed the key that would allow me and my missing prince to open the Halls of Amenti.

'Then what leads you to believe they form a key?' I asked.

He shrugged and shied away from answering. 'Whether they do or not, I'd still query how a mere Roman foot soldier came to possess one of the most powerful weapons on Earth, only to inflict harm upon one of Earth's most adept souls with it.'

I mulled over his theory. 'Perhaps the foot soldier was in league with Christ, and used the weapon to secretly heal and not harm him?'

Emmett was amused by the premise. 'I can see why you write fiction.' He returned to his computer.

'Fact can be stranger than fiction,' I teased, ignoring his insult.

Killian Labontè opened his office door and, ripping the phone set from his head, threw it onto his desk. 'Imbecile.' Then he spied me standing by Emmett's desk and his temper immediately dispersed.

'Killian Labontè.' He held his hand out and walked over to introduce himself.

This was exactly the kind of confidence I would expect from one of the Nefilim, yet oddly enough his light-body appeared perfectly normal. There were a few muddy patches in his aura and light centres, but he had no major hang-ups and was very self-confident for a human of his age — not really surprising considering his cushy upbringing. Killian Labontè came off as a kind of happy-go-lucky rebel in the tabloids; they couldn't get enough of him. His intense blue eyes, handsome features and good physique did make him rather easy on the eye.

'Tamar Devere.' I held out my hand and Killian held it fast in his as he became fixated by my eyes.

'I've never seen violet eyes before ...' His attention shifted downward. 'Or legs that long.'

It was clear that Killian, like me, was used to inspiring awe in the opposite sex. Such an admiring gaze from the heir to a multi-billion-dollar fortune might have made some women feel uncomfortable and nervous, but I was confident.

'And all in one neat package,' I said flirtatiously.

'Indeed.' Killian raised my hand, intending to kiss it, but was interrupted by Emmett crushing his drink can and tossing it into the empty metal bin.

Labontè closed his eyes briefly to suppress his annoyance, as Emmett got up and headed for the kitchenette, then resumed his friendly demeanour. 'I was just on my way to get changed for a function. A friend of mine is opening a nightclub. Would you care to accompany me?'

'Do you think I'll pass for eighteen?' I said. I had to let him know I was a minor.

'As long as you're with me, no one will ask any questions,' he said arrogantly. 'Unless, of course, you think your parents might object?'

'Not at all.' I smiled. 'They encourage me to get out and meet others.'

'It's a date then.' He slapped his hands together, pleased, then checked his watch. 'Meet you back here in half an hour?'

I nodded. 'That'll give me time to change into something more inappropriate.'

Labontè looked discomfited for a second, then smiled. 'I like you already.' And with a wave he was gone.

'Guess I'll be reading about you in the social pages tomorrow,' said Emmett when he returned from the kitchenette and saw me leaving.

I sensed a warning beneath the comment, which was rather sweet. 'Why read the news when you can be the news,' I replied flippantly.

Emmett shook his head, clearly taking me for a social climber, and I decided it was safer to perpetuate that illusion. As I headed back to my sleeping quarters to raid my luggage for a change of attire, I decided I rather liked Emmett Rich.

'Are you insane?' My mother was displeased by my decision to date her employer. 'Your father and I have gone to great lengths to keep you hidden from undesirables, and you decide to date the guy who's been hailed as the world's most eligible bachelor for three years running! The press go ballistic every time he glances sideways at a woman. You'll be world news by tomorrow morning!'

'Exactly,' I said, zipping up my pleated, checked mini-skirt. I reached for my little white shirt, pulled it on and tied it up around my midriff. 'I don't have time to chase up all the Nefilim. We need them to come to me. And they can only do that if they know where I am — not to mention Mathu.'

'Everyone *will* know where you are, that's the point!' Mother frowned as she watched me pull my long white socks up over my knees. 'You can't go out dressed like that. You look like a schoolgirl.' Nevertheless, she couldn't help grinning at my blatant cheek.

'I am a schoolgirl.' I was quite prepared to promote that little fantasy among my prospective enemies and admirers. I pulled on my chunky black platform shoes, and my slim-fit black mohair cardigan. 'The good news is that Killian isn't one of my fallen kin.'

'Yes, I realise that,' Mother said. 'So it would be best if we didn't attract any of the Nefilim to this particular area of the world right now.'

A vehicle pulling into the site camp drew our attention to the window — it was a long gold limousine. A handsome young chauffeur opened the rear door and Morell Labontè and his wife, Sabine, stepped into view. They each had an aura of sparkling gold and a light-body devoid of light centres. Physically, their true stature could be seen looming over the smaller human bodies they sported; they were Nefilim masquerading as humans.

'Too late.' I returned to view myself in the mirror. 'Should I put my hair in pigtails, do you think?' I grabbed my long, silky dark hair and pulled it into high bunches on either side of my head, then turned to my mother for an opinion.

She was horrified. 'Please don't do this.'

'I told you *not* to come here!' It was Killian, yelling abuse at his parents, which sent Mother and me racing back to the window. 'This business venture has nothing to do with you!'

'You can only call an enterprise a business venture if you expect it to make money,' Morell scoffed. 'If you simply want to drill holes in the ground, I'll give you an oil well.'

'This has nothing to do with the money,' Sabine cut in. 'You'll get yourself killed crawling around underground. Please forget this foolishness and come home.' She moved to hug her son, but he backed away.

'We wouldn't want to damage this perfect specimen you've grown,' Killian said harshly. 'You're not my parents.'

'Your blood is thicker than that skull of yours, boy,' Morell hissed before returning to the car. 'You will assume your rightful place in society one way or another.'

'Leave! Or I'll have you arrested for trespassing.' Killian stormed off, leaving his parents loitering or lingering around their luxury car.

'Curious,' I commented. 'If the Nefilim know, or even suspect, there's a Signet station buried beneath Montségur, then why would they want Killian to stop working here? Even if he's not an ally, he's still doing their dirty work for them. So either the Nefilim don't know about the Signet station or, for reasons unknown, they don't want Killian to find it.'

'Do you think Killian's adopted?' My mother was wondering how Killian's parents could be Nefilim when he clearly wasn't.

'The Nefilim ceased to wear their true physical forms aeons ago, as they grew too hideous from their addictions,' I explained. 'Instead, they murder and then assume the forms of human beings who have fallen by the wayside — those seduced by power, money, and who have a complete disregard for their fellow man. It's easier for the emotionless Nefilim to assume the lives of such people.'

My mother recalled the practice from her readings of the journals of our foremother, Ashlee Granville-Devere. 'Those of the blood can be vessels for angels or demons,' she said.

'They suck the life from the human vessel they desire, then don its identity like a brand-new suit of clothes. And guess who their next conquest is going to be?'

Mother looked shocked when she realised I was talking about her boss.

'Although if Killian is indeed of the blood, he could just as easily be a vessel for Mathu as one of the Nefilim,' I added, and my heart skipped a beat at the possibility. I took a deep breath to dispel the rush of joy and gathered my wits. 'I should go.'

'But what shall we do about them?' My mother pointed out the window at the two impostors posing as Killian's parents.

'They must be left at liberty,' I instructed. 'They will lead us to others of their kind.'

'You be careful,' Mother said awkwardly — out of habit.

I reached into my luggage and pulled out a tiny handgun. 'You know how cautious I am.'

'Where did you get that?' Mia was shocked and then enchanted by the tiny gun with its clear chamber filled with liquid light.

'It's something Levi has been developing,' I replied.

Levi was the Council of Amenti's key technologist, along with his partner, Thana.

'Is it safe?' Mother asked, concerned about me wielding experimental weaponry.

'It's completely harmless … to the uncorrupt.'

I tucked the tiny weapon into the top of my skirt at the back, where it was covered by my cardigan. Mia looked as if she was in pain.

'Don't worry,' I told her. 'Focus on *your* mission.' I kissed her forehead and left.

Outside I ran into my father, and kissed him on the cheek too. 'Later, Dad,' I said, and strode off before he started a re-run of my mother's protests.

'You're not letting her go out looking like that?' I heard him protest to my mother.

I didn't look back, just walked on to my date with notoriety.

CHAPTER 3

SOUL TRADE

As I passed the gold limousine, I saw that Morell Labontè had retired to the back seat and was absorbed in a video conference call. There was no sign of Sabine. I continued to the site office, where I'd arranged to meet my date, but it appeared empty. I sensed, however, that I wasn't alone and so moved stealthily across the communal workspace towards the private offices on the other side of the room. The sound of whispering drew my attention to the kitchenette at the back of the common room. I turned away from the private offices and crept towards my target, but as I passed the doorway to Killian's office I was grabbed around the waist and mouth and pulled inside. I broke free and turned to defend myself — my open-handed strike stopping only centimetres from Emmett Rich's Adam's apple.

He swallowed, bewildered by my strength and speed, then raised a finger to his lips to indicate the need for silence. He pointed to the wall in Killian's office that backed onto the kitchenette. There was a rather large hole in it, and I moved at once to investigate.

Sabine Labontè was in the kitchenette, speaking very intimately with André.

'Are you sure it's authentic?' she asked.

'I retrieved it from the chasm myself,' he replied. 'Did you bring what I require in exchange?'

She pulled from between her breasts a vial filled with sparkling particles and I stifled a gasp.

'What is it?' Emmett whispered, put out by my taking over his investigation.

I shook my head and refused to give up my vantage point.

'Molier is gone, but your addiction can live on … for quite some time,' Sabine teased the Frenchman.

Christian Molier had been André's employer on the Sinai excavation at Mount Serabit, where my parents had first got together. Molier was an abomination of nature due to his addiction to Star-Fire — the potions of the gods that gave its users immortality. Star-Fire had already damned the souls of all the Nefilim and it transformed Molier and his followers into creatures of the night, not unlike the vampires of myth.

André grabbed for the vial but Sabine kept it from him.

'The stone,' she said, and held out her hand.

André placed a velvet case in her palm. She opened the case to check the item. I couldn't see the contents, but she smiled and handed André the vial of Star-Fire. André looked relieved to have the vial in his possession, so much so that he didn't seem to mind that Sabine Labontè's seductive manner ceased as soon as she had what she desired.

'Have a lovely, long, young life,' she said with a smile, knowing that André's addiction to youth and all things material would damn his soul for all time.

The more humans with Star-Fire addiction the better as far as the Nefilim were concerned.

I looked at Emmett as Sabine left the kitchenette and held a finger to my lips. We were both silent until she had departed the site office; then I went to speak with André, despite Emmett's whispered protest. I had no time to waste on being discreet.

'*Bonsoir*,' I said, startling André, who instantly shoved the vial he was admiring into his pocket.

'Tamar? Wow!' His lustful eyes scanned my outfit. 'I was just thinking about you.'

I walked straight up to him and gripped his head between my hands. 'What did you give her?' I stared into his eyes ablaze with desire which spiralled into fear as he was overpowered by me.

'Who?' he said, denying all knowledge of what I was talking about, but I could see into his thoughts and they showed me my father's ringstone.

Although I called the ringstone my father's, it never actually belonged to him. It was a stone that took the form of a ring due to the hole at its centre, and such a stone was essential for the casting of an ancient Wiccan spell. During the incantation Ashlee Granville-Devere had called upon the spirit of my father, who agreed to attach his soul mind to the stone so that he might counsel and aid Ashlee during the course of her investigations in the Near East. Many centuries later my mother found the ringstone, and it was through this old family heirloom that she first met my father and helped free him from his curse. The ringstone had been stolen by Molier and cast off a very high cliff in the Sinai, around the time I'd been conceived. Whether my father's soul mind was still in any way connected to the ringstone was a mystery, and one I didn't want unravelled by the Nefilim.

'That was my mother's!' I said, and slapped André's face for the betrayal. He seemed to enjoy it for he smiled. I grabbed the vial from inside his pocket and, as he desperately tried to retrieve it, I knocked him to the ground.

'You idiot!' I said, checking the substance to confirm my earlier assumption. It was Orme all right. 'Time to rejoin the human race, *mon ami.*'

I pulled out my weapon and fired at him. I heard Emmett cry out in the next room as a liquid-light bullet embedded itself in André's body.

'Holy shit, Tamar!' Emmett rushed into the kitchen to find André having a fit on the floor. 'What the hell did you shoot him with?'

'Pure love,' I replied, concealing my weapon again, then racing past Emmett to the door. I hoped to prevent Sabine Labontè leaving with the ringstone. 'He's just finding it a little hard to process.'

The limousine was halfway up the valley road by the time I made it outside. I cursed and went back inside to see how André was faring. He was dry-retching and cursing in French, as black muck oozed from his mouth, nose and ears.

Emmett was speechless as he struggled to process what had just happened. He looked at me and backed up a few paces. 'You're some kind of alien, aren't you?'

'Aren't all thirteen-year-old girls just like me?' I batted my eyelashes at him.

'Of course, I should have known by the stature.' He observed my height with trepidation and awe. 'You're one of the Nefilim.'

'I am Anunnaki,' I barked. 'Big difference.'

The intensity of André's convulsions increased.

'We should call an ambulance,' Emmett said.

'He'll be fine.'

I moved to the sink and dampened a tea-towel. André was running out of fight; exhausted from his purge, he stopped struggling and relaxed as I crouched down beside him and wiped all the black muck from his face. He smiled at me. '*Un ange.*'

I nodded and placed the tip of my index finger on his third eye. His eyes closed in rapture and he grinned intently until I withdrew my contact, whereby all expression dropped from his face. When he opened his eyes once more, he was disorientated.

'What happened?' He clambered up from the pool of black slime he was lying in, repulsed by the smell.

'You were sick,' I told him, and winked at Emmett who was watching the situation with great interest and amazement.

'Sick!' echoed André, observing the black bile all over his clothes. 'What the hell have I been eating?'

'How do you feel now?' I asked.

He ceased being revolted long enough to consider this. 'Why, I feel ... *fantastique!*' he cried, throwing his arms wide, then wincing. 'On the inside.'

The Orme he had ingested had extended his youth somewhat, but time had caught up with him now. The spiritual cleansing inflicted upon him by the liquid-light pellet had returned him to his true age and physique. He was clearly surprised by how his limbs ached, for he had no memory of his previous addiction.

'I should go take a shower,' he said, moaning as he stretched his sore body. 'Emmett, could you —'

'I'll clean up,' Emmett cut in, pre-empting André's request.

André smiled. 'You're a good lad,' he said, and wandered towards the door in a daze. 'Remind me to give you a raise,' he added.

'I will,' Emmett assured him, suppressing his shock. André was usually a miser with funding.

When we were alone, Emmett looked at me in wonder. 'That was *really* amazing.'

I folded my arms and tapped my fingers. 'What to do about you?' I thought aloud.

'Please don't do the finger thing on me,' he pleaded, obviously realising I had tampered with André's memory of events. 'I can help you.'

'I don't need help,' I said. 'It's safer for you if you're ignorant.'

Emmett didn't bother trying to escape — he knew resistance was futile. His adoring gaze touched my frosty heart with its sincerity; it wasn't how I looked that attracted his admiration, but who I was.

'Well,' he said as I came closer, resigned to his fate, 'it was nice meeting you.' Then he delayed my finger gently. 'Wait. Who are you really?'

He was going to forget in a moment anyway so I decided to indulge his wish. I whispered my true name in his ear. As he gasped in astonishment, I pressed my finger on his brow and willed him to forget.

Emmett opened his eyes and looked completely bemused. 'What the . . .?' He observed the mess on the floor.

'Looking at it won't get it cleaned up,' I said.

'Pardon?' He looked at me, puzzled.

'You promised André, remember?' I prompted. 'He's going to give you a raise.'

31

Emmett did have a vague memory of this and nodded. 'It had better be a big raise,' he said, considering the task ahead with disdain.

'Later,' I said, and headed back through the common room. I wanted to find my parents and tell them about the sale of the ringstone, but as I reached the door, Killian Labontè entered.

'Wow!' He looked me up and down and laughed. 'Are you trying to get me arrested?'

'From what I've read, you don't need any help with that,' I said, and moved past him.

'Very true,' he conceded. 'Shall we go?'

'I just need to see my mother for a second —'

'Your parents are down the hole,' he said, sounding a little put out at the delay. 'Why don't you call them on the mobile in my car?'

He led me towards a brand-new Porsche Sportec Turbo in gunmetal grey.

I shook my head. 'It'll keep.' I had my own means of getting my message across to my mother that didn't involve sharing our private affairs on the open airwaves.

The conversation en route to the club in Bordeaux was a little stilted at first. Killian was all riled up about his parents arriving on site unannounced, and was struggling to suppress his anger so as not to bore me with it. He spoke of his wish to be anybody but who he was, and of his utter disdain for his family.

'Your life appears charmed to me,' I said, wanting him to reveal what was so detestable about his parents. Could it be that he knew what they truly were?

'Looks can be deceiving.'

I tried a more leading question. 'Have your parents abused you in some way?'

'No,' he said, glancing at me and then back to the road. 'But they intend to.'

'How do you know that?' Was he aware that he was destined to share the same fate as his parents — was this the pending abuse he referred to?

He grinned at the question. 'No offence, but I don't know you well enough … I'd hate to scare you off.'

'I don't scare as easily as you might imagine,' I said, but he shook his head and remained silent.

'So many mysteries,' I teased, letting him know how intrigued I was.

'Not so many really.'

'Well,' I said, grinning in challenge, 'if you won't confide in me about your private life, perhaps you'll tell me what you expect to find beneath Montségur?'

'I expect to find some answers,' he said, then, seeing I wasn't satisfied, he added, 'to an old family mystery.'

'The Grail family?'

He looked startled by my frankness.

'I just co-wrote a novel on the subject,' I said, easing his suspicion.

'Then you know about the Rod of Power?'

I nodded. 'But I don't think it was ever kept here for any length of time.'

'Ah,' he said, 'but the rod is somehow connected to our mount. There are depictions of it in the labyrinth we've unearthed.'

'But the Grail family have many amazing treasures connected to their legend — what fascinates you about the Rod of Power in particular?'

'It has the power to defy the gods,' he stated.

Perhaps he intended to use the staff to protect himself from his formidable parents? 'You plan to defy the gods, do you?' I asked.

'Only if provoked.' He downplayed his conviction, but beneath the flippant comment I sensed a great severity.

'I want to be on your team then,' I said with an equal amount of humour and assurance.

He gave a half-laugh, amused. 'Not even I want to be on my team. But I'll be thankful for any support you may want to give.'

The paparazzi went into a frenzy when we arrived at the nightclub. We hit the red carpet that led straight inside — as opposed to the other entrance, where hopeful patrons were lined up for miles. When the press asked who I was, Killian replied, 'Isn't it obvious? Tamar is the most beautiful woman on Earth.'

I could already see the headlines in the papers the following morning. My mother would be livid.

'Are you dating?' several reporters were quick to ask.

'We're business associates,' Killian teased them, then escorted me inside, leaving a barrage of questions in our wake.

I turned back to the press and made a peace sign. 'Keep it green,' I said, one of Killian's signature sayings.

It delighted him. 'I didn't think you knew that much about me.'

'I'd have to be from *another planet* not to know about you,' I chided and he forced a laugh.

'Do you believe in other planets, in the existence

of extraterrestrials?' he asked, trying not to sound as interested as he was.

I didn't reply, distracted by the prickly, uneasy feeling that crept over my body as we approached the bouncers at the front door. Their auras showed the telltale signs of Orme abuse, and beneath their human guise I spied Dracon.

The Anunnaki souls who had been on Tara at the time of the explosion had also been cast into this universe. As the Anunnaki were not human, they could not be allowed to evolve through the Amenti system as they would have caused a mutation in the human blueprint. It was hoped that the lost Anunnaki would incarnate into the Anu, who were already on Earth, but the devolution of this race into the Nefilim had made this impossible. Thus, with nowhere else to go, the lost Anunnaki incarnated into the Dracon, the race of lizard drones created by the Nefilim to mine the gold required to feed their Orme addictions. They were enslaved by the Nefilim for a long time, but eventually some suppressed soul minds within the lizard people began to become self-aware — and resentful of the Nefilim's favouritism for the human race. There was an uprising, the lizard warriors overpowered the Nefilim and killed every human they could lay their hands on. The Nefilim fled Earth for thousands of years, sure that as the Dracon were all male, the race would die off.

They did not die, however, and have thrived to this day, becoming one of the primary threats to the Amenti Project. Some of the Dracon formed alliances with the Nefilim, who have long since returned to Earth and re-established themselves in very high places in government, religion and society.

Others formed their own hunting packs and based themselves in third world countries, where large numbers of humans could vanish and never be missed. But others became enlightened to their dormant souls within and slowly began transforming back into Anu, physically, emotionally, mentally and spiritually.

Killian acknowledged the tall, muscular bouncers, who knew him by sight and cleared a path for us, no questions asked.

Inside the club my foreboding trebled. There were Orme-addicted Dracon in disguise everywhere! They all appeared beautiful on the outside — trim, tanned and highly fashionable — but on the inside they were hideous. How had my people become so lost?

'These are your friends?' I asked Killian, who was waving and blowing kisses at various people, human and Dracon alike.

'Just social acquaintances really,' he said. 'My friends will be upstairs, in the VIP area.'

'Of course,' I pretended to hit myself in the head, 'what was I thinking — you down here among the commoners?'

Tonight was an invitation-only event. There was an all-girl early-century revival band on stage, pumping out a song that had been written before I was born; and on the dance floor I recognised a heap of faces from the tabloids — a good number of whom were Dracon, or dating one.

Killian grinned. 'I warrant you'll be thankful to escape to the VIP area before long.' He cast his eyes around the club, having noted that every eye in the room, male and female, was on me. 'It seems I'm not your only admirer,' he whispered.

I smiled at his flattery, but on the inside I was concerned about the company Killian kept. Was he leading me up the garden path, or was he blissfully unaware that his social circle was filled with the same body-snatching beings that had taken over his parents?

I strode, head high, through the ranks of my fallen subjects, unafraid of a confrontation. They weren't sufficiently psychically adept to see through my luscious disguise to who I really was — their judge and redeemer.

At the side of the stage was a staircase guarded by more Dracon, who welcomed my date and me as if we were royalty.

'I want to introduce you to my band,' Killian shouted to me as we scaled the stairs. 'We might play tonight, if we get the urge.'

'Cool,' I replied over the din.

Killian and his band, Daddy's Bitch, didn't seem to take their music career very seriously, but because they were the famous progeny of the social elite they were a charting success worldwide. They never toured, but did surprise gigs, which they streamed to their fans over the net for free. I'd never really listened to their music as it was rather dark and heavy, but it looked as if that blissful oversight was about to be corrected.

The VIP lounge was sparsely populated and it was easy to spot the company Killian sought. The members of Daddy's Bitch and their sycophants were gathered around a lounge setting by the large Gothic fireplace, fiddling with their instruments, drinking and smoking dope. There were three others in the band that Killian fronted. The only female, Co-co Yamamoto, was the daughter of the

Japanese banking tycoon, Taro Yamamoto. Co-co played bass guitar but was more famous for beating unwanted reporters to a pulp, as she was a triple black belt in karate.

Jeb Savage, the lead guitarist, was the son of the American politician Bob Savage, who was set to run for the Republicans in the forthcoming American presidential election. Jeb and Killian had been best friends since junior high and had endured many public debacles together. Jeb and Co-co had been an item since the band formed three years before.

The drummer, Steve Marx, was nicknamed 'Wildcat' for two reasons. The first was that it described his general personality and behaviour to a T. The second reason was that, as the son of the English multimedia magnate James Marx, none of Wildcat's outrageous exploits ever made it into the tabloids or TV news. His father had a strong monopoly on and extensive influence over the European press, and thus the infamous drummer loved to emphasise the fact that, just like a wildcat, he was a protected species in Europe.

I stood back as Killian greeted his best friends warmly and they responded with an equal amount of enthusiasm. I knew the band members by sight — their faces were as familiar to the world as those of their powerful parents. But upon this personal viewing, I learned much more about them than the press ever had. Obviously Killian didn't realise that his close-knit group of rebellious rockers had already joined the ranks of the Nefilim and were his true friends no longer.

I needed to get the band alone if I wished to expose these impostors for who they were. My reasoning was, the faster I took Killian into my confidence, the faster I could discover how much he really knew. He was surrounded by his enemies, who would lead him straight to the same damning fate that had befallen them. And if, as I suspected, Mathu's soul mind was buried in Killian's psyche somewhere, I might lose my prince to the ranks of the fallen if I didn't take action soon.

'Rrraaaw,' purred Wildcat as he turned his attention to me. 'Who's the giant chicky-babe?' He approached me, confident that I'd be flattered by his interest. 'You've been window-shopping in Milan again, haven't you, Kill, my boy?' The big, brawny skinhead circled me, looking me up and down.

'Not at all,' Killian replied, assuring me in an aside that he never hunted for girlfriends on the catwalk — his friend was just trying to make him look bad. 'Tamar's the daughter of the linguist on my excavation project, and she's just co-authored a novel about the Grail bloodline.'

Killian's tone was one of pride, but the news had a different effect on the impostors, who suddenly regarded me in a more threatening light. Why should they see me as a threat, unless they knew the truth about who my mother really was, and who I was?

'So this one has a brain too.' Wildcat finally looked me in the eyes. 'Is that what you're implying?'

Time I spoke up for myself. 'I could pretend to be blonde,' I said, 'if you'd find that less threatening.' I stared the man down — he was no doubt used to being the tallest in the room — and everyone had a laugh at his expense.

'Cute outfit,' he said sarcastically as he withdrew towards his friends.

'Ah, don't mind him.' Killian waved off his friend's behaviour. 'He's very moody.' He took a deep drag on the joint Co-co had shoved in his hand, then passed it to me.

I had never smoked dope before, but as one of Amenti's staff I was immune to the effects. To appear social, I accepted, dragged far more deeply than Killian had and passed it back to him. My human half was inclined to cough and splutter at this point, but the goddess in me maintained a cool, calm reserve and exhaled the stream of smoke without blinking an eyelid.

'Holy shit, girl,' Killian grinned, 'you *are* a kindred spirit.'

I smiled in return, with one eye on his friends who had huddled together to converse. 'Now, how about a drink?' I said.

'What's your poison, *mademoiselle?*'

'Don't bother,' Wildcat cut in, 'we're leaving.'

'We're blowing off the gig?' Killian said. I knew they did this often. Daddy's Bitch never charged for an appearance, so they were never obliged to perform.

'We made an appearance, the press got photos, it's enough!' Wildcat reasoned, and Killian ran with it.

He put an arm around me to ensure we didn't get separated during the exit — when people saw the band leaving before performance time, there was bound to be an outcry. I arched my back a little, aware of the weapon shoved down the waistband of my skirt.

'So where are we going?' Killian asked them.

'Out of town.' Wildcat grinned and raised his brows a few times to heighten the mystery, then turned to barge a path for the band out of the club.

The leather-clad Co-co brought up the rear. Daddy's Bitch didn't need hired security; everyone had learned not to mess with her.

'Band only,' Wildcat said, and pushed aside the members of his entourage who tried to accompany us.

'Why does she get to go?' one of the band's die-hard groupies protested.

'She's a goddess,' Wildcat retorted, taunting me with a wink as he kept us moving.

If I willed it, I could read the thoughts of any soul on Earth, except those with Orme addiction. The golden shield it formed around the light-body was as solid as the Orme-based steel structures the Ancients built to house their greatest treasures. There was no way I could penetrate the barrier around Killian's friends' minds. I was going unknowing into whatever event they'd planned.

The other band members travelled in Wildcat's black SUV and we followed in Killian's Porsche. I was glad that we weren't all travelling together, as being in their proximity made my skin crawl.

You may think I should have felt some pity and compassion for my fallen kindred, but Kali had many bad memories from her time as one of the Nefilim incarnate: she had been widely ridiculed and ostracised for her humanitarianism. What was more, these souls had given the Anunnaki a bad reputation in this universe and the next. It was my job to save them from themselves, but once they returned to their soul group, they would make

41

amends for the pain and humiliation they had caused the Anunnaki, and Kali personally.

'Where do you think we're going?' I asked Killian.

'I'm sorry, this hasn't been much of a date so far,' he said. 'I guess I should have taken you to dinner before we hit the club. You must be starving!'

Now that he mentioned it, I was hungry, but as an Amenti staff member, food was no longer essential for me; I could live on cosmic light and water alone.

'I'm not hungry,' I said, 'just curious.'

'My friends must seem precocious. I know our reputation precedes us, but I assure you they're really quite harmless.'

Killian sounded sincere, but he was so very wrong. His impression may well have been the case once, but not any more.

We followed a provincial road that was winding its way through a forest when the SUV in front turned off into an abandoned picnic area.

The dark atmosphere of the place washed over me in alarming waves that chilled me to the core with their low frequency. The forest was dying here, for the vibratory frequency of the area was not conducive to growth. There were ley line crossings of light and darkness all over the Earth grid that led into the Otherworld, and this was one of the latter.

'What the hell are they up to?' Killian didn't know whether to be amused or bemused.

Wildcat stopped his vehicle and the band members climbed out and approached our car before we'd even shut our engine off. Co-co knocked on the window on Killian's side and he wound it down.

'What's the buzz?' he asked, curious about the remote location.

'We just need to have a little chat with your girlfriend.' Co-co pressed her fingers into the pressure points in Killian's neck and he passed out.

'Come on, princess, let's see what you're really made of.' Wildcat opened my door and, grabbing hold of my hair, dragged me out.

Fortunately this left both my hands free. I drew my weapon and fired point-blank into his gut. He went flying across the clearing and landed flat on his back, squirming to escape the light now spreading through his body.

'That's "Your Highness" to you,' I corrected.

'You Kianist bitch!' he yelled. 'What have you done to me?'

Under the heightening sonic pressure, the impostor could no longer maintain his false human form and his deformed Nefilim body unfurled from it. His cursing and cries of anguish caused a storm to form overhead, the lightning and thunder clashing in response to their master's protests.

'Ishkur,' I said, recognising him now as one of the sons of the leader of the fallen.

Ishkur had once been in charge of the weather on Earth — a storm god. Now he stole his power from the dark arts in order to command the elements, forcing nature spirits to do his bidding lest he banish them into density.

Thunder shook the Earth and several bolts of lightning shot from the sky towards me. I raised my hands and demanded they yield.

'In-a-vho-ki, Ne-ta or-um!' The oldest language on Earth spilled from my mouth — the language of the Anunnaki, once known as Anuhazi. *I invoke you by divine loving command to return to the light* was the English translation of what I'd said, and with my permission the storm quickly dispersed.

'Holy shit, it *is* her.' Co-co was suddenly less confident of gaining the upper hand.

'I told you this was a bad idea,' Jeb said, sounding rather calm considering his friend was now convulsing and spewing black muck.

I turned the gun on Co-co, knowing that she was the noted warrior of the two. The karate queen proved far more nimble than expected, for as I fired she cartwheeled to avoid the bullet. Before I got a second shot away, the gun flew from my hands into Jeband he turned it on me.

'That weapon has no effect on me,' I informed him.

'How about this?'

I turned to see Co-co's heel on a collision course with my face.

I used my will to slow time to a crawling pace, then grabbed Co-co's extended foot, twisted it and thrust her away. I turned my focus to retrieving my weapon, only to find Jeb mysteriously absent, my weapon gone with him. I released time to search for my missing target, but Co-co recovered more quickly than anticipated and rose to come after me. I turned to confront her.

'Stop right there, both of you.'

The sight of Killian with a handgun aimed at us across the roof of his car brought the confrontation to a standstill.

'What have you done to my friends?' he demanded.

'These aren't your friends,' I said, motioning to Wildcat's alien form, still wriggling on the ground.

'I realise that,' he assured me, coming out from behind the car to better aim his gun and his questions at Co-co. 'What have you done with my friends? My parents!'

'It won't matter soon,' Co-co said with a smile.

Killian cracked. The bullet from his pistol blew a huge hole in the girl's head, demolishing half her face in the process, and yet she didn't fall.

'What the …?' Killian gasped, as she reconstituted before his eyes.

'You can't kill a creature that's already damned. Isn't that right, Ereshkigal?' I used her oldest name, the one I had known her by, and she was shocked that I recognised her.

'Ereshkigal!' Killian knew the name too. 'How could you recognise the ancient Sumarian, goddess of the dead …' His words trailed off in shock. 'Who *are* you, Tamar?'

Co-co laughed. 'You don't even know that you are dating the *Destructor*.'

'What?' Killian distanced himself from me, lowering the gun now he realised it was useless.

'I have come for the fallen ones; humans have nothing to fear from me,' I assured him and returned my attention to Co-co. 'I can save you from the inevitable fate that has driven you to steal a human form.'

'Nothing can save us!' Co-co hissed.

'Spoken like a true goddess of doom,' I teased her. 'Then explain how I have returned to life.'

'You are a human myth, designed to trick the Nefilim into conspiring in their own demise.'

'You wish,' I said, and pointed to Ishkur whose horrid physical form was changing into the glorious astral presence of his former Anunnaki soul mind.

45

'Ishkur?' Co-co could barely believe her eyes as she gazed at the splendid astral being — he looked like an angel. It had been so long since she had seen any of the Nefilim appear thus, tears sprang to her eyes. 'Is he dead?' she asked, as he floated before her, all evidence of his addiction gone.

'He certainly is,' I said with a smile, and Co-co gasped, realising that perhaps she did not have to be damned anymore.

Ishkur looked down at himself and wept for joy. *I am free!* he cried out in relief to the night. *My senses have returned; I can feel!*

'It is a trick.' Co-co backed away.

'The righteous do not lie; we are not deceitful or spiteful, or we would not be the righteous,' I said, hoping to vanquish her doubt. But with every step I took towards her, Co-co stepped further back towards the negative epicentre of this dark place. Clearly, aeons of fear and hatred would not allow her to believe me.

'My orders are to kill you,' she said.

'I cannot be killed,' I told her. 'And whether you want it or not, I will save your soul.'

Co-co's inner conflict brought her to a standstill, and she dropped to her knees. 'Take me, great mother ...'

'Stay away from her!'

Jeb stood in the middle of the clearing, a mass of moving shadows at his back. His human guise cast aside, he was revealed as the Lord of the Underworld, once known as Erragal, and he was here to retrieve his mate.

The Underworld was the lowest astral level of the earthly plane, not to be confused with the Inner Earth territories of the physical world frequented by humans, or the Otherworld, or higher astral realms, frequented by the Anu. Just like its higher-dimensional counterpart, the Underworld granted access to the physical world whilst also providing an escape from it. Due to the diminishing beauty of their appearance, and their growing alliance with the Dracon, most of the Nefilim's major bases were, as the name Underworld suggested, subterranean.

I willed time to stop, but to no effect.

Erragal laughed. 'You now stand within my sphere of influence.'

Co-co rose and grinned, having successfully lured me into range of the dark porthole. Yet I could have sworn that her plea to be saved had been heartfelt. She joined her partner.

'There is not enough cosmic light within this ley line crossing to support your power, so do not attempt to enforce your will here,' Erragal warned, the shadows seething behind him. 'We all have ghosts we'd rather leave buried, princess, even you.'

I had assumed that the goddess in me had no fear, but even Kali shuddered at the thought of confronting Pintar again — the Dracon that had raped her in her previous incarnation — and I knew that Erragal had the black magic to make that reunion happen.

'Bring forth her demon admirer, baby,' Co-co implored her lover as she wrapped herself around him from behind. 'This one looks like she could use a good fuck.'

I glanced back to Killian, who looked completely shocked by what he was witnessing. It was typical of the Nefilim to take pleasure in stirring painful memories in others.

'Why not?' Erragal smirked and closed his eyes to summon my old adversary.

As he did, I drew upon all the light within me and began to sing. Killian and the ghostly Ishkur were enchanted by my voice, but those who stood against me found it agonising.

I motioned Killian to the car, still singing as we climbed inside. He started the engine and tore off up the road.

'That was incredible,' he said with great enthusiasm. 'I'm so very pleased you didn't get to hear me strangle a tune.'

You have a good voice too, Ishkur's ghost commented from the back seat.

When Killian spied him in the rear-vision mirror, he nearly crashed the car. 'What's he doing here?' he said angrily. 'He killed my friend!'

Sadly, I have killed many, many humans, Ishkur confessed with regret. *But I can help save you.*

'You've done all you're going to be doing on this Earth, Ishkur,' I advised him. 'It's straight to the Hall of Amorea for you, my friend ...' I turned in my seat to view him, '... as soon as you tell me whose form Enlil is hiding out in at present.'

Enlil? Ishkur seemed perplexed by the question.

'You know, Ill, your lord and master?' I was prepared to probe his mind if need be, although, having been reborn, Ishkur no longer had the capacity to lie or withhold information.

I know who Ill is, he assured me, *but he does not have a human form at present.* The demi-god looked at Killian. *He is still awaiting delivery.*

'What!' Killian freaked at the implication and would probably have pulled the car over to the side of the road if he wasn't already running for his life.

'Is that where you were taking us tonight?' I asked.

Well, yes. Ishkur shrugged, as if the notion was elementary. *We hoped to present our lord with his chosen form as well as the long-awaited human incarnation of Kali.*

'Co-co called you the Destructor!' Killian said, completely bewildered.

As he was clearly incapable of steering the car, I employed my psychokinetic powers to take control of the wheel.

'Only so far as demons are concerned,' I assured him again, as he looked stunned by his car's new automatic pilot function. 'Do you have any demons you need to be rid of?' I added, joking, and he finally cracked a smile.

'Quite a few, as it turns out.' He looked at Ishkur warily.

I also returned my attention to Ishkur, for my interrogation was not done. 'Where is the control centre for your frequency fence?'

'What's that?' Killian was curious, but I hushed him and stayed focused on my subject.

That project is highly confidential and I am not directly involved, Ishkur advised me sadly. *Only Erragal, Suen or Ill himself could tell you.*

I knew he was telling the truth; it was disappointing. Suen, otherwise known as Sin, was another of Enlil's sons. His name meant 'the bright one' as he was so technologically and scientifically minded, but his intellect had never been used to invent anything beneficial to creation. It made sense that the King of the Underworld, the Nefilim's chief technologist and the daddy of all the Nefilim had masterminded the frequency fence project.

'Then Erragal, Suen and Ill are now my primary targets,' I concluded. I wasn't really surprised, as these three Nefilim, along with Ill's firstborn, Ningirsu, had always formed the nucleus of the fallen ones.

'Now you see my need for the Rod of Power,' Killian said. Then he noticed the sun's first rays hitting the sky. 'Surely it can't be morning already!'

'I was forced to screw with time a little, and suspect our adversary did as well,' I informed him. 'So it wouldn't surprise me what time it is, or what day for that matter.'

Killian checked his watch. 'This says it's a quarter past twelve, so we've lost at least six hours.' Which meant the watch would be unable to advise him of the date. 'I'll buy a newspaper in the next town.' He looked back to the controls of his car, which were still operating on their own. 'If you'd care to give me back control of the car, that is.'

Once his hands were on the steering wheel again, I relinquished control. Killian was clearly more comfortable with that arrangement.

'So where are we going?' he asked.

'Back to base,' I advised. 'I need to speak with my parents.'

During the journey back, I took some quiet time to go within and connect telepathically with my mother while she slept — in case the Nefilim got to her, or me, before I had the chance to converse with her. I didn't have time to relay all that had gone on this night, but I enlightened her as to what I had learned about the ringstone. The rest of my discoveries could wait until I saw her in person.

CHAPTER 4

THE TIME LORD

We parked the car some distance from the site camp. It was certain the Nefilim had someone on site to report on our movements, and while I may have taken out those eyes and ears yesterday when I cleansed André, it was best not to take any chances. Ishkur claimed that the Nefilim had the technology to see anyone, anywhere, at any time, but I knew this did not extend to Amenti's staff. The high vibratory rate of our beings cloaked us, and those close to us, from the sight and hearing of any being on this Earth. That said, our comings and goings through the time continuum could be noted, as such instances caused disturbances in the fabric of time-space and the Nefilim had learned how to monitor these.

We crouched on the forest-covered hill that overlooked the dig site. Killian was pleased we hadn't just driven up and announced ourselves, for his parents' limousine arrived as we watched, and I observed Sabine Labontè trick my father into meeting with her alone. As my mother allowed this, I could only assume she hadn't yet processed the information I had imparted to her in her sleep.

'I have to warn him, wait here,' I told Killian and Ishkur, and silently made my way down the hill towards the back of Killian's quarters. It was the largest and most luxurious dwelling on site, so naturally Sabine led my father there to converse in private with him.

Back pressed hard to the wall, I crept towards a window where I was able to observe the lounge area. My father followed Sabine into the room and closed the door behind them.

'Warn who about what?' Killian startled me with his whispered query.

I smacked a hand over his mouth to keep him quiet, and he appeared rather surprised by my strength.

'... I assure you, Tamar has no serious designs on your son or his fortune,' my father was saying. 'I know she looks mature, but she is barely thirteen.'

'*Thirteen!*' Killian's shock was muffled by my hand, and I slapped my other hand over his eyes to prevent him seeing anything he shouldn't.

Sabine had her back to my father, but I could see the ringstone necklace she toyed with in her hands. 'Oh, Albray, Albray, Albray ... I'm not concerned about your daughter.' She spun around to reveal her treasure and my father was near shocked off his feet. 'I am far more concerned about you,' she said, and smiled seductively.

'Where did you get that?' My father recovered, clearly convinced it could not be the same ringstone that my mother had lost down a sheer cliff in the Sinai fourteen years ago.

Sabine's smile turned to a smirk. 'I have my means. You will not try to retrieve this treasure from me at any time.' She became more serious as she made her orders plain. 'Nor will you attempt to harm me or seek retribution. Is that clear?'

'Clear as vodka, madam. But my duty to the ringstone must be voluntary,' he advised, unfazed by her threats.

'So you say. Shall we test that theory?' She moved closer to him. 'Kiss me, crusader, with all the passion you would your wife,' she commanded.

And my father did exactly that. I could hardly believe what I was seeing.

Killian was wriggling so much, I let him go. He too was gobsmacked to see what was taking place in his lounge room.

'That's not my mother,' he informed me in a whisper.

'I know.' I held a finger to his lips. I recognised the lustful games of this one-time goddess of beauty and battle. She was Ishtar, no doubt about it.

Sabine laughed as they came up for air. '*Lovely*.' She wiped below her lip to ensure her lipstick hadn't smudged.

'You don't know what love is.' My father thrust her away, repulsed by what he had done.

'But you could teach me,' she purred.

'Only with repentance will you ever know love again,' he said, backing away. 'What do you want?'

'I want you to fill me up with your angelic babies.' She slid up close to him, pressing him against the wall. 'I want to cause a rift between you and your beloved that will cut through this dimension and into the next!'

'With all you could command of me, this is what you wish?'

He allowed her to get closer and I realised he was fishing for information.

'Well,' she shrugged, 'you haven't lost my favour yet. And so long as you satisfy my desires, I won't ask you to do anything too terrible.'

'My wife and my daughter are everything to me.' My father wore his most handsome and persuasive expression. 'Please don't do this. Be an angel and give me the ringstone.'

Sabine gazed into his eyes, enchanted. 'God you *are* gorgeous . . . too gorgeous to give up just yet. But you need not worry about the guilt . . . I demand that you don't remember any of the details of this affair.' She plastered herself against my father and began to relieve him of his clothes.

'Get away from there!'

I swung around to find Polaris striding towards me.

'You can't be here right now,' he said and pulled me away from the window.

I could hardly believe his gall. 'I don't take orders from you,' I hissed, furious that my father would betray my mother, enchanted or not.

'Who is this guy?' Killian asked, bewildered.

Polaris peered through the window to assess the situation.

'Please, Tamar, go and wait for me up on the hill,' he said.

'You have to stop her,' I insisted. 'She's going to destroy my parents' relationship.'

He wasn't worried. 'I think that you grossly underestimate their bond. And I am here as an observer only.' He pointed to direct me up the hill.

'By whose orders are you merely to observe?' I asked.

'Your father's.' Polaris was growing impatient with me.

'My father's?' This was unexpected. 'How can that be when he doesn't know about the ring —'

Polaris stopped me short of saying too much in Killian's presence. 'Just this once, trust that if you do not do as I say, much progress will be undone.'

His words just confused me further. 'Progress? What progress could possibly come from this?'

'Just wait for me up the hill.'

He was clearly annoyed that I was distracting him from his mission, and so I gave him the benefit of the doubt and retreated, taking Killian with me.

'Who is that guy?' Killian whispered.

'He's . . .' What could I say about Polaris? 'He's a time lord.'

'*Whoa* . . . seriously?'

Killian was rolling with whatever I told him now, way too deep in shock and confusion to question my authority.

We returned to our original observation point, where Ishkur was waiting as instructed.

It's Ishtar, he said, pointing to the building that Sabine Labontè now occupied, pleased to be of help at last.

'I know,' I said, sorry to disappoint him.

'You know?' Killian repeated, disbelieving. 'How long have you known?'

'I identified her as one of the Nefilim yesterday, but I only recognised her identity today.'

He appeared hurt that I hadn't confided in him earlier.

'I didn't know how much you knew already, so I wasn't about to confront you with the truth,' I defended myself. 'Not without you seeing some proof of what's really going on.'

'So my parents are truly dead?' Killian looked tearful as he turned to Ishkur, who nodded.

We cannot keep anyone alive whose identity we have stolen or our assumed identity would be at risk, the demi-god explained as compassionately as was possible for a being who was an emotional novice.

'Well, you're not taking me!' Killian's anguish for his friends and family surfaced in a huge outburst of anger.

'Calm yourself,' I said, willing it so, and Killian did, though not by his own choice.

'Wouldn't you be a bit upset if you were me?' he appealed.

'I don't get mad,' I said, trying to inspire him towards a more constructive approach. 'I get what I want. So if you intend to live, save your energy — you're going to need your wits about you.'

Killian appreciated my reasoning and nodded.

Polaris scaled the hill to join us. 'Time to leave, kiddies.'

'I'm not going anywhere,' I insisted. 'I need to speak with my father.'

'I'll take you to him,' Polaris said.

'I don't need your escort,' I replied, and strode off down the hill. But Polaris gripped my arm to stop me.

'That is your father yesterday,' he advised. 'A day during which he did not see you. Are you getting my drift yet?'

Time travel wasn't my strongest general knowledge subject, and Polaris was the expert.

'Did I miss a day somewhere?' I asked.

'You will,' he replied, looking to the sky.

A great shaft of liquid light lifted us and our company into the belly of the *Klieo* — the time-hopping transport that was the brainchild of Polaris, the guardian entity of Signet Station Nine, and captained by another of his incarnations, Prince Henry Sinclair.

Polaris locked Killian in a cabin on board the *Klieo*, insisting that he wasn't to see any of the ship or be told anything about his situation.

'Tell me what the hell is going on,' My date pleaded as I entered the cabin to try to reassure him.

'You're safer here than anywhere,' I began. 'The Nefilim can't find you as long as you're on board this ship.'

'How long am I going to be stuck here? I have things I need to be doing. Now more than ever.'

I could tell Killian's thoughts were on finding the Rod of Power.

'Time has no meaning here, so you won't lose anything by taking the chance to relax and recoup,' I said. He looked perplexed. 'I'm your best defence right now,' I continued, 'and I'm going to get some answers.'

'Who from?' Killian moved in close, hoping to seduce some information out of me. I certainly wasn't opposed to him trying. 'Let me come with you.' He raised his big blue eyes in appeal.

I brushed his long, dark fringe out of his eyes. 'Absolutely not.'

My refusal didn't stop his advance, however. 'Can I kiss you anyway?'

'Absolutely n—'

I had never been so pleased to be defied. I'd never been kissed before and it lived up to all my daydreams. For a moment I completely forgot who I was. But once our lips parted I remembered Kali's mission very quickly and my first thought was whether Killian was my missing prince. Would my kiss unlock some ancient memory in him, like in the fairytales of old?

'Wow!' He appeared dizzy.

'Did my kiss stir anything within you?' I asked quickly, as I heard the captain coming for me.

'Sure did.' He gave a cheeky grin and motioned to his trousers with his eyes.

'That's not what I meant.' I grinned and tried not to sound disappointed.

As he heard the door opening, Killian grabbed my hand. 'What did you mean?'

'Some other time,' I said as Polaris entered the cabin.

Killian left it at that, and let go of my hand as Polaris was giving him the evil eye.

'We're good to go,' he said to me.

'I'll be back as soon as I have some solutions,' I told Killian, and headed out the door past the captain, who was still staring disapprovingly at my suitor.

'I suppose something to eat is out of the question?' Killian asked.

Polaris gave no response, just closed and locked the door.

'It's all right for you time lords, angels and goddesses,' Killian hollered after us, 'but I'm only mortal! I need sustenance!'

'You seriously think Mathu is hiding in that guy?' Polaris commented as he accompanied Ishkur and me to the exit hatch.

'It's a strong possibility.' I was trying not to let my first kiss colour my instinct, but that proved impossible; I wanted him to be Mathu, my attraction to him was intense.

Polaris was sceptical. 'It's just that I don't ever remember Mathu being quite that full of himself.'

I looked at him, surprised by his observation. 'That's the pot calling the kettle black, don't you think?'

'Yes,' he agreed, 'but I've always had a high opinion of myself. Your beloved has not.'

'A good point,' I concurred as we exited onto the deck of the *Klieo*, parked alongside the great earthern bridge inside the cavern of Mamer.

CHAPTER 5

COMPROMISED

MIA DEVERE — MERIDAN

I awoke at my desk the next morning, pen in hand, the above chapter sprawled in handwritten pages across my desk.

My mobile phone was ringing. Still bleary, I reached into my bag and answered it. 'Hello.' I smothered a yawn. 'Mia Devere speaking.'

'Bonjour, Mrs Devere. I am Sylvie Bruyere, promotions manager for the House of Chanel in Paris.'

Not the first person I was expecting to hear from this morning.

'As in "the little black dress" House of Chanel?'

'*Oui*.' She sounded delighted at my recognition of her brand. 'I am calling in the hope of contracting your daughter, Tamar, to be the new face of Chanel —'

'What?' I was shocked out of my skin. How did she know anything about my daughter?

'I understand this must be very exciting for you,' continued Sylvie.

'Overwhelming,' I said drily. 'We'll have to get back to you, I'm so sorry.'

I hung up the phone and it immediately rang again. I answered it.

'This is Chuck Fix from *Rolling Stone* magazine —'

I switched my mobile off in a state of mild shock. It appeared that Tamar had got what she wanted: overnight fame.

I looked at the pages I had penned in my sleep, thinking that I should read them. I couldn't recall a word of it, not even who the transmission was from.

It was only when Albray walked into our room that I realised that he wasn't still asleep in our bed.

'The morning papers are here,' he said.

He sounded perturbed about the fact. He slapped one down in front of me and I saw that the front page was filled with a large photo of Killian Labontè and our daughter. The headline read: *Le visage de la beauté*.

'That would explain the call I just got from the House of Chanel,' I said.

Albray forced a laugh. 'Are you serious?' He seemed unsure whether he should be deploring Tamar's sudden notoriety or beaming with pride at our daughter's success.

The sound of a car pulling into the site sent us racing to the door — we hoped it was Tamar and Labontè returning from their history-making date. However, it was Killian's parents' gold limousine that drew to a stop outside.

'Not good,' Albray commented.

The chauffeur opened the door and the sole occupant, Sabine Labontè, stepped out of the vehicle and looked straight to us. 'Albray Devere?' she said, ignoring me. 'I need to speak with you — it's about your daughter.'

'Here we go,' Albray said in an aside to me, and put on a smile for our guest.

'Be careful,' I warned, although he knew as well as I did what she truly was.

At the time, I didn't think it odd that Sabine didn't ask to speak with both of us. I was still half asleep, and with my overnight work yet to be read I was happy to let Albray deal with Sabine's concerns. As one of the Council of Amenti, Albray had a far greater psychic advantage than any of the Nefilim and I didn't for a second question whether he could cope with the situation alone.

Half an hour and a couple of coffees later, I was of a very different mind for I had finally read my daughter's transmission.

I scrambled outside to find Albray waving goodbye to the gold limousine, and was relieved to see him apparently unscathed by the encounter.

'All smoothed over,' he assured me, 'for the time being.'

He looked concerned momentarily, then smiled at me and headed off to the amenities block.

Albray joined me half an hour later, freshly showered, shaved and changed. This was a little unexpected, as when we were on location he reverted to his ancient knightly ways and didn't bother too much with his appearance.

'Where are you off to?' I asked, thinking he must be going out.

'Nowhere. I was just feeling a bit grungy.' He noted my astonished expression. 'What?'

'Grungy? You! I didn't think you knew the meaning of the word.'

Albray laughed. 'Well, aren't you pleased I finally

learned?' He embraced me in a very amorous fashion.

'Aren't you going to tell me what Mrs Labontè had to say about our daughter?' I asked, trying to put him off without making my concerns obvious.

My husband was discouraged by my choice of topic and let me go. 'She just needed reassuring that our girl is very chaste and so her son isn't going to wind up being charged for having sex with a minor. She suspects that Killian's only dating Tamar to infuriate his parents.'

'And that took half an hour?' I asked, trying not to sound like the suspicious wife, somewhat unsuccessfully.

'Mia!' Albray placed both hands on his hips, sounding perturbed. 'I thought we had put all our jealousies behind us.'

I was immediately suspicious. Instead of answering my question, he'd turned the subject around to my faults — a sure sign that he was hiding something.

'I have reason to believe you have been compromised,' I informed him calmly.

'Compromised!' He was furious — he was definitely hiding something.

'Sabine Labontè has acquired the ringstone your soul mind is attached to,' I told him, staring him in the eyes to gauge his true reaction and in them I saw horror, relief, sorrow and remorse. 'What happened?' I asked.

'I don't know what happened,' he blurted out, relieved not to have to try and hide the fact. He took a seat and tried to recall what he could. 'I felt horrible afterwards,' he looked up at me in pain, 'as if I'd —' He caught his breath on the recollection. 'As if I'd been close to her.'

'You had sex with her?' I choked on the question in horror.

'No! Maybe? I don't know!' He was close to tears.

I had only ever seen Albray cry in joy, and felt ashamed that I was so quick to assume him guilty. 'Well, that explains the shower,' I said.

'I know she hypnotised me with the ringstone. After that, all I recall is waving her goodbye. She may have just implanted the idea that I ...' He chose not to complete the sentence.

'Holy mother, she could have instructed you to do anything!' I said, realising that a sexual encounter with the woman was a minor inconvenience compared to some of the missions she could have instilled in Albray — and very probably had!

'I need to probe your memory,' I said. 'It's the only way.'

'No,' Albray said quickly. 'You'll only perceive what she wants you to perceive. The only way to truly be sure what happened is to be there when it happens.'

'That's impossible.'

'Not for Polaris,' he retorted.

It was true that Polaris was a time lord, but I couldn't allow Albray to seek out any of the Amenti Council in case he had been hypnotised into killing them or ambushing the Amenti scheme. He was a major security risk now and I had to take him out of the equation until I could brief the Council on what had happened and they could decide how best to deal with the situation.

'Wait here a second,' I told him.

I grabbed one of my shoulder bags and made my way to the bathroom. Inside the bag was a weapon

64

I had procured from a Dracon in battle. It shot debilitating darts that could keep even one of my kind motionless for hours. I had never thought to use the weapon, so it was buried deep in the bag, hidden inside the old hollowed-out book in which I had once found Albray's ringstone. I remembered the ringstone with sorrow now; what I would give never to have lost it.

Weapon in hand, I paused a moment to gather my will to shoot my own husband. Then I burst into our room, took aim and found nothing to fire at. Albray had fled.

Fortunately it was a Sunday and there were very few people on site. I tucked the stun-gun into my backpack and headed down into the major excavation area. I needed to contact my fellow Council members and make them aware of the situation with Albray. I was able to go into a deep trance state and connect with my sisters, but if Albray had been programmed to do me harm, he would predict this action and my body would be a sitting duck whilst my consciousness was in flight.

My mission — to activate my station and then secure it from discovery — was now seriously compromised. I half-expected that Albray had fled into the labyrinth. Still, only I knew where the entry point to my Signet station was, and I was the key that granted access and activation. If I succeeded in activating my station and drawing down the Triogenes pyramid attached, then I could access Giza via Signet Station Four, whose pyramid, Thoth, had already been activated by Lilith. This course of action would kill two birds with one stone. For when I had completed this mission, I would collapse the outer labyrinth to ensure that my Signet station could not be entered from surface Earth. After that I could gain access from any of the other Signet stations, Giza primarily.

I dearly hoped that my hunch concerning my husband was wrong and I would not encounter him en route to Meridan station. Albray's travel sword was missing from our luggage and his skill with his chosen weapon was a primary concern for me. I could only hope that we were not forced into a position of discovering who the swifter warrior was.

CHAPTER 6

THOTH — GIZA

At Giza is the pyramid of Thoth,
the trickster,
the Keeper of Time and
Master of the Game.

Within the Hall of Records
human consciousness is calibrated
and higher experience stored
to fuel the planetary consciousness
for the return of the Sphere
and the opening of Amenti.

The first of the twelve pyramids,
Giza is the base station to all the matrix.
It is the geographical timepiece of Earth
that perpetuates the illusion of the cycles of time.

TAMAR DEVERE — KALI

My rescued kinsman, Ishkur, accompanied Polaris and me through the porthole from Mamer that led to the outer chamber of the Amenti complex beneath Giza. This chamber contained three inter-dimensional passages: one to the cavern of Mamer in the physical world; one to the Otherworldly realm of the Anu, which existed in the higher astral plane; and the third to the Underworld, frequented by the Nefilim and Dracon, which existed in the lower etheric realms. This last porthole only permitted passage *into* the Underworld as the vibratory rate of the chamber was too high for any low-grade entity to pass through it and survive. The vibratory rate inside the Giza complex would have to drop dramatically for any of the Nefilim and their lowlife minions to gain access to Amenti, especially now that the Hall of Records had been opened. The Giza ante-chamber also provided entry to the Amenti complex, which my parents had opened before I was born.

This was as far as Ishkur could go, for none of the Nefilim were ever permitted to enter Amenti, even though the primary entrance to the Hall of Amorea was situated therein. In order to reach Sirius B, where the rest of the Anu race were evolving their emotional beings, Ishkur would have to take the porthole siutated within the realm of the Anu to the Hall of Amorea and pass through the Earth's core. Thus it was that we found Lugh Lamhfada awaiting us to guide Ishkur on that journey.

Lugh was a great prince among my people. He too had once been one of the fallen, but as a son of En Ki he had secretly studied the teachings of Kianism and, like Mathu and me, had eventually overcome his Orme addiction to become a leader among the Anu on Earth. He had led many of the fallen away from the Nefilim centres in the Near East and settled them in Ireland, where they became the mighty Tuatha Dé Danaan.

Tumaz! Ishkur was amazed to see his long-lost

cousin. As they were both composed of the same astral matter, they embraced as brothers.

I have not gone by that name in a long, long time, Lugh said, holding his cousin at arm's length and looking him up and down, pleased to see him restored to his former Anunnaki self.

Ra then? Or Marduk? Ishkur scanned his memory for his cousin's many identities, but Lugh shook his head. *What then?*

I am known as Lugh Lamhfada. The Anu warrior knew the news would sting a little.

You are Lamhfada! Ishkur could barely believe he was standing before the leader of the Anu, who had been ambushing the Nefilim agenda for all recorded history. *They have no idea who you are*, he assured Lugh and then laughed. *Heaven help you if they ever find out.*

Heaven does help me. Lugh motioned to the captain and me. *Heaven helps us all, even those as lost as yourself.*

Ishkur smiled at the truth of it.

Are you ready to go home now, cousin? Lugh motioned to the porthole that led to his dominion.

If I can be of no more aid. Ishkur looked to us and we assured him he was free to go.

Lugh bowed to me. *Excellent work, Your Highness.*

'I know you will see our cousin safely home,' I said, proud of my one-time brother. 'Your assistance is always greatly appreciated, Lugh Lamhfada.'

I am your humble servant. Lugh's smile was full of cheek and flirtation.

He was just like his younger brother, Mathu, and my desire to find my prince spurred me into action. I headed into the Amenti complex.

'We have your father contained here,' Polaris told me, now that we were alone.

'Why here?' I thought this a grave breach of security.

'Arcturus handed himself in as soon as he realised he'd become a risk,' Polaris said, defending my father, which was one for the books. 'And now that I know for certain Sabine Labontè did not instil in him a command to ambush the Amenti Project, he is no longer a danger to us.'

'What about next time Ishtar decides she wants her toy boy?' I said. 'Is this perverse arrangement you have with my father to be ongoing?'

'Ishtar!' Polaris hadn't been able to recognise my kin as easily as I did. 'Are you sure?'

I nodded.

'Oh dear.' Polaris feared for Arcturus's ability to resist the seduction techniques of the goddess of desire, who was once the very embodiment of beauty.

'And what about my mother?' I asked. 'When does she get told about this?'

'Ah yes.' Polaris scratched his head. 'We need to speak with you about that.'

'I'm sure you do. But right now I need to see Denera. I want her to consult the Hall of Records for me,' I finished, answering his query before he could ask it.

He pointed down past the glowing limestone walls of the labyrinth towards where the Hall of Records was located.

The hall was shaped like a keyhole, rounded at the entrance end, with a long passageway extending from the opposite side of the chamber. The walls, floors and ceiling appeared nonexistent upon first viewing, and touching them felt like dipping your hands in thick tepid water.

'Liquid light,' I said in recognition. The substance was a medium for a good part of the time-space technologies of the Ceres, along with their huge crystal generators.

All of Amenti's staff had been chosen from among the Ceres race, bar myself and my absent mate, who were both Anunnaki. Back on Tara, the Ceres race had evolved beyond material existence to become guardians to humanity — as above then so below. My people, the Anunnaki, were seen as the enemy of humanity as a few rogues among them were deemed largely responsible for the catastrophe on Tara and the fall of humanity into this lowest harmonic universe. To atone for this wrong, and those continuing it on this planet, I, Kali, Queen of the Anunnaki people, had volunteered to join the Amenti Project to aid in bringing home all the fallen souls of our people.

I could roughly judge the height of the chamber by the long oblong porthole inset in the wall at the far end of the hall opposite. The portal was deep green in colour, partially reflective and still — like the undisturbed surface of a pond. In the centre of the rounded part of the chamber was a circular mound of solid emerald that rose to waist height. Inset in the milky-white crystal floor of the chamber in front of the emerald mound was a black metallic circular plate. When anyone stood on the plate, a band of emerald green light enclosed them inside a light tube — this was the telepathic shield that ensured only one person controlled the Hall of Records at any given time.

Denera, keeper of the Higher Akasha, and her partner, Zalman, who maintained the Lower Akashic, were deep in conversation when Polaris and I entered the Hall of Records. The instant they saw us, they stopped and gave me their full attention.

'Welcome, Kali, to Signet Station Four, host to the Hall of Records and the Amenti complex,' said Denera. She had once been known as Lilith, but went by her Ceres name since joining the staff of Amenti. 'I am mistress of this station whose pyramid resonates to the frequency of Thoth, the master of illusion, and therefore the cycles of time.'

My heart skipped a beat; Thoth was one of the names my prince had been known by in Earth's ancient past.

'I know what you are thinking, Kali,' Denera cautioned, 'but Mathu borrowed the name of this station's pyramid during the thousands of years he worked, studied and taught here. It was from this very control room that he shut down the Signet Grid and banished the Hall of Records to the astral realms before the demise of Atlantis.'

'So the soul of my prince is in no way connected to this station?'

It was difficult to suppress my disappointment when Denera shook her head.

'However, what is connected to this station is five other Signet stations,' she said with a grin.

Gaia was the primary Signet station to which all the other stations needed to connect. The labyrinth here housed the Arc of the Covenant porthole passage, which was currently hosting the Sphere of Amenti, inside which burned the Blue Flame. The Blue Flame resonated to the frequency of the higher harmonic universe that Tara belonged to. It protected the evolutionary blueprint of humanity and fed the high-frequency energy through the

Earth's natural grid to the other Signet stations. Once a Signet station was activated, the celestial pyramid attached to it was as well; and each pyramid contained the stargate to the home planet of the guardian council assigned to protect that Signet station. If anyone but the true key-holder attempted to activate a station, the portal would be shut down by the guardian council, or could even be remotely destroyed as a very last resort.

My fallen kindred, the Nefilim, were well aware of the Signet Grid and, having failed in their attempts to activate one of the stations, had since been developing ways of damming the matrix in places. To do this, they had developed the dark arts, using the blood sacrifice of innocents to summon demons from the lower planes of awareness into focused areas on the globe. The evil forms then spread evil thoughts and deeds among the Earth's inhabitants, which lowered the harmonic frequency of the area and created a dark blockage in the Earth's natural grid system through which light and energy could not flow.

'You have opened half of the Signet stations already?' I said, pleased they were so far advanced in their mission. Inwardly, however, I was concerned to learn I had less time to make good on my promises of finding Mathu and steering my fallen kindred back towards their soul source.

'That is correct,' Denera replied. 'And you are here to consult the Hall of Records with regard to your search for Mathu.' But instead of helping me as I'd hoped, she shook her head.

'I need a clue,' I implored her.

'I would help you, child, if I could. I have tried!' she said. 'But so far as your Mathu is concerned, there is a void.' She sounded frustrated. 'It is as if the planetary records have been altered and all traces of Mathu's existence removed.'

'Please, no.' My first horrid thought was that my prince had incarnated, and that the Dracon had got to him first with one of their soul-shattering devices.

'I did it,' a voice announced. It was Levi, overhearing our conversation as he approached with a replacement for the weapon I had lost to Erragal. 'I hacked into the planetary consciousness on Thoth's — or rather, Mathu's — behalf.'

Denera looked shocked. 'When?'

'In a past life, before the Hall of Records was elevated beyond the physical world,' Levi explained casually and handed me my weapon. 'Try not to lose this one.'

'Why didn't you mention this before now?' Denera sounded annoyed; finding Mathu was a high priority.

'To tell you the truth I'd forgotten all about it until you mentioned it just then,' Levi said, and then he broke into a smile. 'The scribe probably planned it just so.'

'Then how am I meant to find my prince?' I implored the technologist. 'I thought I would know in my heart when I'd found him, but I do not.'

Levi was staring at me with a dazed look of revelation. 'Déjà vu,' he said, recovering his wits. 'Thoth said he would leave a marker by which you could identify him.'

I was filled with hope, and took hold of Levi's arm. 'Please tell me you know what this marker is.'

'It's a pendant,' Levi said with a smile, happy to help, and from his mind's eye I perceived an image of the said treasure. It was covered with hieroglyphs that I recognised: 'He awaits beneath the lotus,' I read aloud. It made little sense to me.

Levi nodded at my translation. 'Miss Koriche gave it to me before I entered Amenti,' he said.

'Vespera,' I gasped, for it was she who had been Miss Koriche in a past life. 'I need to speak —'

'Vespera is on her way,' Denera said, having already telepathically requested her presence.

I recalled reading of the pendant in Ashlee's journals; according to her account, Thoth returned the pendant to Miss Koriche, following Levi's departure for Amenti.

'The pendant contained a small fragment of Thoth's original form,' Levi explained while we waited. 'It harnessed genetic information about the great scribe that could be accessed by anyone of high psychic aptitude, such as ourselves.'

Vespera entered the Hall of Records wearing a curious look on her face. 'You requested to see me?'

I got straight to the point. 'What happened to the pendant Thoth gave Miss Koriche?'

She looked puzzled a moment, then memories of that far-gone lifetime came back to her. 'As Thoth requested, the pendant became a family heirloom, passed down by my son to his sons. And that's probably where it is today.'

I looked at Zalman. He needed no further prompting.

'I will trace Miss Koriche's family tree,' he said, 'and get back to you with the identity of any possibilities. There may be none; there may be hundreds, it's hard to say.'

'A better staff I could not want,' I told them all, happy to be finally getting somewhere in my search.

'Are we done here?' Polaris asked, having other pressing matters for me to attend to. 'Arcturus will want to speak with you, Kali, before you return to Montségur.'

'Ah yes, my adulterer father.'

'The ringstone to which your father pledged his service acts as a constraint on his will.' Denera spoke up on Arcturus's behalf as I followed Polaris from the chamber. 'Is a rape victim an adulterer? He may have looked like he was enjoying himself, but I assure you he did not.'

I nodded to concede her point. I would reserve judgement until I had spoken with my father myself.

Polaris entered the cabin where my father was confined to explain why I was there to see him. The room was made of Orme-reinforced steel, which blocked all psychic frequency. It had a twin-door entry with a security chamber between the doors; one door was required to be shut before the other could be opened. If the prisoner stuck his or her nose beyond the first door, then both security doors would close and trap the escapee. Even if the prisoner was able to become invisible, the sensors were DNA-sensitive and would identify even the ghost of a person.

When Polaris bade me enter, he looked more sombre than I had ever seen him. 'He's devastated, go easy,' he advised.

It was so unlike Polaris to sympathise with my father that my Anunnaki judgemental streak dulled and I felt deeply apprehensive about having to confront a situation that involved true human emotion.

One look at my father's expression and my

human side knew how deeply he was hurting. He sat hunched forward on the metal bench that was the only object in the round, glowing metal room. I wanted to say something reassuring, but nothing came immediately to mind. However, the uncomfortable silence lasted only a moment, until my father found the courage to raise his head and see my awkward expression.

'How can you even look at me?' he asked, tears of shame in his voice.

'I love you.' The words were finally forthcoming. I may have looked older than my years, but emotionally speaking both Kali and Tamar were still very immature.

'I don't deserve your love.' He couldn't look me in the eye for his own filled with tears. 'Or your mother's.'

'I won't tell her,' I said, moving to embrace and reassure him, but he held out a hand and stopped me.

'I want you to tell her,' he said. 'She should know ...' His words trailed off; pained by whatever he was thinking, he added, 'I cannot tell her.'

His shame consumed him and, although he fought it off, finally reduced him to tears. I had never seen my father cry, nor even unnerved.

'Mum will understand, truly,' I said as he wiped his eyes on his sleeve. He shook his head. 'Look, I saw the whole thing,' I started, then stopped at the look of horror on my father's face. 'Well, not all ...' I tried to backpedal but the damage was done. 'But I saw enough to know you didn't succumb to Ishtar willingly or easily.'

'Ishtar!' Arcturus went as white as a sheet as he recognised the name of the Nefilim goddess of seduction and war.

I took a seat alongside him on the metal bench. 'Arcturus doesn't fear the Nefilim, so why do you?' I asked.

My father cracked a sorry smile. 'Arcturus fears losing Meridan.'

My sympathetic smile did nothing to reassure him. I couldn't predict how my mother would react; whether Ishtar's scheme to cause a rift between them would be fulfilled. However, there was something I could do to ease the healing process.

A pile of paper materialised in my hands, covered with handwritten text. 'Here.' I handed it to Arcturus.

'What's this?'

'My account of what happened as I would relay it to my mother ... including the part of this conversation we haven't had yet.'

I grinned to see my father's sadness replaced by wonder and pride.

'You are a very gifted child,' he said, overwhelmed by my gesture of trust and forgiveness.

Even the Anunnaki half of me had to admit that bringing hope to another felt good.

'Read it and decide how guilty you really are,' I said, knowing he remembered little of what had actually occurred. 'Then give it to Mum when you're ready.' I got up and turned to my father to say goodbye.

Arcturus didn't know whether to laugh or cry. 'You *are* all grown up.'

I embraced him; he had never needed a hug so badly. 'I just want to see you two crazy kids put this behind you and be happy.'

'No one wants that more than I do.' My father held me at arm's length. 'But speaking of crazy kids, what's this I read about you and Killian Labontè?'

'Ah …' I wriggled free of my father's clutches, feeling this was my cue to depart. 'I really do have to go … Gotta save the world and all.'

'His family are dangerous,' my father said. He was living testament of that. 'And in my humble opinion, Killian Labontè is dangerous too.'

'If you think his family are bad, you ought to meet his band.' I made light of my father's worries and could see that a scolding was forthcoming. 'But what if Killian is just some ignorant son of the blood that the Nefilim haven't got to yet?' I went on. 'His auric body is pretty average. No trace of Orme, no huge looming spooks!'

Arcturus hazarded a nod to concur that my reasoning had merit.

'So cut my friend a little slack, okay?' I smiled. 'He's really very —'

'That's your *I've-done-something-naughty* smile,' my father accused, pointing at me. 'You've kissed him, haven't you?'

'Now I really am going.' I turned and headed for the security doors. 'Later, Dad,' I said, and stepped into the security chamber.

'Tell that boy he is *so* lucky I'm detained at present,' Arcturus called after me. 'And if he so much as *thinks* a lustful thought about you —'

'Too late.' I gave him a cheeky wave goodbye as the security door put a great metal barrier between us.

CHAPTER 7

STRANGE AURA

MIA DEVERE — MERIDAN

En route to the dig site, I was acutely aware that my husband could be lying in wait anywhere along the precarious path through the unearthed ruins. So when someone jumped out of the shadows just to my rear, I had a blade at his throat before he could speak.

'Emmett,' I said, surprised to find he was my captive. I sheathed the knife on my left hip, beneath my long jacket. 'Don't go creeping up on people like that.'

Emmett looked stunned to find me packing such a weapon, and more stunned that I had the expertise to wield it so effectively. 'I won't,' he assured me. 'Ever … again.' And he started to back away.

'Did you want me for some reason?' I asked.

'Tamar's not back yet,' he blurted out. 'Doesn't that worry you? If you think she's safe with Killian … sorry, Mr Labontè, you're sorely mistaken. The guy is a complete psycho! He thinks his parents are alien beings, and that down that hole somewhere he's going to find the Rod of Power or a map to find it, and with that weapon he intends to murder his parents —

who aren't really his parents, you understand. And then …' Emmett threw his hands in the air, 'God knows what he plans to do!'

I was going to sound like an uncaring mother, but I needed to get back to my mission. 'What I would be more concerned about is whether Mr Labontè is safe with my daughter,' I said.

'How can you say that? Kali's only thirteen!'

His use of the name shocked me into an about-face, and I found him looking just as perplexed.

'Kali? Where did that come from?' He shook off the conundrum to pursue his argument. 'Nevertheless —'

'Nevertheless, *Tamar* will be back when she's good and ready, and neither you nor I can alter the fact. If she needs me, Emmett, she'll call.'

'Look, I know you think I'm just a jealous loser, but what if Tamar is in trouble?' he persisted, following me, which I simply couldn't allow. I also didn't want Emmett becoming infatuated with my daughter; he was bound to get hurt when she stepped right over him in pursuit of her greater goals.

'Tamar doesn't get into trouble, she *is* trouble,' I said, and he looked appalled.

'How can you say that about your own daughter?'

'Interesting that you called her Kali just now — a Freudian slip, do you think?' I could see Emmett's mind boggling at the question. 'Now, if you don't mind, I'm off to work.'

I didn't look back to see how hurt or frustrated he was, I just kept moving.

'All you history hunters are alike!' he yelled into the stairwell as I descended. 'Why do you think the past is so much more important than the present? Nothing is more important than the present — it's the only reality that actually exists! Where we can have an effect!'

I moved with greater speed to get beyond his view. I was thinking of the present and the future, but it was the past that held the key to a brighter outcome for both. I needed to alert my fellow staff members to the potential threat my husband now posed; my daughter could take care of herself.

The excavation team had only explored the tunnels of the outer labyrinth, for the maze was so extensive they'd been forced to map it as they moved through to ensure they didn't get lost or fall into one of its many hidden pits. So far they had found only dead ends, and that was all they would ever find.

I moved through the maze with sure-footed certainty, yet ever mindful of an ambush. Imagine my surprise when I spied the light of a glowstick up ahead in the darkness, and two figures moving towards me.

'Who's there?' I called out.

'It is Polaris, and I have your husband in my custody.'

'Praise the universe.' I breathed a sigh of relief and ran to meet them.

'I've come to let you know that Arcturus handed himself in voluntarily,' Polaris told me. 'And, having revisited his meeting with Sabine Labontè this morning, I can verify that he isn't a threat to your mission.'

'That's fantastic news.' I flung my arms around Albray's neck and gave him a squeeze, but he was unresponsive. Something wasn't right: both my husband and the captain were acting strangely.

Polaris headed back inside the cavern. 'Time for

me to go. I'm parked in one of the outer chasms,' he explained.

'So what did Sabine do with you for half an hour?' I asked my husband.

He smiled to reassure me. 'Only implanted in me the will to discourage our daughter away from her son.'

'That's it?' I thought the woman an idiot. 'Has she no idea of the damage you could do?'

Albray shrugged. 'I lucked out. Shall we go?'

'Go where?' I was surprised by his eagerness to accompany me, for only I could enter the Signet station.

'If you think I'm leaving you unaccompanied for this mission, you've got another think coming. This project is crawling with Nefilim, and they're bound to be monitoring these tunnels. I'll guard the entry whilst you do your thing.'

This comment struck me as odd, for even if our adversaries were monitoring the tunnels, our light-bodies acted as shields to prevent us being detected by undesirables.

'Sweetheart,' Albray pulled me from my musing with a click of his fingers, 'time is of the essence.'

'That way,' I said, and indicated that he should walk on in front of me.

As I followed him, I used my third-eye vision to check out his aura. I expected to find a Nefilim in my husband's guise; however, Albray's light centres appeared normal and his primary auric hue was as orange as ever — even in the green light of the glowstick he carried. Still, his light-body had a kind of fluid look about it, which was something I'd never seen before in the whole fourteen years since I'd learned to use my etheric sight.

The tunnel we were following ended in an unremarkable-looking earthen chamber.

'I don't get it.' Albray threw up his hands. 'Did we take a wrong turn somewhere?'

'Must have.'

I backed up a few paces, trying to decide what to do. Something wasn't right here and there was no way I was going to open the passage to my Signet station until I knew it was safe. A blade was no good in this instance — I didn't want to inflict harm in case this really was my husband, and it was my psychic sight and not his auric body that was faulty. I reached for the stun-gun in my bag and only then realised that I'd dropped it when I apprehended Emmett, and in my hurry to get away from him I'd left it behind! It was times like this I wished I'd developed the skill of physical teleportation. All the Amenti staff members had the capacity to develop any psychic ability, but our needs throughout our lifetimes had given each of us an aptitude for particular skills.

Time to run, I told myself, and my body was quick to respond. I raced up the tunnel in the darkness, doubly panicked when I didn't hear anyone pursuing me. For if this was a Nefilim ambush, there would be reinforcements to block my escape. I reached for my knife, but was knocked to the ground as I collided with another body, which then fell on top of me.

My victim whimpered as I overpowered him and pinned him beneath me.

'Emmett!' I gasped and released him. He was in grave danger by being here, yet he could be my saviour.

'There are these strange creatures out there,' he told me.

There was so much distress in his voice that I knew he'd seen some Dracon, which left no doubt in my mind that this was an ambush. The Nefilim were attempting to seize Signet Station Twelve!

'My bag, where is it?' I gripped him hard to express my urgency.

He found my hand in the darkness and shoved the bag into it.

'You can't write yourself out of this one, knife girl.' My husband's voice came from behind us, taunting, although clearly it wasn't Albray who addressed me. From the tunnels up ahead I heard the familiar sound of Dracon ground troops scurrying on all fours along the ceilings, walls and floor towards us.

Despite my superhuman strength and resilience, my heart was pounding. Of all the Signet stations this was the only one we could not allow them to take, for the Triogenes pyramid housed the stargate that linked Earth to the lower causal realms of Aramatena in the constellation of Lyra. A highly advanced race of beings guarded the main passageway in and out of this lowest harmonic universe, through which ran the Amenti superhighway between Earth and Tara. If anyone but me tried to activate the stargate within the pyramid, the pyramid's guardian council had the ability to destroy Triogenes at Earth's end — better to leave humanity to its own devices than risk the main porthole to the second harmonic universe being breached or destroyed. Without the consent of the Council of Aramatena, my Signet station would not fully activate and connect to the grid. And without all twelve Signet stations active, Amenti's doors would not open.

I found the stun-gun and pulled it from the bag. 'Stay close to me,' I whispered to Emmett as I dragged him to his feet. 'Your immortal soul depends on it.'

'I believe you,' he replied, and I pulled him in the direction of the dead end.

Albray stood at the tunnel entrance, silhouetted against the light of the glowstick that he'd placed in the annexe beyond him. He formed his hands into fists and glowing blue etheric blades shot out of the fingerless leather gloves he wore. These weapons would leave no physical marks as they injured only the etheric body, but as the physical body could not exist without its etheric double, any vital organs pierced by the blades would go into seizure.

'Time to cooperate,' he advised me.

I shot several darts into his body and watched him fall. 'I quite agree.'

Unless Albray had joined the ranks of the Nefilim and Dracon, this was clearly not my husband, for etheric blades were a weapon of the Old World Order. The Nefilim must have developed a means to disguise their light-bodies, but their shield was not perfect, and now I knew what the fault looked like.

I stepped over the motionless form and into the annexe beyond. 'Come on,' I urged Emmett.

There was a smooth rock wall on the far side of the annexe, which I approached. I took a deep inhalation and sang a very high, very pure sonic, which caused a doorway of glowing white light to carve itself through the stone.

'Holy shit,' said Emmett.

The Dracon reached the chamber entrance, but were put off entering by the high frequency of my note; it drove them crazy.

I held my note, grabbed Emmett by the arm and

pulled him through the light barrier with me. Then I abruptly ended my song and the rock immediately reconstituted behind us.

'Oh my goddess,' Emmett gasped. 'That was totally rad, Doc!'

Although I was flattered by his reaction, I couldn't show it. 'You shouldn't be here at all,' I said instead, annoyed by the breach in security.

He was offended. 'What threat am I to you? Come to think of it, what would you have done if I hadn't brought you your bag?'

He had a point.

'It's not what kind of threat you are to me, Emmett, it's the threat your being here poses to all existence on this planet!' I was turning circles contemplating what to do with him.

'Look ... obviously you're up to some pretty scary shit here, which I'm not supposed to know about, and so I won't even ask,' he said, eyeing the massive quartz crystal formation glowing in front of us. 'Why don't you just tell me what you want me to do?' He turned his baby blues back to me and raised both brows imploringly.

'I want you to stay *right* here,' I said, pointing to the spot where he stood.

'I can't wait in there somewhere?' He nodded towards the crystal structure, sounding hopeful.

'You're not supposed to be here at all,' I pointed out. 'I can't stress enough how important your cooperation is.'

'All right.' Emmett dropped to sit cross-legged on the ground to wait for me. 'What happens if you don't come back?'

I turned and made for the crystal structure. 'I'll be back.'

'Famous last words,' I heard him say behind me.

Still, I was confident that once I'd fully activated the Triogenes pyramid, this vital Signet station would be secure. I would erase Emmett's memory of these events before we returned to the site camp, and all would be well with the world. I did have the slight problem of getting past the Dracon forces that would no doubt be blocking our return route, but my friends in Amenti could help me with that.

I followed the earthen pathway through the outer crystal matrix of Meridan station. These mighty crystal clusters were surface conductors that drew down the vital Blue Flame energy that the station siphoned from the Blue Flame of Amenti via the primary Signet substation at Giza. Thus, pure love force was directed into the Earth's natural energy matrix, subtly lifting the vibrational energy of the planet. Every time one of these Signet stations came online, massive advancements were made in human consciousness with giant breakthroughs in science, medicine, the political arena, the arts and so forth. As I moved along this familiar path I marvelled at what effects my work this day might have on the planet at large.

I had been here before — the first time many aeons ago, when Meridan oversaw the construction of this Signet station; and again when my spirit walked the Halls of Amenti. Yet this was the first time I had physically moved through the structure and I felt an overwhelming sense of 'coming home' — or at least somewhere very close to home. When I emerged from the crystal cavern and the main structure of the Signet station rose high before me, the tears of pride and wonder that had been moistening my eyes overflowed; I had never felt so filled with happiness and purpose.

Each Signet station was a personal reflection of the Amenti staff member and the interstellar council leader that guarded and protected it. Back on Tara, Meridan had been a highly acclaimed etheric architect. My partner, Arcturus, was an etheric engineer; I designed structures and he dealt with their construction. My previous profession was reflected in the glowing white structure before me, for this was the only Signet station whose structure incorporated etheric matter. The outer walls and roof were made of a dense etheric substance, which was so illuminated that it was opaque, and through the white shot periodic waves of rainbow colour. The inner walls and floor were tiled white to match the towering walls, archways and arched windows. The aesthetic had a purpose, for although at present the building looked like a beautiful, majestic cathedral, at my will it would mould into an impenetrable fortress.

The advantage of building with etheric matter was that as it was the basic underlying substance of all matter within the planes of existence of this universal matrix, it could be manipulated to resonate at any frequency from the lowest density through to the physical, astral, mental and causal frequencies of the higher planes of existence. To have mastery over etheric matter was to have mastery over the quantum world. I knew I possessed this capability — I had just used it to open the gateway to this station — yet it was a talent I had been afraid to unleash upon the physical world. In truth, I feared abusing Meridan's power; and yet I knew I must start to explore it if I was to master and use it for the benefit of the Amenti Project.

I moved through my station, each room lighting up as I approached. The chambers were filled with editions of the most revered and inspirational tales of the ages, some already written, some yet to be, each stored in the medium most suited to the age of its earthly creation. For the leader of the Council of Aramatena was Triogenes, the greatest storyteller, who had inspired both the heroes of legend and the scribes who had penned their deeds. Signet Station Twelve was a storehouse for the many works of Triogenes that were, at the appointed time, automatically deposited into the psyches of worthy scribes throughout the ages. These had been placed within Meridan station before the Triogenes pyramid had been taken offline; so even though Triogenes was no longer directly connected to the Earth, his inspirational work here continued. My heart rejoiced at the realisation that today I would meet the great Triogenes himself.

As each Signet station was unique to its guardians, so was each control centre; this meant that only the Amenti staff member assigned to each particular station understood how it functioned. The control centre of Meridan station was suspended in the middle of a deep dark chasm of crystals, accessible via a long bridge. I stepped onto the bridge from the station house, unable to see anything beyond the windows that lined its passageway.

Upon my approach, the doors to the control centre parted before me, the interior flooded with light and the window shields raised, illuminating the chasm beyond. This chamber, like the rest of Meridan station, was entirely white, for that was the light colour frequency to which the Triogenes pyramid resonated. Reflecting its architect's taste, Meridan station was simple and elegant — white tiled floor, white walls, three huge white retractable shields that could be used to protect the curved windows of the rounded-off, triangular, pod-like chamber. In the centre of the chamber floor was what appeared to be a circular pool of ice.

I stepped up to the telepathic control panel to one side of the circular pool and, placing my hands upon it, gave the command to draw down the Triogenes pyramid from its dormant exile beyond the Earth's atmosphere. This event would activate the porthole of liquid light, granting me access to the station's guardian council and all the other stations in the Signet Grid — including those still inactive.

But the first place this porthole would take me was to stand before the Council of Aramatena for verification.

Above me, the huge etheric glistening white pyramid descended through the chasm, sending electric emissions shooting through the crystals on the cavern walls.

Shafts of brilliant white light began to cut through the solid surface of the porthole in the floor, turning its hard veneer to a pool of white liquid light, which swirled towards its centre to form a funnel of light.

I approached the stargate knowing I would soon be in another dimensional realm, in a distant part of our galaxy. Yet I felt no fear, nor even excitement; only a calm sense of duty as I took a running leap into the void.

CHAPTER 8

INTER-
DIMENSIONAL
TERRORISM

I plummeted headlong through the swirling, light-filled vortex and then stopped abruptly. I was still and had form, but the light mass surrounding me continued to swirl and change shape. Although I could not define it, I was aware of having entered a structure that was, to my limited perception, structureless. Within this void I sensed the presence of other light-beings, as formless as their surroundings. I felt insecure, my psyche overwhelmed by the limitlessness of this place, and yet the love I sensed radiating through me was immense.

She was overwhelmed, our heroine, said a masculine voice, the words coming from all around me. *She felt the need to construct, for here was all this wonderful high-quality etheric matter to manipulate, and she was an etheric architect by trade, with a high reputation to uphold.*

Yes, I replied. *But I fear offending my hosts with the*

need to accommodate my insecurities and my desire for form.

Deep inside, Meridan realised that such base emotions and reactions cannot exist in a higher harmonic universe, the voice pointed out. *These were causal beings whom she addressed, who existed purely to put her will into effect; her imagination was their inspiration and her comfort and happiness their highest priority. For she was a master architect of the Elohim and her will was the command of every being of Aramatena.*

This was a challenge to prove I was who I claimed to be. And, given leave to exercise my skill, I invited inspiration to take hold.

White walls manifested and moulded themselves to match the vision in my mind; a council table and chairs appeared also. To break the monotony of all the white, I created oval windows in the chamber and a transparent dome in the ceiling. Through them, the night sky of this region of space was visible, filled with celestial bodies and activity that added breathtaking scope and colour to my creation.

My own view from Aramatena was of two huge planets that revolved around each other and this one, creating a massive light vortex at their centre — the major porthole to the next universal system up from our own. The other two planets were Aveyon, a brilliant aquamarine green, and Vega, which glowed brilliant blue — the remnant of which appeared on the physical plane as the star Vega. These three planets had been the seeding point of life in our time matrix about nine hundred and fifty billion Earth years ago. The councils and planets were all causal in nature and were each connected to one of the final three Signet stations in the Amenti Project, stations ten to twelve. Together, this triad of planetary councils and stargates formed the Cradle of Lyra, which was the birthplace of all life in this lowest harmonic universe.

As I stood before the table in the council chamber in awe of my own handiwork, the members of the Council of Aramatena began to appear in the chairs.

'Our heroine was surprised to see that all the beings before her appeared human,' said the oldest and wisest-looking man, seated at the head of the table.

'Triogenes,' I surmised and bowed to him. 'I assume you could appear as a Dracon if required, but that appearance would not be as conducive to our negotiations.'

He agreed with a nod of his head, and looked to the spectacular view beyond the windows. 'Lovely. There really is a lot to be said for form,' he commented approvingly.

'It's a little sparse.' I added a few plants, some depictions from the Hall of Time Codes, and finished with a spot of high tea laid out on the conference table.

Triogenes chuckled. 'Good show. I couldn't have written it better myself. Tea anyone?'

His associates were glad to take up the offer: selections from the tea tray went floating off in all directions, and the teapot proceeded to pour itself.

'This is surely the work of Meridan, the master etheric designer,' said the woman seated alongside Triogenes, admiring the lovely room, but I believe she was more impressed with the cake.

'To be fair, it's the work of a fabulous patisserie I discovered in Double Bay,' I replied.

'Obviously humankind are progressing. There is no mistake here,' Triogenes decreed once he'd taken a few sips of tea. 'The stargate between our worlds will be open for passage once again.'

'That's it?' I ventured, watching the council indulge in their tea party. 'A good cup of tea is all it takes to re-establish long-severed inter-stellar relations?'

Triogenes nodded and smiled broadly. 'For you, Meridan, this part of your destiny was always going to be a ... well ...' he held up his plate, '... a piece of cake. The causal matter of this lower harmonic universe is, to your true self back on Tara, but one of many primitive building materials to be interwoven into your designs.'

I was overwhelmed to realise that up here in the causal realms I wasn't considered the lowly Earth being I'd imagined, but as a goddess who was greatly revered for her huge contribution to creation in this universe. I made a note to myself: in times of self-doubt, it would serve me well to remember this.

'And now that she felt mighty and significant,' Triogenes waved to me, 'she was ready to return to Earth and finish what she had begun so long ago.'

Everything around me blurred and I was set on a spiralling, roller-coaster ride back to my Signet station.

I was deposited atop the white porthole of liquid light, my flimsy physical form shaking with the after-effects of the high-frequency episode. Still hunched over on the floor, without pausing to regain my sensibilities, I desired to be transported to Thoth Station beneath Giza, where I could finally report on the events of the day to the Amenti Council.

Unfortunately for me, the porthole exit at Giza was a vertical door. I felt the cool splash of its emerald green frequency as I passed through the Thoth pyramid and was ejected through the equally green porthole at the far end of the Hall of Records. Still weak from my inter-stellar adventure, I stumbled on shaky legs into the sacred chamber to land face first on the floor.

'Mia!'

I rolled onto my back to find Polaris rushing to my aid. I smiled, pleased to see him, for through my own life experience and my reading of Ashlee Granville-Devere's journals, he had become as much of a hero in my eyes as my own husband.

'Captain,' I began, 'Albray has become a security risk —'

'We know,' Polaris calmly assured me, his blue eyes twinkling. 'Arcturus handed himself in to me; and since I revisited his meeting with Sabine Labontè this morning, he's been cleared of being a threat to your mission.'

'Déjà vu!' I exclaimed; this was almost an exact repetition of what my ambushers had told me this afternoon. 'Who else knows about this?'

Polaris seemed a little stunned by my reaction, knowing nothing of the ordeal I'd just been through. 'Denera, Tamar —'

'No,' I stressed, 'apart from Amenti staff.'

Polaris's face turned dark. 'Killian Labontè.'

'Do you know where he is now?' I was gripped by panic; was Tamar still with him?

'I dropped Labontè and Tamar back at Montségur

tomorrow morning,' he said. 'Why? What's happened? You secured your Signet station, didn't you?'

'Not before the Nefilim attempted to take it from me.' I filled him in as we walked towards Denera, who was standing behind the control panel of the Hall of Records. 'Our foe have created a new light-body shield that alters their aura to appear like that of whoever they're impersonating. The deception is practically undetectable.'

'Practically?' Denera noted my choice of words.

'It has a very subtle fluid-like flaw in its appearance,' I explained. 'Hence, the labyrinth at Montségur is now crawling with Dracon and at least a couple of the Nefilim.'

Polaris looked horrified. 'We can fetch Tamar back,' he suggested, looking ready to depart that instant.

I wasn't so compelled to rush straight to her rescue, knowing that we could cheat time. There were other more pressing concerns. 'My daughter did say she wanted the Nefilim to come to her,' I mused, 'and we still have most of the night to sort out the situation there before Tamar arrives back. What worries me more is getting Emmett Rich out of my Signet station.'

Both Polaris and Denera gasped.

'I know, I know, but what was I meant to do — leave him to the mercy of the Dracon?' I appealed.

Still their horrified expressions didn't change.

'Tell me you knocked him out, bound him, anything?' Polaris appealed.

I was too stunned by my own stupidity to answer.

'Did you check his aura for the fluid-like flaw you described to us?' Denera said hopefully.

'There was no time.' I felt pathetic trying to defend myself.

Polaris struggled to contain his frustration. 'We have to get back there, right now!' He grabbed my arm and hauled me towards the porthole.

As he did, the Signet Map within the Hall of Records' console activated itself.

'Wait!' Denera called. 'You shouldn't leave until we know this alert doesn't concern you.'

The Signet Map unfurled from the console and projected its image onto the liquid-light dome in the roof. It showed a flattened map of the world with all twelve of the Signet station locations marked; Montségur was blinking red.

'I have a very bad feeling about this,' Polaris muttered.

'Even if someone has breached the station, they can't use it,' I said, appealing to him to stay calm.

'What bothers me is that the Nefilim know that,' Polaris retorted. 'So why would they bother seizing it unless they have a use for it?'

Suddenly I felt nauseated.

'Hey, it won't be anything we can't fix,' he added, trying to reassure me. 'It's not your fault, you should have had more backup. We should have focused on getting the final stations open one at a time, instead of spreading our resources thin and trying to open them all at once.'

'I shouldn't need backup!' I wasn't going to let anyone else take the rap for this one.

'True,' Polaris agreed. 'But as you've only just activated your station, you've only just figured that out. Am I right?'

I smiled. He was right; I was a lot more aware of my personal power now.

'Look, I've made plenty of mistakes, big ones!' he said. 'So don't be —'

'Heaven preserve us!' Denera gasped, and the panic in her tone made my stomach sink.

She had stepped into the tube of light that constituted the telepathic command centre of the Hall of Records and Signet Station Four, which worked in conjunction with the Signet Map to form surveillance for the Signet stations. Denera was staring up at the domed screen on the roof, viewing the situation unfolding in the control room of Meridan station.

Emmett Rich was standing next to the white liquid-light porthole with what appeared to be a can of spray paint in his hand. 'So simple a child could do it,' he chuckled to himself, and sprayed the liquid-light surface, which instantly turned to solid gold.

'No!' I cried.

All kinds of alarming sounds began to emanate from the control panel, and Denera spoke quickly to translate them. 'The breach in security at Meridan station has been reported to the Council of Aramatena, who will destroy the Triogenes pyramid and Meridan station if Meridan does not advise otherwise within one Earth hour.'

'If that is Orme our friend has just sprayed over the porthole, it will harden and deflect whatever energy is sent down the porthole right back to the source.' Polaris sounded devastated by the destructive potential of the simple plan. 'Such a blast would destroy Aramatena, blow its sibling planets off their orbit and effectively shut down the major porthole out of this universe.'

'And also close down the Amenti passage, which means we'll all be trapped here,' I finished.

Superhuman or not, I wanted to be sick. 'So simple a child could do it' — I repeated the words of my adversary. I would never have suspected Emmett to be a foe; he seemed such a sweet, intelligent lad.

Denera urged me to pull myself together. 'No time for regrets, Meridan.'

But my remorse was too great; it felt like a monster eating away at my insides. I couldn't focus on anything but the devastation I was about to cause. 'Don't call me Meridan,' I said, feeling I could never do the goddess within me justice.

'It is your name,' Denera insisted. '*Own it.*'

I took a deep breath to gather my wits. 'Can I warn the Council of Aramatena from here?' I asked.

Denera shook her head. 'But you could quite possibly get a message to them via one of the other two planetary councils within the Cradle of Lyra.'

'Where are Zalman and Castor now?' I queried. They were the key-holders to Signet Stations Ten and Eleven whose stargates connected to Vega and Aveyon respectively.

'Zalman is doing some investigative work for Tamar,' Denera said. 'Castor, however, you'll find at his Signet station. He's —'

I didn't wait to hear the rest. I was gone through the emerald porthole passage, with Polaris hot on my heels.

CHAPTER 9

ARLIS-COCHIZEL —
LAND'S END

The pyramid of Arlis-Cochizel
manifests the illusion of realities in time,
which,
on the Earth plane,
you perceive as lives past.

Seek these lifetimes
within this pyramid,
in the quest to understand
your current existence.

Find yourself in any timeline —
draw upon that myriad of experience,
to remember who you are
and why you came here.

For every end
is the prelude to a new beginning.

We passed through a wash of glimmering silver-black energy and were elevated onto the top of a pool of liquid light of the same colour. Around us was an amazing underwater control station, situated deep in a cavern of crystals under the ocean bed off Land's End, England. The control centre was almost entirely glass, showcasing the vibrant sea life beyond and the glistening silver-black pyramid suspended overhead, which fed bolts of Blue Flame energy into the crystal conductors below.

'Welcome to Lyonesse.' Castor was there to meet us. 'Or at least that's what this area was called when it was above the water. This is the pyramid of Arlis-Cochizel, the revealer of lives past.' He motioned to the celestial powerhouse above.

'It's all beautiful,' I assured him, disappointed that I didn't have time to give it the admiration it deserved, 'but I have pressing need of your aid, Castor.'

I wasted no time in explaining the situation.

'I will go to the Council of Aveyon with your message,' Castor said, and he took our place on the silver-black pool of liquid light, which quickly formed into a whirlpool that sucked him into oblivion.

'We were brothers once, you know,' Polaris told me, making conversation while we awaited Castor's return.

'Yes, I know, I wrote about you both —' I gasped as I caught sight of a treasure I hadn't seen in some time. 'Is that ...?'

'One of the arks? Yes, indeed. But not the one you think it is. The Ark of the Ring is still safely locked away in the Sinai, where you left it.'

I moved closer to the treasure, in awe of its history. 'So this must be ...'

'The Ark of the Rod,' Polaris confirmed.

'So we know where they both are.' I was relieved by this news, as Tamar would need both tools to unlock Amenti.

'Ever since the time of Arthur the rod has been here.' Polaris smiled at me as if I should know this.

'Are you talking about King Arthur?' I asked.

'Yes, of course. That was Castor's last incarnation before he joined our ranks ... don't you remember? You were the one who handed this treasure over to him for safekeeping.'

Pangs of awareness shot through my being as, under the influence of the pyramid of lives past, my memory of meeting with King Arthur was stirred ...

I stood on a misty battlefield at dawn, heavily pregnant and weary from being pursued by those who sought the treasure in my possession. I had used the Rod of Power to spirit myself away from one place of peril to another. The King of the Britons knelt before me, and in his war-torn and battle-weary features I saw Castor.

'I have seen you in my dreams, lady,' he told me, seeking an explanation I did not have the time to give.

'A far greater enemy than the Romans is coming to claim this sacred relic,' I told him. 'Many lives have been lost to see it this far, and I can take it no further. Only you can see it to safety now, old friend.'

'What must I do?' he asked, his voice and eyes burning with conviction.

'It must be taken to the island off the far southern tip of your isle, and there you will find a safe haven,' I instructed.

'Lyonesse?' He sounded confused.

'Your enemies will try to pursue you,' I warned, 'and once you reach the said isle, you must use this treasure to sink it.'

Arthur looked shocked, but only for a moment. 'I will gladly give my life for your cause, lady.'

I smiled down at the noble king who was completely oblivious to his own destiny. 'That will not prove necessary,' I assured him, and placed a hand on his forehead. 'Remember who you really are.'

The vision faded and I was returned to the present, and Polaris, who was still awaiting an answer from me.

'So, it wasn't the Lady of the Lake who gave Arthur Excalibur,' I said.

'No,' Polaris agreed, 'it was the Lady du Lac.'

Du Lac was the name of a bloodline of Grail princesses into which many of my Dragon sisters had incarnated at one time or another. In the Halls of Amenti I had remembered a lifetime in which I too had been born into this bloodline; and some claimed my exploits in that lifetime had been handed down to the present day through the guise of Mary Magdalene.

'But how can that be?' I wondered aloud. 'The historical dates don't match up; Arthur wasn't a contemporary of Jesus Christ.' Was it my own memory that deceived me?

'True, they weren't contemporary, so how do you think the Magdalene and Arthur came to meet?' Polaris prompted.

I gasped at his implication, and observed the ancient treasure in a whole new light. 'The rod can be used to create a time tunnel!'

'Affirmative,' the captain said with a smile. 'But

only someone of your ilk, with supreme control of his or her psychic abilities, with knowledge of the Earth grid and its hot spots, who was privy to secret universal doctrine like the natural biorhythms of the planet, could have created such an accurate porthole. You see, the problem with seeking a location in the future is having sufficient knowledge of future history.'

'Wow, was I really that advanced?' I said, stunned. 'When I walked the Halls of Amenti I recalled my life as a noblewoman, a descendant of the Royal House of Israel. I was of the priestly line of the Maccabees, who reigned in Jerusalem for hundreds of years before the Romans stole it from us. My name at that time was Magdalen, it's true, but that woman's life, beliefs and associations were so different from the stories of Mary Magdalene I know that it didn't seem possible to me that they could be the same woman. If I was the Magdalene of the Bible —'

'You were,' Polaris assured me.

'Then the man I married in that lifetime was a brilliant revolutionary, not at all the passive Jesus the Church has created. His name wasn't even Jesus!'

'History is written and rewritten by the victors, and for a long time the only victors on Earth have been those seeking to hide the truth from the likes of us,' Polaris explained. 'No one has ever been able to give an exact date for Arthur's rule in Britain, or even proof that he existed at all! Why? Because he was such a threat to the Old World Order — they could not beat him, they could not kill him, they could not control him and, in the end, they could not find him ... thanks to you.'

'I remembered Magdalen's lifetime very clearly in Amenti, but I didn't recall wielding the Rod of Power, so how is it I just recalled meeting with Arthur?'

'Because the moment in question is now part of the wormhole system that runs through the Kali rift; it's a station in time that can be used in the inter-time war, and hence the fate of that moment is ever-changing.'

I was confused, and frowned.

'How can you remember the outcome of a moment that has no set outcome?' Polaris said, to try to make me feel better, but by now I was so bewildered I gave up trying to understand.

'So I truly was the Black Madonna?' I asked instead.

'As surely as I was Earnest Devere, or Captain Henry Sinclair. And as the Black Madonna, you are the only one who can unite the ring and the rod to form the key to Amenti for Kali. Which you will do if your daughter proves worthy.'

'And if she doesn't?'

Polaris didn't have an answer. Instead, he willed the lid of the ark to rise, exposing its golden belly and the glowing parts of the staff therein.

I hadn't expected to see it in three parts. 'Is it broken?'

'Not at all.' Castor's response startled us both into an about-face, hands behind our backs like children caught misbehaving. 'The pieces connect to form a sword or a longer rod and blade; hence the confusion through the ages as to whether it was a rod or a sword or a spear.'

This was all fascinating, but I needed to know the result of his meeting with the Council of Aveyon. 'What news?' I asked.

His broad smile reassured me. 'The crisis has passed. The Council of Aveyon were able to warn Aramatena in time to prevent them attempting to destroy the Triogenes pyramid.'

I breathed a huge sigh of relief, glad that I wouldn't be remembered as the person who had destroyed the primary porthole out of this universe.

'However,' Castor continued, 'if we don't do something about booting those invading bastards out of Meridan station soon, they may figure out another way of disabling the pyramid from this end.'

'But don't we need the stargate functioning in order to open Amenti?' I didn't really understand the mechanics of the grid; I was a designer of etheric architecture, not an engineer.

'No,' Polaris informed me, 'we only need the pyramid active, and it's now locked on. Of course, the defunct porthole means we can no longer directly access Meridan station via the grid, nor Aramatena, but it could have been much worse.'

'And still could be if we don't get a move on.' Caster motioned us to the porthole, and the lid of the ark closed as we departed.

'We can pick up *Klieo* from the cavern of Mamer and use her to get us to Montségur,' Polaris suggested.

'And if my husband is no longer a threat, we can recruit him to help with this clean-up,' I added.

Polaris gave me the thumbs up, before we were all swept back to Thoth Station beneath Giza.

Albray was in the Hall of Records awaiting our return with Denera, who appeared much more at ease than when I had seen her last.

'Mia!' Albray embraced me, having been told of my ordeal, then pulled back to say, 'I picked a hell of a time to drop the ball.'

'Well,' I smiled, 'at least now we know why Sabine didn't give you any serious sabotage orders. The Nefilim had their own plans and were just aiming to get you out of the way.'

He returned my smile with one that looked forced. 'We need to talk.'

'No, we don't.' I took him by the hand and led him into the hall, leaving Castor, Polaris and Denera to discuss our next move.

'Mia, *please* ...' Albray urged me to hear him out, bursting to clear his conscience.

'I know what you're going to say,' I told him, for in my heart I did know. 'I know what she demanded of you, and, unless you did it by choice, we have nothing to discuss but the state of your well-being.' I brushed back his long, dark fringe to see the relief upon his face. 'Are you okay?' I asked.

'I'm fine *now*.' Obviously his own well-being had been the last thing on his mind. 'Honestly, I don't remember a thing.'

'Well, if neither of us remembers the event, we can pretend it never happened —'

Albray shook his head and reaching inside his jacket, he produced a sheaf of handwritten papers. 'Unfortunately, Tamar witnessed most of it.'

My eyes welled with tears as I sensed my husband's shame.

'She was surprisingly mature about the whole thing,' he said with a heavy sigh. 'She even managed to make me feel a little better about the episode.' Then his expression changed from shame to annoyance. 'What I don't feel good about, however, is the fact that Tamar is falling for Killian Labontè, and as he's the only one, apart from our staff, who knew I'd been set up, chances are he set you up too.'

'Not good,' I agreed, confused by the events I'd witnessed this day. 'So where does Emmett fit into all this? I got the impression that Emmett and Killian don't get along. Was that an act, like Killian's hatred of his parents? Are they all in on it? And what about Emmett's father, Dr Rich? I didn't find anything even slightly suspect about his light-body, nor Emmett's for that matter. If their bodies were shielded by the Nefilim's new auric simulator, I sure as hell didn't notice it.'

I was distracted by Zalman striding past us into the Hall of Records.

'We need to take some prisoners and carry out some serious telepathic interrogation,' Albray said, and we both turned to follow Zalman and discover the reason for his haste.

'I have traced the various family lines that sprang from Miss Koriche's gene pool,' Zalman informed us. 'She currently has twenty-six living male descendants, from twenty-five different branches of her family tree, and they are spread all over the world.'

'Bugger,' said Polaris.

'Why are we tracing Miss Koriche's family?' I asked, puzzled.

Polaris filled Albray and me in on the breakthrough they'd had regarding the identification of Mathu's current earthly embodiment, via a pendant he had left with Miss Koriche to pass onto her sons.

'Killian Labontè is one of those descendants,' Zalman advised us, and the shock was visible on every face around him.

'Are you telling me Tamar might be right about him being an innocent victim?' Albray said; my husband didn't like to think his instincts might be failing him.

'Sabine knew you'd been set up,' I pointed out. 'Perhaps she set me up too.'

'But Sabine didn't know that Polaris knew I'd been set up,' Albray said. 'So she couldn't have advised anyone of his involvement, nor his appearance to enable one of the Nefilim to assume his form to deceive you.'

'Are you defending her?' I folded my arms, suspicious that he might have remembered more than he was telling.

'*No*,' he stressed. 'I'm just trying to narrow down the possibilities —'

'To Killian Labontè,' I cut in. I believed his fatherly instincts were interfering with his reasoning ability.

Zalman spoke up over the interruptions: 'However, the family most likely to be in possession of the pendant at this time is that of Dr Colin Rich.'

I gasped. 'Emmett?'

I looked up to the dome, where the golden slab that had replaced the pool of liquid light at the heart of Meridan station was still visible. Emmett was no longer in the control centre, however. Perhaps he'd gone in search of an escape route. I wondered how long it would be before he figured out that he was trapped in there until I released him.

'Surely he cannot be Mathu?' I said. 'Why would Mathu do this?'

'The being who disabled your porthole is obviously not the real Emmett Rich,' Denera pointed out. 'Merely one of the Nefilim posing as him.'

'The Nefilim kill those whose identity they assume,' Polaris added, 'so the real Emmett Rich is most likely dead.'

'For all our sakes, I hope not,' Denera said.

I disagreed with Polaris too. 'No, I suspect this identity takeover was a last-minute counterplan.'

'What makes you say that?' Albray asked, curious.

'Emmett confronted me about Tamar's association with Killian today, right before I entered the labyrinth. I'm sure his concern about her was real emotion, which is the one thing the Nefilim can't fake … that's what made me suspect that a Nefilim was impersonating Albray, and then I discovered the auric irregularity.'

'Let us find out. I'll need a memory reference to pinpoint the event,' Denera said. She approached me, placed a hand either side of my head and told me to relax. 'Think back to that confrontation with Emmett,' she instructed.

I did, and Denera released me. 'Very good,' she said, and stepped up onto the circular platform before the control station. The light-tube closed around her and its liquid-light walls relayed images of the event. The almost completely circular room and the dome overhead made it seem as if we were standing right in the middle of the action.

'*All you history hunters are alike!*' Emmett yelled down the stairwell after me. '*Why do you think the past is so much more important than the present? Nothing is more important than the present — it's the only reality that actually exists! Where we can have an effect!'*

'Sounds like something Mathu would say,' Polaris commented to Albray, who nodded; it seemed they both liked this candidate for our missing team member more than Killian Labontè.

Emmett gave up on the argument with me and walked straight past the bag I'd dropped without noticing it, back up to the site camp. The figure of Dr Rich emerged from the shadows to claim the bag, then transformed his appearance into that of his son to pursue me.

'It appears Meridan's hunch was correct,' Denera commented as the telepathic control tube retracted. 'Go and fetch Emmett Rich to safety, but remember, we are still not sure he is Mathu.'

As she finished speaking, Levi entered the Hall of Records loaded with weaponry. 'Heard about all the commotion,' he said.

'Now that one's got my name on it,' Castor commented, referring to a sub-machine-gun-sized liquid-light gun, like the smaller one Tamar carried.

'I don't think so.' Polaris stepped forward to relieve Levi of the coveted weapon, but Levi steered clear of all the drooling men, my husband among them, and said, 'This is for Meridan.' He handed it to me, ignoring the protests of the menfolk. It was surprisingly light.

'Not only will it take out our enemies ten times faster than the handgun, but it has a stream function.' Levi turned the weapon on its side to show me the switch. 'And that ought to dissolve that Orme coating on your porthole fairly efficiently.'

'Oh my goddess, you are a genius!' I said. I hadn't

112

even considered the possibility of being able to reverse the disaster, and I kissed Levi for being so brilliant.

'There is nothing you can do that we cannot undo,' Polaris said, reminding me of his earlier claim as he accepted a handgun from Levi. 'Now all we have to do is arrive at Montségur at the precise time you opened the secret passage through to Meridan station . . .'

'Twelve-fourteen in the afternoon on 29 March 2017.' Denera relayed the numbers as recorded by the Hall of Records and the Signet Map.

'. . . and take the station back,' Polaris concluded. He holstered his new weapon on his belt alongside the many others he'd collected in his travels.

'And save the prince,' I added. 'Both of them.'

Albray and Polaris looked at me as if I was kidding.

'Until we're certain which of them our missing teammate is unconsciously residing within, we must protect both Emmett and Killian,' I explained.

They opened their mouths to argue the issue.

'However,' I cut in, 'I must say it's awfully nice to see you two agreeing on something for a change.'

'Well, that alone ought to tell you something,' Albray said, and Polaris backed him up with an 'Indeed'.

Castor lost patience with the three of us. 'We are on a bit of a tight schedule, people, so if you wouldn't mind?' He motioned us towards the door.

CHAPTER 10

BLINDSIDED

As the priority of the day was to ensure the safety of Emmett Rich, the *Klieo*, skippered by Levi for this mission, dropped our party off in the middle of the site camp.

The site office proved deserted, so the next place we looked for Emmett was in the quarters he shared with his father, Dr Rich. Before we'd even entered we spied the thick red substance oozing from under the door. The smell of death made my blood run cold with apprehension of what lay beyond.

'We're too late,' I feared.

Albray pulled me aside and kicked the door wide open. The room's walls, ceiling and furniture were splattered with blood and shredded human remains.

'Dear goddess!' Even Castor was straining his imagination to envisage what kind of killing technique had been used. 'This is high- level carnage, even for the Dracon; it must be the Nefilim's handiwork.'

'Is it Emmett?' Some warrior I was: I couldn't bring myself to check.

The men entered gingerly, wary that the killer might still be present and of how easily they could slip on the gooey remains coating the floor.

My eyes glued to the ground at the doorway, I noted several faint bloody footprints heading away from the accommodation. 'Tracks!' I advised my company.

Albray was happy to come outside to take a look. 'It's hard to tell, but I don't think Emmett's here,' he said.

'Then who was that?' I motioned back to where I dared not look.

'I'm afraid we're down an anthropologist,' Albray said gently.

'Dr Rich!' I was shocked, but it made sense: the being that had followed me into the caves with my bag earlier today had been wearing Dr Rich's persona before it transformed into Emmett. 'They killed an innocent, brilliant man to get to me,' I realised and my heart sank.

'Can we go back in time and prevent this?' I called out to Polaris, who was still inside the room.

'We've just about exhausted our windows of opportunity in these twenty-four hours,' he replied. 'We can't run the risk of bumping into ourselves. That could cause a catastrophic quantum anomaly, the science of which is far too complicated to go into right now.'

'Hey!' A voice hailed us from the other side of the camp. André. 'What's going on?' he yelled as he made his way towards us.

'Oh crap!' Albray said. We didn't have time to explain this mess, nor our mysterious guests. Luckily, both Polaris and Castor were still inside the room and out of André's line of vision.

'Your modern English is getting better,' I commented to Albray, hiding my huge weapon behind his back. 'I'll take care of this.'

I was careful not to step on the footprint tracks as I met André halfway and steered him towards the canteen.

'Why are you poking around in Dr Rich's quarters?' André demanded as we entered the empty eating area.

'I was looking for Emmett actually. Have you seen him?'

'I only just got back from town,' he explained and then frowned. 'Is something amiss?'

I guessed he was wondering why I was seeking an office boy of no consequence. I vagued out a little as I considered what to do about André, and my third-eye vision kicked in, as it often did at such times, and I spied the fluid irregularity in the Frenchman's aura. This was not André. How stupid of me not to have checked his light-body. How ridiculous that I'd left my weapon with my husband! One scream would bring my male company running, but by the time they got here, I would be dead.

'Oh well, not to worry,' I said and backed away towards the door. 'I'm sure he's around here somewhere. I'll find him.'

My companion knew that he'd been had and grinned at my feeble attempt to depart. 'I don't think so,' he said, and transformed into a huge demon-like being, more human in appearance than the Dracon, but with leathery orange-hued skin, black almond-shaped eyes, pointed ears, and horns protruding from either side of his forehead.

'You are Nefilim.' I stated the obvious in the

hope of getting some information out of him before he tried to kill me.

'They call me the Smiter,' he said, and a metal spike shot out of the metal band on his wrist. 'I have an aptitude for war and plague.' And he moved in on me.

I sidestepped, my heart pumping twelve to the dozen. *I am the greatest etheric architect in this universe*, I told myself as the creature and I circled one another. *Ether is the basis of all matter on every plane of existence, and thus I can manipulate it here as easily as I did on Aramatena.*

'I am a master of creation,' I challenged him, instilling the fact into my own head in the process. 'Let us see which force is greater.'

The creature took a flying leap at me; my knee-jerk reaction was to will the cement floor to rise like a barricade between us. The Nefilim hit the obstacle with all the force one would imagine from an unexpected airborne collision with a cement wall, then fell to the floor, hard. The surface enfolded him and held him fast, as per my mental instruction, then hardened, leaving nothing but my adversary's face exposed.

'Good goddess,' exclaimed Albray. He and my other male companions had arrived in the doorway in time to witness the end of the confrontation.

I grinned, having rather amazed myself, and turned to my husband. 'Honey, I'm home,' I announced.

'You certainly are!' Polaris laughed, astonished. 'And I still haven't worked out what my superhuman talent is!'

'Me either,' Arcturus said with a frown.

'But what about —' Polaris cut himself short.

'What about what?' Arcturus prompted but Polaris waved it off as not important.

'My Lady du Lac never ceases to amaze,' Castor said.

This was the first time in my living memory that anyone had referred to me as the Lady du Lac and I realised that the title didn't refer to any single woman. Once a Grail princess stepped into her power, she was the Lady du Lac.

Polaris squatted next to the demon and glared at it. 'What have you done with Emmett Rich?'

The creature grinned. 'A bit precious, is he?' And it gave a great heave.

'Watch out!' I cried, but too late to prevent the monster vomiting green bile into Polaris's face. The fluid burned into his flesh like acid and he fell to the ground, gritting his teeth and kicking his feet in an attempt to control the pain whilst his heightened metabolism set about healing the wound.

As I rushed to aid our fallen comrade, Albray took aim with my weapon and shot the demon full of cosmic light.

I knelt beside Polaris. 'What can I do?' I asked, but he waved me back to our captive.

As loving energy filled the creature, it began to purge the black residue of its Orme addiction. Before long, all trace of its demonic nature had vanished to be replaced by the glittering ethereal being he'd once been. I restored the floor to its former state, and all the paraphernalia the Nefilim warrior had been carrying was left sitting on its surface.

'What have you done with Emmett Rich?' Albray was in the spirit's face before he had time to realise what had happened.

I am free! He wasn't interested in questions; he just wanted to celebrate his release from his worldly burdens.

Albray spotted the wristband that housed the Orme spike lying on the ground and retrieved it to threaten the witness. 'Answer the question or I'll spray you with this stuff and send you right back to hell.'

I am sure I haven't done anything to him, the spirit replied, looking saddened by Albray's aggressive stance. *Who is Emmett Rich?*

'Great!' My husband flung his arms in the air, knowing the being could no longer lie. Then he turned back to the spirit. 'Which of your brethren are currently attempting to take Meridan station?' He would know that much at least.

Our lord sent Namtar and Erragal to take the station.

'Erragal knows where the frequency fence's control centre is,' I advised. 'He's one of Tamar's primary targets.'

'Well, what are we waiting for?'

We all turned to find Polaris on his feet, his face nearly restored. 'Let's go get them on side.'

Before exiting the canteen, I looked at the discarded technology on the floor and spotted a small module. I retrieved it, guessing it to be the Nefilim's new auric simulator. *This ought to interest Levi*, I thought, and tucked it into my pocket before following my teammates outside.

We escorted our captive to the *Klieo*, which was hovering unseen high above Montségur. Levi flew her down and picked up the Anu stray for safekeeping until we got back.

'This is going to be intense,' Albray commented as we made our way towards the entrance to the caves, which was also where the bloody footprints led. 'Be prepared.' He tried not to sound like he was giving me a lecture as he handed my weapon back to me.

'Erragal wasn't made King of the Underworld and a major confidant of Ill's without good reason,' Castor warned. 'And Namtar is better known as the fate cutter, as he too is a harbinger of disease and pestilence. He usually associates with Ishtar, so I'd say he's probably the Nefilim who's been posing as —'

'Morell Labontè,' Albray and I chorused.

Which raised another concern.

'So what if we do take him out?' I said. 'How are we going to explain all these dead bodies and mysterious disappearances?'

'You don't,' Polaris said simply. 'As it's time for you to disappear along with everyone else.'

I didn't feel ready to face such a huge life change. 'So that's it? My career and my life here are over?'

'What do you mean?' Castor said. 'You're only just embarking on your true vocation now.'

'But what about my publishing deal?' I felt very disappointed about that. I'd been told by Lugh Lamhfada that it was my destiny to share the story of my bloodline with the general populace. 'I still have book three to hand in.'

'If the last manuscript shows up anonymously, do you think your publisher would hesitate to capitalise on that?' asked Albray, who was used to operating outside the boundaries of time. 'Especially considering that huge advance they paid you.'

'True,' I conceded, 'but without proof it came from me, then —'

'If it means so much to you, I'll personally take you back in time and you can hand your publisher the last two manuscripts at once,' Polaris offered.

'Wow!' My mind boggled, as this meant that in some future reality I'd already finished writing my trilogy. 'I'd greatly appreciate that, Captain.'

'Then consider it done.'

Polaris took out his liquid-light gun as we descended the deep, dim stairway that led into the caves beneath Montségur. At the bottom, I took the lead and, each employing our third-eye vision, we proceeded in darkness. I followed the contours of the cave's light-body, which were as plain to me as if I'd been wearing infra-red goggles.

As we drew close to the tunnel entrance that led to the annexe containing the hidden gateway to Meridan station, I noticed some dark shadowy anomalies up ahead. When the shadows began to move towards us, my companions opened fire. As the liquid light spread through the shadows' forms it was plain to see that they were Dracon. I needed no further prompting and opened fire myself, blazing a trail with my superior weapon to the annexe where the Nefilim who had posed as Albray earlier awaited us. Only now he was wearing his Nefilim persona and was no longer incapacitated as I had left him. He exhibited the same demon-like features as the Smiter, only he was far more sinister and much better dressed, in a stylish black suit, glittering gold cape and wide-brimmed hat.

I didn't stop to chat, I just opened fire.

Namtar wrapped the cape around himself and bowed his head — his Orme-reinforced clothing formed a shield that my light-bullets bounced off. All four of us fired upon the target at once, but, unable to get a clear shot, we ceased wasting ammunition.

Namtar chuckled at our attempts to take him down and raised his head slightly to view us. His focus came to rest on Albray. 'Well, if it isn't my wife's toy boy. She just can't wait to see you again.'

Albray fired upon the beast, who resumed his protective stance and then vanished completely. 'Shit!'

'He's not called a god of dis-ease for no reason,' Polaris advised my husband. 'Don't let him bait you.'

The captain gestured to me to open the gate. 'We'll get Namtar later,' he said. 'The priority is to get Erragal out of the Signet station.'

I closed the gateway behind us and we followed the path through the crystal formations that led to Meridan station. When the station itself came into view, my company were completely in awe of the celestial structure, but there was no time to stand around and discuss the dynamics of my design.

We were hurrying down the main hall to the control centre when a whistle brought us to a halt outside the historical reference room, located through an arched doorway to our left. There we found Erragal, still wearing Emmett's form, comfortably sprawled on a lounge reading a book.

'Interesting stuff, Meridan,' he said, tilting the book to show us the cover. It was entitled *The Black Madonna* and I was shocked to see I was the author. 'It's the final book in your trilogy,' he told me before shifting his gaze to Albray. 'Haven't you been a naughty boy,' he grinned.

Albray was riled by the comment, but before he, or any of us, could fire, a shadow moved past us, spraying all our torsos with a thick coating of gold. It hardened like stone, completely incapacitating our upper body and arms. The shadow was a *jinn*, a demon conjured through blood sacrifice from the lower etheric world. The Nefilim and the Dracon used these creatures for protection from higher ethereal forces and frequencies, as they acted like a low-grade etheric shield, too dense for higher frequencies to penetrate. They could also perform physical tasks for their masters — like coating us all with the dregs of Erragal's spray paint.

The *jinn* took a second pass at us, spraying the men's feet to immobilise them completely.

'Goddamn you!' Albray cursed.

'Yes, he has,' Erragal said, getting up to remove our weapons. He was especially impressed with my gun. 'Just what I need,' he taunted me.

'That is a creating weapon, what could you want with it?' I spat back.

Erragal didn't know about my rediscovered talent of manipulating matter, so I wanted to pump him for information while he still felt he had the upper hand.

'Before I became engrossed in your book, I was reading this.' He motioned to an old scroll unfurled on one of the tables. 'It's the true story of King Arthur,' he glanced to Castor, 'as written by Magdalen.' He turned back to me. 'It tells me that Signet Station Eleven is where the Rod of Power has been hiding since the Dark Ages, and as you've now supplied me with this weapon, I can reactivate the porthole and use it to get to any damn Signet station I please.'

Obviously he didn't realise the station was being monitored from the Hall of Records. 'Only I can use the porthole,' I warned. I didn't want a repeat of today's emergency.

'Not true,' Erragal said, to my annoyance. 'Only you can open the porthole, it's true. But once you have … it's free passage for all who manage to gain entry to your station.'

I looked to the menfolk, hoping he was lying, but judging by the looks of horror on their faces it seemed he was right.

'I know all you bloodline bitches have a superpower of some sort,' he went on, and produced the stun-gun I'd used to restrain Namtar earlier. I'd left it in the Signet station as I didn't want to be carrying weapons during my audience with the Council of Aramatena. 'Still, I wouldn't get any grand ideas if you cherish your teammates here.' The demi-god emptied the gun of its incapacitating darts and replaced them with a cartridge from his pocket. 'These darts are filled with Orme, and although it would be a great waste of life-juice to off your friends without sucking them dry first, my spook …' he tossed the weapon to the *jinn*, which instantly aimed it at my husband, '…won't hesitate to damn them all to hell if you don't cooperate.'

My companions looked at me, wondering if I was going to call his bluff. Exposing my abilities to one of the enemy wasn't a wise idea, but I couldn't stand back and do nothing. I focused on the stun-gun and willed it to melt.

'Are we clear?' Erragal interrupted my concentration.

My mental instruction seemed to have no effect on the weapon. I could only conclude that my will was unable to penetrate the *jinn*'s dense, low-grade etheric matter. Erragal must have summoned this demon from the deepest, darkest realms of density and I shuddered to think what kind of blood sacrifice he'd arranged to secure its services.

'I understand,' I said.

My companions looked stupefied that I hadn't rearranged the universe to our advantage, but I shook my head at them, hoping they would understand that my hands were tied.

Erragal didn't know what I was really capable of, so I might still be able to play my hand when we were beyond the range of his demon.

'This shadow and I are telepathically joined and it sees all I see,' Erragal warned me. 'The second he suspects you of dicking me around, he'll damn all your lovers beyond where even this,' he raised the liquid-light machinegun, 'will bring them back.'

'What does he mean "lovers"?' Albray looked at Polaris and Castor.

'Don't let him bait you,' Polaris reminded him.

'Because I might find out something you don't want me to know?' Albray spat back.

'Oh, this is too much fun!' Erragal cried. His attention shifted from me to my teammates. 'I would stay, divide and conquer some more, but Meridan and I have many an important engagement to attend before your little superwoman returns in the morning.'

How could he know that Tamar wouldn't be back until tomorrow?

'Let's go, angel.' Erragal grabbed me with one hand, still holding my huge weapon in the other, and dragged me towards the station's exit, leaving the men to stew under the guard of his demon.

'What have you done with Emmett Rich?' I asked, making conversation.

'It's a shame you need your mouth to open the gateway, because I would truly love to close it permanently,' the demi-god said without breaking his stride. 'Still, then I couldn't do this.' He turned and shoved his tongue in my mouth. I gagged.

'Every time you ask me a question, I'm going to do that, and next time it won't just be my tongue I stick in your mouth,' he said with a grin. 'Anything else you want to know?'

When I declined to answer, he resumed dragging me along the pathway through the outer crystal structure. He was obviously expecting to find his Dracon friends awaiting him on the other side of the gateway, but when I opened it he would behold a bunch of Anu angels instead. So I complied with his order to open the porthole, and was stunned when Namtar and a horde of Dracon greeted us.

'There is nothing you can do that we cannot undo,' Namtar explained with glee as he pushed past me into Meridan station. 'Time to go fetch your husband for my wife.'

I was so tempted to retaliate with a show of force, to bring down those huge crystals on top of these destructive beings, but that wasn't my mission. My mission was to save every living soul on Earth; besides which, the *jinn* that was linked telepathically with Erragal had an Orme bullet aimed at my husband. I had to bide my time, and try to get Erragal into the control centre so that Denera could see what was unfolding here.

I began to sing the note that closed the gateway, but Erragal clamped a hand over my mouth. 'Leave it open,' he said, and shoved me back inside the station.

Namtar was keen to get to Albray, and Erragal directed him to the historical reference room. Namtar disappeared through the archway and his Dracon troops positioned themselves down the station hallway and at the entrance, to fortify their position.

Erragal dragged me down the hall. I wasn't as resistant now, as I wanted to reach the control station as quickly as possible. Still, if I didn't put up some kind of fight, he would become suspicious. We reached the bridge to the control station, and Erragal could not fail to be awed by the sight of the crystal walls of the cavern glowing with Blue Flame energy, which they drew down into the core of the Earth from the huge pyramid above.

'The frequencies of this porthole are going to tear you apart, you know that, don't you?' I said.

'That was a question.' The demi-god turned to me, more furious than before.

'It was rhetorical,' I protested, but he merely grunted, eager to keep moving. 'Worry about your own skin,' he advised.

Upon our approach, the doors before us parted. When we reached the porthole, Erragal let me go. He flipped the switch on the side of my weapon and fired a stream of liquid light onto the Orme-coated surface, dissolving the solid gold layer. Then he tossed the weapon aside.

'Now,' he said, 'if I end up anywhere but Signet Station Eleven, you know what's going to happen, don't you, angel?'

This was the perfect opportunity for me to summarise the situation for Denera's benefit without Erragal suspecting we were under surveillance.

'The *jinn* you have guarding my menfolk with an Orme gun is going to shoot them,' I said, trying not to appear smug. If the Nefilim thought I was going to allow them to get their hands on the Rod of Power, they were sadly mistaken.

We arrived safely at the beautiful underwater station hosting the Arlis-Cochizel pyramid. I was surprised that Erragal had not perished en route; Nefilim technology was becoming more and more innovative and I could not understand why any species would go to so much trouble to ensure that they and everything around them were damned.

Erragal seemed surprised that I hadn't attempted to thwart his voyage here. 'That's the trouble with being good, isn't it, angel, you have to be honest and forthright.' His chuckle turned to delight as he spotted the Ark of the Rod nearby.

Even we angels get to twist the truth a bit, I thought, but suppressed my smile and faked distress. 'Touch the ark and it will strike you down.'

'You open it!' He pushed me towards the treasure. 'I want to see the Rod of Power.'

I obliged from where I stood, using my skill of manipulating matter — although to Erragal it seemed I simply employed a telekinetic talent. The ark's ornate lid lifted to expose the three parts of the Rod of Power.

Pleased that all was as it should be, Erragal motioned for me to replace the lid. He drew a small metallic box from his pocket and opened it, releasing millions of tiny dark airborne particles, which converged in a swarm upon the ark and it vanished.

'Nanobots,' I surmised. The Nefilim were famous for their nanotechnology, but I'd had no idea it had advanced so far. 'They have made the ark invisible.' I clapped as if it were a cheap party trick, but in truth I needed to know if the technology had teleportation ability or if it was merely an invisibility cloak — for the Nefilim truly loved to boast.

'I am sorry to inform you that the treasure you have dedicated your many Earthly existences to protect is now safely residing in my realms, where you'll never find it,' Erragal said with great pleasure.

So that was how Namtar had vanished earlier, and how Erragal had escaped my daughter's time warp last night. It also explained the Dracon's ability to teleport.

Erragal grabbed my arm once more. 'After I've ensured Meridan station is secure, you and I are going to do a tour of the Signet Grid and see what other treasures we can pilfer.'

'Sounds like fun,' I said flatly, thankful that my sisters were coming to my aid as I spoke.

CHAPTER 11

CRAFTY WOMEN

SUSAN DEVERE — TALORI
Solarian and I were at Signet Station Five in Xian, China, when Denera's face appeared in the blue liquid-light porthole pool in its ceiling. She explained the situation at Meridan station and urged us to report there as soon as possible to assist. As it was our partners that Erragal's *jinn* was holding hostage, we had a vested interest in aiding our sister in her plight.

Fortunately, following a quick inter-stellar audience with the Council of Alcyone in the Pleiades, I had just succeeded in activating the Teco-Porima pyramid, and as my Signet station was now secure, Solarian and I were able to leave for Montségur immediately.

Before we arrived at Meridan station I assumed the form of a Dracon warrior; morphogenetics and DNA dynamics was my area of expertise. As we were deposited on top of the glistening white porthole of Signet Station Twelve, I nearly scared the wits out of Solarian.

'*Susan*, don't do that without warning me!'

Solarian often called me the name she had

known me by in her last incarnation as Ashlee Granville-Devere.

'How about a kiss?' I teased her.

'Spare me.' She shoved my ugly moosh away.

I spotted Meridan's weapon discarded on the floor. 'The universe always provides,' I said, retrieving it and heading for the bridge into the station complex. 'Be back in just a tick.'

I slung the light-gun over my right shoulder and proceeded down the corridor. It was lined with Dracon, whose ugly appearance and low-grade energy made my skin crawl; they were a vulgar contrast to the spiritual architecture and pure white décor. Not one of the warriors attempted to address me as I passed, for I was wearing the insignia of a Dracon captain. As I entered through the archway into the historical reference room, I moved the weapon into firing position, where I found Castor and Polaris under the guard of the armed *jinn*.

'Best-looking reptilian I've ever seen,' Castor commented to Polaris, for my partner could see through my disguise.

I opened fire upon their captor. The stream of liquid light seemed to have little effect at first, beyond blinding it with its brilliance. But it provided sufficient distraction for me to fire on my menfolk, dissolving their golden restraints. They turned to help me face the Dracon onslaught. The guards were confused by my reptilian form and they focused their fire on the escaped prisoners. Castor and Polaris had been relieved of their liquid-light guns by Erragal, so were forced to resort to lesser weapons and hand-to-hand combat. In the meantime, I finished off the demon. The shadow slowly broke down under the pressure of so much light and released its fatal Orme weapon, which I was quick to snatch up and hook onto my own weapons belt.

'*Ah-Ta P'tah Or-um!*' I chanted, inviting the demon to be blessed and return to the light divine.

But the shadow struggled to the bitter end, and instead of being redeemed by the divine light it chose to retreat to the hell from which it had been summoned; a decision I could not understand and pitied greatly.

I turned the stream of light upon the Dracon that were giving my partner and Polaris so much trouble, and the beasts dropped like flies exposed to insect spray. As they convulsed themselves into a higher state of being, I finally got to ask the question foremost in my mind. 'Where's Arcturus?'

'Namtar took him and vanished,' Polaris said, extremely agitated by the fact. If we lost even one member of Amenti's staff to an Orme death, there would be no going back to Tara for any of us. 'We have to get him back.'

'And how do you plan to do that?' I asked. None of us had any idea where Namtar had taken our teammate.

Polaris was perplexed but determined. 'By ensuring that Arcturus isn't here to be taken in the first place.'

MIA DEVERE — MERIDAN

When my captor and I arrived back at Meridan station, I wasn't surprised to find Talori waiting for us. She took aim at Erragal with my liquid-light gun

132

and he was flat on his back before he knew what had hit him. Emmett Rich's form dissolved away and for the first time I saw Erragal as the beast he truly was. The irises of his eyes burned yellow and the whites were bloodshot with hatred. He began to contort and convulse, mumbling venomously to himself.

'What's that he's saying?' Talori asked, but I was unable to translate. There was only one tongue that we staff of Amenti did not understand and that was the language of the dark arts.

A dark shadow began to form around Erragal, slowing the light flow through his body.

'Perhaps that demon is re-forming,' I said, and advised Talori to fire upon Erragal again.

Talori did, but discovered that she was out of ammunition — my weapon had been used a lot more during this mission than we had anticipated.

Erragal reached into his pocket and produced the little metal tin of nanobots.

'Don't let him open that!' I cried.

'Mine!' Solarian called out, and willed the object to herself, but due to the shadow now protecting Erragal, her will was not as effective. Erragal had to struggle against her intent to unlatch the catch on the item, but the lid popped open nevertheless and a swarm of nanobots covered him and they and he vanished.

'What the hell just happened?' Polaris demanded.

'We just let one of Tamar's primary targets escape,' I replied, and my tone discouraged him from trying to place blame in any quarter. Then I noticed someone missing and my heart sank in my chest. 'Where's Albray?'

No one wanted to be the one to tell me, and they didn't have to. *Time to go fetch your husband for my wife* — I recalled Namtar's words and they made me sick to my stomach.

'How is it that the Nefilim could identify Albray and me as Amenti staff members?' I asked. 'Who was their informant? André perhaps? Or Molier?'

'It wouldn't be the first time that damned vampire has brought one of us to the attention of the Nefilim,' Solarian commented, having been exposed by Molier herself in the past. 'The Nefilim have probably been tracking you since you laid Molier to rest in the Sinai.'

'Meridan,' Castor interrupted, looking sorry to bother me with other concerns right now, 'did Erragal obtain the Ark of the Rod?'

I shook my head. 'He thinks he did. But what he got was a very beautiful replica with no power whatsoever.'

'The illusionist returns,' Solarian said with a smile, pleased I had tapped into my higher abilities.

'Still, for all my talent, I couldn't prevent them taking my husband,' I said. 'His last confrontation with that goddess of depravity hurt him enough. I can't allow her to inflict her will on him again.' I choked back my urge to weep. 'What do I do?'

'Remove all the Anu soul minds from this mountain,' Solarian suggested.

'Collapse the outer labyrinth that leads to the gateway,' Talori advised, 'and secure the station.'

'And we should report back to Giza, as there's no threat awaiting Tamar here now.' Castor put in his two cents' worth.

I looked to Polaris, wondering if he had anything to add; he was deep in thought. 'We're going about this all wrong,' he said at last. 'We need to go back in time and open the remaining stations.'

'How far back?' Solarian queried.

'As far as current circumstances will allow, so that the Nefilim have no chance of undoing any good we do.'

'Are you telling me that I have to go through opening this station all over again!' I asked, on the verge of freaking out.

'It won't be so harrowing this time, I promise,' Polaris told me. 'And it means none of this will happen.'

'And what about Albray? His is one of the stations we need to open,' I pointed out.

'I'll see to his rescue immediately after we've locked down this station and delivered the redeemed Anu soul minds from this battle to Lugh Lamhfada,' Polaris said. 'I can retrieve Albray from Montségur before he requests me to take him captive after his run-in with Ishtar.'

'Can't we avoid that incident altogether?' I appealed, but Polaris shook his head.

'As I explained before, the time line is too tight around that incident … I can't risk running into myself. However, my plan will avoid Arcturus being taken a second time, and if we go back to the past to open and secure Meridan station, then chances are the labyrinth beneath Montségur will never be discovered, therefore you won't be called in to investigate and —'

'And Ishtar and Albray will never meet,' I concluded, excited by Polaris's foresight. 'But will Ishtar still get the ringstone?'

Polaris grinned. 'Not if we get it first.'

CHAPTER 12

TWO PRINCES

TAMAR DEVERE — KALI

Killian and I were deposited back at Montségur, just outside the site camp at dawn on Monday morning. As soon as we hit the ground, Killian ripped off the blindfold that Polaris had insisted he wear. 'So your time lord friend still doesn't trust me,' he said.

'I still don't trust you,' I replied cheekily.

'Why not?' Killian grinned and I could tell our kiss was on his mind. 'I know you know that I'm not one of those creatures.'

'But you have the potential to be,' I bantered as we walked into camp.

'And you don't?' He had a point. 'At this stage of the game, don't you think it's harder for me to trust you than for you to trust me?'

'What choice do you have? You need me.'

'And you don't need me?' Killian wasn't just pretending to be insulted now.

I shrugged, maintaining my playful manner. 'I'm still deciding.'

He was amused by my response, but as he moved in to kiss me again I walked on. All seemed quiet

136

and calm in the site camp; the project team were yet to arise. My first priory was to find my mother.

'Hey, not fair,' Killian protested. 'Don't I get the chance to prove my worth?'

I rolled my eyes and looked at him as he caught up with me. 'I don't measure worth by a person's —'

'Labontè! Tamar!'

The call came from the site office. We looked in that direction to see Emmett Rich running towards us, distraught. 'Thank God you're back!' As he came closer it was plain to see that he'd been crying. 'Everyone is dead!' he blurted out.

'Everyone?' I panicked for my parents.

Killian was more concerned about his project. 'What do you mean, dead? How?' He took hold of Emmett as if to shake information out of him.

'I don't know,' Emmett said. 'I went out yesterday looking for you,' his gaze turned my way, 'and when I came back . . .' He choked up and shook his head, unable to say the words. 'See for yourself.' He pointed towards the site accommodation.

Killian released Emmett and ran over to the sleeping quarters.

'My parents?' I said, preparing to race off myself.

'From what I can tell, they're not among the dead.' Emmett allayed my worst fear. 'The last time I saw your mother she was heading into the caves.'

I set out in that direction.

He came after me. 'It's no use. The entrance has been filled in.'

I stopped. 'It's collapsed?'

'No,' he insisted. 'It's as if the caves never existed.'

I frowned as I thought on the situation. *Perhaps Mother succeeded in opening the Signet station?* The notion almost brought a smile to my face, but for the sound of violent vomiting coming from the accommodation area. 'Oh dear,' I said, and headed towards Killian, now slumped on the ground outside one of the residences.

Again Emmett came after me. 'I don't think you should go over there,' he said.

It was very sweet of him to attempt to spare me the horror, but it only made me more determined to see for myself what had happened.

'Please, Tamar.' He grabbed my hand to pull me to a stop, but Killian, now recovered somewhat, called out, 'Let her come.'

I went over to see the bloodbath for myself.

'*They* did this, didn't they?' Killian was seething with rage at having to add his business partner and crew to the Nefilim fatality list.

I nodded, wanting to throw up myself until my Anunnaki sensibilities kicked in. My heart chilled, stifling my repulsion and allowing me to be more analytical. 'There can be no doubt about that,' I said.

'They? Who are *they*?' Emmett asked.

Killian and I looked at each other a moment, considering how much he should be told.

'Look, I'm not an idiot! I know no human being could have done this,' Emmett said. 'So just cut the bullshit and tell me who *they* are.' As we were still hesitant, he became more demanding. 'I deserve to know!'

'The Nefilim,' I replied bluntly, aware that he knew quite a bit about my fallen kindred.

'*The Nefilim?*' He took a step back, more shocked than sceptical. 'Why would the lords of the spook world want to do this to us?' Clearly he remembered nothing of the André incident yesterday.

'Apparently, it's me they're after,' Killian said, lifting his designer T-shirt to reveal the mark of Cain upon his chest. 'They've killed my parents, my friends, and now this.' He dropped his shirt and looked at the blood drying on the dwelling's step, his eyes filling with tears of remorse.

Emmett looked shocked when he saw the mark of Cain on Killian. He was silent a moment, thoughtful. 'But I saw your mother only yesterday,' he said eventually.

'No,' Killian corrected, 'you saw an evil being wearing the guise of my mother.'

Emmett looked ready to take out his anger on the playboy he despised. 'You *knew* there were evil beings loitering about but you —'

'I only suspected,' Killian assured him. 'My fears were only confirmed last night.' He frowned and looked at me. 'Or was that the night before?'

I shook my head; we weren't permitted to explain why we had missed a day.

'You don't know?' Emmett barked.

'I've been a little out of it.' Killian tried to gloss over his slip. 'I seem to have lost a day somewhere.'

'While my father and everyone else here was being mutilated,' Emmett shoved Killian in the chest with both hands, 'you were getting stoned!'

'*No*, I wasn't stoned!' Killian shoved him right back. 'Where were you anyway?'

'I told you, I was looking for Tamar. I was concerned for her well-being.'

'But she was with me,' Killian said with a frown; he knew Emmett had known my whereabouts.

'Exactly,' Emmett said, and Killian suddenly realised he had a rival for my affections.

'Jealous?' he accused with a grin.

'*Concerned*,' Emmett replied.

'Frustrated!' I interrupted them both. 'This is getting us nowhere. Neither of you could possibly have foreseen this or prevented it from happening. So stop arguing and let's get on with finding out what's going on here.'

I wondered if my mother knew. There was no point checking my parents' quarters; she would never leave a message lying about. But if I could just get a moment to meditate, I could see if she had left any thought transferences for me.

'I need a change of clothes,' I said, counting on my companions not following me into my room.

'What if *they*'re still lurking about?' Emmett said, moving to pursue me.

Killian held him back. 'She'll be fine, believe me.'

'You're a regular knight in shining armour, aren't you?' Emmett brushed Killian's hand away in disgust and kept going.

'You think I'm afraid?' Killian grabbed Emmett's shoulder and swung him around to pursue the issue.

'*Please!*' I called to them, and their punches froze in midair. 'Try not to kill each other before I get back. Emmett, why don't you tell Killian what's happened to the caves,' I suggested, thinking that ought to keep them distracted until I'd had time to meditate and change, for the situation demanded that I don the Amenti staff uniform.

Finally in the privacy of my room, I put on the full body suit, which was made from etheric fibre and allowed me to mould it into whatever attire I chose. For the present, I'd selected a pair of jeans, a singlet top, a leather jacket and biker boots, all with the resilience of Orme-based metal.

'That ought to keep the rain out,' I said, eyeing my reflection with a grin of approval.

I sat down to see if I could make contact with my mother or any of the Dragon Queens. I breathed deeply to shut out the external world and focus my attention inward.

'Where are you going?' I heard Emmett yell from some distance away.

'No more!' Killian yelled back. 'Not one more human being dies on my account. If the Nefilim want me so badly, they can have me!'

Uh-oh, I thought. *I'd best go see what's happening*; but before I'd even opened my door, I heard Killian's car start up on the road above the site camp where we'd left it several days ago. 'Shit!'

I ran out into the main clearing, where Emmett was still standing, looking livid.

'Where the fuck does he think he's going?' he said. It was a fair question given the mess Killian was leaving behind.

'I'd say he's going to pay dear old Dad a visit. Have you got a driver's licence?' I asked hopefully.

'Only a learner's permit.'

'Not to worry.' I shrugged it off as a minor detail. 'Is André among the dead?'

Emmett nodded.

'Then he won't mind us taking his Humvee.' I headed towards the vehicle.

'You can't drive!' Emmett insisted. 'You're only thirteen!'

'Oh, come on,' I said. 'Who on Earth is going to believe that?'

I climbed into the Humvee's driver's seat and, reaching under the steering wheel, willed the engine to life.

'How did you do that?' he said as he crossed in front of the car to get to the passenger seat. 'Do you even know how to drive?' He climbed in and slammed the door closed.

'Sure I do,' I lied. You didn't need to actually learn how to drive if you were psychokinetic; you just had to make a good show of it. 'Do you know the Labontès' home address?'

Emmett nodded and I directed him to the global positioning system. 'Then punch it into the GPS and let's go.'

'Whoa!' Emmett was thrown back in his seat as the vehicle took up off the road at my mental bidding. I just hung on, pretending to steer.

Our destination was the Loire Valley region of France where the Chateau Labontè was located. I was worried about Killian rushing off to confront the Nefilim on his own; what on Earth was he thinking?

'What did you say to Killian to get him so incensed?' I asked my passenger, who was sinking further into shock by the minute.

'I didn't say anything,' Emmett insisted. 'I just showed him what had happened to the caves and the next thing I knew he was storming off.'

'Weird,' I commented. 'Perhaps it was just a delayed reaction to the carnage.'

'How can you be so cool with both your parents missing?' Emmett asked.

'Why did you come looking for me, Emmett?'

'Well, when three members of Daddy's Bitch showed up dead yesterday morning, and you were last seen with them, I naturally ... Where the hell *have* you been?' he blustered when I appeared surprised. 'It was all over the papers yesterday afternoon. Their fathers are appealing for information pertaining to the whereabouts of Killian Labontè and his mysterious new girlfriend.'

I'd been wondering how the Nefilim were going to handle the disappearance of Killian's band members. They must have kept their victims' bodies on ice in the spook world for just such an occasion as this.

'They obviously want to find Killian and me *very* badly,' I said.

'*They?*' Emmett was taken aback. 'Are you implying that Taro Yamamoto, James Marx and the man who may be the next President of the United States are Nefilim?'

'It's a strong possibility,' I replied. 'Morell Labontè definitely is.'

'All right!' His eyes came to rest on the gearstick, which was changing gears all by itself. 'Who the hell are you, Tamar?'

'Not a very good mimic, that's for sure.' I sat back and openly allowed the car to drive itself. 'How much do you know about the spook world, Emmett?'

He shrugged. 'I consider myself fairly well read on the subject for a mere mortal. But I'm not letting you change the subject again until you explain exactly who you are.'

This rescue was going to be a hell of a lot easier for me if Emmett knew the truth. I placed my index finger onto his third eye and returned the memories I'd stolen from him a few days before.

When he'd recovered from the influx of information he was excited, and angry. 'You knew! And you've got the power to have stopped this slaughter.'

'I'm sorry —'

'Sorry doesn't cut it!' he yelled, and moved to open the car door.

I gave the mental command to lock the doors and drive faster.

'Let me out of this car!' he shouted.

'I couldn't take down my best lead to the lord of spook world.'

'My father is dead!'

'And every other human being on the planet will join him if I don't succeed in taking Ill out!' I said harshly. 'Either you help me rid the world of those responsible for your father's death or you can just get out of my way!'

Emmett was stunned to silence by my outburst.

'So,' I adopted a more civil tone, 'how much *do* you know about the spook world? Is Irkalla still the capital?'

He nodded. 'It's run by Erragal and his consort, Ereshkigal —'

'Ha! In my day Ereshkigal ran the place,' I said. 'Even in the Underworld women have been forced into subservient roles.'

'In your day?' Emmett was confused, then his memory of me whispering in his ear returned. 'Kali,' he uttered, white as a sheet, and promptly lost consciousness.

'Some help you are.'

I wondered if I should just drop him on the side of the road and spare him from the nightmare I was about to lead him into. But it didn't seem fair to leave him to face the mountain of questions that would have to be answered in the wake of the massacre at the dig site. And as fate had seen fit to spare him from that awful demise, the least I could do was protect him until he found his feet. Killian was far more of a worry. He knew how much danger he was in; could he really be so selfless that he would invite his own damnation in order to stop the killing? There was only one soul I knew to be that selfless, for he felt he owed this world nothing less: Mathu.

With Emmett out to it, miles of road to cover and the car on automatic pilot, I decided to go into a meditative state and touch base with my mother and the other Dragon Queens.

Once I had removed all thought of the future and the past and sat centred firmly in the present, I called out to my mother. When there was no response from her, I began to convey my mental account of the last few days to her anyway; she would discover it when she found time to rest and seek within. However, my transmission was interrupted by my mother's far more urgent conveyance.

Praise the goddess you contacted me, Tamar. Now you must listen intently to what I have to say — our continued association depends on it!

So listen I did as she disclosed to me the staff of Amenti's intention to change the past twice over, firstly to save my father from torture at the hands of the Nefilim, and in the second instance to open all the Signet stations over a decade sooner. The news tore my heart in two. I had to find Killian quickly, for if the Signet station at Montségur was opened and secured at a much earlier date, he would never discover the caves and we would never meet. I'd only just found him and now was about to lose him when history rewrote itself. The only way to prevent our separation in this current reality was to get Killian out of this physical time-controlled plane of existence and into the

Otherworld. I needed to get us both to the Amenti complex beneath Giza as soon as superhumanly possible or we would both lose touch with this reality, and the events and people within it.

CHAPTER 13

ILL WILL

The Chateau Labontè looked very dramatic against the night sky. At a guess the forbidding castle-like structure dated back to the sixteenth century, but the dark energy emanating from the site was cultivated much further back in time.

The gates were open and I spied Killian's Porsche parked at the end of the long drive.

Emmett was sleeping like a baby in the passenger seat, so I locked him inside the Humvee and moved to feel the bonnet of Killian's car. It was still warm.

I raced to the front door and blasted it from its iron hinges. A large foyer appeared before me, a curved staircase rising each side to the upper level; obviously of a much later period than the exterior structure. Directly ahead, beneath the landing where the staircases met, was an archway and there stood one of my fallen kindred, with an Orme spike poised at Killian's neck.

'I'm just bait for you,' Killian tried to warn me.

The spike grazed his neck and my heart almost stopped beating, but I couldn't allow my foe to sense that I gave a damn.

'Namtar,' I said, for even in his wretched state I recognised him, 'given up wearing Morell Labontè, have you? There seems to be a mass shedding of identities going on at present.'

'There are plenty more where those came from,' he assured me, shaking Killian to include him in the equation.

'Nice suit,' I commented. I knew from my mother's advice that his glittering gold cape and wide-brimmed hat would deflect my weapon's liquid-light darts.

'I wouldn't confront you without it,' he bantered, and gave me a devilish smile.

'I think it's going to take more than a piece of fabric to protect you from me, cousin.'

'I have your father up here, half-caste.'

The voice came from above, and I looked up to see Ishtar on the landing. She was wearing a glittering gold evening gown and was still in the shapely form of Sabine Labontè.

'Honestly, I've had him and had him and had him,' she boasted, and Namtar chuckled at my dismay. 'Just smell me if you don't believe me ...' She caressed herself between the legs. 'His heavenly scent is all over me.' She giggled and my rage welled to bursting; I wanted to kill her!

'How dare you ruin so great a spirit!' I yelled.

'Tamar, they're going to damn my soul!' Killian pleaded.

I'd avoided telling him that little detail about the fate of his friends and family, not wanting to add to his grief and distress.

'You can't save both of them, my darling,' Ishtar said, and an Orme spike extended from the wristband she wore. She went back upstairs, while

Namtar disappeared into the downstairs shadows with Killian.

At this point I had no idea whether my hunch regarding Killian Labontè was true, but my father was definitely an Amenti staff member and I couldn't risk his damnation. I launched myself towards the upstairs landing, and was amazed to achieve enough height to vault the banister and land in the hallway behind Ishtar.

'Come, princess,' she beckoned, leading the way into a room ahead.

I was almost upon her by the time she made it through the door, but she teleported herself instantly across the luxurious bedroom to the stone wall where my father was chained. I found her ability remarkable, as my fallen kin were supposed to have lost their supernatural powers.

'Albray, my darling, I've brought you a gift,' Sabine crooned.

My father was crouched to hide his nakedness, even though this meant his arms were stretched high above his head. His head hung low in shame — I had never seen him so broken.

'Come, come, my angel, I've brought you the most precious thing in your whole wide world.' Ishtar grabbed a handful of Albray's hair and yanked his head up to look at me. He screamed his protest at the top of his lungs.

'Use the fucking spike,' he challenged his abductor. 'There's nothing more you can take from me.'

'Oh yes there is,' she assured him with a smile.

I was so devastated by my father's anguish that it took a moment for my Anunnaki rationality to overcome my distraught human side. I drew my weapon from the back of my jeans and aimed it at Ishtar. Sure she was wearing an Orme dress, but her head was unprotected. I fired, but as the light began to disperse throughout her body, her atomic structure sparked, fizzled and collapsed. A nanosimulator, I realised, and thought the diversion rather clever — Ishtar wasn't even here. As the replica of Sabine Labontè disintegrated so did the threat to my father's life.

'Kill me,' he pleaded nevertheless, unable to look at me. 'Please, Kali.' He broke down in tears, shaking uncontrollably.

At my mental bidding he was released from his bonds, and I conjured clothes upon his body so that he might feel less exposed. I crouched beside him and spoke gently.

'Arcturus, right now Amenti's staff are preparing to go back in time and pluck you from this plight before it ever occurs. You will not remember any of this, for indeed it will never happen.'

'*You* will remember.' He remained hunched up, refusing to make eye contact.

'And I shall admire you all the more,' I said, all the time praying for my mother to get her plan in gear and get my father out of this reality.

Her plan, or rather Polaris's plan, was to rescue my father prior to the Amenti taskforce going back in time to open the dormant Signet stations, as my father's station was among those needing to be activated. Once Albray vanished from this time line, I would only have a very short window before the second part of Polaris's plan was launched. For although their mission would take some time in the past, the changes their actions would cause here in the present would be practically instantaneous.

'I need you to come with me now,' I urged, expecting a flat refusal. 'You are my only indication of how much time I have left.'

He attempted to stir his weary, shaken form, unsuccessfully.

'Namtar is taking Killian to Ill in the Underworld. If he is Mathu, I'll lose him,' I appealed, and burst into tears without even considering that this was the one thing that never failed to rouse my father to battle.

'I'll need a sword,' he said.

I wiped my eyes to see my father the knight staring at me. He forced a supportive smile, which I returned as a sword appeared in my hands. 'I thought you didn't like Killian,' I said.

'What I feel about him is irrelevant.' He took the sword and motioned for me to lead the way.

I flew over the upstairs banister and landed in the foyer; Dad took the stairs. We both made for the archway through which Namtar had taken Killian.

'Tamar!'

I turned to find Emmett eyeing the front door I had blasted from its hinges earlier. Then he looked at my father in astonishment, wondering where he'd sprung from.

My father was relieved to see him. 'Thank god you weren't kidnapped, or murdered!' he said.

'You know what happened at Montségur?' Emmett said, even more puzzled.

'No time to chat,' I called back to them. 'If you want to come along, keep up.'

We reached the manor's large kitchen, where my father pulled me to a stop. My senses heightened to full alert and I realised we were standing in the epicentre of the porthole to the Underworld — it was directly beneath us.

'Basement,' my father and I said at the same time, as we spotted the thick timber door. It had no handle, only an electronic keypad.

'Chase over?' Emmett asked as he caught up with us.

I approached the keypad and mentally bade it to *unlock*; the keys punched out a sequence of numbers and the door opened to reveal a set of stairs leading down.

Emmett looked at my father. 'You must be very proud.'

I jumped down the staircase in a single bound, my companions following at a more sedate pace. Up ahead was a stone wall with a gap in the middle; I ran through it straight into a labyrinth of stone walls and passages.

'Keep up,' I called back to the others. 'I know the way through.'

I could sense the right way to go; I just followed the strongest flow of negative energy.

'I'm feeling sick,' Emmett said, stumbling to a halt. 'And really angry!'

'It's a by-product of this place,' my father advised, urging him to keep going. 'The atmosphere here is pure evil, and the fact that you're adversely affected by the negativity indicates that you're one of the good guys.'

'That doesn't make me feel any better,' Emmett grumbled.

'Just think happy thoughts and don't buy into where the energy is trying to lead you,' Dad instructed.

While Emmett recovered I went on ahead; we

were so close to the end of the maze. 'This way,' I called back to them as I passed through a final doorway and into a huge diamond-shaped chamber. Black illuminated stairs led down on all sides to a central platform that was a seething pit of dark energy. On the edge of this abyss stood Namtar with Killian.

'You can come visit your little friend in Irkalla,' he called to me, and jumped into the mass of darkness.

'Tamar!' Killian yelled, holding out a hand towards me as he was dragged down with his captor.

I was halfway down the stairs when Emmett emerged from the labyrinth and shouted, 'Stop! Your father's vanished!'

I halted, my heart pounding in my chest — I was running out of time. 'Of course,' I mused, looking towards the dark vortex: the Underworld was outside the constraints of physical time, just as the Otherworld was. Killian would not be transported out of this current time line, but I would be. That meant I had to follow him into the abyss; but what of Emmett?

'You're not seriously thinking of going down there!' Emmett raced down the stairs two at a time towards me.

'Listen,' I told him, 'you have a choice to make.'

'What do you mean?'

'Just listen!' I said, running short on patience. 'The time lines of your current reality are about to change.' I held up a finger to warn him against interrupting. 'If you stay here, you'll find yourself in a reality where your father won't become involved with the Montségur dig, and so he'll still be alive and well. Everything will be as it was before Killian Labontè came into your lives.'

Emmett took only a second to process that information. 'Which means we'll never meet,' he said.

I shook my head as I backed away towards the dark abyss.

'That hole leads into the spook world, doesn't it?' Emmett weighed up all the knowledge he'd obtained from me against returning to his past. 'My father will still be resurrected whether I'm here to see it or not,' he said, following me a step at a time.

I nodded. 'But if you follow me, which I advise you don't, there's a very good chance you won't live to see him.'

'But if I don't go with you, I'll never see you again.' The sadness in his voice caused tears to well in my eyes; how could his feelings for me run so deep? 'I'll forget all about you.'

'That's right,' I said. I felt a lump form in my throat and realised that my own heart was aching at the thought of parting from Emmett. Still, the idea of leading him to the slaughter of the Nefilim was even more heartbreaking. 'I can't allow you to come with me,' I said firmly.

'But why do you have to go?' he asked.

'I have to save Killian.'

'Because he is of the blood? But I am of the blood too.'

He ripped open his shirt to expose the mark of Cain on his chest, but I was more shocked by the gold pendant around his neck that glowed dimly in the darkened room.

'Where did you get this?' I asked, almost choking on the words as I reached out to ensure it was real.

'My dad ... it's an old family heirloom,' he said, surprised by my interest. 'It means ...'

'. . . he awaits beneath the lotus,' I concluded for him.

He looked stunned. 'Yes. It makes no sense to me, but the inscription means a lot to my family . . .'

Struck by the same thought, we both looked up to see a huge golden lotus flower carved into the ceiling directly above the dark vortex. I was overwhelmed by delight, relief and a million other emotions. 'Mathu?' I said tentatively.

'Who?' Emmett's eyes were nearly popping out of his head. He backed away from my suddenly seductive manner. I willed him to a standstill as we were a little pressed for time.

'Is that really you in there?' I asked.

'What are you doing?' he cried, protesting the loss of control of his body.

I grinned as I stepped closer. 'Hold still, this won't hurt a bit.'

Emmett looked absolutely horrified, and I would have been insulted had I not realised his gaze was fixed on something behind me. I turned to see the dark energy mass at the centre of the porthole rising at a frightening rate.

'Ill,' I said, recognising his energy.

'Tamar!' Emmett implored me to release him, which I did just in time for him to embrace me and hold me close.

The dark mass surged out of the pit and engulfing us, we were dragged down into the Underworld.

PART 2

TIMEWALKERS

CHAPTER 14

SOPHIA-HOKHMAT
— NOVA SCOTIA

This is a Signet station,
one of twelve pyramids of light
placed on the Earth plane by design.
Each station is as unique in frequency and purpose
as the twelve Masters who are the keys.
They are the Council of Amenti,
who incarnate as the teachers
and healers of their timelines
to oppose an enemy
that transcends time and space.
The keeper of this station
is the soul frequency Polaris,
the Master of Time, Space and Realities.
The battle of good versus evil,
light versus darkness,
may be viewed here.
And you will know what you must do.

Once the Signet station at Montségur had been secured and the light-filled souls of our Dracon foes had been delivered to Lugh Lamhfada for ascension through the Hall of Amorea, the staff of Amenti directed their attention to saving Arcturus from the Nefilim.

Polaris's plan was to pull Arcturus out of Montségur, just as he had following my husband's first private meeting with Sabine Labontè. We could not spare him from Sabine altogether as this option was the one that would cause the least disruption to the time lines.

'If I go back any further, then Tamar's reality is going to be altered too, and she will lose any progress she's made on her mission in the interim,' Polaris explained. 'This way, I arrive to collect Arcturus a few moments before I did last time, and only his recollection of events will be altered. Tamar's reality will remain the same. So, if you would all be so kind as to meet me at Polaris Station, I will return there with Arcturus presently.'

'I'm coming with you to collect him,' I insisted.

Polaris wasn't keen on that idea at all. 'Your husband's feelings are still going to be confused and raw in the wake of his meeting with Sabine. I don't know that you being present when he arrives on the *Klieo* is going to be all that helpful … no offence.'

With a wave of my hand, I made myself invisible. 'He won't even know I'm there,' I said, and reappeared to the applause of my staff mates. 'It's all only matter, which is of no matter to me any more,' I explained.

Polaris was still wary. 'You have to wait on board

the ship,' he said, caving in to my wishes. 'I don't want to risk losing you in the process of rescuing him.'

'Agreed.'

'I'll send the others to Polaris Station ahead of you,' Denera said as Polaris, Levi and I headed off to the *Klieo*.

'Much obliged,' Polaris said with a bow.

With Levi at the helm, Polaris and I stood in the teleportation station within the *Klieo*'s belly while she melded into the time-space continuum to return to yesterday once more. As the ship was engulfed by the Blue Flame energy that enabled it to move through time, I unexpectedly made contact with Tamar and was able to fill her in on all that had transpired this day. But the Blue Flame faded and we were cut off before I had the chance to learn anything of her situation.

The huge round crystal plate inset in the timber floor of the round chamber melted into a light vortex that swirled downward.

'Better make yourself scarce,' Polaris suggested, and I assumed my invisible form. 'Back soon,' he said, and jumped feet first into the swirling light matter.

He ascended again in seconds, with my husband in tow.

'Thank God you heard me,' Albray said as the porthole hardened beneath them. 'I never thought I'd be so glad to see you.' He slapped the captain's shoulder and gave a laugh.

'Me either,' Polaris said, not taking offence.

'You must lock me up immediately,' Albray implored, grabbing hold of the captain's jacket for emphasis. 'One of the Nefilim has got her hands on my ringstone and I fear that I'm now a great threat to the Amenti Project.'

'No, you're not.'

'Yes, I am!' Albray insisted. 'I need you to go back in time and —'

'I already have,' Polaris cut in. 'Sabine didn't instil any covert mission in you.'

'Really?' Albray was reassured but confused. 'But how did you even know about our meeting?'

Polaris grinned. 'I am who I am.'

'So what happened with Sabine?' Albray wondered. 'Did I . . . I mean to say, did she . . .'

Polaris winced.

'Please tell me she didn't.' Albray was looking ill now.

'The Nefilim being who has taken the guise of Sabine Labontè is Ishtar,' Polaris told him.

'The ancient goddess of lust and war?'

'What hope did you have?' Polaris broke the news as gently as he could. 'What hope would any man have?'

My husband almost collapsed under the weight of his distress. 'Curses!' He paced about as if trying to evade the truth, then stopped still to look at the captain. 'Does Mia know?'

Polaris nodded. 'Kali witnessed a good part of the seduction and wrote down what transpired for both your own information and Meridan's.'

'Goddess, no!' Albray was horrified.

'It wasn't your fault,' I said, and dropped my invisibility. 'I was the one who lost the damn stone.' Tears of remorse fell from my eyes as Albray embraced me. 'I'm so sorry,' I blurted.

My husband held my head in his hands and said firmly, 'This was not your fault.'

'It wasn't yours either,' I was quick to respond, and the conviction in my voice reduced him to tears. 'We're going back in time to open the Signet stations, and when we have, Sabine and André will never meet, and we'll ensure that we get the ringstone before she does.' My tears were streaming now, for all I knew that he did not. 'And although we'll remember your abuse at the hands of this being, you have already been spared the worst of it, which was yet to come.'

As we clung to each other for comfort, Polaris quietly left the room.

Albray pulled back to look me in the face. 'I've missed something, haven't I?'

I nodded and smiled. 'Praise the goddess … and Polaris, bless him. The dear captain has been your greatest supporter and a *very* good friend to you. Even though you will never recall it, we are deeply indebted to him.'

'Seriously?' Albray was a little stunned. 'The captain and I have been *friendly*?'

'Your *greatest* supporter,' I repeated.

'Well, he did owe me a favour or two,' Albray pointed out in an effort to explain the anomaly.

'Please don't be an ass about this,' I implored him. 'Just be thankful.'

'I am,' he said, then, unable to recall exactly what he was grateful for, he frowned. 'I guess.'

I returned his frown with one more perturbed and he quickly changed his tune.

'All right! I promise I'll be nice … and *thankful*.'

At Polaris Station we were met by the entire Amenti team, apart from Denera, who was to remain at Giza to monitor the grid and the time lines from the Hall of Records.

Our meeting took place inside a large boardroom that, like the rest of Polaris Station, had a very nautical feel. It was filled with priceless furniture from the thirteenth century, collected by Polaris's last incarnation, Captain Henry Sinclair.

Polaris explained that Zalman would not be coming with us on the mission either. 'As Zalman's Signet station, Ta-She-Ra El Amun, played such an integral role in bringing us all together, we can't go back in time past the year 2003 when it was opened.'

'Wasn't that station active in the nineteenth century?' I asked, recalling how Ashlee Granville-Devere's journal recounted her meeting with Zalman there.

Solarian was amused by my lack of comprehension. 'Yes, but once the station was activated in 2003, six months before Zalman and Jamila made contact with you at Giza, Ta-She-Ra El Amun rose out of physical existence and was no longer constrained by time. Just as we are outside of time here in Polaris Station at present. Now that the station is active, it can be accessed from any point in Earth's history, if the guardian of that station so chooses.'

'So you don't really need the *Klieo* to travel through time?' I asked Polaris.

As time-space architects, Polaris and Solarian easily understood these principles; it was the rest of us who were having trouble.

Polaris shook his head. 'Signet stations don't time travel, they exist outside of physical time. You don't enter a Signet station and then exit it in a different era.'

I recalled this was true of Ashlee's experiences in Ta-She-Ra El Amun; she may have lost a night or a week while passing through Otherworldly realms,

164

but had never lost any great chunks of time.

'As the guardian of this Signet station, once it's activated I could will anyone from any time to enter it,' Polaris explained further, 'but I can't physically step out into their history.'

'Then how did Zalman do it?' I asked, and all eyes turned to him.

'It was merely an astral projection of me that went to meet Ashlee and her party,' he enlightened.

'That's why you didn't have a shadow!' Solarian finally realised.

'This is all very interesting,' Dexter said, flicking his dark hair from his face, 'but can we please get on with the mission brief? I suspect you've picked the year 2003 as you plan to use the Eye of Ra portal passage to hook into the Montauk wormhole within the Kali rift and thus cloak our mission from the Nefilim and their Illuminati lackeys. Am I right?'

Most of us looked at Dexter as if he were speaking another language.

'What?' he said with a shrug, as if his conclusion was elementary.

Dexter was the guardian of Signet Station One, Xerthaneus, whose porthole connected to Parallel Earth from Antarctica. What and where is Parallel Earth, you ask. At this point in my tale I had no idea. Still, it did seem fitting that Dexter was the Amenti staff member in charge of extraterrestrial communication and activity. As J.E. Taylor in Ashlee's time, he'd been held captive by the Dracon long enough to develop his own telepathic capabilities, which enabled him to tap into the Dracon telepathic hive. Dexter worked closely with the Anu recruiting disillusioned Dracon to return to the ranks of the Anu, and by so doing had collected vast amounts of information about the Dracon, their secret agendas and their allies among the Nefilim and humankind.

'The Kali rift?' I was curious. 'Does it have anything to do with my daughter?'

'The Kali rift is a tear in the fabric of time-space,' Dexter replied, hoping to speed things up. 'The rift separates this current Earth reality from its greater, original reality within what is known as the Ranna time flow.'

I looked back to Polaris for answers.

'There are different nodes or ports of interface within this time rift,' he explained further, 'which can be used to slip in and out of time without being detected by the Nefilim's monitoring systems. These ports of interface, which you might imagine better as wormholes, are already existent so there's a better chance of escaping detection, as the Nefilim are more likely to note new wormholes being torn through the fabric of time-space.'

'Okay, I understand that,' I said, 'but how did the rips get there in the first place and what have they got to do with Kali?'

'Oh, for heaven's sake!' Dexter sighed impatiently, but Polaris held up a hand and silenced him.

'Let me see if I can explain this ...' Polaris pondered a moment. 'As the result of a sentient will —'

'The Nefilim,' Dexter clarified.

'— pursuing a course of action contrary to that of the true consciousness of the Ranna time flow, certain occurrences —'

'Atlantis, Project Rainbow, Montauk and Cydonia,' Dexter added.

'— came together in Earth's time construct as a

synchronous event causing a fracture in time, a breakaway reality known as the Kali time flow. The Kali rift is the gap that exists between our true time flow in the Ranna and where we currently reside in the Kali continuum. Your daughter's Anunnaki soul mind was sent to heal this rift.' Polaris ended his explanation with a shrug, as though stating the obvious.

Many, many questions were fighting for precedence in my mind, when a massive wave of energy welled in my heart and flooded my entire being with a sudden burst of awareness — my silent watcher was serving to remind me that I already understood trine time.

In the expansion of spirit into greater dimensions of experience, a sudden separation occurred in its light grid resulting in a universal tear — the Kali rift. As a result, two light spectrum grids were created: the Ranna time flow — the full-light metatronic spiral of undescended light; and the Kali time flow — the half-light oritronic spiral of descended or fallen light. The universal tear exposed the central node where all energy ley lines of this universe conjoined: the Eye of Ra. The three star councils of Orion, the Pleiades and Sirius maintained a high-light energy pyramid to act as a capstone over the Eye of Ra to keep this universe from self-destructing. The Sun Lords of Sirius guarded this pyramid structure, known as the Telos Aarkhara. The Telos Aarkhara recreated time event horizons that fed to and from the Eye of Ra, so that time fractures could be contained and not perpetuated throughout the entire universal grid. The Ranna time wave was the higher light-body of Earth that did not become formative as a physical manifestation. Ranna was the realm of the ultimate observer, from where I, and all silent watchers, operated. Ranna was the complete hologram of time as it flowed uninterrupted through the time-space dimensions of the multi-verse. The Kali time wave was where that part of Earth that had descended into matter now resided; the realm of the observed. From developments in the inter-time war between the years 2012 and 2022 would spring another time wave, which would form a fusion point where the lower parts of Ranna would meld with the higher portions of the Kali wave to form a third time wave. Whether that new reality would be more akin to the Ranna than the Kali time flow was entirely dependent upon the efforts of the Amenti staff members at this time.

Parallel Earth, into which the Xerthaneus pyramid granted entry, was split by a thick band of frequency into two possible future worlds. Shadow world — what Tamar called the spook world — existed in the lower etheric realms deep beneath the Kali time flow; it was the Underworld of the Nefilim and Dracon, where the enemies of mankind were progressing full steam ahead towards the destruction of the Earth and the harvesting of its inhabitants. The Xerthaneus porthole also granted access to the Otherworld of the Anu, which existed within the full-light metatronic spiral, where the Earth was still evolving along its predestined path of evolution in the Ranna time flow. Which of these two worlds Dexter arrived at via the Xerthaneus porthole depended upon whether the frequency of our current physical reality was high enough to attune to the Ranna time flow existence of the Anu, or, as the case was more often than not, the Earth's harmonic frequency was attuned to the shadow world.

My rush of revelation took but an instant, and I returned to the discussion around me to discover I hadn't missed any part of the brief. I immediately turned my mind to pondering the incidents Dexter had cited as being the cause of the wormholes that ran through the universal tear.

'I know the incident that sank Atlantis caused the Signet Grid to be shut down,' I said aloud, 'and I know Montauk and the Rainbow Project had something to do with the Philadelphia Experiment, but Cydonia ...?'

'An ancient Nefilim capital on Mars that is no longer one of their strongholds,' Dexter informed me.

'Oh.' I frowned, confused again.

'The Rainbow Project, which was the testing of an experimental electromagnetic technology on the premise of producing radar invisibility, took place on 12 August 1943,' Polaris explained. 'The experiment created a bridge through time to a similar project taking place at Montauk on 12 August 1983.'

'You might be interested to know at this point,' Dexter chipped in, now enjoying sharing his knowledge, 'that although the Long Count calendar used by the Mayan civilisation of pre-Columbian Mesoamerica completes its thirteenth cycle on 21 December 2012, the calendar's mythical starting point was on 12 August, according to the proleptic Gregorian calendar. The time count used was based on the initial Mayan numeration, a kal, which is the number twenty!' He grinned at me excitedly, as if I should understand the relevance.

Polaris jumped in to save me. 'In our present time-space reality, the fabric of space spirals around to fold over itself in twenty-year cycles ... the Earth has a 12 August twenty-year biorhythm. Therefore the electromagnetic wormhole created by the Rainbow Project between 1943 and 1983 also cut straight through 12 August 1963, creating another node, or exit point, in the continuum on that date. On 12 August 2003, another project, HAARP —'

'High-frequency Active Auroral Research Program,' Dexter interjected.

'— tested another form of experimental electromagnetic technology on the pretext of studying the properties and behaviour of the ionosphere.'

'Which was bullshit.' Dexter coughed into his hand. 'What it really had to do with was the enhancement of and interference with communications, the development of new types of radio transmissions, and large-scale modification of global weather patterns via ionospheric disturbances. HAARP's Earth-penetrating topography capabilities can reveal the existence of underground installations, as well as oil and mineral deposits —'

'And even ancient, long-buried technologies.' Polaris cut in on Dexter for a change.

'Like our Signet stations,' I gasped.

'Unless they are active,' Solarian interjected, 'in which case they rise above our reality here in the Kali time wave and into their true place within the Ranna time flow, where no Earthly technology can find them.'

'HAARP also has many weapons and mind-control uses,' Dexter went on, emphasising the seriousness of what we were dealing with. 'It's experimenting with extremely low frequencies to communicate with submarines worldwide. These ELF waves can be attuned to the same frequency as human brainwaves in order to manipulate a human's mind against his or her will.'

I gasped when I realised where the lesson was leading. 'It's the frequency fence!'

Polaris nodded. 'On 12 August 2003, the Illuminati convince factions within the interior government to orchestrate another electromagnetic experiment in the belief that it will stop severe climate change in the future by reinforcing the ionosphere. The HAARP project will focus multiple transmitters on the same location in the sky and the gravity waves generated will open a channel to a similar experiment taking place deep beneath the surface of Mars hundreds of years in the future.'

'Hence my rationale that the captain selected the year 2003 in order to use the Eye of Ra portal passage to hook into the Montauk wormhole within the Kali rift and thus cloak our mission from the Nefilim and their Illuminati,' Dexter summed up. And then added for good measure: 'For incorporated into the Eye of Ra is an inter-dimensional passage from one side of the Kali rift to the other, which is protected by another energy structure, the Telos Aarkhara, which is intricately linked to the Cydonia complex on Mars.'

Finally I made the connection between Dexter's explanation and Polaris's. 'Are you telling me that we're going to swing by Mars in the future in order to reach Earth in the past?' I said, rather breathless at the prospect.

'Exactly.' Polaris applauded me, and the rest of the staff followed suit. I grinned in excited anticipation.

'We'll be landing in the past at the precise moment all HAARP's new systems come online,' Levi advised. 'The faster we can secure the remaining Signet stations and get back to the future, the faster we can get on with shutting down the frequency fence for good.'

'Why wait?' I wondered. 'Why not shut down the frequency fence in 2003, before it has a chance to do any damage?'

'Only to have our adversaries rebuild it, bigger and better, by the time we get back to the future?' Dexter posed.

'Point taken.'

'We're not going to 2003 to change the past,' Polaris stressed to everyone. 'In fact, our objective is to change the past as little as possible, because the more subtle we are, the less chance of a Nefilim counterattack that could see us return to a darker future than the one we are leaving behind. For a good part of the time we will be operating in the Otherworld and outside of physical world events. Our aim is to raise the consciousness of the past; and the increased high-quality frequency being generated by the fully operational Signet Grid will limit the sphere of influence and future potential of the frequency fence considerably.'

We all nodded.

'Any questions?' Polaris asked.

Arcturus put his hand in the air and Polaris tried not to flinch. 'Where is the Eye of Ra to be found?' my husband asked.

A good question, I thought, and realised I knew the answer. 'If the Sun Lords of Sirius guard the pyramid structure of Telos Aarkhara, we might want to enlist their help,' I suggested. 'Whose Signet station connects to Sirius?'

'That would be mine,' Solarian raised a hand, 'but unfortunately it's still inactive. The Nefilim, having had their HAARP technology in operation for some thirteen years now, know of its whereabouts and are observing the area closely.'

This was shocking news. 'So my Signet station isn't the only one under Nefilim threat at present?'

'Of the Signet stations still waiting to be activated, Talori's is the only one not being closely monitored,' Polaris confirmed. 'It's located in China, and the US still don't share their deepest secrets with the Chinese.'

'The Sun Lords of Sirius guard the Telos Aarkhara it's true,' Levi offered a solution, 'but it's the Blue Fire Command, who exist on Rigel in Orion, who guard the Eye of Ra and its porthole passage. The porthole within the Dreamkeeper pyramid of my Signet station is linked directly to the Blue Fire Command. As the guardians of the Eye of Ra, they oversee the ongoing disparity of energetics that exists between the full-light and half-light intelligences in this universe, and intervene in the name of the metatronic consciousness when appropriate ... so I believe they'll support our intention.'

'I didn't realise the *Klieo* doubled as a spaceship.' My husband was concerned about our mode of transport for the journey.

Polaris smiled at his own ingenuity. 'She'll survive anything this universe can dish out,' he said proudly. 'And as far as her intergalactic capabilities are concerned ... she won't need any. The Blue Fire Command will transport the ship for us.'

'All we have to do is take the ship to the Dreamkeeper and I'll see to the rest,' Levi concluded.

CHAPTER 15

THE DREAMKEEPER — AUSTRALIA

In the Pyramid of Dreams
dwells the Dreamkeeper,
and within the matrix of his Dreamtime,
one discovers the ability
to move back and forth between realities.

Here, a soul learns that
what is created in Dreamtime
becomes manifest in the physical,
and that each soul mind fashions
their own earthly experiences.

For our dreams are the future,
where anything
and everything
is possible.

Levi filled me in on the nature of the pyramid within his Signet station as he led me to the *Klieo's* flight deck. I'd never before been granted the privilege of admittance onto the flight deck; for security reasons Polaris preferred that even Amenti staff members entered on a needs-only basis. So I was rather surprised when Polaris directed me to follow Levi; I couldn't imagine why I was being awarded the honour — unless the captain was up to his old tricks and attempting to annoy my husband, which he succeeded in doing. Solarian also questioned why I was being granted entry when she was Polaris's partner and never had been. The captain decided to escort her to the flight lounge, with everyone else, to reassure her that it was nothing personal.

'So your station's in Australia, Levi?' I said as I followed him upstairs to the front of the vessel. This section was composed of a white material with a dim, mutable otherworldly glow about it, unlike the rest of the *Kleio* which was constructed of dark polished timber — although not your average mahogany as it also glowed in periodic waves.

'My station's *over* Australia, in the future,' he said, opening the flight deck door then turning back to smile at me. 'AD8885, to be exact.'

'What?' I was stunned. 'How the hell did you ever find and activate it if it only exists in the future?'

'KOALA came to my aid.' He grinned at my disbelief; I'd assumed he was making an Aussie joke. 'Kemesos Ordis Alsais Leduc Alkemestra.'

'You're speaking another language, right?'

'KOALA is an acronym that I'll explain some other time, but basically it's the Inner Light Network research centre located in the future, on the same terraform island as my Signet station ... you might say that KOALA is the counterbalance of Montauk.'

Levi waved his hand past a plate on the flight deck door and it opened to grant us entry. When I stepped into the round chamber, all my other questions were forgotten and a whole new batch arose. 'Oh my goddess!' I said. There was such an array of technological wonders all around, most of which I couldn't begin to fathom the function of.

The most notable features were two round mounds of white rising up from the floor. Each was supported by a large foot, the base of which was the same circumference as the top surface area, but whose leg curved inwards to a slim point and then out again to support a table top. Both mounds were positioned beneath tubes of the same width that dropped down from the ceiling above, stopping several metres above the tabletops. Although the two features were of similar design, one was bigger than the other with two steel plates set in the wide lip of its tabletop. Inset in the centre of the mound was a large round metal plate of a fine-mesh texture.

The smaller mound was perfectly plain, but its tabletop dropped into a hollow, which, upon closer inspection, disappeared deep into the bowels of the ship. The tube above it was also hollow.

'Blue Flame energy funnel ... it directs Blue Flame energy from the sails into the engine,' Levi explained, before moving towards the larger mound.

'And that one's the control panel?' I assumed.

He nodded, and placed his hands on the two metal inset plates. Light shot up through the mesh plate to fill the space between it and the tube above with a holographic picture of the *Klieo*; the illumined vessel slowly turning circles in the 3-D space so it could be seen from all angles.

Welcome aboard, Levi, said the *Klieo*'s control station as it identified him. It brought a tear to my eye to discover that Polaris had programmed his ship to speak to him in Solarian's voice.

'How lovely,' I said, clasping my hands in front of my heart, truly moved by the sentiment.

'For the captain, maybe,' Levi grinned, 'but in my last incarnation, Solarian was my mother!'

I had to laugh. 'So how did you merit the esteemed honour of being the captain's crew mate?' I asked.

'The term is *first* mate,' he said, giving me a cheeky glance. 'After I'd served my hundred years beneath the Blue Flame of Amenti, I went undercover into the Montauk Project to become one of their timewalkers and so I became familiar with the wormhole system that resulted.'

'Didn't that project employ horrible brainwashing techniques?' I asked, then became distracted as all the exterior doors on the holographic ship lit up.

Exterior doors secure, the *Klieo* announced in response to Levi's telepathic order.

'The techniques Montauk employed had no effect on me,' Levi said, but his grin looked forced. I could see in his eyes that it had been a traumatic experience and one he'd rather not discuss.

Setting course for Signet Station Eight, the *Klieo* confirmed, and I returned my attention to its brilliant graphic display.

The holograph of the ship transformed into a full-colour map of the world, with our current location in Nova Scotia and our destination in the Central Desert region of Australia pinpointed. Then the map folded in on itself until the two points aligned and lit up.

Initiating command, the *Klieo* warned, and the holograph morphed back into the form of our vessel, her sails now lit up. *Blue Flame Energy Function initiated.*

I turned my sights to the Blue Flame energy funnel: a beam of blue-green light burst downward into the base mound and continued to flow in a steady stream. I was drawn to the pure energy; this was my colour frequency and it resonated perfectly with me.

Within moments streams of the blue-green light began to engulf the walls, ceiling and every feature of the ship. I was mesmerised by the liquid-light plasma that spread across all surfaces like sunlight reflected off a disturbed body of water. A deep peace filled me; only to be broken moments later by a very anxious feeling.

I heard Tamar crying out to me, wishing to transmit a thought transference, only her voice sounded strained and drawn out, as if she were speaking through a thick layer of water; or, as was more likely the case, through a thick layer of frequency. Whatever the source of the interference, it caused her transmission to fade in and out in places.

When you retur— 2003, you —orced to land! It is Castor they seek and the Ro— tauk started 1923— the Black Sun. Beware the Montauk Boys. If they obtain — permanently extend their wormhole system all the way back in history to th—

When the Blue Flame energy of our passage subsided, I was left feeling shaken rather than relaxed. My first thought was to wonder if Tamar's warning to 'beware of the Montauk Boys' was somehow a warning against Levi, who had just admitted to being involved with the project.

'Meridan? Are you all right?' Levi queried. I must have been as pale as a sheet.

'I've just had word from Tamar,' I said, struggling to remember the broken transmission. 'There was a lot of interference so I can't be sure I have her message straight.'

'What did she say?' he asked, but the captain entered before I could answer. He looked surprised to find us standing around talking.

'We're on the Nefilim's scope for this short leg of our journey,' he said. 'Why aren't we already in contact with KOALA?'

'Meridan has had word from Kali,' Levi advised, and turned back to the ship's control panel. The holograph of the ship morphed into a symbol of three interlocking golden rings atop a winged staff. In the centre of the rings was a beautiful sapphire sphere of light, and inside that a number sequence appeared: 44, 44, 2, 5, 9.

'A contact number?' I commented to Polaris, who grinned in response.

Contact with KOALA established, the *Klieo* informed us.

'You've got to see this,' Levi said aside to me, as the holograph transformed into our vessel again and the front shields on the floor-to-ceiling windows surrounding us lit up.

Front shield window screens deactivated.

The shields vanished, and suddenly we were standing miles above a vast, sun-soaked panorama of the Central Australian Desert. 'Oh my.' It took my breath away. 'I could never hope to create something so awe-inspiring.'

'Don't be modest, Meridan,' Polaris said. 'We've all contributed to the creation that is our Earth. Besides, this is nothing in comparison to your garden back on Tara.'

I was completely taken aback by the comment, and enchanted too. 'You remember life on Tara?' I asked. I remembered very little myself and had wondered how much my fellow staff members recollected.

Polaris shook his head. 'Just the tiniest bits and pieces really ... and yet I recall your garden.' He gave a half-laugh. 'It was so very exquisite.'

I thought this a great compliment, and would have said so had I not spotted a funnel of spinning white cloud erupting in the otherwise clear blue sky right in front of us. 'Captain?' I pointed to the anomaly, and was stunned to see one end of the funnel opening as it came towards us.

Alignment with KOALA funnel confirmed.

The funnel hollowed further to form a tunnel with luminous clouds swirling around its interior. I could see the electrical activity sparking inside.

'We're going in there?' I asked meekly.

I saw Polaris wink at me and then everything inside the ship, including my own physical form, was reduced to a fine-particle state and sucked into the funnel.

At the other end of the tunnel, time and matter slowed and reconstituted.

'What a rush!' I gasped, and held my forehead and stomach to steady myself. I fixed my gaze on the floor; I confess, I was hesitant to see how the Earth appeared in the year AD8885.

The lush wilderness I beheld when I finally

looked up was so massive and hardy that it seemed prehistoric. 'The Earth's future is bright indeed,' I remarked, overjoyed that humanity had overcome its own selfish needs to achieve such perfect beauty and harmony with nature.

Levi shattered my illusions. 'This is not the Earth; it's a terraform island that floats above the planet.'

'So we're no longer in the physical world?' I wasn't really surprised as everything here appeared hyper-real.

Levi shook his head. 'But these thriving islands are all connected to the Earth via hypercords, which are anchored in the great oceans of the planet at prominent ley line crossings. Through such hypercords this terraform, and others like it, are able to nourish the Earth and replenish her.' Levi's voice was hoarse with pain suddenly.

'Ocean?' I wondered if we were still in Australia. 'But this was a desert!'

'The Earth is somewhat topographically challenged at this time,' the captain answered, as Levi was finding it difficult to discuss the subject.

Topographically challenged? 'There's been a flood then?' I said.

Their looks weren't encouraging. 'Only the deep-sea creatures survive ... those that no longer need sunlight,' Polaris explained. 'The Earth has been blanketed by thick dark cloud for aeons. All that remains of humanity are the light-workers, who were evacuated at the eleventh hour into the bases that exist beneath these terraforms, and those human tribes that dwelled in the cities of Inner Earth.'

'If nothing survived then how was all this created?' I asked.

'It was grown from prima matra,' Polaris explained.

'Unviolated first matter,' I translated. I was familiar with the substance from Meridan's work: this was nature's blueprint as it was before the Kali rift; the way it was always intended to evolve within the Ranna flow of time.

I looked out at the terraform landscape: it was teeming with life and I recognised many species from Earth's past and present. Still, there were a few animals I suspected might have developed here in Earth's future. I switched to third-eye vision and realised I hadn't seen the half of it. On an etheric level the terraform was also teeming with light-beings, from the tiniest of nature spirits to the huge deva being that oversaw the work of the elemental minions. 'Fairyland,' I said, entranced.

'Dreamtime,' Polaris corrected. 'Terraforms were the brainchild of the Ennead, but the construction and running of the Earth's life support system is a cooperative venture between the Anu and the Inner Earth tribes.'

I understood from Meridan's experience that the Ennead were a multi-dimensional cell comprised of nine units of intelligence, who hailed from the harmonic universe to which Aramatena belonged — which, in the cosmic scheme of things, was three harmonic universes closer to the Sovereign Integral than Earth. On Tara, the Ennead hailed from an ascended race known as the Elohim, who were even more advanced than my tribe, the Ceres. Here on Earth they were known as the Seraphim, the architects of light and order in this universe.

'This was their last-resort plan to ensure humanity's evolution should we fail to open

Amenti before the current SAC alignment ends,' Polaris explained. Then added confidently, 'But our current mission is going to change the plight of surface Earth.' And, with a clap of his hands, he snapped us out of our melancholy.

Levi gave *Klieo* the command to land and unlock her exterior doors. 'I'll see you at Blue Fire Command,' he told us as he disembarked.

'You're meeting us on Orion … are you Sirius?' I jested.

Both he and Polaris rolled their eyes at my attempt at humour. Levi gave us a wave and departed.

'So what did Kali have to say?' Polaris asked as he took the helm, seeming to sense my concern about my daughter's missive.

'Well,' I began, perplexed, 'as I was explaining to Levi, there was a lot of interference —'

'No problem,' Polaris said and, taking hold of my shoulders, he guided me into place behind the helm in his stead. 'Just place your hands on the command plates and mentally convey what you heard to the *Klieo*.'

'But I —'

'Pushed for time,' he said, indicating I just do as instructed. Exasperated, I complied.

Meridan? Why are you here? the *Klieo* asked as she verified me.

'Be nice, my lover,' Polaris instructed. 'This could be important.'

Very well. The computer still sounded perturbed. *Commencing download.*

I closed my eyes to focus and was startled when the *Klieo* announced almost instantly: *Transmission downloaded.*

'Can you clean that up a bit?' Polaris asked.

Anything for you, Captain.

I looked at Polaris, surprised. 'Is your ship's computer flirting with you?'

Polaris grinned. 'She's the ultimate vessel.'

I had to laugh. 'Solarian would never say, "Anything for you, Captain."' I mimicked the computer's flirtatious tone.

Would she not? the computer asked curiously.

'No,' I assured it. 'She would say —'

Polaris slapped a hand over my mouth to prevent me spoiling his little piece of paradise. 'I confess the voice is Solarian's but *Klieo* has her own character entirely,' he said, and released me to find me grinning with mischief.

'No wonder you don't want to bring Solarian up here,' I remarked.

Transmission restored, advised the computer. *Two per cent inaudible.*

Polaris was grateful for the distraction. 'Run transmission, thank you, *Klieo*.'

When you return to 2003 you are ambushed and forced to land. It is Castor they seek and the Rod of Power. Montauk started in 1923 with the Order of the Black Sun. Beware the Montauk Boys. If they obtain the Rod of Power they can permanently extend their wormhole system all the way back in history to the time of . . .

Remainder of transmission inaudible, the computer advised.

The Montauk Project was a series of secret US government experiments conducted at an underground facility beneath Camp Hero and

Montauk Air Force Base, Long Island, between the 1950s and mid-1980s. The project was steeped in conspiracy theory: tales had surfaced of human abductions and torture to enhance psychic ability, time-travel experiments, alien contact and much more. What had really gone on there was still something of a mystery to me.

'Levi said he'd been involved with the Montauk Boys —' I began.

'I'm fairly sure Kali wasn't referring to Levi,' Polaris cut in, flattening my fear before I could verbalise it. 'What I find curious is her reference to 1923. Our intelligence makes no mention of a wormhole to that year.'

'What I find even more curious is that she claims we're going to be ambushed when we reach our target year,' I added. 'Should we alter our plans?'

'We don't have to … we have you,' Polaris commented flippantly, and looked out the front shield windows.

I was confused by his confidence. I followed his line of sight to see another huge ethereal funnel erupting.

Alignment with Blue Fire Command funnel complete, the *Klieo* announced.

'It's all one way from here,' Polaris squeezed out as the pressure of the vortex engulfed us.

Everything within the *Klieo* was reduced to an atomic state once more. Our destination in this instance was the Eye of Ra porthole passage, within the proximity of Rigel, some seven hundred and twenty-three light years away.

When my universe again took form, I found myself with an entirely different view of it. A huge blue sun bathed me in its rays, so potent with my colour frequency that I could barely move from sheer euphoria. There were many large stars in this area of space, and the massive gas clouds of the Witch Head Nebula were like moving castles in space as the strong solar winds churned them. I could also see thousands of lights darting between planets and space stations.

'Are the lights spacecraft?' I finally found my voice, but couldn't bring myself to move a muscle.

'Some are.' Polaris came to stand beside me at the huge windows. 'Many are light-beings who no longer need a vehicle to travel through space.'

Tears welled in my eyes. The grandeur of the view filled me with gratitude to be who I was, and the intensity of my joy left me breathless.

'Why did you award me this moment, Captain?' I asked. 'Wouldn't it have been more romantic to share it with Solarian?'

'Two reasons,' he advised. 'When we enter back through Earth's ionosphere, a cloud of electromagnetic energy is going to take out all the *Klieo*'s systems. As the HAARP array goes online, the natural frequencies of the Earth grid will be disrupted and the *Klieo* will be unable to draw Blue Flame energy through the natural matrix of the planet. You are the only independent living conduit of Blue Flame energy on Earth, so I need you to —'

'— power the *Klieo* whilst we go about our mission in 2003,' I concluded for him, feeling a little overwhelmed by my task. 'No pressure, of course.'

'I won't lie ... it will be a drain on your energy. But I wouldn't ask if you weren't completely capable of doing the job. It's your forté,' he added to make me laugh.

'I'm here to serve,' I accepted the task. 'But you said there were two reasons?'

'Well, more importantly than your use as a power source, you're the teller of our story,' he said with a charming smile. 'So I wanted you to see our passage from the best seat in the house.'

His response struck at my heart and filled it with a deep sense of purpose. Of all my Dragon sisters, who had been so prolific in their lifetimes in recording their grand adventures, I was the one who had been awarded the honour of telling this tale — the grandest adventure of them all. I felt inspired to begin writing then and there — if I could have freed myself from the paralysis of my awe.

Blue Fire Command request permission for extraction.

'Permission granted,' the captain replied to the *Klieo*.

With a slight jolt, which startled me and set me off balance, the ship began to slowly ascend.

Polaris helped to steady me and then pointed upwards. 'Station dock,' he said.

'We're beneath a space station …?'

I was distracted by the sight of a large glowing vaporous being that was peering in at us through the control deck windows. Within seconds, many other such beings, of different sizes, shapes and hues, had joined it. Their forms were mutable and transparent, which made them fascinating to watch; they thought the same about us, clearly.

'Humans are a bit of a rarity in this neck of the woods,' Polaris explained.

I had a little chuckle at this, then turned my gaze to the underside of the station we were entering. It was enormous, and the closer to the docking area we rose, the more dense the activity of the locals outside our windows became — the underside of the space station appeared to be a nation within itself!

As the *Klieo* rose, she slowly turned and was behind us — the most awesome sight I will ever behold.

I was staring straight into the great universal tear and the light was intense, saturated in the prima matra of the Ranna time flow. *No wonder Rigel appears so damn bright in the night sky back home*, I thought. I attempted to open my eyes wider but the pain was too intense. Instead, my third-eye vision came into focus and so did the wonder before me.

It was a huge gaping window in space that led into another universe — as if one section of a labyrinth had opened to another. Much of the light was coming from the universe that lay beyond the tear and its source was the Eye of Ra, where all the ley lines of the Ranna and the Kali time flows merged. The eye itself was a light vortex, but around it was a golden light structure like two interlocking diamonds, which converged with a blinking-type motion and flashed in response to the quasar-like pulsing caused by the touching of the two universes. This double-diamond structure was the capstone of the Eye of Ra, known as the Telos Aarkhara, which prevented the universal tear from extending any further into the Ranna time flow. As a point of leakage between our time flow and the Ranna, this was where prima matra could be harvested for creation purposes throughout our harmonic universe. This was where the Ennead had acquired the base material required for their terraforms on future Earth.

From the space station above, a golden beam of light extended into the Telos Aarkhara. From deep space, two more beams extended from the Pleiades and Sirius into the universal tear at different angles to form a pyramidal structure that met at the centre of the Telos Aarkhara; these energetic golden beams powered and reinforced the capstone.

'Are you taking mental notes?' the captain queried, respectful of my awe.

'So many,' was all I could say, my joy so immense it caused tears to flood from my closed eyes.

As we entered the Blue Fire Command space station everything went dark outside the *Klieo*. I opened my eyes, deflated to be deprived of the splendid scenery. 'Now what happens?' I asked. 'Do we have a stopover?'

I was excited by the notion, but Polaris shook his head.

'Even though our souls are of the Ceres, and therefore spiritually more adept than those beings in command here, our physical composition is human and therefore ...' He shrugged.

'Unreliable?' I suggested, and he nodded.

'Well, although ultimately the Nefilim are responsible for the advent of the Kali rift, humans helped.' Polaris explained humanity's bad reputation.

With a slight jolt, the ship docked. Outside the shield windows, all was dark. I held my breath in anticipation of the next occurrence, and when the door to the control deck opened I nearly jumped out of my skin.

'Back again,' Levi strode across to take his place behind the *Klieo*'s control panel. 'Prepare yourself,' he advised as he placed his hand on the metal plate. 'This is going to feel like a bit of a whirlwind, as we'll be moving through both time and space to get to our destination.' Then he looked at me. 'Oh dear.'

'What is it?' I asked.

'Advising you of my involvement with Montauk was ill timed,' he replied.

I realised he must have been telepathically advised of the computer's translation of my daughter's missive. He looked devastated at having unintentionally undermined my trust in him.

'Can I assure you —' he began, but I cut him off.

'The captain has already assured me that Kali wasn't referring to you, Levi. And in all honesty I knew she wasn't. Still, I thought you might have some idea of who she was referring to.'

Before Levi could answer, the huge chamber surrounding our vessel was flooded with Blue Flame light, which poured in through the ship's sails and down through the light funnel. I was standing by the windows to admire the view and was completely bathed in the light frequency to which I was so empathetic.

'See you in 2003,' Levi said, and waved to me.

'But what about our pit stop on Mars?' I asked.

'There is no pit stop,' Levi clarified, 'but when you become conscious of movement again that means we're slowing down and we've passed the Montauk interchange po—'

Reality dissolved into beautiful, awe-inspiring light and I couldn't have cared less where I found myself afterwards. The bliss of the moment washed over me in ever liberating waves as I was propelled to the Earth's not-so-distant past.

My passage through the light energy felt both eternal and instantaneous. I seemed to drift in the wholeness of that illumined benediction for an age, yet gradually the light and energy ebbed and I was downcast to realise I was individualising. My union with the immensity of the quantum world had ended all too soon.

The light began to thin and take on shadow and colour as it streamed past me. My perception was my own once more but I had yet to take physical form. The soaring sensation was rather pleasing and I began to feel better about my return to the realms of physical expression, until I saw the spirit of a beautiful young boy go screaming hysterically past in the opposite direction — towards Mars in the future — with several other young male souls following him.

Then the *Klieo*'s control deck reconstituted around me and I was again inhabiting my body. 'Those children?' I immediately asked. 'They were Montauk Boys?'

'Timewalkers. Given the opportunity to go from destitute orphan to elite secret agent in a couple of weeks ... what homeless boy wouldn't jump at the chance?' Levi said with a distinct chill in his tone.

'They use orphans because no one will miss them,' I realised, shocked.

'A particular kind of orphan ... the blond-haired, blue-eyed Aryan-Nordic type.' Levi turned his baby blues my way, having just described his own appearance, and I understood how he'd managed to get himself enlisted. 'Still, if you prove reliable as a timewalker, you might be inducted into the Secret Crew. Only a few years of excruciating torture and you too can become so desensitised that your brain severs contact with all your pain sensors, making you so fearless that you can be programmed to perform superhuman feats.'

'But why seek to foster psychic power thus, when it can be achieved as easily through love and compassion?'

'That would involve the psychic realising they are the source of their own power, which means they could not be controlled,' Levi pointed out. 'So much for the Montauk Project being shut down in 1984.'

'What are the Secret Crew capable of?' I asked.

'Given one strand of hair,' Levi held his thumb and forefinger together, 'they can track a person, see and hear all they do, no matter where they're located on Earth. What's more, they can influence the thoughts of their victim and even possess their mind completely. They also have telekinetic powers … they can move objects, shatter windows, or even a victim's vital organs. That's what they're independently capable of, but when coupled with the Montauk Chair, the elite among the Montauk Boys can create unstable passages through time. The only difficulty is finding the means to source reliable information about the distant past and the future.'

'The Montauk Chair?' I asked.

'Not now.' Polaris came up behind me, placed his hands on my shoulders and steered me towards the Blue Flame funnel, which was no longer streaming with light. 'Showtime for you, Meridan.'

Spread out before our craft was a huge body of extremely dark clouds alive with electrical activity and waves of coloured light. It looked like the aurora borealis, which was truly spectacular on the eye. Inside the ship, the lights and instruments began to flicker on and off.

'Are we losing power?' I asked, and felt a lurch of panic in my gut that I would let everyone down.

'We certainly are,' Polaris said, sliding his arms beneath my own and raising them so my hands were aimed into the funnel. 'So be a goddess for me and channel your flame into my vessel.'

I was so surprised by his cheeky banter that my insecurity vanished. 'Anything for you, Captain,' I said, mimicking his adoring ship's computer, and shrugged him off to stand alone. I'd done this before, and having just been doused in Blue Flame energy I was radiant with excess. I felt the force gathering to my will, and at my command a stream of Blue Flame energy burst forth from my chest, down my arms, out through my palms and into the funnel that powered the *Klieo*.

CHAPTER 16

DESCENT INTO THE UNDERWORLD

TAMAR DEVERE — KALI

Into the darkness I fell, my only wish to keep hold of the soul I was clinging to, for he was my beloved and the missing link in the Amenti chain, even if he was yet to remember his destiny.

Emmett seemed even more determined than I not to lose contact in the abyss. His embrace felt sincere, like my mother's or father's; although he did not feel like a relative — rather, as if I were clinging to some long-lost part of myself. A massive orb of energy was building between his chest and mine; its intensity caused tears to stream from our eyes. The power, beauty and excitement of this energetic fusion reinforced our auras, preventing the dark energy surrounding us from penetrating beyond the outer reaches of our light-bodies. I felt great peace in knowing that, after a millennia of waiting, I was finally embracing my lover in the flesh. Even if I died this day, I would do so in the arms of my soul mate and prince. How cruel fate was to have revealed this now, when our only route back to Amenti was via the seven gates of hell.

The rolling and spinning motion of our descent slowed and our feet touched down in a dark cavern. Above us we could see only darkness; all around the walls were dismembered skeletons, visible in the grey light of the electric torches positioned either side of the only exit.

'Where the hell are we?' Emmett eyed the human remains.

'The seventh and most outer gate of Irkalla,' I replied, looking around for the keeper of the twin stone doors. 'Each gate is guarded by an evil thought form that embodies one of the seven stages of death.'

'So I guess these souls didn't meet with the gatekeeper's approval?' Emmett asked, and figured out the answer just as I replied.

'They didn't have the toll,' we both said at once, then had a quiet laugh at our common knowledge and interests. Obviously Emmett was familiar with the ancient Sumerian text *The Descent of Inanna*, which detailed Inanna's journey into Irkalla to save her lover.

'You are totally amazing, Kali,' Emmett said. 'It just figures that when I finally meet a girl I relate to, she's an ultra-terrestrial ... No offence to ultra-terrestrials, of course.'

I smiled, delighted by how completely clueless he was about his own true identity. 'You think that supernova that occurs when you hold me close is because we relate well?' I thought that a bit of an understatement.

'You felt that?' He was surprised and delighted. 'I thought it was just me.'

'You couldn't be that in love with yourself, surely?' I rolled my eyes and headed towards the large rectangular stone doors.

'That's not what I ... Hey! You're not seriously going to go through the stages of death in order to save Labontè, are you? Can't a superwoman like you just fly us out of here?'

'I'm afraid not. The low frequency and lack of cosmic light in the Underworld ensures that goodwill receives very little support here. And quite apart from that, if I take you back up into our previous reality where time lines are about to change, I'll lose you, remember?'

'Sorry,' Emmett said. 'I'm new to all this inter-time war business.'

'Besides, it's not really a question any more of whether I'd go into hell after Killian,' I added. 'There's only one route out of here for us, and that's through those doors.'

'But what about the tolls?' Emmett made haste to catch me up. 'What's the first stage of the death process?'

'Shock, of course.' And before I could even consider what toll Shock might extract from us, my Amenti suit vanished, my weapon, which had been tucked into the back of my jeans, dropped to the ground and I was left completely naked.

The human in me stopped in her tracks, stunned, but my Anu side allowed me to shrug off the shock quickly and see the loss for the minor inconvenience it was. I pulled my long dark hair around me like a cloak just as Emmet wrapped his jacket around my shoulders.

'Why didn't Shock take your clothes too?' I wondered.

The huge stone tablets before us vanished, to reveal a stone tunnel stretching ahead. *It is you who must honour the sacred rites, Kali,* a voice said, *for it is you who has business in Irkalla. Your companion may travel toll-free alongside you. Ill has decreed it.*

Shock manifested as a huge fellow who looked like a reject from the punk era. He wore only a leather vest on his upper body, which was covered in obscene tattoos and bound with chains. The studs on his wristbands were like knives, and it was easy to see how the souls who had not made it past this gateway had died. His legs were clad in tight leather chaps, which left his buttocks and genitals exposed, emphasising his huge erection. His hair had been fashioned into a mohawk using coagulated blood, and his eyes were deeply sunk in his pale, gaunt face.

Should you fail to meet any toll along the way, however, Shock added, *your companion shall, of course, perish along with you.* He grinned horribly.

Emmett retrieved my weapon from the ground and placed it in my hands. It was all I had left, and I still had six tolls to pay between here and Irkalla. I knew that Ill was trying to humiliate and degrade me in the eyes of my love.

'Can't I leave my companion here, and retrieve him when my business in Irkalla is complete?' I asked, hoping that Ill was not yet aware of Emmett's true identity.

Shock eyed Emmett with relish. *Trust me with your prince, would you, goddess?*

'I'll take my chances in hell,' said Emmett, stepping around me and away from the demon, 'if it's all the same to you.'

I was left with no choice. I just hoped the fire that burned so brightly between us now would still hold a spark by the time this journey was over.

It seems your mortal friend wishes to stay with you. Shock shrugged, as if unable to understand it, then gestured towards the dark tunnel ahead. *Enter, my lady. May you find all you seek in Irkalla.*

'What choice do I have?' I said.

There is always a choice ... I could use a little company. The demon sidled up beside me and slid his hand over my behind. *And without your suit, you're a half-attractive proposition.*

I clutched his throat in retaliation, and he vanished.

'Come on.' Emmett took hold of my hand to encourage me forward. 'I have complete faith in you.'

'The whole point of this exercise is to diminish that faith,' I said, holding a hand to his face and caressing his cheek.

'Then it is a pointless exercise,' he assured me with a smile so broad that it melted the frosty Anu coating over my heart. I wanted to kiss him, until I noticed the stone doors before us were beginning to close.

'Trust me,' he pleaded, and I responded with a huge smile and ran with him into the passage that led to the next gateway, that of Denial.

The huge squared-off tunnel was composed entirely of large stone blocks and I felt dwarfed by its immensity. Behind us the stone doors closed, leaving us to walk in darkness.

'Why did Shock call me your prince?' Emmett asked, made braver by the lack of light.

'Because he suspects that you are,' I replied honestly.

We kept moving forward in silence for a while, but I could feel that the palm of his hand that gripped my own so tightly had begun to sweat.

'And what do you think?' he said timidly.

'I think . . .' I had to consider carefully how to put this. I didn't want to shock him with too much information, and all the walls in the Underworld had ears. 'I think that the supernova that occurs when you hold me close isn't just because we relate well.'

Emmett chuckled at this, then noticed a light in the distance. 'Look there,' he said, and pointed.

Instantly, the light rushed towards us whereby we were swept up and deposited in a dark and squalid cavern. There were human remains around the periphery of this chamber also, only, unlike the corpses before Shock's doorway, they weren't dismembered; rather they were huddled in fear. The doors here were made of glossy black onyx and even larger than the stone doors we'd passed through previously.

And so they found themselves at the gateway of Denial, said its demon guardian. When Killian Labontè manifested before us, I nearly had heart failure.

Women! he appealed to Emmett. *You just can't trust them; they are so very fickle.*

'This isn't Killian,' I warned Emmett.

Can you deny that up until you saw that trinket our friend here has around his neck, you were just as sure that I was your prince? Killian demanded.

I could not deny it lest I fall straight into the demon's trap. At the same time, I could not tell the truth lest I confirm the true worth of the marker containing the soul essence of my beloved.

'It is our sonic resonance and not an heirloom that will identify my prince to me,' I replied.

Really? he challenged in a very charming manner. *And what if I told you that I also have such a pendant.* Killian ripped open his shirt to show me.

'No,' I said, refusing to believe the demon.

Yes, he stressed. *I showed the pendant to Emmett once and he admired it greatly.*

I looked at Emmett, who was staring at the demon in utter bewilderment. 'No,' he said, turning to me, 'it was the other way around.'

Denial, teased the demon, delighted by his victory.

'One usually does deny a false accusation!' Emmett said angrily.

'What do you ask as toll?' I intervened, wishing to get beyond this demon before it shattered our trust in one another.

The demon assumed his true form. He was tall and emaciated, with long, greasy grey-streaked hair that fell around his sun-deficient naked body. Despite being all skin and bone, he moved so fluently that it was creepy — like watching a skeleton dance.

You could not pay my toll, he warned, approaching me and running his bony fingers over the jacket that covered my nakedness. *Goddess indeed! Ishtar was not afraid to walk naked into Irkalla,* he challenged.

I removed the jacket and handed it back to Emmett, who politely averted his eyes. The demon eyed me with relish and jerked at his erection with one hand while he reached out with the other to stroke the smooth dark hair that fell over my breasts.

I prevented his hand from making contact with a forearm block. 'What do you want as toll?'

I want your hair. He grinned, as this would leave me entirely exposed. *Do you agree to my toll, princess, or will you deny me?*

Denial chuckled at my predicament, and continued to jerk off vigorously before me, licking his cracked, dry lips as he awaited my reply.

I drew deep upon my Anunnaki resilience and nodded. 'I agree to your toll, gatekeeper.'

The demon ejaculated, groaning with delight.

My head instantly felt lighter as my beautiful healthy hair appeared on Denial's head. He looked delighted by his acquisition. The chill of complete nakedness enfolded my body and I looked to Emmett to catch his reaction. His eyes were still averted from me and his jaw was clenched in rage. I put a hand on his shoulder to reassure him.

'It's just hair, it will grow back.'

'I just wish I could contribute to the cost of this quest,' he explained, offering me his coat once again without looking at me.

I gently pushed his offering back towards him. 'I am not ashamed,' I said. 'And I am not afraid.'

The black onyx doors began to part.

'I'll walk ahead of you,' Emmett announced gallantly. 'I trust you'd find that arrangement more comfortable?'

'I would,' I said, but in reality felt that Emmett was more discomforted than I was about my predicament.

Go forth, goddess, into Irkalla, Denial bade me, stroking his long silky hair. *You have honoured the ancient rites of Ereshkigal.*

As I entered the tunnel, I shuddered to think how much more disgusting and degrading this journey would become, with five gateways left before I reached my destination.

We found ourselves before two massive doors of steel, in a prison cell cast of the same metal.

Emmett took in the repressive environment. 'What stage is this?'

Now that really makes me mad! The guardian's voice boomed around the room.

Emmett guessed the response to his own question. 'Anger.'

No aspirant to Irkalla ever has the common decency to appear in my chamber clothed!

'Shock took my clothes,' I appealed.

That's what they all say! Anger appeared before us as a gladiator, hung about with weapons and wearing a metal helmet that protected his skull, ears and eyes but left his ugly mouth exposed. His extremely muscular body was naked and glistened with oil, but, unlike his two predecessors, his penis hung limp between his legs. *I am sick to death of Shock and Denial getting all the best spoils.*

I looked around the chamber — there seemed to be an excess of bodies here. Anger was obviously not easily appeased.

Well, at least you have a weapon! he roared.

'Yes, I do, don't I?'

I fired upon the demon thought form and infused him with love. His penis became instantly erect and a smile of pleasure graced his face.

Wow ... a weapon that actually makes you feel GOOD. The demon was intrigued, and discarded his own weapons before confiscating mine. *I haven't felt this good EVER!*

'Gate?' I prompted him to unlock the metal doors

before he shot himself again and became so high he couldn't function.

Of course, lovely lady, he leered, admiring my naked form.

'You're only allowed one toll,' I said, and pointed towards the doors.

May you find love, peace and contentment in Irkalla, my friends. The demon waved us goodbye.

As we departed through the gateway of Anger relatively unscathed, I looked back to see the demon dancing about admiring his new weapon.

'I think that toll might have rendered that gatekeeper completely useless,' Emmett commented as we entered the metal tunnel. 'You're getting better at this.'

'Perhaps, but I'm running out of items to barter.'

Emmett rooted around in his pockets to see if he had anything of value, and pulled out a set of car keys, his wallet, some gum and a portable games unit. Nothing of much value to the Underworld there. 'What about my pendant,' he said, returning the items to his pockets and going to take off his treasure.

'No,' I insisted. 'If that's the authentic item —'

'If?' He questioned my doubt.

I ignored him and went on: 'We can't lose it or allow it to fall into Nefilim hands.'

'Why not?'

I came up close behind him and whispered in his ear. 'The Nefilim would do terrible harm to my prince with that pendant and I'd rather give up my life than see any more horror befall him.'

Emmett seemed appeased, and touched by my resolve. 'I hope he appreciates you, your prince,' he said. He wasn't yet confident about it being him, but obviously wished it to be the truth.

'My prince gave for me until there was nothing left of him to give,' I said. 'I desire nothing more than to find him and reward his aeons of selfless devotion to me.'

The next chamber was bronze and held very few skeletal remains. Either not many aspirants made it this far, or the demon of Unfinished Business had more mercy than the gatekeepers before him.

Hello, princess.

As the evil voice of the demon echoed around the chamber, I realised my first assumption was the truth. Shudders ran through my being as I recognised Pintar's lecherous tones.

'It's not possible. You're dead,' I said, wanting desperately to convince myself of the fact.

'Who's dead?' Emmett asked, looking everywhere but at me as he searched for the source of the voice.

The huge, hideous, half-human, half-reptilian beast that had been destroyed centuries ago by Amenti's staff and my prince, manifested before us. *You think I'm dead? I'm not. I live on in your memory, little girl; your own DNA ensures I can always come back to haunt you.*

I was frozen with fear as the monster loomed closer.

Emmett dashed between us. 'What do you want?' he demanded of the Lord of the Dracon. 'State your toll and cease tormenting her.'

Pintar burst out laughing. *You don't really aspire to be the mighty Mathu, my creator and soul brother, do you?*

Emmett was confused by the question, but was too smart to be drawn in by it. 'It doesn't matter who I am, great ugly one. Just answer the question.'

His cocky response actually brought a smile to my face. The demon didn't like it one bit, and raised a hand to strike Emmett down.

'Ah-ah,' Emmett cautioned. 'I'm to travel toll free, Ill's orders. If you strike me down that would be considered a toll, would it not?'

The beast roared, vexed by the truth of it.

'Still,' Emmett continued, 'I will gladly pay such a toll on behalf of my companion, if that is what you desire?'

Shut the fuck up! Pintar roared. *I am not interested in making you appear gallant, horny boy! So go fuck yourself whilst I extract my toll from little Miss Modesty here.* Pintar eyed my naked form. *We have unfinished business.*

Emmett spread himself in front of me, and I huddled to hide myself from the lustful eyes of the demon. All I had left were my prince and my virtue; at this rate I would lose both and still not make it to Irkalla.

CHAPTER 17

HATHOR — MOUNT SHASTA

The soul who oversees this pyramid
has many names and seven faces,
she is the feminine aspect of all
that moves through the matrix.

She is the Earth Mother,
the creator of life and evolution!
She perpetuates reality
in which souls may manifest.

Among the Elohim, she is Hathor
and her pyramid brings the matrix full circle,
for she is Creator and Destructor
all in one.

ASHLEE GRANVILLE-DEVERE — SOLARIAN
Upon arrival in our predesignated year, Polaris and
Levi joined the rest of Amenti's staff in the *Klieo's*
rec room.

'Where's Meridan?' Arcturus was immediately concerned when the two men entered without her.

'She's resting,' Polaris advised quickly, hoping to skirt around the issue.

'Meridan doesn't need to rest.' Arcturus was wary. 'What's going on?'

'Nothing is going on!' Polaris insisted. 'Meridan wore herself out powering the ship for the last leg of this journey. The electromagnetic cloud we flew through on re-entry would have forced us to land, but she intervened.'

'And you conveniently had her on the control deck at the time!'

'Arcturus!' I strongly advised him to take a breath, and, due to our continued mutual respect, he refrained from taking a swing at my partner. It didn't stop him haranguing him though.

'Why didn't you tell me you intended to use my wife as a battery for your ship?'

'Meridan was fine with the arrangement,' Polaris rebuked. 'And I didn't tell you because I knew you'd be a girl about it.'

'*Excuse me?*' Talori, the woman closest to Polaris, thumped him. 'Let's get back to the essentials: we're currently functioning within the time continuum, which means the Nefilim can see the Signet stations and this ship, *speed* is our only advantage. So ... where are we?'

'Mount Shasta,' Polaris replied, returning his attention to Arcturus.

Arcturus was delighted that his was the first Signet station on our mission agenda, as he was the only male member of Amenti's staff not to have activated his pyramid. 'So we're all going?' he assumed.

'All except Castor and Talori,' Polaris said.

The pair immediately demanded to know why they were to stay behind.

'Because Meridan has had word from Tamar: the Nefilim are seeking Castor,' the captain explained.

Talori was appeased, Castor was not. 'I'm not going to spend this entire mission babysitting the ship,' he objected.

Polaris gripped his shoulder. 'Face the fear, my friend ... accept it.'

'Goddamn it.' Castor turned away to quietly curse his misfortune.

'That leaves five of us to cover Arcturus,' said Polaris, nodding to Dexter, Thana, Vespera and me. 'Let's make it snappy, folks ... we need to get this job done yesterday.'

He turned to Talori and Castor once Arcturus had left the room. 'This *should* take less than an hour, but I'm expecting a delay.'

'Why, because this is Arcturus's station?' I asked, thinking he was underestimating our old friend.

'Precisely. I just worked it out,' he said with a confident grin and headed out the door.

'Worked what out?' I asked, making haste after him, but he just shook his head.

The entrance to the great labyrinth beneath Shasta was a little stone annexe comprising two standing stones with a capstone. The annexe was inset into the east side of the mountain and at present was filled with rocks. As Arcturus moved ahead of us, the boulders shifted to form a tunnel leading into the mountain.

'You might want to block your ears for a moment,' he warned us.

'Why?' I asked.

'The Yaktavian bells. They're made of astral substance and undetectable to the human eye, but they alert —'

A deep sound began to vibrate within the cavern; as it drew closer it increased in intensity and shook the entire mountain. I hastily thrust my fingers in my ears, and only removed them when Polaris flinched beside me.

'Ouch!' He pulled a small dart from the side of his neck.

'Nice shot,' Arcturus said to our invisible assailant. 'But your ammunition is wasted on the staff of Amenti.'

'Albe-Ra!' cried a chorus of high-pitched voices, and an army of little red-skinned men appeared around us, all bowed on one knee, their heads lowered in homage.

'Red-skinned gnomes,' I uttered under my breath, and looked to Arcturus, amused. 'You truly are the spirit of the red gnome.' This was the title Ashlee Granville-Devere had used to summon Albray to her ringstone and service by means of an old gypsy spell.

Then the strangest thing occurred. The auras of the worshipping mass rose as a single ball of energy and took the form of a glowing ethereal head.

'They are a collective consciousness,' Arcturus whispered to us. 'They cannot abide humans as a rule and choose not to appear to nor speak with them.'

The spirit head tapered off into a ghostly tail at the neck, which trailed the entity as it approached to speak with Arcturus.

'What did humans do to them to cause such a rift?' Vespera asked quickly before the entity got too close.

'The same thing we do to any species or race that appears smaller and weaker than ourselves,' Dexter cut in, having a wide knowledge of the ET and other non-human races of this planet. 'Like so many now extinct species or races that once shared the Earthly realms with us, their collective consciousness appealed to the spiritual guardians of this part of the Earth matrix to raise their frequency slightly. Thus they are still physical beings, but due to their high frequency they can drift between the Earthly realms and the lower astral and are no longer forced to associate with us.'

'Are you saying that many of the species that have become extinct on Earth still exist here, but in a higher realm of frequency?' Thana questioned.

'Not some of the species,' Dexter corrected, '*all* of them.'

The disembodied head glanced at Polaris, who was still rubbing his neck where the dart had hit, then spoke to Arcturus. *A thousand apologies to your associate, lord. With the activation of the Nefilim's new facility this day, we feared the worst.*

'No harm done, Skell,' Arcturus replied. 'I am, however, in something of a hurry.'

Of course. Skell bowed his head reverently. *Please follow me. The Ladies of the Elohim will be eager to speak with you.*

'Not half as eager as I am to speak with them,' Arcturus assured Skell, then looked back to us. 'This won't take long.'

He followed the spirit into the tunnel, and then the miniature red warriors, the ethereal head and our comrade vanished.

'There's going to be a delay,' Polaris said, contradicting Arcturus's last words.

I scowled at his negativity. 'Don't keep saying that.'

Polaris smiled confidently. 'Mark my words.'

We'd not been waiting very long when the army of little men and their collective talking head manifested before us again.

Our lord has requested that we lead you to him at once, and apologises for any delay this may cause.

I looked at Polaris who gave me a 'Told you so' smirk.

The wee army, who looked more akin to the native races of America than the fairytale images I'd seen of gnomes, did an about-face to lead us into the dark depths of beyond. As we moved to follow, the cavern filled with light and in the blink of an eye we were moving down a tunnel with sparkling jewelled walls, which melded into a high arched mirrored ceiling that reflected a floor of glowing gold. It was so rich in colour it appeared orange and bathed the whole passage with that colour frequency.

'Doesn't it feel like Albray?' Thana said to me; in her lifetime as Lillet she had known Albray very well.

'That might explain why I feel on edge,' Polaris commented before I could respond.

The passage's decorations were reminiscent of the exotic palaces of Persia, and thus this Signet station did feel very akin to the soul I knew best as Albray, whose mother had been born in the Near East. 'It is exquisite,' I said, admiring the jewelled mosaic walls.

Why, thank you. The floating head turned to smile at my praise. *We Skell are rather fond of jewels, and my kinsmen craftsmen take great pride in integrating them into precious treasures with which to honour our benefactors, the wise and powerful Elohim.*

Skell bowed his head to us, then continued to lead us towards a huge glowing oval disk of gold at the end of the passage. As we reached the disk, which seemed to be a solid gold barrier, Arcturus stepped straight through it to join us.

'The Ladies of the Elohim have made a request,' he said, staring at we three women in a strangely apprehensive manner.

'They want you to retrieve the ring from the ark at Serabit while you're here in 2003, don't they?' Polaris guessed.

'But if I comply, then Molier won't be killed.' The request had clearly thrown Arcturus into a state of conflict. 'And when we return, he'll still be at large and will have had thirteen more years to damage the Earth and her people. I hadn't done the math when I agreed to do this for the Ladies of the Elohim, and now I have I'm ...'

'— conflicted,' I concluded on his behalf.

Dexter gave his advice. 'This is something you should decide for yourself.'

'There is no decision,' Polaris objected. 'The Ladies of the Elohim would not ask you to do anything that was going to be detrimental to their plan.'

Arcturus looked at Polaris, a little stunned. 'You don't know, do you?'

'Know what?'

'*They* are the Ladies of the Elohim.' Arcturus motioned to Vespera, Thana and me. He nodded to Thana and said, 'Hathor removed her mask in my presence and revealed her true identity to me. It seems you were present at my showdown with

212

Molier all those years ago ... not as Lillet's conscious self, but as her higher self.'

Thana gasped at the suggestion that her soul mind would someday evolve beyond even her Ceres consciousness on Tara, up to Gaia's evolutionary scheme where the great female energy known as Hathor of the Elohim resided.

'We are all destined to become Elohim,' Arcturus stated, rather overwhelmed by the fact.

'That seems to indicate we do something right down here on Earth,' Polaris said, slapping Arcturus on the shoulder to snap him out of his shock. 'I know for a fact that you do retrieve the ring in this instance.'

'How do you know?' Arcturus looked relieved initially, although when Polaris smiled like the know-it-all he was, he seemed sorry he'd asked.

'I retrieve the ring from you when we get back to the entrance of this cave ... at least, the me I was back in 2003 retrieves it,' Polaris enlightened him. 'I give the ring to a trusted friend of ours, and it's been residing on the hand of your wife for the past thirteen years and more recently on the hand of your daughter.'

'The invisible ring.' Arcturus smiled.

'Just like our clothes, which are of an etheric nature, the Ring of the Ark can be willed to take the form of any ring one desires, which helps to keep it hidden and protected,' Polaris explained. 'But only in its coiled ring form can it be used in conjunction with the Rod of Power.'

'On the bright side, André will never get his hands on Albray's ringstone,' I commented, referring to the Elohim's request. 'In fact, the ringstone, in theory, will never be lost.'

213

'So we simply make another stop here in 2003,' Dexter said with a shrug.

'No, no,' Arcturus corrected, 'there's a hidden porthole incorporated into the site at Serabit that connects that complex to the porthole in this Signet station.'

'Really?' I was fascinated, being familiar with the ancient temple in question. 'I wonder where in the temple the porthole is hiding? In the Ark Chamber perhaps?'

'Would you care to accompany me?' Arcturus said.

I knew he saw a chance to get back at my partner for exclusively inviting Mia onto the *Klieo*'s control deck, but as I was curious, and a little annoyed at my partner myself, I took hold of Arcturus's outstretched hand. 'I'd love to,' I said.

'Me too,' Thana said, having also had past experience with the Star-Fire Temple.

'Come on then.' Arcturus was more than delighted to take hold of a hand each and lead us through the golden barrier and into his Signet station.

As I passed through the glowing disk, I was overwhelmed by that 'sense of Albray' Thana had commented on earlier and I felt the old attraction to him begin to stir. Fond memories and sensual thoughts about him flooded my mind — orange was, after all, a vibrant and primal colour.

'Wow,' I said, trying to shake off my arousal before it landed me in strife.

'All right!' Thana shimmied like a Latino dancer aroused by a fiery tune.

'Is something the matter, ladies?' Arcturus couldn't wipe the smile off his face; he knew full well that this place was potent with his personal essence.

'Orange is my new favourite frequency,' Thana boldly teased him, 'at least until we get to the next Signet station.'

I laughed at her insight and glanced back to the entrance barrier, expecting Polaris to come storming through after us.

'He's locked out,' Arcturus said, and pouted to mimic my husband's reaction to the fact.

I had to smile at his cheek. 'Why must you bait him constantly?'

'One should always have a goal,' he replied. 'But quite apart from that, I really enjoy it.'

Inside, the Signet station had all the grandeur of a Turkish mosque. The main chamber was round and defined by great pillared arches of solid amber crystal that rose to support a transparent dome in the ceiling. Beyond the dome was a sky of orange, which rained bolts of Blue Flame energy upon the Signet station.

'Is that the base of the Hathor pyramid?' I asked. It was so huge I couldn't see its sides.

'It certainly is,' Arcturus confirmed. 'It encompasses the entire mountain.'

'My goddess!' Thana was awestruck by the etheric pyramid's sheer magnitude.

'Indeed,' Arcturus agreed, his eyes resting on Thana. 'Is it any wonder our lives have been so intertwined when you are the goddess of my stargate?'

Thana was charmed. 'You always did have such a lovely way of putting things.'

Between the arched pillars were huge windows giving a view of a cavern that hosted a lake of bubbling molten magma. Unlike the other stations, whose crystal conductors were outside the control centre, the Blue Flame energy here was drawn down through the inside of the huge amber pillars and then directed into the Earth through a central funnel that ran from beneath the control centre and deep into the planet's crust below the molten lake.

'That's why it's so warm in here,' I commented.

'I thought you looked a little flushed,' Albray teased, holding a hand to my cheek.

This was the first time I had been with my knight outside of Polaris's presence since Albray had been reunited with his physical form, and his personal sonic was radiating through me intensely, even more so than the times his spirit had possessed my body.

'Stop flirting,' I said and walked past him towards the middle of the chamber where the solid amber crystal plate of the station's porthole was set into the polished gold floor.

'I never flirt,' he defended himself, but when Thana and I couldn't stop laughing, he reconsidered. 'Well, maybe once or twice … but definitely not just then.'

'You flirt and you don't even know you're doing it,' I argued, 'that's how chronic it is with you.'

'Well, orange is my frequency,' he said. 'What's your excuse?'

'My excuse?' I gasped, surprised. 'I've never flirted with you!'

He stared blankly at me.

'All right, maybe once or twice … but definitely not just then.' I grinned, as did he.

'Well, I'm glad we've sorted that out,' he said very charmingly.

'Yes, quite,' I agreed, and looked around for the control panel for the porthole.

Arcturus stepped straight onto the huge, round amber plate. 'All Inner Earth technologies are telepathically operated,' he explained, waving to us to join him.

'So you just focus on Serabit?' Thana asked.

He directed us to stare into the amber plate. An image began to materialise within the crystal and I found myself looking down upon the central platform of the circular entrance chamber of the Star-Fire Temple at Mount Serabit.

'How can that be?' I asked. 'This platform has a great gold dome above it.'

Arcturus looked at me as if I were stupid. 'The dome *is* the porthole,' he said, raising his eyebrows.

I wanted to hit myself, but refrained as the glowing amber stone beneath our feet began to liquefy into a whirlpool; then its centre opened wide and the three of us dropped straight through onto the red-Orme-gold floor of the Star-Fire Chamber.

It had been hundreds of years since I'd set foot in this ancient place, and the last time I had, it near killed me, twice over. Thana's experience here had almost been fatal too, and had hindered her spiritual development for hundreds of years.

The golden dome we'd just dropped through had reconstituted and gave no hint of its secret function. The round central platform we'd landed on marked the intersection of two red-Orme-gold paths that crossed through the chamber — from the outside entrance to the Ark Chamber, and to opposing annexes on either side of the sacred dwelling that housed the ancient keys that opened the Ark Chamber. There were also concentric circular paths of stone radiating out from the central platform, separated by deep pits that could be filled with flammable liquid via a lever located near the entrance to the tunnel to the outside world.

Arcturus was gazing at a pile of bones near the tunnel entrance, which were his remains from his days as Albray the Crusader knight. His first visit to this site *had* killed him, and had seen him cursed to be a ghost for over seven hundred years.

'It's odd to think those bones are the very same ones holding me up right now,' he said.

Mia had visited this site soon after this present time and seen Albray resurrected. Still, in the future reality we now inhabited, this would not happen — Albray had already become Arcturus and so long as he was operating outside of space and time, any changes to the events of his past would not affect him.

Around the exterior walls of the round chamber were flaming torches, put there for illumination. I found this puzzling. 'I wasn't expecting to find the temple all lit up like this,' I commented.

'It is a little surprising,' Arcturus said, 'given that it should have been vacant for the last two hundred years! Would you ladies be so kind?'

He directed us to the annexes where the keys to the Ark Chamber were kept, then strode down the path that led to the tunnel up to the surface.

I made haste towards the white-pillared annexe, which contained the Highward Firestone vial, otherwise known as the Star. Thana moved off in the opposite direction to fetch the Firestone vial from the red-pillared annexe.

But when Arcturus reached the path that ascended to the surface, he stopped abruptly. 'The temple is open!' he cried out.

'What?' I came out of the annexe holding the glowing white Star vial.

'Molier must have got the chamber open long before he even contacted Mia,' Arcturus said, turning on his heel and striding back to the central platform to meet us. 'The whole thing was staged purely to get Mia here to retrieve the keys and open the Ark Chamber for him.'

'Well, doh!' Thana mocked as she joined us with the Fire vial, for she had been similarly deceived by Molier many centuries before.

'That means he's here right now!' Arcturus looked ready to finish off the Orme-filled vampire and be done with it, again!

'Albray, I know you want nothing better than to finish Molier again,' I sympathised, 'but if he was to be killed while you are operating within the confines of time and space, you will cease to exist, for his death now will affect your resurrection then.'

'What?' Albray was understandably alarmed to learn this.

'Trust me,' I advised. 'I'm a space/time architect and such an encounter would be very bad for you.'

He looked perturbed, but nodded.

'While we're standing around here, the clock is ticking,' Thana reminded us, and handed her vial to me. 'You two retrieve the ring,' she said, and pulled out her liquid-light gun. 'I'll keep watch for Molier.'

On either side of the golden door to the Ark Chamber was an inset designed to house one of the vials. Once each vial was placed into its holder, the door vanished to reveal a small connecting chamber hosting a golden breastplate and a copper bowl and pitcher. We had no need of these safety measures today, for we were here with the consent of the Elohim. Two more keyholes for the Star and Fire vials were to be found on the inner door to the chamber.

'This is very exciting,' I said to Arcturus as the door to the central chamber materialised once more behind us. 'I never got this far into the temple before.'

Aside from the glowing contents of the vials, the room fell into darkness.

'This ought to be a rare treat then,' Arcturus said, sounding pleased to be the one to indulge me. He placed the vials in the holders provided and the massive doors of the Ark Chamber parted.

A red pathway led to a central ringed platform, around which flowed a sea of the same flammable fluid that filled the canals in the outer chamber. I couldn't make out much of the detail of the chamber as it was in darkness, although I could see the light from the vials in Arcturus's hands reflected at an odd angle in the ceiling.

'Wait here,' Arcturus said as he retrieved the keys. 'I'll turn the lights on.'

He walked onto the central platform and placed the Star vial and the Fire vial in their separate conductors atop a large object. As soon as the vials were housed correctly, a current of electricity formed an arc of light between them. Their glowing contents were vacuumed into the belly of the object, which flared with golden light to reveal itself as one of the ancient arks of myth.

It was about one hundred and fifteen centimetres in length by seventy centimetres in height and appeared as thick as it was tall. Hieroglyphs featured along its sides and at each corner stood a leg support of rich polished timber. On the golden lid, known as 'the mercy seat', two metal points rose up and curved inward towards each other. These held the Star and Fire vials, the electric current running between them illuminating the entire chamber.

The place exceeded all my expectations with its grandeur and I gasped in amazement. Its walls were of highly polished gold, as were the several large pillars that upheld its roof and the inverted golden dome in its centre. The unusual dome hung directly above the central platform and mirrored the entire chamber, the golden ark at its centre.

Arcturus held his hands out over the ark, as if warming himself on its glow. Orange light beamed from his palms into the ark's lid and the golden mercy seat rose slowly into the air to expose a coiled red crystal ring. The ring levitated out of the ark and Arcturus reached forth and claimed it. As he did, the ark's lid slammed down and the chamber lights went out.

After a moment, the two vials atop the mercy seat began to refill, their glowing contents providing some light in the darkness. As soon as they were full, Arcturus retrieved and pocketed them. 'Best get them out of harm's way while we're at it,' he said.

With no more light by which to admire the beautiful chamber, I turned and followed him out.

Arcturus placed the vials in the keyholes either side of the door leading back into the central chamber of the Star-Fire complex. The doors to the Ark Chamber closed behind us then the exit door vanished to expose us to the comparatively light-filled main chamber. To our great horror, we were met by the sight of Molier and three companions, two male and one female, standing upon the central platform beneath the golden dome.

There was no mistaking Molier: his pale, sun-deprived skin, his dark hair and even darker eyes were burned into my memory — along with his many other guises, animal and demon. He had not aged a day in over two hundred years!

The group appeared mystified to see us emerging from the ancient chamber they so desperately sought access to. But it didn't take Molier long to recognise our faces among those he'd known during his seven hundred years upon this Earth.

'Sir Albray Devere and Lady Ashlee Granville-Devere — fancy seeing the two of you together, and here of all places!' He began to chuckle, although clearly a little nervous about the implications of this event — and his eyes darted to the entrance to check that Albray's body still lay where he had left it to rot in the thirteenth century. Then he grinned as the truth dawned on him. 'You found your way into the inter-time war, you lucky devils,' he deduced, and his eyes narrowed as he prepared to take on his demon form.

Where is Thana? I wondered, until a light-bullet shot down from the golden dome above Molier and sent him flying onto his back. Three more light-bullets and his companions joined him on the ground, all writhing as the Orme spewed forth from their bodies.

I was horrified by the event and, concerned for Albray's continued existence, I shoved him towards the porthole. Thankfully Thana was on my wavelength. She swirled down in a whirlwind of liquid light to retrieve Albray and immediately shot back up into the Signet station with him, safely delivering him into the Otherworld and away from the consequences of the time-space continuum of this Earth plane.

In a moment Thana returned to join me in the Star-Fire temple. 'All safe,' she commented upon touchdown. 'And now we won't have to worry about the mischief Molier might cause in the future.'

I was still gaping at the ease with which she'd despatched Molier. 'What I wouldn't have done for one of those weapons two hundred years ago!' I said.

Thana smiled. 'I must confess, it did feel awfully good.' She looked down at the vampire, who, having vomited up an excessive amount of black bile, was now returning to his true age and rotting into a gooey pile of flesh and bone.

His comrades, who had only recently fallen victim to their Orme addictions, had passed out from the effort of their purge, but would be as right as rain after a good sleep and a shower.

'Let's drag these guys out,' I suggested. 'We can't leave them to be trapped in here for all eternity.' For once the sun set, the entrance to the temple would close and, without an abundant supply of Orme powder, could never be opened again.

I looked down at one of the bodies — André Pierre, the man who was destined to bring Mia onto this project. 'Well, this reinforces the fact that André will never get his hands on your ringstone,' I told Arcturus. 'Chances are he'll never even know of its existence.'

'What, for the love of the goddess, took you so long?' Polaris fumed when we returned.

223

'We kicked Molier's butt into oblivion,' Thana boasted, raising her arms in victory. 'And his mates.'

'We're not supposed to be changing history,' Polaris stressed.

'But you said that we would ...' Arcturus held up the red-coiled ring he'd been instructed to retrieve and offered it to Polaris, '... and so we have.'

Polaris declined to take the treasure. 'No, you don't give it to me now, you give it to me then,' and he motioned back down the tunnel towards its entrance.

'Then our work here is done.' Arcturus led the way along the tunnel.

As we followed him, I noted the drop in the cavern's vibratory frequency as the spectacular jewelled tunnel faded back into the grey rock surface.

'I think I should wait here for a bit,' Polaris suggested as we reached the entrance to the cavern, not wanting to meet his other self during the handover of the ring.

'Sure,' Arcturus said, and went ahead alone. The rest of us waited with Polaris until Arcturus reappeared and beckoned us into the daylight. 'It's done,' he said.

'I was here?' Polaris wanted to be sure all had gone as he'd remembered.

'You were,' Arcturus assured him. 'Don't you trust me to do something as simple as handing over a ring?'

Polaris didn't want to answer that. He pointed to a small tear in Arcturus's Amenti suit. 'What happened there?' he asked.

Arcturus shrugged. 'I must have caught it on something.' He held the tear together and it mended itself. 'Good as new. Can we move on now?' And he led us back to where the *Klieo* was parked.

The rest of the team followed, but Polaris hung back, looking perplexed.

'What is it?' I asked.

My husband declined to answer.

CHAPTER 18

DECEIVING APPEARANCES

MIA DEVERE — MERIDAN

I awoke to find the concerned faces of Talori and Castor staring down at me. As I stirred, their worried looks changed to broad smiles.

'There, I told you, your Lady du Lac is perfectly fine.' Talori sounded like she was having a little dig at her partner as she ruffled his hair.

'We were worried,' Castor explained, but Talori appeared more interested in the idle control deck.

'What does all this stuff do?' she asked. She didn't dare touch anything, but she had a good close look and a sniff as well. 'Blue Flame energy,' she concluded after a whiff of the funnel.

'Should you two be in here?' I asked.

'The captain said it was okay to keep an eye on you,' Castor assured me, as I found my composure and sat upright.

'Oh my goddess.' I felt the old familiar sensation of a trinket hanging about my neck, and I reached inside my shirt to discover my ringstone had returned to my possession. 'Praise the heavens!' I gripped it tightly, resolute that it would never leave my sight again. 'If this has returned to my possession, then the past has been altered somehow, so that I never misplaced it.'

'Curious,' frowned Castor.

'Where are Polaris and Levi?' I wondered out loud.

'They've gone with the others to assist Arcturus in opening his Signet station. They should be back any time now. They've already been gone longer than expected.'

Talori looked over. 'The captain did mention before he left that he expected a minor delay.'

'Why?' I wondered. 'Because Shasta is Arcturus's station?'

'I really couldn't say,' Talori commented diplomatically, not willing to buy into the long-standing tension between the two men.

'Ouch!' I searched through my pockets to find whatever it was that had been sticking into me as I slept. 'Gotcha.' I held the offending item up to examine it, and Castor recognised the little module.

'Is that —'

'— one of the Nefilim's new auric simulators? It certainly is. I meant to give it to Levi to pull apart.'

'Ooooh, interesting.' Talori came to take a closer look. 'Is it still operational?'

I hadn't thought to check. 'Let's find out.' I clipped the module onto the back of my trousers. 'It has to have a telepathic command sensor as it's too darn small to be operated any other way. Okay …' I stood up to focus better.

'The amazing Meridan will now transform into …' Talori announced with gusto, taking a seat beside Castor to watch the show.

I looked at Castor, and before I'd even finished sizing him up Talori was applauding. I gazed down at myself, amazed to view Castor's form.

'Two of you!' Talori hugged Castor and nuzzled her forehead against his cheek. 'What a delicious idea.'

A great crack sounded and a sphere of light erupted in the middle of the room and steadily grew larger.

Remembering what Tamar had forewarned about Castor being hunted down, Talori immediately suggested he use his shamanistic powers to disappear.

'Flea,' Castor said without a second's hesitation, transforming and hopping into Talori's pocket.

I heard Talori call out to me, but my attention was on the sphere of light, which had now widened into a tunnel. At the far end was Killian Labontè, appearing rather the worse for wear.

'Tamar is in trouble ... you have to help us. Come!' He beckoned me urgently. 'Please! I know you don't know me, but if you're one of the Amenti staff, you have to help!'

I was confused by his words until I realised I was still in Castor's form.

'No, don't!' a man shouted from behind, and I turned to see Levi enter the control deck. The fear on his face plunged a dagger of warning into my soul.

I attempted to pull back, but the tunnel was shortening rapidly, dragging me towards Killian. Something grabbed at the back of my trousers ... one of my teammates attempting to pull me back ... but they lost their grip and I was torn away. I recalled Tamar's warning: *It is Castor they seek,* but it did nothing to reassure me. I knew there was only one place on Earth at this time in history that could have produced a porthole like the one now drawing me in.

I was about to get an inside look at the secret operations that went on deep underground at Montauk.

Ashlee Granville-Devere — SOLARIAN

The sad news of Meridan's abduction via a transient porthole was compounded by the fact that Levi had pursued her. There was nothing Castor or Talori could have done to prevent the incident, even if it hadn't been over before they'd even realised what was happening.

'We have enough stored Blue Flame energy in the backup generators to keep the *Klieo* cloaked for a few hours,' Polaris warned. 'But without Meridan, we have no fuel to move her.'

'Without Meridan, the staff of Amenti are fucked. Period!' Arcturus was about to lose his mind. 'She is the Black Madonna; without her the Ring and Rod are useless! Could that be why they took her?'

'They thought they were taking Castor,' Talori pointed out.

'We can only hope the Montauk Boys don't figure out who she really is,' Polaris added.

'Is hope the best we can do?' Arcturus barked.

Thana placed a hand on his shoulder to calm him. 'Levi is the greatest authority we have on the operations at Montauk, and he won't allow any harm to befall your wife,' she assured him.

'I'm sorry.' Arcturus calmed down as he realised that Thana shared his sad predicament, and he embraced her. 'We'll get them back,' he vowed, and looked to Polaris, hoping that, as usual, he had a plan.

The frown upon Polaris's face was not reassuring, however.

CHAPTER 19

IRKALLA

TAMAR DEVERE — KALI

The gatekeeper of the fourth level of Irkalla, Unfinished Business, was getting a little tired of having to deal with me through Emmett, so he swept him away from in front of me and then leered down at me.

This is not my archenemy, I told myself, searching for the courage to stand tall before him. *He's just another demon from my past trying to prevent my soul mission.*

'State your toll or move aside,' I demanded, hoping to call his bluff so that he stopped the dramatics. In a past life I had been raped by this creature, after which I'd killed myself out of shame. I was not ashamed now, however; nor did I fear anything that tried to stop me achieving my final goal. Still, I hoped the creature did not intend to rob me of my virtue.

The demon grinned, exposing his razor-sharp teeth, and his breath wafted over me — the smell of a thousand rotting corpses. I wanted to gag, but refrained.

I want the ring your mother gave you, the one the

time lord used to track you to me, Pintar said.

I was taken aback, having forgotten all about the invisible ring on my finger. 'Why do you want it?' I asked. It was a novelty, yes, but it had no great value or function that I was aware of. It was true that it had enabled Polaris to track me, and maybe that was why the Underworld wanted to take it from me, to prevent me being tracked. That didn't worry me; I could take care of myself.

I could name another toll . . . one more intimately taxing, the creature threatened, beckoning me with its long claw-like fingers to hand the item over.

I needed no further prompting; I'd do whatever it took to get out of this chamber intact. I gripped the ring and twisted it from my finger.

'Hold on,' Emmett said. 'If you actually have an invisible ring, surely that's more valuable than the treasure I carry?'

'What treasure could you have, mortal?' Pintar swung around to Emmett.

'Don't answer that!' I ordered. The thought of handing over what was possibly my prince's soul essence to this creature and its Underworld masters was too distressing even to consider. I thrust myself between the demon and Emmett. 'Here's your toll,' I said and tossed him his prize, then gripped Emmett by the shirt and hauled him towards the huge bronze doors.

'Mention your treasure once more on this journey and I'll personally punch your lights out,' I hissed.

'I was just trying —'

'To save me, I know,' I finished for him. 'But every time my prince tries to save me, he ends up dead, damned or lost! So just take a break! I'll handle this challenge on my own, if it's all the same to you.'

'If that's your wish, I'll stay out of your negotiations,' he said haughtily.

'Thanks. I'd greatly appreciate it.'

The bronze doors closed behind us and plunged us into darkness again.

We were propelled into the next chamber, where the silver walls and doors were tarnished and lustreless. The skeletal remains here were few, but their final resting poses were tortured.

'I'll just be over here then,' Emmett said, and to make completely clear his disengagement from the situation, he pulled his portable games unit from his pocket and began playing.

I felt this was a rather childish reaction to my request, but if it kept him out of my business, it worked for me. I approached the silver gates, waiting for the guardian to show himself.

What do you want? moaned a voice imbued with misery.

'I wish passage to Irkalla,' I replied, trying to sound upbeat and not discouraged by the gatekeeper's tone.

The spirit howled, too caught up in his woes to consider mine. *Go away!*

'Go where?' I appealed.

I don't care!

'Look,' I said, 'I can tell you're depressed —'

Depressed! the voice wailed. *I AM depression! I have no hope, no interest, no aspirations or desires, NOTHING. I'm stuck here for all eternity, and if you can't change my fate, why should I care if YOU rot here too? At least you'll see some end to the monotony, and watching you decay will give me something to do.*

Listening to the gatekeeper started to make me feel depressed too. I was thinking that I should have saved my happy gun for this gate, when I heard Emmett chuckle behind me.

'Yes!' He gave a victory cry, then looked up to explain his outburst. 'I finally cracked that level. So sorry, I'll be quiet now.' He returned his attention to the game but was unable to wipe the grin from his face.

What's that he's doing?

A tiny hunched-over man appeared next to Emmett. He was huddled beneath a dark hooded cloak, the putrid sleeves of which he used as a tissue.

As I watched Emmett selling the demon on all the functions of the game machine, I had to adore him for defying my wishes and helping me out of a stalemate with this guardian. We couldn't make the demon truly happy, but some amusement wasn't a bad substitute.

'That's the way,' Emmett encouraged as the gatekeeper took the game and began to play.

Once the demon got a feel for it, Emmett slapped his shoulder. 'Now, how about those gates?'

You can't leave! the demon protested, eyes glued to the screen of his new toy. *How will I know what to do next?*

'Well, that's the beauty of these games,' Emmett explained. 'What happens next is always a surprise.'

Really? Depression sounded delighted to learn this. He was now eager for us to leave him be, and turned away from us so as not to be disturbed further. *Then by all means, go!* he said, and actually chuckled as the silver gates began to part.

'Thank you, Emmett,' I said as we stepped through the gateway of Depression.

'Two gates to go,' Emmett said simply. Nevertheless, I could tell he was pleased to have been of assistance.

In a chamber of gold stood a demon in the fairly handsome personification of a man, adorned in fine robes and calm in his demeanour.

'Who might this be?' Emmett asked, curious about the non-threatening appearance of this gatekeeper.

'He is Acceptance,' I said.

'Well, that doesn't sound too bad.'

'That depends on what you're being asked to accept,' I replied.

Welcome O Queen of Queens to my chamber of surrender, the gatekeeper said with a smile of greeting, or perhaps it was a challenge.

'And what does Acceptance require me to surrender this day as toll to pass through the golden gates?' I asked, getting straight to the point. I was so close to my destination I could almost smell victory. Once I got to Ill, the rest of the Nefilim would drop like flies.

My toll is a kiss, he advised winningly.

'*Just* a kiss?' The request seemed too simple.

A kiss that he must watch, he motioned to Emmett. *So that he might see you for the femme fatale you are, willing to stop at nothing to achieve your goal.*

'This is supposed to be *my* toll,' I objected.

Your little friend chose to be involved, the guardian pointed out. *So I'm involving him.* The demon took the form of Killian Labontè. *Do you accept my terms?*

This toll would have psychological ramifications but I felt I was prepared for them. My worry was how Emmett would see my acceptance. Ill wished to destroy Emmett's high opinion of me, and who better to do that than the person Emmett despised most, Killian Labontè. And if I was wrong about Emmett, and Killian proved to be the soul I was looking for, a bad experience here could damage my image of him too. Ill was covering all his bases.

Emmett spoke up to quell my fears. 'With every humiliation you make her endure my admiration for her will only grow stronger.'

I'm sure you'd like to think so, Acceptance quipped, and looked to me for my decision.

I nodded silently and the demon beckoned me to approach.

The gatekeeper may have looked like Killian, but he still smelled like a demon from the sixth plane of hell. My plan was to close my eyes and mind until it was over, but Acceptance had other ideas.

The demon turned me about to face Emmett then pulled me back close to him. My limbs felt sedated. Even when the demon cupped his hands over my breasts, I couldn't find the will to retaliate.

See? the demon taunted Emmett. *She likes it.*

I wanted to deny the fact, but when I tried to speak only moans of pleasure came from my mouth. The demon slid a hand between my legs and I felt so humiliated that I wanted to throw up, but I lacked the will even to do that.

'You said a kiss only.' Emmett made a move to retrieve me from the demon's clutches.

Accept she is a whore or you'll never get out of here, the demon demanded, holding Emmett at bay with his power and rubbing between my legs more frantically. I groaned again, ashamed and yet exhilarated at once. I tried to focus on not being aroused by the probing of the demon's nimble fingers, but was unable to resist, my physical pleasure aiding him in his cause to humiliate me.

'Stop it!' Emmett demanded, confused by my lack of protest.

She doesn't want me to stop it, do you, darling? the demon leered over my shoulder.

'All right!' Emmett said. 'I believe you. Now let her go!'

And leave her, a goddess, wanting? the demon taunted. *That just wouldn't be right.* He licked my cheek and my stomach turned, repulsed.

I did not want my first sexual experience to be at the hands of a demon. Summoning all my will, I turned my head and kissed the creature's cheek, breaking his spell over me. I cast him off.

'You have taken enough for a thousand tolls,' I hissed, ready to rip him from limb to limb with my bare hands. 'Open the damn doors!'

Yes, surrender to your killer nature, princess, the demon advised with a grin. *It will serve you well in Irkalla.*

I hated that the negative energies of this descent were getting to me, and feared what I might be provoked into doing by the time I reached Ill. If I was still entertaining these negative emotions when I confronted the Nefilim leader, love could not prevail.

I stormed through the huge golden gates ahead of Emmett, too rattled to look him in the eye.

'I'm so sorry,' he said as he came after me. 'I didn't realise you were restrained. I —'

'I really should thank you for accepting the Underworld's portrayal of me as a whore,' I returned, 'or I might never have broken loose.'

I kept moving, deeply upset that he could accept such a lie about me.

'But I don't know you!' he appealed in his own defence. 'Not really.'

My emotions were all over the place and if I didn't pull them into line and regain my equilibrium, all would be lost. 'I know you don't,' I conceded.

But if he really was my prince, my true love, surely he would not doubt me? The further I progressed towards Irkalla, the more I doubted that Mathu lay dormant in this boy. This was why Ill had invited me to take this journey: to test my faith in my own instincts. Whether Emmett was my prince or not, Mathu was out there somewhere, and with this knowledge I regained my inner strength.

'I will do whatever it takes to achieve my goal,' I said, confirming that much of the gatekeeper's claim as truth.

'And what is your cause, Kali?' Emmett was curious. 'Surely you haven't endured all this just to save Killian Labontè?'

The notion coaxed a laugh out of me. 'I hardly think so.'

'Then what?'

'I am the Destructor of the great unreality,' I announced loudly, so that Death might heed my approach. 'I am Time and none can escape my all-consuming march. I am Quietus to the ignorant who fear for their lives; the ego recoils in my presence, seeing in me its own demise.' I strode on, more confident, as the golden doors closed behind us and the passage fell into darkness. 'I am the Blackness that awaits the deceivers of cosmic law. Demons, your liberation is nigh, for I AM.'

*   *   *

Death's chamber was constructed of the most resilient and prized metal on Earth, Orme-reinforced gold, and the walls and doors gave off their own bright illumination. There were no remains in this chamber — Death would take anyone, and as for a final toll, if nothing else one still had a soul to exchange. This made the choice of material for this chamber ironic, for an Orme addiction would also cost your eternal well-being.

'So this is Death's door,' Emmett joked, trying to lighten the moment. 'In one way this is an adventure beyond imagining; on the other hand I've never been so —'

I clasped a hand over his mouth. 'Never fear Death,' I advised sternly. 'Lest you invite his wrath upon you.'

Emmett nodded silently, and I let him go and approached the massive Orme doors that stood between me and the courtroom of Erragal and Ereshkigal.

A massive demon manifested before me, taking the form of the Grim Reaper. His facial features could not be seen beneath his hooded cloak that fell to the ground, but his hands were skeletal.

Toll, he demanded.

'Name it,' I replied.

Your singing voice, he said gravely.

Emmett wondered if this was a joke. 'Is Death thinking of going into the entertainment business?' he asked.

'The high resonance of my song drives low-frequency beings insane,' I explained.

With this toll, the Nefilim would feel confident

238

that they had stripped me of all my weapons. Due to the lack of cosmic light in Irkalla, my psychic skills were useless. However, I had a secret weapon that my adversaries had overlooked; it was hidden in the last place the Nefilim would ever consider — my heart.

'Take it,' I replied.

Emmett gripped my arm. 'That will be a sacred gift lost,' he whispered, imploring me to reconsider.

'A small price to pay for a paradise found.'

The demon gave a wave of his huge hand and Emmett was cast aside. Death lowered his sickle around me and encouraged me closer. *Sing your last note, angel.*

I breathed in deeply, almost retching at Death's stench, then released the highest, purest note I could reach.

With a howl of agony, Death snatched the sonic from me. The beautiful note ended abruptly and my enlightening song was forever silenced. The demon gave a menacing laugh of victory as he released me.

I moved to join Emmett and was touched to find tears streaming down his face. 'Are you all right?' I asked.

'That note.' He shook his head, unable to express himself fully. 'I know it —'

Irkalla welcomes you, Death said, cutting Emmett short, *O self-proclaimed saviour of the Nefilim —*

'I have come for the Anunnaki!' I corrected. 'So save your prophetic speeches for someone who *cares* and open the gates.'

Death vanished in an infernal huff, and the huge glowing gates to the seventh plane of hell ignited before us in a fiery blaze.

'Awesome,' muttered Emmett, trailing behind me as I headed for the dark tunnel that led into Irkalla's courtroom.

'My relatives like to put on a good show,' I replied.

'I was referring to you.'

The comment made me smile, but I didn't look back. I had cleared a path to my objective; it was time to focus.

'Stay close,' I advised.

'My very thought.' He took hold of my hand; his own was freezing.

'You're so warm.' Considering my naked state he found this surprising. 'How come?'

I looked at him as we passed through the gateway, noticing the mist on his breath and that he was wearing his jacket. 'I can't say.'

'I thought hell was supposed to be hot?'

'You shouldn't believe everything you read,' I said. 'Hell is a state of living without cosmic light, without which there is no warmth, no love and no illumination.'

'Now *that* makes sense,' Emmett conceded, his teeth chattering as we entered an area of deepest shadow. Not even the golden glow of the walls and floor made this entranceway inviting; a foreboding sense of death, oppression and danger hung in the dank air, urging every molecule of one's being to retreat. Then the cries of the lost souls that inhabited this realm began to filter through to us. *Help us,* they begged, screamed, wept.

'Look.' Emmett was drawn to look more closely at the Orme wall glowing alongside of us, the surface of which had become transparent to reveal large holding tanks crammed with lost souls. Many of them were tiny newborns, wailing in torment.

240

'So many babies,' he said in an anguished tone. 'What could they have possibly done to be stuck here with the damned?'

'These souls are not the damned,' I explained. 'The damned fragment upon death, leaving nothing to be tortured. These are the souls of the human sacrifices carried out by the Nefilim, the Dracon and the Illuminati through the ages in order to summon demons to do their bidding and give them power over mortals. All these babies did was to be born to women who sacrificed them to the dark arts in exchange for worldly power. Because these souls were murdered, they are not damned, for they have not sinned; rather, they are cursed, and as all curses can be lifted, they may yet be released from this eternal darkness. Until then, the demons of the subplanes thrive on their suffering.'

Emmett brushed tears from his eyes. 'Our world sucks!' he said. 'How could we let this happen?'

'Don't let the negativity of this place get to you,' I advised. 'You've been doing so well.'

He was becoming angry now, wanting to make someone pay. 'But —'

'Just know that the time when this behaviour will no longer be tolerated is fast approaching,' I said confidently. 'I am the herald of their salvation.'

'How, Kali?' he appealed. 'How can you fight such pure evil?'

I smiled, sympathetic to his grief and doubt. 'With pure love, of course. And now you must summon all the love inside you and wear it as a shield, for pure unconditional love for all beings, good and evil, is your only chance of salvation in Irkalla. Don't lose faith.'

He obviously saw the truth in what I was saying, for he shook off his negativity and found a smile. 'I have faith in you, Kali.'

I placed a hand on his shoulder, proud of him. 'And I have faith in you, Emmett Rich.'

'I'm touched,' added a third voice. It was Erragal, Lord of the Underworld.

I looked up to see that the passage of lost souls was morphing into the great courtroom of Irkalla. Its perimeters could not be seen as the walls and ceiling were consumed by darkness. Emmett and I were standing on a raised platform above an abyss that dropped into nothingness. The space around us was alive with demon activity; we couldn't see the Underworld inhabitants but could sense their ominous mass circling. Across the void, on a much larger raised platform, were the thrones of Irkalla, upon which sat Erragal and Ereshkigal, today wearing their youthful human personas of Jeb Savage and Co-co Yamamoto.

These forms had been rendered useless by my recent deeds in the physical world, but the staff of Amenti were in the process of altering time, which meant history would change and these human forms would once again be of value to the Nefilim. If they had realised this, then they must know what my fellow staff members were up to. How they knew was another question.

Suspended above the two thrones, secured to a metal cross by metal wrist and ankle bands, was Killian Labontè.

'They want to use you as bait for someone named Castor,' he yelled to me. 'Something to do with Montauk and expanding a wormhole sy—'

Erragal waved his hand and Killian fell silent. I

could see his mouth moving still, but could not hear a word.

'You'll have plenty of time to chew the fat once our business is concluded,' Erragal told me.

Why Castor in particular? I wondered, then realised the answer was simple. *The Rod of Power.* For the rod had the power to create paths through time, provided you knew exactly where you wished to go. But none of the Nefilim would be able to wield the mighty tool of the Elohim; only the Black Madonna had the twelve-strand DNA required to fully control the rod's awesome power. So what could my lost kindred possibly hope to do with the treasure once they had obtained it?

'My business in Irkalla is with Ill,' I said aloud. 'If he has the guts to come forth and stand before me himself.' I would not expose my secret weapon until I had the Nefilim ruler within my sights.

'My Lord Ill could do as you ask,' Erragal proffered, 'but as your friend here,' he motioned to Killian, 'is his next embodiment, my lord would have to drain the mortal's vital fluids to obtain his life force. Instead, in his great generosity, Ill has decided to give you the chance to negotiate for this man's eternal soul.'

I attempted to show indifference. 'And why should I place this man's soul above all the other souls on Earth?'

Erragal and his consort began to laugh, highly amused by my response. 'She doesn't know,' he managed amid his hysteria.

'You suspect that my prince lies dormant in this human,' I observed. 'Why would you think so?'

'He has the marker.' Erragal waved his hand again, and a mass of demons ripped open Killian's shirt to reveal the pendant identical to the one Emmett wore.

But how could the Nefilim have known about the pendant at the time Killian was kidnapped? My concern grew; that information had come directly from Levi's unconscious to me — was it possible we had a traitor on staff? How were the Nefilim obtaining such inside information?

I turned back to Emmett, experiencing déjà vu from my encounter with the demon of Denial.

Emmett offered up the first explanation that came into his head. 'Killian must have had it copied ... he got me stoned, I crashed out ... he could have done anything.'

Erragal removed the silencing spell in time for us to hear Killian's vehement reply.

'That's bullshit!' he insisted. 'This pendant has been in my family for generations! What do you think initially sparked my curiosity in my bloodline?'

'Your father's one of them!' Emmett said, pointing to the Underworld rulers.

'He wasn't always one of them,' Killian replied, tears spurting from his eyes. 'Please believe me, Tamar, you're being deceived.'

'By him!' Emmett was quick to point the finger back at Killian. 'Up until a few days ago, these two,' he indicated our hosts, 'were his best friends!'

'These creatures aren't my friends!' Killian spat back. 'They devoured my friends!' He hung his head and began to weep.

The true pendant held a small fragment of Mathu's form and thus would radiate with his life essence; once I held both pendants in my hand I would know which one was authentic, no psychic skill required. However, if I attempted to discover the truth now, it would expose my prince to our enemies. Whichever of these young men was not the lucky incubator would be immediately disposed of. Until the Nefilim knew the truth, both Emmett and Killian were safe.

'Well, princess, it seems one of your suitors is lying to you,' Erragal taunted. 'And with no cosmic light in Irkalla to support your psychic powers of deduction, I can't imagine how you plan to figure out which one. However, as I'm feeling benevolent today, I'm going to allow the three of you some time alone to figure out which of these mortals will be Ill's new persona, and which will get served to our Dracon for supper. Fair enough?'

'Don't you dare leave!' I demanded, so tempted to use a show of force to support my will.

'You're not really in a position to negotiate, Your Worshipfulness!' Erragal laughed as his demons, bearing huge Orme blocks, closed in from every side.

Don't allow them to force your hand, I cautioned myself, as Killian was released from his cross and thrown in the impenetrable golden room with us. A huge Orme block crashed down above us to enclose us completely.

'You lying sack of shit!' Emmett took a flying jump at Killian and the fists started flying.

These two had been dying to rip into each other for so long that I thought it best to let them expend some of their frustration before I attempted to get any sense out of them.

When they had exhausted themselves and were taking a breather to nurse their wounds, I asked for their pendants, which they both willingly handed over.

'Why are you naked?' Killian asked at last. 'Not that I'm complaining.' Despite his banter, he attempted to keep his eyes from straying below my shoulders, as did Emmett.

'In the attempt to save your worthless arse, the demons that guard the seven gates of Irkalla stripped her of more than just her clothes,' Emmett informed his rival.

'So I see.' Killian brushed a hand over my bald scalp, sorry for my loss. 'You did this for me, Tamar?'

'Ha,' Emmett laughed, 'you wish!'

'I have other business in Irkalla,' I advised, before turning my attention to the pendants. As I focused on the separate pieces I was enthralled to feel Mathu's essence so close; the only trouble was, I was detecting an equal amount within each of the pendants. 'That's odd,' I said.

'What is?' Killian and Emmett demanded at the same time.

I flipped the pendants over and, sure enough, there was a very faint join through the centre of each. 'The pendant has been split in two and then fused with half of a replica,' I deduced.

Both my suitors yelled in outrage then laid into each other anew.

'Stop!' I shouted. Their fighting was beginning to annoy me. 'This separation could have occurred any time within the last two hundred years! So until solid evidence proves otherwise, could we please run with the premise that you're both telling the truth?'

They looked completely stunned by my reasoning, but were still hesitant to submit to my suggestion.

'If we're all to make it out of Irkalla alive, then we're going to have to work together,' I said.

'Who's this prince Erragal was talking about?' Killian asked, to avoid having to agree to trust Emmett.

'How about you tell me why the Nefilim are seeking Castor?' I responded, feeling that was more important right now.

'I don't know that much about the Montauk Project, so I didn't understand a lot of what I heard,' Killian explained.

'I'm fairly well read on the subject,' Emmett offered, urging Killian to spit out what he knew.

'Well, they said the Montauk wormholes could be extended further back in time by using a time rift created in 1923 as a bridge between the wormholes of the past and those more recently created.'

Killian shrugged, perplexed, but Emmett and I both nodded, greatly interested.

'What happened in 1923?' I probed.

'Some Nazis apparently tried to create a time hole back to the time of King Arthur. They were seeking the Grail for Hitler —'

'Project Phisummum,' Emmett broke in. 'It's said they harnessed all natural and supernatural forces, from modern technology to medieval black magic, from the teachings of Pythagoras to the pentagram incantation, to create a wormhole back to the time of King Arthur's final battle.'

This confirmed my belief that the Nefilim were seeking the Rod of Power, for it had made its final appearance in the physical world at the battle of Badon Hill.

I was deep in thought when Killian spoke up again. 'Now can I know who this prince is?'

'He is my soul mate in the next dimension above Earth's evolution,' I explained. 'We consented to

247

come to Earth together with the sole purpose of redeeming our lost kindred. However, as with all the lost souls banished to this lowest dimension after the catastrophe on Tara, only by evolving through many lifetimes did we remember our soul quest and our connection to each other. As punishment for the sins of our fallen brethren, Mathu and I were only permitted to incarnate together twice. Once, when we first incarnated into the dying line of the Anunnaki here on Earth, and the second time in this, our final lifetime as human beings. The only problem is ... I'm yet to find him in this lifetime.'

Killian appeared enchanted by the tale and smiled winningly to realise he was suspected of being my prince.

I glanced at Emmett and was surprised to find him in tears. 'No, that's not right,' he said.

'What's not right?' I asked, but he was engrossed in his own contemplation.

'That note,' he muttered, 'I've heard you sing it before.'

'You think *you*'re her prince?' Killian scoffed.

Emmett's gaze suddenly became focused on me and I saw the truth in his eyes. 'In a cathedral filled with great works of art —' he began.

'Oh, come on!' Killian rolled his eyes but I hushed him.

'The Hall of Time Codes,' I said, completely transfixed by Emmett's words.

'— you sang that note,' he went on, tears flowing down his cheeks, 'and the sonic drove me to my knees.'

I gasped as I too recalled the event he described, for indeed he spoke a truth that even I had forgotten. Mathu's spirit had been present the day

248

we took down Pintar, leader of the Dracon, for Pintar was the embodiment of Mathu's alter ego — all that was evil about him from his time as one of the Nefilim. Mathu had used an incantation of the dark arts to separate this evil alter ego from himself and had transferred it into one of the Dracon. He planned to kill the Dracon once the purge was complete, thus destroying his dark side forever. But after the purge, Mathu had no bad will left in him at all and let the Dracon go, and the evil thought form, Pintar, became Mathu's nemesis throughout the ages. Until, in the Hall of Time Codes, as I sang my enlightening song, Mathu's spirit bonded itself to Pintar and, in claiming his dark half and forgiving himself, Mathu finally defeated his adversary.

Emmett was shaking violently, overwhelmed by the sudden waves of awareness. 'What is happening?' he stammered as I gripped his shoulders.

'Sorry,' I apologised in advance, 'but I have to do this.'

As our lips met, my heart exploded in my chest. I felt a stream of light energy burst forth from my heart centre into Emmett's heaving chest, and vice versa. His kiss lost all its reserve and became as hungry as my own. I felt his young body transforming in my arms. The teenager matured into a being equal in stature and maturity to myself.

'Hey, guys, there's something going on,' Killian called out.

My eyes were closed but in my mind's eye there was light everywhere. Being in Mathu's arms felt like coming home after a long and perilous solo voyage, and I wasn't prepared to cut short this sensation for anything!

'I'm serious, folks!' Killian's tone was more desperate this time. 'I think we're being gassed!'

I opened my eyes and saw my beloved standing before me. His eyes were deepest violet, and his hair was like snow cascading over his shoulders. I wanted to greet him, but a stinging chemical aroma invaded my nostrils and throat. My eyelids closed again, as heavy as lead, and my body collapsed beneath me.

My last awareness was of Mathu whispering 'My queen' as he fell to the ground alongside me, and fate stole us from each other once again.

CHAPTER 20

MONTAUK — LONG ISLAND

MIA DEVERE — MERIDAN

I was very grateful to be a master of etheric matter as I headed into such hostile territory; I was invisible before I even entered the facility located deep underground beneath the Montauk Air Force Base, Long Island.

When the vacuum of the porthole died away, I was left standing on a platform inside a massive, almost completely spherical metal chamber. Before me was a pod suspended over the void at the centre of the chamber via a long walkway. It held one seat and was entirely enclosed. Its shield window was facing me and so I could see it contained one occupant, but, due to the ambient lighting inside the pod and the outer chamber, I could not define his or her features. There were large metal umbrellas attached to the top of the pod and its underneath — most likely a transmitter and receiver, I deduced — along with many coils and other conductors coating its exterior.

The Montauk Chair?

I looked around the chamber. There was another control deck set higher up in the structure, where several military men and a few Dracon were obviously overseeing the proceedings in the pit below. Behind the control panel I could see two small alien beings, known as Greys.

The platform I was standing on overlooked the deep dark void where the floor should have been; an antenna dropped from it an indeterminate length into the darkness. An enclosed observation deck circled the rim of the entire room, its transparent tubelike structure ensuring an unhindered view of all areas of the chamber. Behind me was a huge white cement screen, the wormhole now fading on it like the ending to a film.

I was horrified to see that Levi had followed me through the porthole. He stood with Killian Labontè on the landing platform, looking bemused not to find me there too.

A trapdoor opened in the platform between Levi and myself, and one of the Nefilim, accompanied by several armed Dracon, rose up through it.

Levi bowed his head to the new arrivals. 'My Lord Erragal, Timewalker 456143 returning to report on Project Horse.'

'What the hell?' The towering Nefilim looked baffled and turned to those at the control deck above. 'Why do I have an operative returning from a mission in AD6037, when all I ordered was a wormhole to the other side of the planet?'

Everyone looked confused.

Erragal turned to Killian, who was standing as far from the aliens as possible. 'Is he one of the Amenti staff?' he demanded.

'I don't know.' Killian was puzzled. 'This isn't the

man I persuaded to follow me.'

'So where *is* the Amenti staff member you were instructed to bring back?' The demi-god was beginning to lose patience.

'How should I know?' Killian spat back. 'He was right behind me, then ...' He shrugged. 'Look, I did what you said. Now I want to see Tamar.'

My heart skipped a beat. How on Earth had the Nefilim got their hands on my daughter? And how had Killian Labontè ended up back in the year 2003? Was *I* still in 2003? They were all good questions and only Killian had the answers.

'How many life forms came back through the porthole?' the Nefilim lord asked the control tower above.

'Three,' came the response through the speaker system, and the Dracon snapped to attention, realising there was one unaccounted for.

'Fucking shamans!' Erragal hissed. 'Castor can change form.' The lord's dark eyes scanned the huge void before him for any sign of movement. 'If there is so much as a flea within this chamber I want it caught!'

Dracon and military personnel alike jumped into action all around the observation deck.

'And you, Timewalker 456143, are coming with me,' Erragal said, sounding disbelieving of Levi's claim. He gripped Levi around the neck and pulled him onto the moveable platform, followed by two Dracon hauling Killian. As the lift appeared to be the only way on or off the launch platform, I was quick to hitch a ride too.

I was surprised to find it no effort to hold my breath all the way through the descent — just one of the many perks of being an Amenti staff member that I was discovering on a daily basis. The lift continued past the observation deck and down several floors to the correctional facility — I really didn't like the sound of that.

'Humans ... you literally make me feel sick!' Erragal complained to his captives.

The doors opened behind me, startling me, and I leapt backwards into the corridor to avoid being steamrollered by the other occupants. Thankfully, there was no one waiting for the lift or I would have surely bowled them over.

'Take him back to the holding cell,' Erragal instructed the Dracon holding Killian. They went one way, and Levi was dragged by Erragal and the remaining Dracon guard in the opposite direction.

Levi knows what he's dealing with, I thought quickly. *I need to get some answers from Killian Labontè first.*

The young rebel was tossed into a corner of the cell. He didn't get up and retaliate as I'd expected; it seemed his will to fight had abandoned him. His dark fringe fell over his bruised face, and his long lean body looked rather beaten too. I could see why young women the world over were going nuts over this guy; even 'victimised' looked good on him.

'Where's Tamar?' I asked. I expected to hear Castor's voice coming out of my mouth, but it was my own. I reached around to check on the auric simulator and found it was missing.

'Mia?' Killian moved to rise.

'Stay as you are, in case you're being watched,' I said.

He returned to his slouched pose. 'They could be monitoring sound too,' he pointed out.

'This is a large correctional facility, they'd go insane trying to monitor audio in every cell.'

Nevertheless, I crouched low to speak with him softly. He reached out and made contact briefly.

'You're fucking invisible!' He was flabbergasted. 'You're one of them, aren't you? Those Amenti angels that have got the freak show around here so shit scared.'

'An eloquent assessment,' I said. 'Still, let's talk about you. How you ended up in 2003, for example?'

'I'm in the past?' Killian suppressed his shock. 'When I saw the set-up they have here, the control deck and all these fucking *aliens*, I thought I was surely in the future!'

'Bugger,' I muttered, realising he wasn't going to be much help. 'How did the Nefilim get hold of Tamar?'

'She marched naked into Irkalla and confronted Erragal and his bitch directly, demanding to see Ill.' Killian's eyes filled with admiration. 'Even though it seems I'm not her prince, I'm really grateful for what she did for me.'

'Tamar found her prince?' I was breathless with anticipation for more information. 'Emmett Rich,' I realised, before Killian could say it. He nodded and I grinned. So Albray and Sinclair had been right about that after all. 'Where are Tamar and Emmett now?' I asked.

'I don't know. I don't know where *I* am! If it's 2003 ... damn, there's an eight-year-old version of me here somewhere.'

Then a thought hit him like a meteor falling from on high. I saw it land in his consciousness and ignite his being into action. 'I could warn my parents about the Nefilim and they could —'

'Oh no.' I was quick to squash any such thought. 'The repercussions of changing history —'

'— would be great for my family!' he interrupted.

'No, Killian, nothing would change. Don't you see? Your parents, love them as you do, were driven by power and money. And unless that were to change, the same fate awaits them no matter how you try to get around it.'

Killian gave a defeated sigh.

'That was their way,' I said on a more encouraging note. 'But it doesn't have to be yours.'

'What can I do?' he said despairingly. 'I rebel ... that's all I do.'

'Rather than rebel against an enemy, I find it better to outwit my foe.'

'How am I expected to do that?' He waited for a response that never came. 'Mia? Mia! Don't leave me here! They're going to feed me to the Dracon!'

'I'll be back,' I assured him, then melted through the metal wall and into the corridor.

I heard Killian run to the door and slam up hard against it. 'She just moved through a solid wall,' he mumbled,' and gave a half-laugh. 'Fucking unreal!'

I retraced my steps to the lift where I'd last seen Levi, and continued down the long corridor that stretched in the opposite direction from Killian's cell. It was deathly silent, but not a peaceful hush; it felt more like the repressed quiet of an awful secret.

Some way ahead a door opened and the sound of hundreds of children screaming shattered the stillness. A Dracon stepped out into the corridor, the door closed behind him and the eerie silence returned.

As soon as the guard had passed me, I hastened to investigate the source of the disturbing cries. Through the observation window in the door, I saw rows of medical cots with young boys strapped to them. Electrodes were attached to their eyes and genitals and they were being subjected to some form of shock treatment. I had to look away as my empathy sensor went into overdrive and I felt a rush of pain. *I have to stop this.*

A Dracon guard emerged from a door opposite and interrupted my potential heroics. 'You can't do what you plan to,' he advised, looking directly at me.

I was startled into looking down at myself, but I was still invisible. How could he know I was there? *Was it Levi?* I couldn't voice my suspicion or I'd give myself away.

The Dracon came closer. 'We're not here to change the past,' he reminded me and I knew my guess was correct — Levi had changed to Dracon form.

'You grabbed the auric simulator from the back of my trousers on the way through the wormhole,' I said. 'But how did you locate me here?'

'It was easy for me to sense your positive presence in this horrid place.' Levi's gaze shifted to the boys being tortured in the room I'd been peering into. 'You could not desire to shut down this project more than I —' he began, then gasped and moved closer to the glass. 'I have to check something,' he said and entered the lab.

Curious, I followed.

The current had been switched off and most of the poor boys had passed out; those that hadn't were only semi-conscious and moaned quietly with the little energy they had left.

Levi came to a stop by the bed of a young dark-haired boy who stood apart from the others, who were all Aryan types — blond and blue-eyed. He opened the file hanging from the end of the cot. 'Damn ... I thought I recognised this one.'

Upon second glance, I was stunned to recognise a pre-teen Killian Labontè. *There's an eight-year-old version of me here somewhere*, he'd commented earlier, but it hadn't occurred to me that he'd meant 'here' in the building! 'Killian is one of the Montauk boys,' I uttered under my breath, as I struggled to comprehend the ramifications of the discovery.

'It explains a lot,' Levi agreed. He plucked a hair from the unconscious boy's head and tucked it into his Dracon disguise.

'That's how the Nefilim have been aware of our every move,' I realised as I cast my mind back over the events of the past few weeks.

'If Killian is one of the Secret Crew, all he'd need is a strand of your hair, or Tamar's, and he'd be privy to *everything*,' Levi said.

'Even this?'

'Even this.' Levi's tone was unsurprised as he nodded towards the glass plate in the door. I followed his gaze to see a flock of reptilian guards in the corridor.

They did not enter, however; they stood back for Lord Erragal, who was accompanied by Killian Labontè. Strangely, Killian behaved as if he were in charge. He stormed into the lab ahead of his Nefilim company, hand out, demanding, 'I'll take the auric simulator and that strand of hair you just plucked from my head, Timewalker 456143, aka Levi Granville-Devere, aka Signet Key Eight, *Dreamkeeper*.'

Levi complied, knowing it was futile to resist. As he handed back the auric simulator he returned to his true form — which I much preferred, especially as humans were grossly outnumbered by aliens in this instance.

'Show yourself, Mia,' Killian ordered, 'or I'll have your daughter and her long-lost lover dipped in a vat of liquid Orme.'

'So you sold your soul too,' I accused as I appeared right in front of Killian's face.

'My soul was shattered long ago, before I had a choice in the matter.' He motioned to the unconscious boy on the bed.

'So stop it happening!' I implored him.

'I don't want to stop it happening!' he yelled back defiantly. 'I am the most powerful human being on the planet! And pretty soon I'll become one with the most powerful god in history!'

'Ill isn't a god,' I said. 'He's a misguided, damned entity who wants to take every living thing on Earth along with him to his ultimate demise.'

The room fell silent and every one of our enemies glared at me.

'I'm afraid you're the one who's misguided, Dr Devere,' Killian, livid, stared me down, 'aka Signet Key Twelve, Triogenes, aka the Blue Flame Bearer, aka the Black Madonna.'

'Bingo!' Erragal finally spoke. 'Even better than Castor to retrieve the Rod of Power for us.'

I was amused by the suggestion. 'I would never —'

'Never say never,' Killian warned, 'not when we have your daughter.'

'Prove it,' I said, calling their bluff. I had only Killian's word on the matter, and that was obviously worth very little.

'Follow me,' he said, striding off.

I looked at Levi, who raised his brows and moved to accompany me.

'Not you, techno boy,' Erragal said, grabbing him. 'I have other plans for you.'

'He stays with me,' I insisted. 'Or I turn this entire operation into a demolition site right now. Your choice.'

'What about Tamar?' Killian turned back to threaten me.

'What about your wormhole system?'

A tense moment passed, then Killian smiled. 'You're not afraid of me at all, are you?'

'Not in the least.' I surprised myself, for it was the truth, and with Killian's telepathic link to me he knew it.

He glared at me. 'Do you know what I could do to you?'

'More importantly, you know what I could do to you,' I replied flippantly, 'and that's why you're trying to intimidate me, which clearly isn't working.'

I walked out of the room, past the Dracon, and Levi followed. When Killian, Erragal and their guards attempted to move, they discovered that the soles of their shoes had mysteriously melded with the floor.

'Mia! I'm warning you, don't fuck with me!' Killian yelled after us.

'Should I let them go?' I asked Levi, who was smothering his amusement as we proceeded down the corridor unaccompanied.

'We really should find out what they know about Tamar,' he replied.

Just as our captors had removed their footwear, they came unstuck from the floor.

'I thought this was supposed to be a hostage situation,' I taunted them.

Two barefoot Dracon finally raced into the corridor and took aim at us.

'Now that's more like it,' I said and Levi nodded in agreement.

Killian may have been smiling as he emerged from the room, but his body language conveyed that he was ropeable.

'Don't push me, bitch!' He grabbed hold of me and stared into my eyes. I felt a sharp pain in my sinuses and then my nose began to pour with blood. Levi couldn't help me, restrained as he was by the Dracon guards.

'How fast do you think you can regenerate an imploded heart?' Killian asked nastily, and let me go.

'It's all just matter.' I was more emotionally rattled than physically harmed, but wouldn't show it. I undid the damage to my sinuses and the blood vanished from my face. 'There is nothing you can do that I can't undo, not now or ever,' I told him.

Killian looked taken aback, and I took advantage of his brief confusion to examine him with my auric vision. I had to find the piece of me that he was using to spy on us all; it had to be on his person somewhere. The Blue Flame energy being emitted from the strand of my hair caused it to light up like a neon sign against his aura. It was wound tightly beneath the wristband of his watch. Upon my bidding, the hair dissolved to nothing, with Killian none the wiser.

'Tell that to your daughter,' Erragal said, using his great height as an intimidation tactic. 'She'll have the sixty plagues of Nergal brought down upon her if you don't start cooperating.'

He pointed to a doorway further down the hall, and I headed over to see what proof they could show me of Tamar's imprisonment.

Inside the room I found a long table of black onyx. Lying on its top was an etheric fibre suit like those worn by the Amenti staff members. Beside it was a long thick coil of silky black hair which, viewed psychically, glowed richly violet. There was no doubt it was my daughter's beautiful hair, every strand of which could expose her every move to our enemy! There was also a liquid-light gun, a small treasure chest, a metallic ball and an electronic hand-held games unit. I reached for the latter item knowing it did not belong to Tamar, and found the name Emmett Rich programmed into the display; *still*, I thought, *anyone could have entered that name into the unit.* Next I opened the treasure chest, to find it empty.

'There's nothing in here,' I said.

'Oh yes, there is,' taunted Killian. 'Let your fingers do the seeing.'

My heart skipped when I felt the invisible ring; as far as I knew, there was none other like it.

'I'll take that now, thank you.' Killian snatched it from my fingers. 'Aren't you going to ask about the metallic ball?'

My gut told me that I didn't want to know.

'Touch it,' he prompted. 'Go on.'

As my fingers made contact with the cold metal, the sound of Tamar's inspirational singing voice filled my heart with joy and then sadness.

'What is it?' Levi asked curiously, for only the person touching the ball could hear the voice; a precaution that prevented these damned creatures being driven insane by the purity of her song.

'It's a recording of Tamar —' I began.

'No, no,' Killian corrected, 'it's not a recording of Tamar's singing voice, it *is* Tamar's singing voice. She gave it up to pay a toll to enter Irkalla, where she is now, sedated, naked and quite subdued.' He smiled, convinced that he now had the upper hand.

Contrary to his expectation, I didn't attack him. Instead, I felt deeply sorry for him and the emotion showed on my face.

'What?' he asked, wanting an explanation for my sad look.

'How much pain must you have endured to be able to knowingly betray your greatest ally in such a manner,' I sympathised.

He revelled in what he'd done. 'Beautiful, isn't it?'

'Does she know the truth about you?' I asked, and the query took a little of the wind from his sails.

'I suspect she will soon,' he responded, 'now that you know. You Dragon Queens have your own communication network, don't you?'

He obviously knew of our telepathic connection. He also knew that my link with Tamar was strained at present, and indeed her detainment in Irkalla explained the interference during her last attempt to contact me.

'So the next time you ladies chat,' Killian continued, 'you can tell Kali that Ill and I greatly look forward to wedding our most powerful rival. And in return for her complete cooperation, we won't summon her love's alter ego from the darkest depths of hell for another rematch of wills.'

I had expected a death threat, but Ill knew of Mathu's existence, and where he was, which was far worse. I refused to be intimidated by them, however, and continued to pity their naivety.

'You and Ill are insane if you think you'll be able to control my daughter,' I said.

'Kali *is* under our control!' He pointed to the table. 'How much more proof do you need?'

Erragal came forward, his dark presence towering over us. 'And that means you're going to retrieve the Rod of Power for us.'

'Only I am genetically capable of wielding the rod,' I pointed out, hoping to discover what they planned to do with the item.

'*Until* ...' Killian raised a finger to stress his point, '... you reunite the rod with the Ring of Power to form the key to Amenti. Which you will then hand to Kali, my intended, and she and I will have the honour of opening the doors of Amenti.'

I was perplexed. 'The doors will not open for you.'

'Nor for *any* thereafter,' he concluded with a smile. 'Not for another twenty-five thousand years anyway. Plenty of time for us to utilise your stargate system to conquer every guardian race connected to this pathetic little backwater planet!'

This was no longer Killian speaking; for a moment he was possessed by a darker, much more sinister presence. Psychically, Killian did not seem to have any malign entities attached to him, but perhaps his own psychic skills allowed him to connect with the dark presence he was allied with.

'And to ensure you don't supply us with another fake,' Erragal said, still annoyed by the memory of our last meeting, 'Killian will accompany you back to the battle of Badon Hill, where he can see you retrieve the Rod of Power from the hand of Arthur himself!'

'What?' I could hardly believe my ears. 'That

plan is beyond foolish, it's pure insanity! The battle of Badon Hill was a significant event in history —'

'Which no one can really pinpoint in terms of location or date,' Killian cut in. 'Hell, historians can't even prove Arthur existed! Ever wonder why that is?'

I opened my mouth to reply but Killian was on a roll.

'Because the battle of Badon Hill is such a significant event in the inter-time war that its outcome is ever-changing.'

'There is no wormhole back to the battle of Badon Hill,' Levi said, being fairly knowledgeable on the matter.

'Not a direct one,' Killian granted. 'But a brief changeover with the Illuminati sects of pre-Nazi Germany will see us all the way back to our destination.'

Tamar had warned me about all of this and I'd still ended up becoming embroiled in it.

'If you're talking about Project Phisummum, that wormhole was highly unstable due to the dark powers that were summoned to create it,' said Levi. 'It will never be able to withstand the traffic of a permanent wormhole interchange; you'll be lucky if it stays open long enough for you to get back through it — that is, if the Illuminati don't kill you for crashing their inter-time party in the first place.'

'Once the Black Madonna holds the Rod of Power, she will be able to cut a path to anywhere in history.' Killian was more certain of this fact than I was.

'And should you deviate from our orders,' Erragal warned me, 'we'll know of it, and I'll see to it that your daughter is raped by every demon in Irkalla, before Nergal's sixty diseases go to work on her.'

He certainly painted a vivid picture and I felt sure he meant every word he said.

'Your technological friend will stay here with us, as insurance,' the Nefilim added, but I didn't find the terms acceptable.

All Amenti staff were psychically gifted to a certain degree, but I didn't know enough about Levi and his skills to be confident he could defend himself alone against the dark forces assembled here at Montauk. True, he had done it before undercover, but now he was exposed as a threat, and I had a good idea of how the Nefilim would deal with such a potential menace. I began to protest but Levi quashed my objection.

'Forget about me,' he said, 'your primary concern must be Tamar.'

The way he spoke, with such insistence, led me to believe he was inferring more than he could say.

'Understand?' he insisted.

Only semi-sure that I knew what he was asking of me, I nodded.

'I want him where I can see him,' I insisted, 'before I leave and when I arrive back.'

'If you arrive back,' Levi chided Killian, doing nothing to boost my confidence. But then I realised what he was saying: he didn't want me to return to Montauk, not even for him.

Forget about me; your primary concern must be Tamar.

Once I had the Rod of Power in my hands, Levi was suggesting I head straight back to 2017 to Tamar's aid. But what about our other stranded Amenti team members — they were sitting ducks here in 2003 with the *Klieo* out of commission.

'Take him to the general observation deck,' Erragal instructed his guards, and Levi was removed from the room.

'You won't succeed,' I told Killian and Erragal, but they just smiled.

'We knew you'd say that.' The Nefilim motioned to Killian, who pulled a copy of the third book in my trilogy from a backpack sitting on the same table where Tamar's tolls lay. He slung the pack over his shoulder.

'I've already read the book, you see,' he told me.

'Then you know my prediction is correct.' After all, if I wasn't victorious, then I'd never get to write the book in the first place.

Erragal gave a hearty laugh. 'You're in for a few nasty surprises.'

I wanted to grab the book from Killian and read it myself. 'You're bluffing,' I said.

'Am I?' He shoved me towards the door. 'We'll see about that, won't we?'

I was escorted, under guard, back to the Montauk Chair chamber. One floor below the timewalkers platform, Erragal and his Dracon guards exited the elevator, and Killian and I were left alone to wait for our cue.

'Once Ill takes you over, nothing will remain of you at all,' I said, wanting to see what reaction I'd get.

'I hold all the true power,' Killian assured me. 'Ill has no power over me that I do not allow.'

'That might be the case now, but —'

'You think they control me?' he snarled, obviously threatened by my lack of belief in him.

'Of course they control you,' I said frankly, 'or else you'd be on the side of humanity and not in cahoots with the fallen!'

He scoffed. 'Where was humanity when I needed it? You overvalue our species. For the most part, they're all fucked!'

'So you go and join forces with the beings who corrupted our evolution in the first place?' I tried to fathom his reasoning.

'I am on *my* side!' Killian emphasised, as the lift began its ascent towards the timewalkers platform. 'Whatever works!'

The calm smile on his face was so odd, and in such contrast to the situation unfolding, that I suspected his mental programming allowed him to completely detach from his emotions, which made him very difficult to read.

On the platform, the first thing that struck me was the wind sweeping around the circular chamber. The air was alive with electromagnetic energy, which was being drawn from the Earth's natural energy grid via the huge inverted antenna extending into the void beneath the chamber. The Montauk Chair sat suspended in the null field at the centre of the disturbance.

I glanced over to the observation deck and spied Levi, under guard. He waved me goodbye and I returned the gesture.

'Come on, we haven't got all day!' Killian swung me around to face the huge inward-swirling porthole. It extended so far out ahead of us that it was impossible to perceive where it ended. 'To Camelot, my lady,' he said, making light of our situation.

'Via a bloodbath orchestrated by your friends,' I chided. 'What fun.'

'You're Aryan-looking — you've got nothing to worry about.'

Killian pushed me ahead of him, and I was drawn into the vortex of light and energy and transported another huge leap away from my home time in 2017. As I felt myself swept up in the quantum flux of the time phenomenon, I closed my eyes and focused all my will on contacting my Dragon sisters.

CHAPTER 21

POINTS OF INTERFACE

As I projected my thoughts across time and space to my fellow Dragon Queens, something amazing occurred: my spirit separated from my physical form in transit and soared beyond the phenomenon that held me captive. I had experimented with astral projection in the past, but it usually required great concentration and willpower. It hadn't even occurred to me that I might use this talent to my advantage in this instance.

Beyond the light and turbulence of the wormhole, I was drawn through darkness until I found myself in a grand and ancient chamber. It did not appear to be of the physical world, yet the architecture borrowed from many of the different cultures throughout human history. The room was round, with pale yellow ethereal walls, and a floor and ceiling that glowed like sunshine. Huge pillars of jade green were carved with different dragons representing the varied civilisations across the globe. The dragons were not stationary depictions, however; they clung to their pillars, tails swishing, heads cocked, guarding the chamber below. In the centre of the room was a round table of emerald surrounded by seven tall-backed chairs cushioned with deep green velvet.

Meridan.

I looked around and was relieved to see Denera. *Praise the universe!* I embraced her spirit with my own. *Where are we?*

This is the true Dragon Court, she said. *It is a place of telepathic interface for the Dragon Queens, a conclave that only we may enter.*

As I recovered from my awe, my thoughts turned to why I had sought out my sisters; and in the next instant I was sitting at the table addressing them — bar one, for Kali's seat remained empty.

I advised of what had befallen Levi at Montauk, what I knew of our enemy's plans and the sad news of Tamar's imprisonment in Irkalla after finally finding Mathu.

I am sure Levi does not wish me to return to Montauk with the Rod of Power, so what should I do? I finished.

Killian has Tamar's invisible ring, you said? Solarian queried.

When I nodded, she, Thana and Vespera looked very concerned.

Then they already have the Ring of Power, Thana stated.

No, I objected, *that can't be, it's still safe inside Mount Serabit.*

But when Solarian filled me in on what had happened at Mount Shasta, I realised their claim was completely justified.

Oh my . . . I said as everything around me swirled into a blur and then back into focus. *I feel giddy.*

Meridan, listen, your transmission's breaking up, Denera said urgently.

What about Tamar and Levi? I protested as the dizziness washed over me again.

Leave them to us, Denera said. *Only you can unbeach the* Klieo. *You must use her . . . to . . .*

My perception blurred completely and I was drawn away from the warm glow of the sunny chamber, through the darkness and into the vacuum of the wormhole back to the past.

ASHLEE GRANVILLE-DEVERE — SOLARIAN

After we lost Meridan, my consciousness lingered in the Dragon Court long enough to hear Denera's advice on what she felt to be our best course of action.

As soon as the *Klieo*'s conference room doors opened, Arcturus was upon me, demanding news.

'Denera confirms that your plan is sound,' I said. 'We must use the Inner Earth transit system and the already activated Signet stations to reach and open the remaining stations.'

'And to get to Montauk,' Arcturus added.

'Montauk is no longer your destination,' I replied.

He objected, wanting to go to his wife's rescue.

'Arcturus,' I took hold of his hands to calm him, 'Meridan is no longer there, nor anywhere you can reach her. Your daughter, however, is being held prisoner in Irkalla and is being used to blackmail Meridan into doing the bidding of the fallen.'

Arcturus was floored by the news. Before he could voice the many questions he had, I relayed all Meridan had told us.

'So the Nefilim have the Ring of Power,' Arcturus said, glancing at Polaris who had insisted on giving the ring to Tamar. For once my husband was humbled.

'She wasn't to know what she was giving away,' I defended her.

'Great goddess!' Castor was looking pale too. 'They're going to attempt to take the rod right out of my hand!'

'Meridan won't relinquish the treasure to anyone, but she is relying on us to free Tamar so she won't suffer for her,' I explained.

Arcturus's mind boggled at his task, desperate as he was to take action. 'How the hell do I get into Irkalla?' he said.

Dexter held his hand up. 'I can get you there. It's a fairly dark time on Earth at present, so my Signet station should take us directly in the back door.'

Arcturus was confused. 'But your station leads to Parallel Earth in the future. How will that help Tamar now?'

'Parallel Earth and Irkalla exist outside of time,' Dexter pointed out. 'If Tamar is being held there, then we'll find her.'

'I'm up for an adventure,' Castor piped up.

I forced a grin of apology. 'You have to stay with the *Klieo*.'

'Why?' he demanded, frustrated to be left behind again.

'Because Meridan is currently screwing with the events of your past, which means your reliability will be in question until she returns.'

Castor didn't like it but he couldn't refute the reasoning.

'Tell Meridan to deliver the *Klieo* back to my station, and we'll meet you in Nova Scotia after we've retrieved Levi,' Polaris instructed.

Castor nodded.

'Not to worry, my love.' Talori moved to console her partner. 'There's plenty of action awaiting you in 2017.'

'Keep in touch,' Castor said to his male colleagues, tapping his finger against his temple. They had a telepathic interface, just as we Dragon sisters shared our own communication network.

'Fingers crossed we'll hear from Levi soon,' Polaris said, heading towards the door. 'Every hour counts,' he reminded us. 'The longer we're here the more we're prone to change the future.'

'Beat you back here then,' Arcturus challenged.

'My friend,' Polaris said with a grin, 'in your dreams.'

Mia Devere — MERIDAN

As the draw of the wormhole lessened, its already ominous frequency increased dramatically, warning me that the most nefarious energy I had ever felt lay dead ahead. With every ounce of my being I wished to flee in the opposite direction; not because I feared confronting the source, but because the extremely low vibratory frequency made me feel physically ill and weak.

When my consciousness rejoined my physical body I was standing in the midst of a horror that completely shattered my hope in humanity; for although there were reptilians and Nefilim present, disguised as human beings, most of the willing participants were human. This evil gathering was taking place in a huge underground grotto, its walls hung with the symbols of the Third Reich. There was a deep pit in the centre of the space, piled high with tiny human skeletal remains, rotting corpses and the mutilated bodies of the dead from this day's activities. Around me, an orgy involving the rape and torture of young children was in full swing, along with several blood sacrifices including the murder and consumption of newborn babies. I have no desire to describe this horrendous scene any further; suffice to say that only the most debased human acts have the power to attract and excite demons to such a level that they will cooperate in creating a tunnel through time for their conjurors.

The master of ceremonies overseeing the proceedings had the darkest aura of any human being I had ever seen. He was focused on channelling the empowered demons, which were feeding off the fear being generated by the mass victimisation, into a whirlwind over the pit of death in the centre.

I looked at Killian, who appeared impassive. 'Feel pride in your associations now, do you?' I asked.

'I don't feel,' he replied.

The master of ceremonies remained focused on his evil creation, but all other eyes diverted with awe to Killian and me as we made our dramatic appearance. The porthole we had come through had rocked the chamber on arrival and again on departure.

I held my breath, sure we were the next targets for the bloodthirsty gathering. I longed for an excuse to end this horror for all involved.

Killian noticed my itchy fingers. 'Take action and Tamar dies,' he warned.

I tried to calm myself but the rage built inside me. The demons were penetrating my aura — but if I allowed hatred to become my motivating force, I was little better than the lost souls I wanted to punish.

'The proof of our power,' shouted the master of ceremonies. 'Behold the timewalkers I promised you.'

They are expecting us? I was stunned by this as we had just come from the future. Was this dark human a prophet? Or had this event been planned since the early 1900s?

'Mercy, be gone!' he cried, turning my way and grinning horribly to reveal a mouthful of teeth sharpened to razor-like points. 'Damn those who pity! Drag down their souls to awful torment, laugh at their fear ... spit upon them!'

Upon his instruction, the debauchery resumed with a vengeance.

'Get ready to move,' Killian instructed. 'They'll only manage to open this porthole for a few seconds.'

The dark master raised his hands in the air and the wind tunnel in the centre of the room reached maximum momentum. 'I am the god of war and vengeance! I will give thee a war engine and none shall stand before thee!'

The wind tunnel fell on its end, a huge burst of energy crackled through the room and a passage through time opened.

'Go!' Killian grabbed my arm and charged us forward, taking a flying jump over the pit of death and into the wormhole that was already collapsing in on itself.

My passage through the dark vortex, which had been constructed from human misery, was like being stabbed with ice-cold daggers all over my body. I felt overwhelmed by sadness, shame and guilt; my heart ached with such vengeance that I wished I could rip it from me to stop the agony.

I landed with a thud, and could do little more than lie there as my entire body trembled violently from overexposure to the low-level frequency. I was the Blue Flame bearer and had my own inbuilt source of Blue Flame energy, yet it seemed as if that open channel had been clogged so I couldn't draw upon it. *What must Tamar be experiencing right now?* I wondered, for surely the frequency of Irkalla must be even more violent than what I had just endured. I wept for my baby girl and for the great burdens she had been born to bear.

'Mia?'

For a moment I couldn't focus; I felt so weak, so miserable and guilty, I could only sob.

A warm, gentle hand came to rest on my forehead and a rush of beautiful energy flowed through my third-eye chakra and into my body with such force that it set my eyelids fluttering. The energy felt so familiar to me. I couldn't place where I had encountered it before, but in my soul I knew this frequency belonged to someone I had admired and loved very much. As the wave of healing rolled down through my chakra system, my damaged light centres were cleared of the recent stress and my vitality levels were restored. I ceased feeling sorry for myself and sat upright, to confront Killian's smiling face.

'Are you okay?' he asked, as if he was genuinely concerned.

'What do you care?' I said, and moved away from him, looking around for the being that had just healed me.

'It was me,' Killian said, then turned his attention to the spectacular, pristine coast of the southernmost tip of Britain.

I was stunned. *How could such a healing energy have come from this man? Surely he has been far too damaged in his lifetime.*

I examined him with my third-eye vision and found a well-developed light-body with dark patches over the throat and lower chakras, but surprisingly clear gut, heart and mind centres.

'Look at that!' He sounded as excited as a kid at Christmas as he directed my attention to an island city that stood at the end of a long stretch of beach running out from the headland at Land's End. 'Lyonesse,' he said, and laughed like a madman. 'I made it!' He threw his arms in the air and collapsed to his knees. 'I am in the *fifth fucking century* where *no alien being* knows that I exist!' He flopped back onto the ground and took in a deep breath. 'We are going to screw those *fucking* bastards, Mia ... *so badly*.'

'Hold on,' I said. 'You're on *humanity*'s side now? Killian, I can't keep up with your personality switches —'

'I have always been on humanity's side and I am in complete control,' he assured me.

'Then why didn't you help me do something about that holocaust we just passed through?' I challenged.

'If we stopped that holocaust it would have spoilt our chances of influencing the only event that will prevent all the holocausts!' Killian said wisely.

'And when you tried to bleed my brain out through my nose?'

'Well, I had to do something, you were walking all over us,' he said, using flattery. 'This is what I planned all along. Those Montauk buffoons never had control over me. I've developed my psychic abilities so well that I control them! Now they trust me so implicitly they didn't even send a Dracon escort with us ... *Losers!*' Killian was up on his feet again, too pumped full of adrenaline to sit still.

I found this young man quite baffling; he was so full of aggression and anger, and yet he could obviously transmute that violent energy into a healing force. He was a complete contradiction, and yet that appeared to make him the perfect balance of good and evil, love and hatred, light and shadow.

'How can you be so sure the Nefilim aren't aware of your presence here in ancient Britain?' I queried. 'Those Nazis we just left behind were clearly expecting our intrusion.'

'Oh, we weren't an intrusion, we were the main event,' Killian advised. 'A bit of forward planning never goes astray and the Nefilim have had plenty of time to plot their course to world domination.'

I needed to make it clear that I had my own plans. 'I'm not going back to Montauk.'

'Absolutely not,' Killian agreed. 'We're going to take the Rod of Power back to 2017 to free Tamar so that she can uncreate this whole mess!'

He was sure I would be with him on that count, but I shook my head.

'Delivering the Rod of Power to the Nefilim's capital city is not on the agenda either,' I told him. 'The best thing we could do is leave the rod right where it is, with Castor.'

'We can't leave it, we need it to get home,' Killian pointed out, annoyed by my resistance.

'Not entirely true,' I argued.

'I've spent my entire life trying to find that treasure. There's no way I'm going to leave it behind!'

'You can't wield it!' I warned.

'You didn't think I was capable of healing either.'

He had a point. 'Who are you, Killian?'

'I don't know!' he said defiantly. 'I'm just a dumb fuck unlucky enough to be born into a brainwashed, power-hungry family who didn't give a fuck about him.' He shrugged.

'So how did you do it? How did you manage to stay sane and keep your heart?'

'I learned about the enemy of my enemy,' he replied, looking deep into my eyes. 'The staff of Amenti.'

'Who told you about us?'

'The Sanat Kumara. He told me he was this planet's guardian entity and that if I endured, one day I'd be in a position to assist you.'

I didn't know what to say.

'Is it true that all the souls ever lost to the bloodlust of the Old World Order will be freed from darkest density if the Halls of Amenti open?' he asked.

'It's true,' I confirmed, 'if we succeed in raising the consciousness of humanity high enough. It's not vengeance that will free those souls. Only love of all things great and small, good and evil, will void the reality that is the Kali rift.'

'Love?' Killian said, surprised. 'To the Nefilim, love is a weakness to be exploited —'

'The fallen are disillusioned, and incapable of understanding the power of emotion,' I interjected before he worked himself into a tizz. 'Unconditional love is the greatest strength to be found within the five harmonic universes. It can heal *anything* ... but I believe you already know that.'

The expression on Killian's face was one of relief and awe — perhaps even a little lovestruck. 'Do you know how long I have waited to stand in the presence of someone who is on the same side as me?' he said. 'Someone I don't have to pretend with?'

'Someone like Tamar?'

I felt it best to remind him of his attraction to my daughter, as his dark eyes were observing me far more intently than I liked.

'Tamar is a goddess,' he said, moving towards me, 'but for some reason I feel more of a connection to you.'

'A connection?' I asked, backing up a few paces to maintain some distance between us.

He stopped at my retreat. 'I feel like I've known you before.'

'Well, perhaps you have.' I tried to make light of his now obvious attraction.

'You don't feel it then?' he asked in all seriousness.

'I don't.' I looked deep into his soulful blue eyes for emphasis … where I found myself drowning, mesmerised by the light I saw in them.

'What about now?' He placed a hand to my cheek.

My face melted into his palm; his touch, his aura, was so familiar, so intense, that tears welled in my eyes. Yet my memory still failed to make the connection — I couldn't place where and when we had met before.

'Mia?' He removed his hand when he saw I was upset. 'I —'

He stopped as a rumbling vibrated through the earth beneath our feet; it was slight at first but built rapidly.

'Earthquake?' he guessed.

I shook my head; it wasn't moving fast enough for a tremor. 'An army.'

I looked to the north-west and saw the force starting to spill over the horizon. There was a lone rider some distance in front of the pack — he had nearly reached the cliff face a little further down the coast.

'Castor,' I said, and moved towards the cliff face, intending to meet my old ally on the beach.

Two aircraft, more advanced even than those of my home era, swooped down from the cloudy sky and dived at the lone rider, who abandoned his startled horse and made a run for the cliffs.

'Goddamn it!' Killian yelled, freaked out by the unexpected appearance of the advanced craft. He grabbed me from where I was standing, mystified, out in the open and hurried me to the cover of the cliffs. 'Go, go, go!'

He guided me into a large crevice, where we crouched low to watch what was unfolding.

The aircraft had circled around and were now firing laser bullets at their target, who was scrambling down the cliff. He jumped to the beach, grabbed the long covered object he'd thrown down ahead of him, and started running towards the island.

'The rod,' Killian said. 'He'll never make it on foot.'

I listened to the aircraft as they turned for another pass at their target. In my mind I saw the two craft collide, and instantly they crashed into one another and plummeted to the ground. The impact shook the cliff face and sent rocks tumbling onto the beach below.

'Yes!' Killian cheered. 'I did it!'

'You did it?' I queried his boast.

'And here I was thinking it was me.' A third voice startled Killian and me to our feet.

Our mysterious intruder stood in the shadows, his face cloaked by a hood. When I turned to him he gasped, astonished. 'Forgive my insolence, lady,

I did not realise it was you.' He removed the hood and I beheld Castor, scruffy, long-haired, bloodied and unshaven.

'How can he recognise you if you meet in the future?' Killian asked.

'My lady came from the past. Although her colouring and attire have altered,' Castor said, 'I would know her anywhere. She gave me this.' He raised his cloak to expose the hilt of a golden sword.

'The Rod of Power!' Killian nearly choked on the realisation that his search was at an end. 'Where's the rest of it?' The rod had been shortened to its sword form.

'I could tell you, but then I would have to kill you,' Castor replied. 'As you are a friend to my lady, I am loath to do that.'

Killian had a chuckle. 'He thinks we're friends.'

'We are friends,' I said, startling Killian. 'Unless, of course, you've been lying to me?'

'No,' Killian insisted, intrigued by my sincerity. 'You believe me then?'

'It is our mission to believe in you,' I said, including Castor in my comment, 'and in all humankind.'

'I see.' He sounded a little disappointed by my generalisation, but I didn't want to encourage his attraction to me.

'So the runner is a decoy,' I said to Castor, looking over to the island. The man had made it as far as the vegetation bordering the island city. The enemy army were swarming down the cliffs like a plague of insects and racing across the narrowing strip of beach.

'Once all our enemies are on the island, I will sink it,' Castor said.

'And what of the good citizens of Lyonesse?' I asked, concerned about the repercussions of the order I had given in another life.

'Evacuated, my lady,' he advised. 'They considered their beloved city a small price to pay to get the Saxons and their demon allies off our backs. This show of power will hopefully deter the murderous invaders, at least until the memory fades into legend.'

'Demon allies?' Killian took a closer look at the pursuing army and discovered that many of them were reptilian, and that they were being led by one of the Nefilim, disguised as a man. 'Erragal.' He said the name with loathing.

'Aye,' Castor said, 'he took on the guise of my son, Mordred, and made chaos from the harmony I spent a lifetime creating.'

'Well, what are you waiting for?' Killian cried. 'You could destroy Erragal right now! You have the rod, there's the target; shoot!'

Castor and I both shook our heads.

'I have already explained to you that the object of the game is to love thine enemy, not to destroy him,' I said.

Killian was both encouraged and perplexed by my reasoning. 'His worship here is about to kill an entire army when he sinks that island!' he said. 'What's the difference?'

'The difference is that all the humans who perish will reincarnate,' I explained.

'And will become more constructive human beings, if they learn their lesson from this day,' Castor added.

'The Nefilim lord and the Dracon won't perish, they'll just be shaken up a little,' I concluded.

Killian sighed. 'To what end? So they can return nastier and in greater numbers than before? I happen to believe that the destruction of their kind is a constructive move.'

'He seems a little unsure of which side he serves, my lady,' Castor commented, and I had to laugh at how quickly he'd summed up Killian.

'Understatement of the century,' I replied.

Killian objected to being assessed. 'Hey, I know I'm confused, but what do you expect after my upbringing? Why do you think I'm so desperate to find somewhere to sort my head out, somewhere the Nefilim won't be waiting to screw me over! This isn't going to be quite the holiday I expected,' he went on, 'but they don't know I'm here, so my plan is still sound … I think.'

'Your plan?' I queried. 'I've already told you that I'm not —'

'What month is this?' Killian asked Castor, ignoring me.

'It is the month of Coll. Why do you ask?'

He turned to me. 'What month is that?'

I ran through the old Celtic calendar in my mind, matching it to the modern calendar. 'August.'

Killian looked pleased. 'Just as I suspected. You see, all of the Nefilim's time tunnels run through August in twenty-year cycles. So if you cut a hole back through time today to 2003, you'll succeed in creating a new superhighway in the Nefilim's wormhole system, straight back to here with portholes every twenty years in between.'

'That is a lot of history to play with,' I emphasised. 'So what are you saying — that we're stuck here?' I finished.

'Only temporarily. In ten years and six months, we can cut a wormhole back to the future at the opposing end of the cycles of time, and then there'll be no chance of the wormholes being joined.'

'Ten and a half years!' What was I going to do in the fifth century for all that time? Still, I couldn't see any other way to avoid aiding the enemy to do exactly what they'd sent me here to do.

'If we depart from here in February in fourteen years' time,' Killian said, expanding on his theory, 'we'll arrive in 2017 a couple of months early to save Tamar —'

'Our target year must be 2003,' I insisted, throwing a spanner in the works.

'I just got through explaining that you can't go back along the time line that leads through that year. If we wait here eighteen years, we could get to 2001, but even then you're cutting close to the twenty-year cycle of the Nefilim's wormholes.'

'If that's what it takes to meet up with my teammates where I left them and prevent this entire Montauk debacle from interfering with our original mission, then that's what I'll do,' I said firmly. 'In the meantime, you can give me the lowdown on what you've learned of the Nefilim operations here on Earth — starting with how you channel Ill.' I was still most curious about that. 'And how you came in contact with the Sanat Kumara.'

'What?' Castor was astounded. 'How could you possibly be able to channel both the purest and the most evil entities in this entire evolutionary scheme?'

'Not at the same time, I can't,' Killian clarified. 'The hemispheres of my brain have been completely split in two and function independently, but I can switch sides at will.'

'Incredible!' Castor said.

'What can I say?' Killian shrugged. 'Those Montauk fucks really screwed with my head.'

Castor was baffled by the response. 'Well, not to worry, I know someone who may be able to shed some light on the matter. And after today's events, I'm going to have to seek his assistance to disappear myself.'

This raised a question that Killian had wanted answered for a long time. 'Where on Earth does one go to disappear from the Nefilim and their lizard drones?'

'Why, the Otherworld, of course,' Castor replied with a grin.

After an initial moment of shock, Killian looked my way. 'Is he serious?'

'Probably,' I said. 'After all, he is the legendary King Arthur who had quite a few Otherworldly contacts.'

Killian turned back to Castor. 'Do you know Lugh Lamhfada?'

'Why should Lamhfada interest you?' I asked before Castor could reply.

'Because he is so greatly feared by the Nefilim.' Killian seemed to regard him as something of a superhero. 'Do you think he would speak with me?'

Castor eyed the young intruder. 'With your unique talents and connections, I'm very sure Lamhfada will want to make your acquaintance.'

CHAPTER 22

THE RECRUIT

ASHLEE GRANVILLE-DEVERE — SOLARIAN

As we were exiting the conference room, Castor experienced a strange giddy episode, which delayed our departure.

'Meridan made it back to the fifth century,' he mumbled.

'Did he say Meridan?' Arcturus edged his way closer to the patient.

'I remember now,' Castor said, chuckling at the memory he was having for the first time, amazed by the process of simultaneous time. 'I left her and her companion in the care of Lugh Lamhfada, before I entered the Halls of Amenti.'

'Her companion?' Arcturus queried and Castor nodded.

'He was really quite amazing,' he said. 'Lamhfada took a great interest in him. If the lad could really do what he claimed, then his genetic profile would be very telling.'

'What did he claim?' Talori queried, having an interest in genetics.

'Never mind that,' Arcturus cut in. 'Who was he? Where are they now?'

Castor thought on this and then burst into laughter. 'Meridan is right out front.'

We all gasped, and Arcturus rushed ahead of us through the *Klieo* to confirm the claim. I'd never seen a man so relieved as Arcturus as he embraced his beloved.

'I was so worried,' he told her.

'There was no need,' Meridan replied gently, and sought comfort in the long embrace.

The touching reunion came to an abrupt halt, however, when Arcturus spotted Killian Labontè standing a few steps back in the clearing. 'What's *he* doing here?' he demanded, and then the penny dropped. 'This is the man you've been time-hopping with? You told your Dragon sisters that he was an enemy! He's the one responsible for our daughter's imprisonment!'

'No.' Meridan corrected him calmly, but with a warning note in her voice. 'Ill is responsible for Tamar's imprisonment. Killian has only done what was needed to get himself out of the Montauk Project.'

Arcturus was observing his wife as though she were the enemy now. 'And save himself he has, whilst Tamar rots in Irkalla!'

'Killian is here to help get her out,' Meridan explained, but Arcturus wasn't to be appeased. He addressed Killian directly.

'We don't need any more of your help.'

'You know your way around Irkalla then, do you?' Killian responded.

Arcturus looked to Dexter for backup.

'I said I could *get* us there,' Dexter said. 'I imagined we'd just wing it, as we usually do, but a guide would prove useful, not to mention time-saving.'

This wasn't what Arcturus wanted to hear. 'You're prepared to trust this two-faced turncoat?'

'Meridan obviously trusts him,' I said. 'We should hear her out before deciding, don't you think?'

'Lamhfada saw something in him too,' Castor advised.

'That's good enough for me.' Polaris waved Killian forward.

'I'd be moving your ship fairly promptly,' Killian advised, as the *Klieo* appeared in the clearing behind us.

'We're out of juice,' Polaris said, beckoning Meridan to go with him to the helm.

Meridan cast an apologetic look at Arcturus, then hotfooted it after the captain.

Arcturus turned back to Killian. 'I don't trust you.'

'Well, that's allowed,' Killian smiled. 'Good to know though.'

He turned to the rest of the team. 'So many legends in the one place ... I feel like a kid who's just stepped into a *Marvel* comic! It is truly an honour to meet you all.'

Castor was the first to step up and shake Killian's hand. 'You survived Lugh's tuition then.'

'His guidance, and yours, saved my life and my sanity,' Killian replied warmly and openly. '*Thank you.*'

'I expect you'll return the favour some day,' Castor said, looking upon the lad as he would one of his bravest knights.

I wasn't too sure what to make of this young man myself, but his auric hue was just amazing. It sparkled gold, as the Nefilim's did, but the light centres of his body whirled with a brilliance I'd only observed in Lugh Lamhfada and others of the Fey. If this aura wasn't another cheap Nefilim deception, then clearly this lad was an extraordinary human being, more spiritually adept than us all.

CHAPTER 23

ENOCH —
NEW MEXICO

In the pyramid of Enoch —
Keeper of the Keys —
observe the dwelling places of the righteous,
from which goodness flows like water.

Their mercy is like dew upon the Earth
as they petition and intercede in
the fate of mankind.

They are keys
that fit together
like a puzzle,
forming the totality
of human experience.

MIA DEVERE — MERIDAN

I stood in the splendour of the high court chamber addressing several lofty beings of Lamhfada's ilk. My heart welled with excitement to know that one of the splendid beings before me was my angelic father, the Lord Ki.

'Are you the being we know as the Sanat Kumara?' I asked.

The spiritual being, who was only loosely inhabiting an Anu body, chuckled. *It seems that one of your Dragon sisters is using you as a channel, Solarian.*

I suddenly sensed Solarian's astral self all around me and realised I had somehow tapped into her astral projection.

'I do apologise,' Solarian said, addressing the council. 'This was only meant to be a transmission to Meridan, not a possession.'

Quite all right, came the response. *As your sister is unconscious she cannot be held accountable for her actions, and it is a very pertinent question she has asked. The answer, my dear Meridan, is yes. I postponed my spiritual evolution in order to aid the Queen of the Anunnaki to repair the damage done on Earth by our people.*

'Lord,' Solarian appealed, 'please continue with what you were telling me before this interruption ...' She sounded a little agitated by my unintended invasion of her astral self.

I had so many questions about Killian, and this being had all the answers, but I realised I had intruded enough. I allowed the ethereal scene to fade into the blankness that marked the prelude to conscious awakening.

As my eyes opened it took me a second to realise that I was lying on a lounge on the control deck of the *Klieo*. The last thing I recalled was Polaris commanding the ship to Signet Station Six while I channelled Blue Flame energy into the turbine funnel. *I must have passed out again.* I sat up, wondering where everybody was.

Out beyond the front shield windows rose a huge rock wall. An ancient grotto was carved into its face, now crumbled into disrepair. I looked around — there was rock surrounding us. It seemed the *Klieo* was parked inside a huge desert crater.

'New Mexico,' I said to myself, recalling where Signet Station Six — Solarian's station — was located. Solarian must have opened the Enoch pyramid and stargate, and made contact with the Azurline Council on Sirius B, while I slept. Sirius B was the primary planet of the Anu these days, which explained why those on the council had appeared to be of Lugh Lamhfada's kind, and also why En Ki was with them.

I wandered out into the corridor and headed towards Solarian's voice, which was coming from the ship's conference room.

'Our father spoke of the Elect One who has been under his wing,' she was telling the rest of the staff as I entered. 'He said that he would send his elect before us, and that the righteous would prevail and be without number before him forever.'

'Him?' Polaris queried. 'I'd have thought that Kali was En Ki's Elect One, as she's the primary key that opens Amenti.'

'But Kali was sent to raise Nefilim consciousness, not humanity's,' Talori pointed out. 'The Elect One En Ki spoke of is the second coming of Christ.'

'He's talking about Killian Labontè,' I said from the doorway.

My husband looked stunned by my words.

'Here she is,' Solarian said and grinned at me, 'my sassy sister who psychically hacked into my meeting with the Council of Azurline.'

'She took control of your astral body?' Talori gasped, impressed.

'Only long enough to ask a question,' Solarian clarified, 'but, yes, she did.' She seemed rather proud of me.

Talori was fascinated. 'I've never heard of that being done before. I must take some of your blood when we get back to the future. For analysis,' she explained. 'I think your DNA might be braiding.'

'After what I've been through in the past twenty years, I wouldn't be at all surprised by what my DNA is doing,' I told her cheerfully.

'You've been gone for twenty years?' Arcturus was most concerned to hear this.

I nodded apologetically, feeling that twenty years of distance rapidly unfolding between us. 'A full cycle of time — eighteen years in the past, two in the present. It was the only way to avoid inadvertently building the Nefilim a superhighway back to the early Roman Empire.'

'Smart thinking,' Polaris said, following my reasoning.

I shunned the credit. 'Thank Killian. He was the one who worked it out.'

'What makes you think that Killian is En Ki's Elect One, Meridan?' Solarian got us back on subject.

'Killian Labontè is not Christ!' Arcturus couldn't believe we were even entertaining the notion. 'If anything, the exact opposite is true and he's the Antichrist!'

'He is both and neither, but has the potential to be either.' I offered what I felt to be the truth. 'Yeshua, better known as Jesus, wasn't born with Christ consciousness either. He became one with the planetary Christos in his later years, because, when tested by Satan, he chose the path of Christ even though it meant pain, ridicule and hardship for him.'

'Having been married to the man, you should certainly know,' Castor commented, then immediately regretted it. He was usually far more tactful.

'You believe Killian is Yeshua incarnate?' my husband said incredulously.

'I recognise his energy,' I confessed.

'So you were married to Killian in a past life?' Arcturus was thunderstruck by the information. 'And have spent the last twenty years in his company? *Twenty years.*'

I knew why he'd stressed the point; he and I had been together for less than fifteen.

'I didn't recognise him until we were back in the past,' I explained, but Arcturus had left the room, unable to process how he felt about the news whilst surrounded by others.

'I'm so sorry, Meridan,' Castor said. As he spoke, the room fell into darkness.

'What now?' Polaris grumbled, but before he'd reached the door, the ship's systems came back online. 'I'd best go see what that was all about,' he said. 'Meridan?'

As his power source, I accompanied him.

Apologies for any inconvenience, Captain, the *Klieo* said as we entered the control room. *I detected the shockwave of an electromagnetic pulse approaching and temporarily shut down all systems to avoid corruption.*

'Was the source nuclear?' Polaris asked.

Negative, Captain, the lack of radioactive particles suggests a non-nuclear source.

Polaris looked intrigued. 'And the blast origin?'
Long Island, New York.

He gave a knowing smile. 'Levi,' he said.

My memory was suddenly catapulted back twenty years to the moment I'd left my fellow staff member in the secret underground facility beneath the Montauk Air Force Base. 'Levi is able to command electromagnetism?' I asked, stunned. 'No wonder he wasn't worried about being left alone.'

A holograph of the *Klieo* appeared above the control panel and her sails lit up. *Blue Flame Energy Function is detecting an incoming current*, the ship told us.

There was a great crack of metal above us and Polaris and I turned immediately to the Blue Flame energy funnel. A beam of blue-green light burst downward into the base mound and continued to flow in a steady stream.

The captain was delighted and began to laugh. 'So much for not changing history,' he said. 'It looks as if Levi has cast a spanner in the works of the new HAARP grid, which will keep the Nefilim off our backs whilst we activate the rest of the stations. And the best news is that you're off the hook as our only energy source.'

'So I can go with Killian to free Tamar?' I asked. I shuddered to think of my husband accompanying Killian into Irkalla, as they would both end up dead. In my heart I knew I was right about Killian, but if it turned out I was wrong, I wanted to be the one to deal with the repercussions.

'I gather you've activated your station at some time in the course of the past twenty years?' Polaris asked, and when I nodded he thought quietly for a few moments. 'Come with me to the lab,' he said eventually. 'Castor is running a few tests on our new friend.'

'What kind of tests?' I was concerned, as Killian had been subjected to enough scientific probing in his short life.

'Just blood tests and so forth, nothing too drastic,' Polaris assured me. 'The aura can be simulated, but genetic information cannot. Come on,' he urged. 'Let's go and see what our friend Killian is made of.'

'I didn't even know there was a lab on board,' I commented as I followed him out the door and to the upper hatch stairs.

The captain smiled as he twisted one of the metal upright supports on the stairwell. The staircase rose upwards and then collapsed flat against the ceiling to expose an elevator beneath.

'How thirteenth century of you to have a secret passage to the lab ... and yet so futuristic.' I was amused at how the captain had adapted to his history-hopping lifestyle. 'You are truly a lord of time.'

We descended to the lab, which was an entire deck unto itself. Not only did Castor have a lab down there, but Levi had a huge work station as well. A transparent walled walkway connected the two labs and as we walked along it I peered into Levi's workshop. It was filled with all manner of intriguing technological marvels, both futuristic and ancient.

'What is all this stuff?' I asked.

'Things I've collected, been given or stumbled upon in my travels.'

'What does it all do?'

'In truth, we're still trying to work that out. Levi likes to tinker when he gets a chance ... which, lately, seems to be never.'

'Shouldn't we be heading to Montauk to retrieve Levi?' I asked. No one else seemed concerned about this.

'He's already on his way back to us, I expect,' the captain replied. 'Or have you forgotten about his other little talent?'

'Levitation . . . of course.'

'In the interim, we need to give Killian the all clear to move through the Signet stations in order to get to Irkalla via the Xerthaneus stargate in Antarctica.' Polaris paused before entering the lab where Castor was observing Killian. 'If he gets the all clear, Solarian will see you through her stargate. From there you can access Dexter's Signet station. The rest of us will activate the remaining stations and meet you back at Nova Scotia.'

'And Arcturus?' My husband posed our biggest dilemma.

Polaris winced. 'Obviously, considering the current situation,' he glanced in at Killian who was chatting with Castor, 'Arcturus can't go with you.' He looked pained. 'This was his mission and he's not going to like having it taken away from him . . . especially by *me*.'

'But you will tell him?'

The captain forced a smile and gave a hesitant nod.

I breathed a huge sigh of relief and gave him a hug. 'Thank you.'

'Are you trying to get us in more trouble?' he joked.

'I'm just so very grateful,' I said, reining in my emotions. 'Really, you're such a good friend to us . . . It's a shame Arcturus doesn't realise it.'

The captain had to laugh. 'I do believe that my partner has found occasion to say exactly the same thing to Arcturus, so in that regard I believe I owe him a karmic debt.'

He turned to look at Killian again then back to me. 'You haven't ... I mean, you wouldn't ...' He was suddenly awkward, which was very unlike him.

I guessed his concern and put him out of his misery. 'I love my husband, Captain. But I also have a lot of faith in Killian. I know in my heart that he's integral to the plan.'

'The question is, whose plan — the Nefilim's or ours?' Polaris was still sceptical, and I couldn't blame him.

'Killian has managed to suppress his dark side for twenty years and during that time I saw him channel nothing but the good of the Sanat Kumara,' I said. 'Who, I recently confirmed, is En Ki himself, our angelic father. So why would our father send us the Antichrist?'

Polaris cocked his head to think about this, and finally opened the door to the lab. 'Gentlemen,' he greeted Castor and Killian, then noted the mess the lab was in — there was glass shattered on the floor, tools scattered everywhere.

'We meet again, time lord,' Killian replied with a grin.

'It seems you're something of a time lord yourself these days,' Polaris said, still assessing the damage to the lab.

'Killian's dark half didn't like giving blood,' Castor explained, far more interested in the magnified holographic blood sample he was viewing at his work station.

I was appalled, as Lugh had spent twenty-odd years teaching Killian how to avoid engaging his dark half. 'You didn't make him regress, did you?'

'It was only for a couple of minutes,' Killian said in defence of Castor's actions. 'It was fine really, and I'm curious to know more about me too.'

'This is just incredible,' Castor said, beckoning the captain and me to join him around the holograph. He indicated the image of a DNA strand. 'Average human DNA,' he stated. 'And this is Killian's DNA.' Another two double helixes entwined into the existing double helix to form a six-strand DNA code.

'And this is what happens when Killian channels the Sanat Kumara.' Castor gave a telepathic command and the six DNA strands doubled and rebraided to form a twelve-strand DNA code.

Fortunately, I had an understanding of ascension dynamics, which enabled me to understand the DNA braiding process. There was a double helix for each of our bodies — the physical, the emotional or astral, the mental, the causal, the spiritual and the monadic. Beyond this point, the being reached a state of complete enlightenment whereby it transcended into the higher evolutionary scheme of the next harmonic universe. As each body developed, another double helix activated within the non-coding DNA the being already carried. Even the most modern technology on this planet could not detect the presence of these bodies nor follow their development, as our current scientific community was still oblivious to their existence. Fortunately for us, the races that chaired the guardian councils of our Signet stations were not so spiritually ignorant and had developed technologies that assisted the staff of Amenti to do their jobs here on Earth.

'Twelve-strand DNA,' Castor concluded. 'We staff members average about a ten-strand genetic code.'

'Christ!' The captain's eyes shot to Killian, who smiled broadly at him.

Castor held up a finger. 'Not exactly, as this is what happens when Killian switches to his dark half.'

The holograph of the twelve-strand DNA code shrivelled to a mere two-strand code, way lower in frequency than the average human being who normally sported four- to six-strand DNA.

'Oh dear,' Polaris said. 'That makes him a huge security risk.'

'I am in control, Captain,' Killian pleaded his cause. 'Please let me do this. How else am I to prove myself an ally?'

'You have already proved it,' I reassured him, but Killian was more interested in convincing the males on staff of his allegiance.

He looked over at the room of technological wonders across the transparent walkway. 'There must be some sort of restraining device in amongst that lot. I'll risk anything, swallow anything, wear anything you like, just let me go.'

Polaris was thinking, but Killian took his silence to mean he was still reluctant.

'If Tamar hadn't cared enough to come after me, I'd still be on the inside,' he argued.

'And now you want to go back in,' Polaris responded. 'You could end up right back where you started!'

'Lamhfada has taught me the art of psychic self-defence,' Killian countered. 'I don't fear the Nefilim any more, and, more importantly, I don't hate them. They no longer hold any power over me.'

Polaris still wasn't sure. 'I need . . .'

'Hello,' a voice interrupted.

'... Levi,' Polaris said with a grin as his first mate entered the laboratory.

'It seems the Montauk Project was finally shut down in 2003,' Levi said sheepishly, having acted contrary to our objective — not to change events in the past.

'It certainly seems that way,' Polaris replied, reserving judgement.

'The good news is it'll probably take HAARP a few days to get back online, so we're off the radar for a while.' Levi smiled, hoping to avoid a reprimand.

'Then we should get moving.' Polaris headed towards the door. 'Better get our new teammate a suit,' he said to Levi on his way past, who looked stunned to hear Killian described that way.

'So I can go?' Killian sounded hopeful.

'I'm sure Levi can come up with some way of ensuring your loyalty,' Polaris said, and glanced to Levi, who didn't ask questions, just nodded.

'I think we still have some remotely detonated liquid-light capsules that we used on Taejax when first he joined our ranks,' Levi suggested.

'Make it happen yesterday,' said the captain. 'We still have three stations to activate.'

Once Killian was suited up and had recovered from the novelty of being able to transform his attire at will, Levi gave him a capsule of liquid light to swallow.

'This works pretty much like a liquid-light bullet, but the shot is administered remotely,' he explained as Killian swallowed the device. 'Should you lose control, this remote detonator will trigger the capsule to burst and give your personal frequency a positive boost.'

'Excellent.' Killian sounded most reassured by this.

'I suggest that Castor looks after the remote,' Polaris said, and Levi passed it over. Castor was pleased to finally be allowed to leave the ship.

'Our weapons will work in Irkalla, but our psychic powers aren't supported there,' Dexter briefed Castor, Killian and me in a closed meeting in the captain's quarters. 'Obviously the negativity levels are intense, so don't let anything get a rise out of you. Try to stay as light-hearted as possible ... and believe me, it will be near impossible.'

Levi had armed us to the gills, with our preferred weapon of choice the liquid-light gun. During my stint in the Dark Ages I had learned to wield a sword, so I'd added one to my cache, in addition to my usual collection of knives. Castor was a little light on: he carried only a liquid-light pistol as his preferred weapons were the jaws, fangs and claws of the animals he could transform himself into. Dexter, on the other hand, seemed to be sporting every weapon known to humankind and a few yet to be discovered. Killian, our guide, wasn't permitted to carry a weapon, but in all honesty he didn't need one — he could summon more power than the entire staff of Amenti put together and could have destroyed us all at any time.

'Solarian is waiting to guide you through to her station,' Polaris announced at the end of the briefing.

Arcturus appeared at the door. 'What's going on?' he asked, but from the disappointed look on his face it was clear he'd already worked it out. 'What, I'm off the mission now? She's my daughter too, you realise!'

'We don't have time for this right now,' Polaris said, making the call. 'They have to go, and so do we.'

We filed from the room, and when Killian passed Arcturus I saw daggers in my husband's eyes. I was the last to leave and when Arcturus looked at me, the pain on his face broke my heart.

'I love you,' I told him, 'but when you're jealous you're dangerous. And there's really no need for it.'

'Isn't there?' he asked quickly, although his tone wasn't aggressive. 'Shouldn't I be concerned that you've spent the last twenty years with another man?'

'It wasn't something I *chose*,' I said. 'And I wasn't in his company for all that time. I caught up on my writing, honed my psychic skills and learned how to wield a sword! I missed you, Albray. And twenty years is a long time to miss someone constantly.' My tears welled, but I sniffed them back; this was no time to crumple into an emotional heap.

'Constantly?' he said, his annoyance melting away.

I nodded and moved in for the hug we both so badly needed. 'Please don't let us part on bad terms. Just trust me,' I pulled away to look him in the face, 'can't you?'

'You're a surprise a minute, Mrs Devere,' he said with a smile. 'It just takes me a little time to catch up.'

'Oh, for heaven's sake,' called Dexter from the corridor outside. 'Will you just kiss her so we can get on with the mission!'

We did kiss, our first kiss in twenty years, and how I wished I could linger with my lover and finally fulfil all the lustful thoughts I had been

305

entertaining about him for what seemed like an eternity.

'On second thoughts,' Dexter called impatiently, 'forget the kiss or we'll never get out of here!'

'Go get our daughter,' my husband said and gave me a nod of encouragement. Then he escorted me out into the hall where the rest of my party were already leaving the ship.

'Maybe you should come,' I said, suddenly regretting that I'd underestimated my husband's understanding. I should have spoken with him before agreeing that he should be ousted from the mission.

'I don't need to come,' he told me. 'I trust you. It's him I don't trust.' His dark eyes turned to Killian, who smiled serenely back at him.

'You dislike me because you suspect I am in love with your wife and daughter — and you'd be right on both counts,' Killian said, much to everyone else's dismay, especially my own. 'These two women rescued my soul from a lifetime of torment — how could I not adore them? They were once my wife and daughter too.'

'You remember,' I gasped, for in twenty years Killian had never mentioned regaining his memory of our past life together.

'I thought he knew,' Arcturus said, further relieved of his unfounded suspicions about us. I shook my head.

'Clearly these angels were only loaned to me in order to lead me to my full potential,' Killian went on. 'My only connection to them now is my indebtedness for their self-sacrifice and assistance.' He smiled broadly. 'Truth be known, being apart from you nearly drove Mia — and therefore me — insane.'

Everyone made sentimental noises as I bashfully admitted that I had been a bit obsessive about getting back, and the rest of the crew emerged into the corridor to see what all the fuss was about.

My husband so wanted to hold on to his suspicions about Killian, but in Killian's actual presence he found it impossible to dislike him.

'Well, don't think this changes anything,' he said sternly. 'You still tried to seduce our daughter.'

Killian chuckled. 'Our father would like to point out that you have seduced many of his daughters during your lifetimes, Arcturus, but he does not hold it against you.'

The entire crew collapsed into laughter, and even Arcturus cracked a smile.

'Well ... I'd have asked their fathers if I'd known them,' he said, making a feeble attempt to defend himself.

'Sure you would have,' Thana mocked.

'I'm certain my father would have appreciated you asking for permission to seduce me,' Solarian said, delighted by the premise.

Talori was leaning on Solarian, so amused she could barely hold herself up. 'Not to mention our poor husbands,' she choked. Her face morphed Arcturus's for a second, which looked ridiculous on her frame. 'You don't mind if I just borrow your wife's body for a few hours, surely?' Talori said in his voice, raising another round of laughter at his expense.

'Will you just go!' Arcturus urged our party, wanting the embarrassment to end.

And, in a daze of merriment, we left for the depths of the Underworld.

CHAPTER 24

HELL OF ETERNAL SLEEP AND DARKNESS

The defunct sleep therein
in incorruptible forms,
they wake not to see their brethren,
they recognise no longer their father and mother,
their hearts feel naught towards their wives and
children.
This is the dwelling of the god All-Dead.
Each trembles to pray to him,
for he hears not.
Nobody can praise him,
for he regards not those who adore him.
Neither does he notice any offering brought to him.
This god is Karmic Decree.

TAMAR DEVERE — KALI

There was no cold on Earth like the cold in hell, for here even my will had frozen solid. My reality was a potpourri of my personal demons, a neverending string of nightmares woven carefully together by my

308

foe. At a higher level of consciousness I knew my captors were altering my perception of reality, but the implants were every bit as vivid as memory. Whenever I attempted to seek comfort in my memories and dreams, they immediately turned dark and sordid.

My parents became two people who despised each other and me most of all. I experienced every kind of abuse at their hands and grew to hate them, myself, the world and everyone in it.

My prince never came for me. Having taken human form, he'd been seduced by the pleasures of the physical world and had forgotten all about his love for me and our mission. Every time I thought of Mathu, I saw him in luxurious surrounds, lavishing his affection upon a multitude of other women. He would turn to look in my direction and laugh at my humiliation and disappointment.

Then there was Killian. Like a spark of hope in this world of utter darkness, I had a vision of him coming to save me. It wasn't clear how he had got past the Nefilim to come to my aid, but we were alone in hell and he was intimately close to me.

'I know you want me,' he whispered, and his moist breath upon my neck sent warm shivers through my freezing soul.

'Yes,' I replied. 'I am yours.'

NO!

My higher self screamed out to me to resist the filth I was being fed. I had to wonder why Ill was going to such lengths to make Killian look good to me, but then my body was racked by agony and the thought fell from my mind. I was losing myself, and I feared for my sanity. No one heard my cries for help, no one came, no one knew I was here or that

309

this place even existed! Except for him, the Lord of all Ill.

We went back a long way, Ill and I, for in my lifetime as Kali I had done some secret genetic work at his request; so top-secret that only he and I knew about it. Ill would have had a complete riot on his hands had the Dracon known he was working on creating a female of their species; and had succeeded, way back before the first Dracon uprising.

With the brief memory, pain shot through my body again — a warning. The memory vanished, to be replaced by the belief that all the Dracon females I had created as Kali had been destroyed after my death.

I dared not allow my mind to think at all, in case every part of me was stolen in this way. In this cold darkness I had lost all sense of time, for every second was an eternity of yearning to be anywhere but here. And the longer I was here, the less I felt, the less I cared, the less I mourned and craved the life and identity that was slowly being torn from me.

CHAPTER 25

XERTHANEVS — ANTARCTICA

*Within this station lie
links to extraterrestrial days gone by,
for during mankind's predestined birth,
malign beings disturbed evolution on Earth.*

*Xerthaneus guards the porthole
to Gaia's uncertain future,
moulded by the intent of
all who live upon her.*

*If the ice melts from this place,
antiquity shall surface,
buried to date.
And we shall know the consequences
of leaving destiny to fate,
and understand all that is extraterrestrial
too late.*

MIA DEVERE — MERIDAN

Passing from the highly intellectual indigo frequency of the Enoch pyramid porthole passage in

311

New Mexico, down through the spectrum to the vibrant, erotic red frequency of the Xerthaneus pyramid passage at the South Pole, proved to be quite a rush and rather arousing. Castor, Killian, Dexter and I were deposited on top of the glowing red surface of the Signet One porthole, all a little flushed by the experience.

'Word of warning,' Dexter announced as he headed straight for the holographic work station, 'the frequency of this Signet station is akin to your base chakra, so it's likely to stimulate a few primal urges.'

'You don't say,' commented Castor, trying to ignore the sultry vibrations of the ice palace, which was awash in the red light of the glowing Signet porthole.

Here I was, with three gorgeous men, submersed in primal urges, and I hadn't made love to my husband in twenty years! I decided to attempt to distract everyone with a science question. 'How do you know that the consciousness of the planet is low enough at this time to link this porthole to our dark future in Irkalla rather than our bright future in the Ranna?'

'By this point in 2003, the US has invaded Iraq, which triggers a steep incline in suicide bombings. There has been an outbreak of the SARS disease and the hottest heatwave on record has swept through the UK and France — it all adds up to a lot of angry, greedy, unhappy people,' Dexter replied. 'Even once we get this grid up and running, I fear it may be too little too late. Humanity isn't waking up fast enough, and the Nefilim have dammed the grid in so many places that frankly I despair at the task of clearing them all.'

'You sure know how to kill the mood,' Killian said, to the amusement of all. 'Holy mother of the universe!' he exclaimed as he noticed a large object frozen in the ice beyond the walls of the chamber. He stepped back to get a broader view. 'Is that a —'

'Spaceship? Yes, it is,' Dexter said. 'And so is that, and that,' pointing to others held in the ice around the station. 'They belonged to the Nefilim but were frozen here during the last Ice Age. They've been working on defrosting them ever since.'

'Global warming,' Killian realised. 'The Nefilim do everything to promote it through their Illuminati operations.'

'My station was located here for the very purpose of keeping an eye on this lot,' Dexter explained, returning to us after he'd programmed our request into the porthole.

'There's something I don't understand,' I told him. 'Each porthole has a guardian council, but does the guardian spirit of this station, Xerthaneus, reside in the Underworld of the Nefilim or the Otherworld of the Anu?'

'Both actually,' he replied.

'But how is that possible?' It took me a moment to figure out that one of the Nefilim must have been a double agent — an enlightened Anu posing as one of the fallen in order to protect the stargate that provided a back door into the realm of eternal darkness.

'We all have little secrets from our past,' Dexter said, and grinned at me.

Red liquid light broke the surface of the crystalline porthole beneath our feet and we dropped into the depths of darkest density.

We landed in the middle of a beautiful garden thriving inside a huge dark tower, which was constructed from massive stone blocks not employed since the most ancient of times. High overhead, the porthole was set into the ceiling the tower and beamed infrared light down upon the flourishing plants.

'Not exactly what I'd expected Irkalla to look like,' Castor commented, then spotted a beautiful Anu woman waiting to welcome us. Her blue aura was radiant amid the red light of our surroundings. 'Hello,' he said, charmed by her beauty.

'With eyes like bluest cornflowers and hair as white as snow, she was tall, slender and elegant, and a wonder to behold,' Dexter quoted before embracing her. 'Ereshkigal ... I did not expect you to meet us.'

She returned his fond embrace. 'Heracles, it seems an age since I saw your friendly face.'

'It has been an age if that's the name I was using last time we met,' he joked. 'It's Dexter these days.'

'This is not Ereshkigal!' Killian exclaimed, then watched, shocked, as she morphed into the ugly Nefilim demon he knew, and then into Co-co Yamamoto. 'You're the double agent?' he cried. 'You killed my friend!'

'I took her life in the short term in order to protect the chance of saving her soul in the long term. Would you have done differently?' she asked him. 'I'll bet you have done the same yourself and turned a blind eye to injustice for the sake of the larger plan.'

I knew for a fact this was true.

'I, like you, have learned to separate the best of me from the worst,' Ereshkigal went on, 'in order to alternate between the worlds of light and shadow, and maintain my sanity and my cover.'

Killian was suddenly seeing Ereshkigal in a whole new light. 'I would never have guessed you were really on my side,' he said.

'I would never have imagined that anyone could beat the Montauk mind-control program,' she said in return, grinning broadly. 'That's very impressive for a human.'

I hated to interrupt the reunion but I was concerned. 'Is Tamar all right?' I asked. 'Where is she?'

'Follow me.' Ereshkigal led us through the garden towards the high stone outer wall of the tower. 'Ill has put her in the Hell of Eternal Sleep and Darkness.'

'That's a drug-induced brainwashing program.' Killian was concerned, having undergone such torture himself. 'Where is Mathu?'

'I have been unable to siphon that information out of Erragal yet, but I will,' she assured him.

'It must be difficult hiding who you really are from the man you love,' Killian said sympathetically.

She laughed. 'I hold no love for Erragal, beyond hoping to save his soul like the others'. My Underworld was once a beautiful place ... before I was forced into marrying Erragal and surrendering my realms to him. Now all that is left is this garden, one tiny oasis of light in a realm of utter darkness. I despise how Erragal, Ill, Namtar and the rest of them have corrupted my elementals and turned them into destroyers instead of creators! But not all my elementals have been turned; there are still a goodly number that are loyal to me and protect this place from discovery.'

At the wall of the tower, Ereshkigal joined her hands in the prayer position, her middle fingertips touching the stone. Her hands passed through the solid barrier and parted it as if it were a curtain of silk.

'I was going to ask how you had managed to keep this place secret for all time,' I said quietly as we followed her into a dark stone walkway.

'No need to whisper yet,' she replied. 'We are still in my secured zone.'

Ereshkigal allowed the wall to close and the corridor fell into utter darkness, until Dexter cracked a glowstick. Our hostess moved across to the opposing stone wall, which she opened for us in the same manner as the first. This time we stepped into an entire labyrinth of dark halls.

'This is my labyrinth, which leads absolutely nowhere,' she said, and patted the wall that had closed behind us. 'Only I have the ability to move through these walls and find my way without getting lost. It is the one part of my kingdom that Erragal never claimed, simply because he doesn't know it exists.'

I was surprised to see that she had retained her tall, angelic Anu form. 'Isn't it dangerous for you to wear your true form here?' I asked.

'Of course,' she said. 'But if I am seen in your company, I'd rather my kin believe I am an invader rather than reveal myself as their trusted ally.'

I saw her point.

We followed Ereshkigal through her maze and eventually came to an archway that led into a huge chasm. In the middle of it I could see the huge, hairy behind of a sleeping beast; I couldn't define the species from this distance, but its stench was all too apparent. 'What's that?' I whispered as we moved through the cavern to get to the cave beyond.

'Oh, that's just Cerberus,' Dexter replied.

I knew that name from mythology. 'The three-headed hound?'

'The very one.' Dexter let out a loud whistle to get the beast's attention and its large snake-like tail began whipping around in an annoyed fashion.

'Don't wake it!' I appealed; too late, for the beast began to growl.

With a wave of her hand Ereshkigal sent the multiheaded pooch back to the land of Nod. 'Now is not the time, old friend.'

'This beastie and I go way back,' Dexter objected.

'So you do,' I said, recalling the legend. 'Heracles was loaned Cerberus by the Queen of the Underworld, Persephone.' And suddenly I saw the story of this goddess in a new light: why she lived half her life in the dark and half in light. It was a metaphor for being a double agent in the inter-time war. I began to outline my theory but Ereshkigal said, 'Shh,' and winked at me as we moved into the arched corridor ahead.

'We are fortunate in that the porthole is underneath the main palace in Irkalla,' she explained, 'as are all the halls of torture and the science labs.'

'So we won't get to see outside the palace walls?' I asked, a little disappointed. Irkalla existed in one of Earth's possible futures, and even though this was the planet's worst possible future, I was curious to see more.

'There is nothing to see!' Ereshkigal scoffed. 'The planet is covered by lifeless oceans of toxic water and blanketed in cloud. Nothing of beauty survives.'

'You survived,' Killian piped up.

Ereshkigal forced a smile. 'Some blessings are truly a curse.'

At the end of the stone corridor was a very modern elevator, whose doors opened on our approach.

'This will take us straight to the labs,' she advised. 'Most of my kindred are distracted by some mysterious disaster that has befallen their HAARP project in 2003,' and she looked at us, obviously suspecting our involvement. Each of us looked about aimlessly and whistled innocently.

'I believe their biggest fear is that they will never be able to retrieve you from the past,' she said to Killian, and expressed her own curiosity as to how he had managed to save himself without extraterrestrial assistance.

'Surprise!' Killian said, not wanting to give any details without a full understanding of how much this double agent knew about the staff of Amenti, our means and mission.

Ereshkigal grinned. 'While you are here, my elementals will shield you all from the awareness of my kindred's demons, which serve as the security system in Irkalla. They may sense something is not right, but they won't be able to perceive what it is. Hopefully they will remain baffled long enough for us to get Kali out.'

The one-time goddess of the Netherworld closed her beautiful large eyes and waved her arms before her in a subtle gathering motion. 'E-Ta'-TA HA'-A'Rha KE'-a ...' she chanted.

'What's she saying?' Killian quietly asked Dexter.

'It is the Anuhazi language,' Dexter explained. 'She is summoning the beings of the Eternal All-One to her.'

'*OOR, UN UR'-A-Or'-Nam* ...'

'Anchor in this moment,' Dexter translated in a whisper, 'the Divine Sea of Liquid Light.'

'*A'-DA Um-A'-Ta!*' Ereshkigal concluded.

'Empower and strengthen my will.'

A wind filled with a dazzling display of tiny coloured lights came rushing towards us through the still air of the dark tunnel. It swirled itself into the elevator with us, filling the small space with the scent of a spring garden and the goodwill of a Christmas Eve. It was a delightful sensation, causing me to tingle all over.

'*Ah-Ta' Ah-Sha-Lum,*' Ereshkigal instructed the elemental body.

I guessed she had requested that they be still and at peace, for the lights vanished, their pleasant smell faded and the excitement level in the elevator — and in us — returned to normal. Ereshkigal's elemental taskforce had gone into camouflage mode in order to conceal us from the spies of our enemy. Still, they wouldn't be able to hide us from the eyes of the Dracon guards nor the Nefilim. We would just have to hope that the disaster Levi had created at Montauk kept them distracted long enough for us to achieve our goal.

The lift doors opened into a corridor that was entirely white, but lit with deep red lighting — the colour frequency most effective for keeping base desires thriving.

A couple of demonic elementals came flying down the corridor to check who was exiting the lift.

When they could see no one, they hissed in annoyance at the wasted effort and flew away up the corridor and around a corner at the end.

There were doors off both sides of the corridor, but no peepholes in them or any windows. Although the place was deathly silent, I knew in my soul that behind the closed doors were souls suffering immeasurable pain and torment; I could sense their distress even though I couldn't hear it.

'Quickly,' Ereshkigal urged, leading us to the third door on the left. She opened it wide and ushered us quietly inside.

'Dear goddess,' I gasped when I saw my daughter. She was suspended, naked and unconscious, inside an upright transparent flotation tank full of a heavy golden liquid. Tubes extended from her nose and mouth, connecting her to a life-sustaining apparatus. A tentacled helmet encompassed her skull, with a long tail that dropped down to hug the nape of her neck.

'Shut it off, drain it!' I felt suffocated by anguish.

Before anyone could react, the machinery responded to my will.

'You still have power here?' Ereshkigal said, stunned, then she looked at me more closely and smiled. 'You are the Blue Flame bearer. I was wondering why I felt such an affinity with you — we resonate to the same frequency.'

This was true for all of the Anu race. I was the first human ever to resonate to the frequency of the Blue Flame.

I watched as the metal headgear detached from Tamar's head, leaving bloody marks at her temples and at the base of her neck where its long spikes had penetrated her skull. I whimpered, wanting to disintegrate the transparent shield between us and hold her in my arms.

'Wait for the fluid to drain,' Dexter warned. 'That is diluted liquid Orme, designed to deaden the psychic senses. If your powers are still working here, it'd be best not to coat yourself in that stuff.'

'Here.' Ereshkigal removed her long velvet cloak and handed it to me. 'Use this to dry her and wrap her.'

As the fluid drained away, Tamar collapsed in a heap at the bottom of the tank. I used my will to make it and all the tubes disappear, then enfolded her in the cloak and hugged her to me. 'Tamar?' I couldn't feel her breathing, so I shook her.

Killian gave her a sharp slap on the back and she vomited fluid all over the place. She remained unconscious but her breathing stabilised.

'Oh thank you, goddess!' I burst into tears of relief.

'She's going to be out of it for quite a while,' Killian advised, 'so we're going to have to carry her out of here.'

I looked at my unconscious, helpless little girl; it seemed she did still need her mother after all and I wasn't going to let her down.

'We can't leave without Mathu,' I said, knowing her one desire. 'He's one of our major objectives, and if we don't take the opportunity to find him now, we'll regret it later.'

'But we don't know where he's being held,' Ereshkigal reasoned.

'And we need to get Tamar out of here as quickly as possible,' Dexter added.

'Make your best guess about Mathu,' I said to our Anu guide. 'Of all the hells the Nefilim have created to torture the unfaithful, which would hurt Mathu the most and aid Ill's cause at the same time?'

Ereshkigal thought a moment. 'A virtuous prince, devoted only to his queen, would most likely be broken in Ishtar's Hell of a Thousand Pleasures.'

'Do you know the way?' I asked.

'Yes, but we'll run into opposition if we venture that far. Ishtar likes to watch the torture, and she won't take kindly to us waltzing off with her victim.'

The mere mention of Ishtar's name made my blood boil; she'd already hurt my husband, and now she was probably doing the same to the love of my daughter's life. I looked at Dexter, Castor and Killian. 'Take Tamar back to the porthole,' I said. 'I'll deal with Ishtar.'

'Like hell you will,' Dexter said.

'Look,' I took a deep breath, trying to work out how I could state my reasons without causing offence, 'I don't mean to sound condescending, but men are completely useless when it comes to handling Ishtar.'

'That is *so* true,' Ereshkigal said before the men could protest.

'Ereshkigal and I are the only ones with any psychic power down here,' I went on.

'That's not true and you know it,' Killian interrupted.

'Please, you'll just have to trust us girls to handle this one.'

Dexter was concerned. 'I don't know … I imagine you have a lot of pent-up anger towards Ishtar.'

'That won't be a problem,' I assured him, hoping to reassure myself in the process.

Dexter sought a second opinion. 'What do you think, Castor?'

'My Lady du Lac has never steered me wrong before,' Castor said with a shrug, 'so I'll go wherever she asks me to go.'

When Killian nodded to agree with Castor's reasoning, Dexter took my unconscious daughter from my arms. 'Be careful and be quick,' he said.

'I can send word to you in the porthole cavern via one of my elementals should the situation get out of hand,' Ereshkigal assured him.

'It won't,' I said, and kissed my daughter's head in parting. 'Don't worry,' I whispered to her, 'you saved my love and now I'll save yours. I promise.'

CHAPTER 26

TAMING THE SHREW

Ereshkigal assumed her Nefilim form as we moved towards the more densely populated part of Irkalla. 'You'll need a disguise,' she said, and was considering where she might obtain one, when I made myself invisible.

'Will this do?'

'Perfect. Now be warned: Ishtar's little corner of hell is all about lust, debauchery and betrayal, which you might find shocking.' She kept her eyes dead ahead as she spoke to me.

We entered the palace proper, which was a spiritual architectural nightmare with all its sharp edges and clean straight lines, lack of natural light and growth of any kind — no plants, no fish or birds, no nature period. Due to the freezing temperature of Irkalla there were huge open fires everywhere, run on gas; no doubt there were no longer any trees left on Earth to burn.

'The fires of hell,' I commented, realising the relevance of the term.

There were statues all around, depicting the now fallen gods in their glory days, torturing their human victims via various means. Instead of paintings there were large screens on the walls displaying live footage of souls being tortured with painful and perverse acts. I felt as though I was taking a tour through the darkest depths of cyberspace.

We passed several sets of Dracon guards, but the palace seemed devoid of the Nefilim. I was beginning to hope I'd get really lucky and find that Ishtar was no longer here, for then I wouldn't be forced to deal with my hatred and contempt for her. These were detrimental feelings and I knew it; it was horrifying to think that I doubted my own ability to live up to my high spiritual awareness in this instance.

'How do you forgive your kindred in order to do what you do?' I whispered to Ereshkigal once we'd reached an empty corridor.

'Empathise,' she replied in a word, and it was a revelation to me — a reminder of a lesson I had learned long ago. For with empathy came compassion, understanding, unconditional love and forgiveness.

'We must be close,' I commented; the live feeds on the screens were depicting sexually and emotionally torturous atrocities and the statues were more erotic. I stopped before a screen showing a young man, more Anu in appearance than human, being overpowered and seduced by many human females. 'Where's that taking place?' I asked.

'Main chamber, end of the hall.' Ereshkigal nodded ahead. 'Once we're inside that room, you're on your own. I must protect my cover at all costs.'

'I understand,' I said and sped up the pace. I hoped Ereshkigal had more of a plan than I did.

We entered what I could only describe as a fully equipped porn studio, where Ishtar was the director and Mathu the star stud, but one that wasn't being very cooperative.

'Leave me alone!' he was yelling through his tears as naked women slid all over his restrained body, trying to engage him in sexual activity.

'Enjoy yourself, my lovely … the camera adores you,' instructed Ishtar, who was still sporting Sabine Labontè's body. She was standing at a console of screens, monitoring the recording of Mathu's seduction from all angles. 'In the whole of Earth's history this may be your only chance of getting laid … as your little princess is now fulfilling the needs of Ill's mighty erection.'

'Liar!' Mathu yelled, which frustrated Ishtar no end.

'Hit him with another dose of Viagra, ladies, and dope him up again,' she ordered her sexy extras. 'Give me some decent footage to feed his sweetheart, or I'll toss your sorry arses into the Hell of a Thousand Wrinkles!'

That threat got the girls moving quick smart.

Ishtar turned to address her visitor. 'Ereshkigal, this is a surprise. Are you finally getting over your frigid streak and coming to watch me work?'

'Where are all the men?' Ereshkigal asked, with some resentment in her voice — obviously she and Ishtar didn't get along. I wasn't really sure if any of the Nefilim liked one another — they were too self-serving and emotionless.

'They're at Montauk,' Ishtar replied. 'Is there a problem?'

'I have had a report of a disturbance down in wash and emboss,' Ereshkigal stated. Although I had no idea what she meant, Ishtar understood well enough.

'The lab,' she said, concerned. 'Kali?'

'I don't know.' Ereshkigal was most unhelpful.

'Then why didn't you go and look?' Ishtar sounded exasperated at being expected to do everything herself.

'Because I thought my Lord Erragal would wish to be informed first. But as he's not here,' Ereshkigal said cattily, and moved towards the door at a snail's pace, 'I'll go and investigate myself.'

Ishtar caught her up and had passed her in seconds. 'Do us both a favour,' she said, 'stay here and organise this lot. I'll go and see what's happened.'

'I'm not interested in your peep show and I don't take orders from you!' Ereshkigal said, following Ishtar to the door. She looked back briefly, perhaps to say goodbye or give me leave to complete my mission.

Ishtar spotted the glance and stopped in her tracks. She turned back to face Ereshkigal, her hands on her hips. 'Ha!' she cried, as if catching her out.

'What?' Ereshkigal challenged. No doubt her heart was in her throat; mine certainly was.

'There just might be a pervert in you after all,' Ishtar said with a leer.

'Sex is about as mysterious as your sterility,' Ereshkigal responded coldly and pushed past Ishtar and out the door.

'Fuck you,' Ishtar retorted, and her angry footsteps pounded off into the distance.

The women left in the room burst into tears, all too distraught even to attempt to flee.

'Please, help me,' Mathu mumbled deliriously, but none of the women dared to release him from his bonds — so I did, to their great shock. When I made clothes appear on their bodies they were doubly stunned, and when I appeared amongst them one of the girls actually fainted.

'Don't panic, I'm here to get you out,' I explained.

I switched off the camera transmission then moved to the bed to see how Mathu was faring. I held his angelic face gently between my hands and his beautiful violet eyes focused on me a moment. 'Can you walk?' I asked. When his eyes rolled back in his head I figured the answer was no. *Not good,* I thought.

I looked at the women, now cowering in a corner. 'Do you want to get out of here?' I asked.

'We dare not,' one of them ventured.

'Stay and you will surely perish,' I told them.

They went into a huddle to discuss the issue and it didn't take them long to decide to take the risk. One of them began slapping the cheeks of their unconscious companion to wake her.

'But there are guards everywhere,' the bravest of the girls said. 'How do you propose to get us out?'

'I have an idea ...' And it was a good one in my opinion. 'I'm an illusionist,' I explained, and transformed into a Dracon guard. The women looked scared, but when I turned them into Dracon too, they screamed and ran from each other.

'It's just an illusion, ladies,' I stressed, which calmed them enough so they dared to touch themselves and feel their own forms beneath their hands despite the Dracon guise they were wearing.

Their spokeswoman smiled. '*Very* cool,' she said. 'I am Celestia. Who are you? The guardian angel of whores or something?'

When I considered the reputation that history had fabricated for me during my past incarnation as the Black Madonna, I considered that could well be.

The women, led by me, dragged Mathu's dead weight through the palace. I could feel the tension in them every time we passed a group of Dracon guards, but when none of the guards bothered to question us, the women's confidence grew.

'Hey, Angel,' Celestia whispered, keeping pace with me, 'I think it's working.'

I had to smile at her nickname for me.

As we approached the lift that would take us to the lower levels, we encountered a demon patrol. Sensing fear, the evil elementals flew in close to inspect one of the guards holding Mathu. Not surprisingly, their target was the most faint-hearted among our company and I feared she would black out again. She almost whimpered under the pressure of the close scrutiny, but I snapped at the demons with a growl and they hissed at me and moved on.

'That was close,' Celestia said with a sigh of relief as we reached the lift. But she gasped along with everyone else when the lift doors parted to reveal Ishtar inside.

'Out of my way!' she demanded. 'Ill's bride-to-be has escaped and I must get word to him.' Then she saw Mathu. 'Where are you taking my subject?'

I shoved Ishtar back into the lift and my companions piled in behind me. The goddess had no weapons, no guards, and no true psychic power any more. The only threat she posed to me right now was if she had an opportunity to raise the alarm.

'Are you insane?' she yelled as the door closed behind us and I hit the button to the lowest level. 'I'll have you all drawn and quartered for this,' she threatened, seeing only our Dracon disguises.

'Your time among the Nefilim is at an end,' I told her — for I couldn't allow her to return to their ranks; it wouldn't take her long to put two and two together and blow Ereshkigal's cover.

She realised she wasn't dealing with a Dracon. 'Who are you?'

I pulled out my liquid-light gun and held it to her temple. 'Your judge and redeemer,' I said.

There was genuine fear in her eyes as the lift door opened onto the cavern that led to the lair of Cerberus. 'Kali?' she said.

'Guess again.'

The women dragged Mathu from the lift and I grabbed hold of Ishtar to escort her out as well.

'Why are we down here?' she asked, playing the vulnerable female in the hope that the male I seemed to be would take pity on her. 'You're scaring me.'

I cracked a glowstick, tossed it to Celestia, and pointed into the dark cavern. 'Go quietly to the entrance to the labyrinth and wait for me there,' I told her.

'There's no way out of here,' Ishtar warned. 'You'll never get away with this. However, I might find it in my heart to help you,' and her dress conveniently dropped down her arm to reveal her beautiful bare shoulder.

I assumed my true form. 'You have been enough help.'

Ishtar pulled her dress back up, disappointed that I was female, but she smiled just the same. 'Well,

well, if it isn't the wife of my favourite toy boy,' she said and folded her arms defiantly.

I was tempted to fill her full of liquid light and be done with it. However, Levi had warned that if we converted the Nefilim to the light by force, without giving them an opportunity to realise their mistakes, we ran the risk of their souls having to learn the same lessons all over again once they rejoined the ranks of the Anu, which could lead to a repeat of the entire Kali rift disaster. I recalled Ereshkigal's advice: *Empathise.*

'I've managed to undo the damage you did to Arcturus,' I advised Ishtar. 'He remembers nothing of your abuse.'

'My abuse!' Ishtar laughed. 'I was the one left bruised by *his* enthusiasm.'

Again her words got a rise out of me, and I was forced to restrain my compulsion to lash out and make her suffer for all the hurt she had caused others. *She is controlling you,* I warned myself, *why are you allowing her to waste your energy on a lie? Arcturus despises her. And she certainly holds no true love for him, as she has no idea what true love is; or does she?* My memory of this goddess's legends reminded me that she was once very much in love.

'What happened to you, Ishtar?' I asked. 'Why must you destroy the relationships of others in order to feel good about yourself?' My heartfelt concern seemed to unnerve her a little. 'You were once a goddess of beauty,' I went on. 'You were happy and in love, don't you remember?'

She shook her head adamantly, but she remembered all right.

Before their Orme addiction, the Nefilim had been mentally advanced spiritual beings who were developing emotional bodies. But with their addiction, their natural descent into physical matter had been rushed and their underdeveloped emotional bodies had perished under the pressure.

'What happened to your love?' I asked.

'Marduk happened!' she snapped. 'He filled Tammuz's head with all that Kian em-bed-path rubbish!'

'Your love is one of the Anu?'

'He ceased to be my love when he chose the Kian way over me,' she spat back.

'So you would rather be damned than admit that Tammuz loved you enough to try to save your soul?'

Ishtar appeared stunned by the question; obviously no one had ever presented the scenario to her in that light before.

'I didn't realise the long-term effects of Orme when I first started taking it,' she defended. 'Tammuz did try to warn me, but I didn't listen.' She gasped at the thought that he may have been acting out of love and not selfishness. 'It was against the will of Ill not to ingest back then,' she explained. 'I thought Tammuz was trying to get us expelled from the Pantheon!'

'I understand your reasons, and he will too,' I said, encouraging her to be brave. 'The past is history, tomorrow is a mystery, but you can alter your destiny right now.'

Ishtar shook her head and grinned. 'I see what you're trying to do. But I won't relinquish my power on a false hope.'

'Is that what you told Tammuz when he told you that he believed your souls could be saved?' I retorted, and the goddess gasped; clearly I had touched on a memory.

She dropped to her knees, clutching her hands over her heart as if it pained her so much that she wished she could rip it out. 'He was all I ever wanted and I drove him away!' she wailed. 'I couldn't conceive ... and I wanted his baby so desperately. I didn't know that my addiction had already ruined me for motherhood ... I should have listened to him!'

I saw the blackened heart centre in her light-body burst open and light come shooting out. She cried out in pain and tears gushed from her eyes. She raised her fingers to investigate the strange wet sensation on her face. 'Tears?'

'Emotion,' I concurred. 'There is no going back for you now, Ishtar; your heart has opened.'

'There is too much horror!' she cried. 'My crimes have been too great!'

The thought of facing her lover after all these aeons spent in darkness was just too overwhelming. Her voice cracked with shame and she collapsed to the floor to weep out her despair.

'I forgive you, Ishtar,' I told her honestly. I felt my heart burning strong with Blue Flame energy and it poured in a great stream towards her.

'No,' she begged, humbled by the heightened frequency she was experiencing. 'Punish me!' She tore away her beautiful persona to reveal the true monster she had become. 'Throw me to the demons I have fed! Please! I would rather die than have Tammuz see me like this.' She bowed low at my feet, overwhelmed by her newly found emotion.

'You have suffered enough,' I said, and placed a hand on her head in comfort. Then I shot a bullet of liquid light into her body and moved back — her purge was bound to be a messy one.

'Steady on!' Dexter called out, running down the tunnel towards me. 'Do you plan on taking the whole of Irkalla back with us?'

Ereshkigal, wearing her true Anu form, followed Dexter and was stunned to see Ishtar's horrible physical form convulsing and spewing black muck all over the floor. 'Oh no,' she said.

'I had no choice, she would have exposed you,' I told her apologetically.

Ereshkigal looked worried. 'This is inconvenient. Ishtar is everyone's favourite squeeze ... my kin will certainly notice her missing.'

'And Tamar, and Mathu.' Killian arrived, counting off our rescues on his fingers. 'And you're going to cop the blame for it, Ereshkigal, whether it was your fault or not.' He knew well enough how the Nefilim operated. 'Perhaps you should also return with us?'

'Then who will guard the porthole,' she said light-heartedly. 'Not to worry, I'll convince them that Ishtar was tricked by Lamhfada, and that he rescued Mathu and Kali. Whenever anything like this happens Lamhfada gets the credit, which is why his legend has grown so great. He's had nothing to do with half the feats accredited to him.'

Killian found this amusing. The two of them stood staring at each other for longer than either of them realised. The Anu agent broke the spell. 'I should really be getting back. I left the porthole open for you.'

We all thanked Ereshkigal for her help.

Killian trailed her to the lift. 'So how long are you planning to stay undercover in Irkalla?' he asked.

'As long as it takes,' she replied.

'You never get a weekend off, no down time?' he joked, sorry that he didn't have time to get to know her better.

Ereshkigal shook her head.

'No chance of a dinner date then?' Killian said, and she laughed at his wit.

'We are soul minds apart, you and I. Perhaps in the next universe?' She waved as the lift door closed.

We had a bit of cleaning up to do after our journey to Irkalla. Castor saw our ladies of the night to safety via his station at Land's End, England. Dexter delivered Ishtar to Lamhfada via the interchange beneath Giza; which left Killian and me watching over our unconscious patients at Polaris's station in Nova Scotia.

'How are they doing?' Killian asked when I returned to the conference room, tired of watching them sleep.

'They seem fine,' I said, collapsing into a chair and resting my upper body on the table. 'Oh goddess, that feels good. I can hardly wait to get back to 2017 so I can have a bath and recoup.'

Killian smiled. 'How long until the others get back, do you think?'

'Hard to say.' I closed my eyes.

'Hey.' Killian roused me with a shake on the shoulder. 'I don't know about you, but I could really use some fresh air.'

I found the idea hugely appealing after being in the Underworld so long. 'What a sterling idea.'

It was dawn outside. The sun sparkled on the soft blue waters of the bay in the distance and the view through the trees from up high on the side of the island mountain was spectacular and invigorating to the soul.

'I hope she'll be okay,' Killian said, his gaze fixed on the horizon.

He didn't have to specify who he meant. 'Ereshkigal has been a player in this war for longer than you and I put together,' I said. 'She knows how to take care of herself.'

'As do you, Meridan — you were amazing in the field today.'

This was the first time Killian had used my staff name; he'd always called me Mia up to now. I guessed it was his way of removing any possibility of intimacy from our relationship, and I appreciated it.

'You did pretty well yourself,' I replied.

Killian scoffed. 'I didn't do anything! It was predicted that some day I'd be of aid to you, but I don't think today was it. At least, I hope it wasn't.' He gave a half-laugh, disappointed. 'I've survived so much, I'd like to think it was for a valid reason. Still, I learned a lot on our journey.' He turned to look me in the eye at last. 'Thank you for taking me with you, and trusting me, and mothering me for the past twenty years.'

This was sounding suspiciously like a goodbye.

'I have some really firm ideas now about what needs to be done,' he went on, looking back out to sea.

Now I was getting really concerned. 'What are you talking about?'

'I'm going to take your advice, Meridan: don't rebel, excel! And I've bought myself an additional fourteen years to do it.'

I took his arm. 'You must come back to the future with us.'

'Must I?'

'Yes,' I insisted. 'This isn't your proper time zone, Killian. Leaving you here could cause all kinds of disasters!'

'Thanks so very much for the vote of confidence,' he jested, 'but the Lord of the Earth wills it.'

'The Sanat Kumara?' I didn't wait for his answer; it didn't matter. What mattered was talking him out of doing something potentially disastrous. 'Killian, listen —'

'No, Meridan, it is you who must listen. I have something of a mystery to share with you before I go.'

Trying to dissuade him was like ramming my head against a brick wall, so I allowed him to sit me down and prepared to listen to what he had to tell me.

'It concerns the Ring of Power,' he began.

'You told me you'd given it to Lamhfada for safekeeping,' I said. 'That's what I asked you to do.'

'Well, that's the mystery,' he said. 'It turns out that I never had it to give him in the first place. The ring I gave Lamhfada was nothing but a small strip of material.' He pulled the fabric out from behind his wristwatch and placed it against the leg of the Amenti staff suit he was wearing. 'An exact match, wouldn't you say?' He handed the sliver of material to me.

'So you don't know where the true ring is?' I asked in a panic.

'No, but one of your staff members surely does.'

'Damn it! Every time I think that ring is secure, it disappears again!' I stood up to take a few deep breaths and calm myself.

'Just thought I owed it to you to let you know.'

'I appreciate your honesty,' I said, but found myself alone.

'Killian!' I screamed out my frustration over the chasm, but my anger was short-lived. *I am in so much trouble*, I thought.

'You just let him take off?' Polaris freaked when he heard about Killian going AWOL in 2003. 'We'll have to go and find him.'

'You won't find him,' I said. 'He's smarter and faster than us. Castor has the genetic proof of it.'

'So you think we should just let him loose in the hope that he uses his powers for good and doesn't fall back in with his old company now that he's *twice* as powerful as he was before?' My husband was finding it difficult to understand my reasoning. 'That's a big ask!'

'The risk factor is enormous,' Dexter agreed.

Castor and Levi remained silent, reserving judgement; and my Dragon sisters held their tongues too.

'Killian claimed it was the will of the Sanat Kumara that he stay here in the past,' I told them.

'To do what?' Dexter asked.

'I don't know!' I said, exasperated. 'I'm not Killian's keeper! He has his own will, his own ideas, and I don't know what they are any more than you do.'

'But you spent twenty years in his company,' my husband pointed out again.

I was tired of hearing it. 'I often avoided his company during that period, as I didn't feel comfortable spending a lot of time with him,' I said, wanting to lay his curiosity to rest once and for all.

'He spent most of the time with Lamhfada. Ask *him* for a character reference!'

'I will certainly do that,' Polaris assured me.

'Speaking of mysteries and Lugh Lamhfada …' I pulled the piece of fabric Killian had given me from my pocket and held it up. 'Which one of you does this belong to?'

'What is it?' Solarian asked.

'It's supposed to be the Ring of Power,' I said.

She looked perplexed. 'But it looks like a strip of fabric from one of our suits.'

Both she and Polaris looked at my husband, who was edging his way towards the door.

'You've had the ring all along!' Polaris said, incensed.

'Which meant it never actually fell into Nefilim hands, so you ought to thank me for saving your arse!' Arcturus said with a grin, then ducked out of the room.

Polaris went after him. 'I can't trust you to do something as simple as deliver a ring! Hand it over!'

'It really doesn't matter what century you're in, some things never change,' Solarian said, rolling her eyes, and I quite agreed.

'So what do we do about Killian?' Dexter seemed the only person still concerned.

'Show of hands for taking Killian at his word and leaving him at liberty?' Solarian requested.

All bar Dexter raised his hand. Even if Polaris and Arcturus were in the room, the vote would have gone against them.

Solarian made the official announcement. 'Killian stays! The ring and the rod are both secured, our missing team member has been found, and all the Signet stations are operational. That would seem to be mission accomplished, people.'

We all applauded.

It was time to go home and face the new future we had created during the past few days. I prayed with all my heart that it would be better than, or at least on a par with, the future we had left behind. Trusting Killian was an enormous leap of faith for the staff of Amenti. In my heart I felt he would accomplish great things; but in my mind there was still a tiny shadow of a doubt that perhaps this boy genius was playing both sides in this war to his own advantage. Left to his own devices, would Killian continue to walk in the light or fall back into shadow? Only time would tell.

Due to the breakdown of the Nefilim HAARP project in 2003 we could not be tracked, and so the captain decided to take the direct route home through time using the *Klieo*'s time-hopping function. Thus, I would soon discover if my instincts about Killian were correct, or whether I had led the entire plan to ruin in the quantum blink of an eye.

PART 3

QUANTUM WARFARE

CHAPTER 27

SPHERE OF THE BLUE FLAME

Mia Devere — MERIDAN

Upon our return to 2017, Polaris parked the *Klieo* in the cavern of Mamer and our entire crew proceeded to the Hall of Records beneath Giza for the debriefing. As Kali and Mathu were still unconscious, they were transported to a recovery room within the labyrinth incorporated into the Amenti complex of Signet Station Four.

Denera and Zalman awaited us in the Hall of Records chamber. They were both smiling, which I took to be a good sign. Denera's eyes were focused on me as we assembled before her. 'Come forth, little sister, I am so proud of you,' she said, and met me halfway across the floor with a huge hug.

'What did I do?' I asked. I was used to being the one who screwed up.

Denera gave me a look that implied I was being too modest. 'Come now,' she urged, but I couldn't guess. 'Okay, I'll show you.'

She went to the Hall of Records' control module, which enclosed her in its telepathically sensitive security tube. 'Christian Molier, 1 April 2017,' she commanded aloud, to give us a hint of what we were about to witness.

'But I dealt with Molier in 2003!' Arcturus said, confused.

'Who dealt with Molier?' Thana placed her hands on her hips.

Arcturus nodded, giving her the credit. 'The point is, he should be dead!'

The liquid-light walls of the chamber lit up, giving us the sensation of standing on an open platform in the middle of a huge crowd of people in Central Park, New York. There was a lone speaker standing behind a podium, his back to us. Dark-haired, tall and slender, he certainly looked like Molier.

'Why the hell have all these people gathered to hear Christian Molier speak?' Polaris asked.

There was something else very odd about this. 'It used to be hard enough to get Molier to meet with his closest business partners,' I said, stunned, 'but to address a crowd of thousands?'

'Shh,' urged Denera, 'listen to what he's saying.'

'What we ask is that during the time we're running this experiment in the Big Apple, YOU, the people of this city, give us more than just your attention. We want some of your greatest, purest, most compassionate and peaceful INTENTION!'

The crowd let loose a roar of support.

'In cities the world over, the Peace Project has made an astonishing difference to the quality of life. In Washington, one week of intensive positive focus, en masse, reduced crime and sickness in that city by fifty per cent in the following year!'

The crowd applauded.

'So please, give the people working on the Peace

Project down here in the park for the next week your fullest support and let's see if we can't all make this city a happier, healthier and safer place to live.'

The speaker waved to the crowd in every direction and to the cameras before he turned to leave the lectern and then we saw his face.

'It's Killian!' I gasped, relieved and excited.

Now Arcturus was getting a clearer picture. 'We disposed of Molier and Killian stole his identity.'

'Not to mention Molier's business holdings and huge fortune,' Denera added, 'which he has channelled into this Peace Project.'

I was flabbergasted. 'I know Killian looks a lot like Molier, but he's very obviously not him. How —'

'— did he do this?' Denera cut in, and stepped down from her control platform. 'As you said just now, Molier wasn't a very social creature ... hardly anyone in this century knew what he looked like. As to the few who did, Killian has psychically persuaded them that he is Molier. He's very powerful, your student, and we have extremely high hopes for him. So what did you do, my dear Meridan? You managed to identify and train the Chosen One, who in turn has spent the last fourteen years establishing an elite following of psychics and scientists, and, using quantum physics as his doctrine, has managed to clear many of the primary blockages in the Earth grid!'

Dexter had a chuckle as his greatest concern about the opening of Amenti was washed away. 'It seems he worked out how to be of assistance, after all. You just have to love the little SOB.'

'He's been promoting the science of photo-sonics,' Denera explained — which was Dexter's and Vespera's area of expertise — 'and he's raised scientific awareness of the possibility of twelve-strand DNA.' Castor's and Talori's field. 'He's also put forward a thesis on how HAARP and other such ionospheric modification facilities might use their climate-control capabilities to refreeze the Antarctic and the North Pole.'

'Cheeky,' Dexter said with a grin. 'The Nefilim have been working a long time to get their mother ship out of the deep freeze.'

'Is he being hailed as the next Messiah?' Solarian asked, concerned this might end up being a repeat of the Jesus episode.

Denera waved off her concern. 'Well, of course he is. But Killian, or Chris as he's now known, has stuck firmly to the science angle and so far it's served him well. The lad is as charismatic as he ever was, but instead of playing the rebel, he's reinvented himself as an innovative, proactive instigator of all things positive for the future of the planet, in both a scientific and a spiritual sense. He leads by example and, due to the influence of the activated Signet stations, people the world over have been open to his theories and discoveries. Chris Molier has inspired millions to create peace, love and beauty with the power of their intent.'

My heart welled with pride that a little bit of understanding, faith and compassion could have such long-reaching positive repercussions.

'But surely the Nefilim have figured out who Chris really is?' Levi was amazed he was still alive.

'He's too powerful, psychically and socially, for the Nefilim to take him out. As you see, he leaves himself completely vulnerable to attack.' Denera motioned back to the screen where Killian was moving freely through the crowd, meeting people and chatting, with no bodyguards, no security, no weapons. 'He wears his fearlessness like a shield and people adore and admire him for it. There have been a few assassination attempts, but Chris never flinches and is never hit. His reputation for dodging death has reached superhero status, but he insists that his only defence is his *intention* to live.'

'So the boy did good.' Polaris sounded a little surprised. 'Sorry, Meridan, I should have trusted your instinct.'

Solarian gave my husband a nudge, as he also owed me an apology.

'Okay, so you were right about him,' Arcturus admitted. 'But he didn't turn out to be Mathu,' he was quick to add. 'We were right about Emmett.'

'But your wonderful work with Killian isn't the only reason I'm so proud of you,' Denera said, looking at me again. 'You managed to deliver Ishtar via non-violent means. Your daughter could still learn a thing or two from you.'

'Were there any repercussions from Ishtar's premature disappearance from history?' I asked, recalling Ereshkigal's concern.

'Nothing too drastic, we suspect.'

'You sound unsure,' I prompted; which was very unlike Denera.

'The Anu have heard nothing from Ereshkigal since that time, and I can't see into Irkalla through this device.' She indicated the control desk. 'But she's stayed out of contact for long periods in the past, so it's probably nothing to worry about.'

'I'll go and retrieve her.' Dexter was halfway to the door.

'She's Lamhfada's concern at present, not ours,' Denera said firmly, bringing Dexter to a standstill.

'You have other work to do. Not everything you did in the past has come up roses.' Her gaze turned to Levi.

'Montauk,' he guessed. 'They've rebuilt it?'

'No, you managed to shut down that project for good.' Denera didn't sound as impressed as I'd expected.

'And HAARP?' Levi prompted.

'There are now facilities of its kind all over the world.' Denera delivered the sting. 'And, thanks to the way you brought Montauk down, all the systems have EM pulse guards, which will detect any oncoming threat, shut down the systems momentarily and reboot a few minutes later when the charge has dissipated.'

'Bugger,' muttered Levi.

'Had you pulled the same stunt in December this year, you might have been able to decommission the entire anti-grid in one strike. But now it's going be a little harder,' Zalman added.

'But Levi's act prevented Killian and me being pursued in the past!' I said.

'And we'd have had the Nefilim breathing down our necks whilst we unlocked the last three Signet stations,' Polaris added. 'As it was, our task was incident free.'

'We're not saying he did the wrong thing.' Denera grinned, pleased by how fiercely we defended each other, as siblings should. 'We're just informing you of its repercussions. There's more, but that can all wait as I feel some rest is in order. But first, there's one last thing I really must show you.'

Denera led us deep into the heart of her station, to the huge round chamber that hosted the Halls of Amenti: six perfectly round portholes, each crafted from a different shade of gold — red, orange, yellow, pink, blue, and the last, a stunning and rare violet. All of the passages were filled with liquid light that reflected the colour of each doorway; it streamed from top to bottom like a waterfall.

We had all visited this chamber before, and walked the halls that led to humanity's root races past and future, hence we instantly realised there was something spectacularly different about the chamber today. The added attraction lay in, or rather above, the large round pool at its heart. Directly above the horizontal porthole, the ceiling disappeared into the huge funnel of the Arc porthole passage. The beautiful silvery stargate therein was shedding considerably more light than usual onto the indigo liquid-light pool beneath.

The light was so potent in Blue Flame energy that it sent me into seventh heaven. I took a great leap onto the pool and slid gracefully across its surface to bask in the light. Inside the enormous funnel sat a huge glowing sphere, just beyond its liquid barrier. The sphere was white at its edges, and faded into the beautiful blue-green projected from the Blue Flame at its heart, but deep in its centre lay a much smaller, intense violet flame: the staff of Amenti's ticket home to Tara.

'It is the Sphere of Amenti!' I called back to my teammates who were still catching me up.

'Wow!' Dexter slid to a stop beside me and gazed up into the light. 'Now all we have to do is drop that little baby down into the Earth's core … and *bam*, a porthole link between Earth's core in dimension two and Tara's core in dimension five.'

'We'll be back in the Ranna time flow,' Polaris finished.

We all stared up at the cosmic wonder whose return we had been preparing for for all eternity.

'Has the planetary consciousness been raised enough to host the sphere?' Talori asked Denera.

'Not quite,' she admitted, trying not to sound discouraging. 'But at the rate Chris Molier is clearing the dams in the grid, and encouraging people to free their minds from religious barriers to embrace the power of their own positive intent, it won't be long before the frequency scale finally tips in our favour.'

'Well, I suppose we should go see if our "little miracle on Earth" needs a hand with anything,' Arcturus said, and I could tell by his tone that he still didn't trust Killian.

'Exactly right,' Denera said, looking at me.

'You want me to go to New York? But Tamar will need —'

'You know him best; he trusts you,' she appealed gently.

'I'll be here for Tamar,' Arcturus said, although he couldn't have been keen for me to hook up with Killian again. 'I'll let you know the second anything changes.'

'I'm sending Vespera and Talori with you, as they can aid Chris's scientists with their research,' Denera concluded.

Talori and Vespera both nodded, inspired by the thought of going undercover into the field.

'But rest first,' Denera insisted. 'The pleasures of my labyrinth are at your disposal. Refresh yourselves and enjoy.'

The staff gave a cheer, and everyone hugged their significant other. Everyone except Arcturus and me; we stood apart, eyeing each other reservedly.

350

Polaris noticed our hesitation. 'Come on, you two, you're not going to let a wee difference in opinion spoil a perfectly good celebration, are you?'

Arcturus and I each went to speak, then both stopped.

I tried again. 'I'm not mad, I'm just frustrated.' I turned on my heel, slid across the pool and jumped onto the chamber floor.

'That's what I was going to say.' My husband came after me and followed me up the six flights of stairs to the security cavern that led to the labyrinth.

Even for someone with superhuman stamina, I was breathing heavily when I got to the top. 'You'd think that with all the technology at our disposal we could install a goddamn lift!'

'But the view on the way up wouldn't be anywhere near as splendid,' Arcturus said with a lustful grin, and I caught my breath — the moment of our reunion, the moment I'd dreamt of for twenty years, was finally upon me. 'I miss married life,' he confessed.

'Me too.' I burst into tears, relieved to finally be on the same wavelength, and threw myself into my husband's arms and kissed him repeatedly.

'I vote we forget about saving the universe for a bit ...' Arcturus hoisted me up and I wrapped my legs around his hips as he carried me over the extension bridge, '... and take advantage of Denera's hospitality.'

'I couldn't agree more.'

I cast off all thought of the outside world to focus on the centre of my universe for a change.

CHAPTER 28

PSYCHOSIS

ASHLEE GRANVILLE-DEVERE — SOLARIAN
The staff members were particularly chipper after a rest period in Amenti's magnificent accommodation, built and designed by our ultra-terrestrial selves to cater for the very few occasions our mortal selves were able to relax and recoup our vitality. Still, after eight hours of surface Earth standard time, play break was over and we all reported for duty.

While Polaris transported Meridan, Talori and Vespera to New York in the *Klieo*, I accompanied Arcturus to the recovery area, where Castor was keeping an eye on Mathu and Kali, in separate rooms for the present.

To our delight, when we entered the observation area between the two recovery rooms, we found Mathu sitting upright on the edge of his bed. Levi was visiting him, having a chat. They were old friends from way back.

'We did it!' Mathu was groggy, but his voice was full of relief and excitement. 'I knew you would find me,' he looked from Levi to the rest of us, 'all of you! You have all been my star pupil at one time or another.'

He nodded at Castor with great affection. 'Arthur, my master shaman, the saviour of the Rod of Power. How are you coping with the consciousness shifts from that time junction we created off Land's End at the end of your reign?'

'Dear Myrddin, how I have missed your conversation.' Castor returned the fond sentiment. 'I'm doing just fine, thank you.'

'Aleka.' Mathu's sights turned to me; I too had spent a few lifetimes in the company of the master scribe. 'When you saved the plan with your bravery during the demise of Poseidonis, I was so very proud of you ... and look how far you have come!'

I was flattered. Mathu was far more charming than I remembered, but of course he had never fully occupied a human body before and so now he had an emotional side.

'I could say the same of you, Master Hermes.'

He waved off my adulation and looked to Arcturus. 'Vishtaspa, my greatest patron,' he said, and Arcturus smiled. 'I wrote hymns about you and the Kavi, you know.'

The Kavi were a semi-mythological dynasty of ancient Persia and Central Asia.

'Yes, Zoroaster, I know and I am very honoured,' Arcturus replied. Noticing my interest, he added to me in an aside, 'Persia, sixth century BCE.'

'Yes, I've read the *Gathas*,' I replied, for the ancient doctrine of Zoroastrianism had formed part of my studies within my lifetime as Ashlee Granville-Devere. 'You were one of the legendary kings of the Kavi dynasty then?'

'Indeed, or so the third hall of Amenti revealed to me.'

In the other recovery room, Tamar gave a groan of what sounded like pleasure.

'Tamar is waking up,' Castor informed Levi and Mathu through the intercom.

Arcturus was in the lab faster than anyone could deny him access. Mathu followed at a slower pace, staggering into the room with Levi's aid.

'Come closer,' Tamar whispered in a sultry tone, her hands caressing her thighs.

Arcturus and Mathu looked at each other across the bed, neither man sure who had precedence in this instance. Was it her father or her lover-to-be she needed most right now? Arcturus stepped back and motioned for Mathu to take a seat beside his sleeping daughter.

'Yes,' Tamar gasped, as if overwhelmed by desire. 'I am yours.' Her hands slid over her gown to clutch her breasts.

Arcturus looked alarmed and very uncomfortable.

'My queen.' Mathu leaned over to caress Tamar's cheek and wake her. 'My love.'

Tamar's arm came up forcefully and held Mathu at bay. 'Killian?' she said.

'No. It is I, Mathu.'

'Deceiver!' Tamar yelled, sitting up, and the force of her anger sent Mathu flying into the far wall. Although she was upright, her eyelids were still closed. 'Go back to your whores!'

Arcturus stepped in. Sitting down next to her, he gripped her shoulders to attempt to shake her to consciousness. 'Sweetheart, wake up.'

'Leave me alone!' she yelled in his face. 'I hate you!'

'Tamar? It's Daddy, sweetheart.'

'I don't want you here!'

Arcturus went flying across the room to join

Mathu on the floor. Tamar threw herself backwards and, gripping her head, went into a screaming fit.

Castor sprang from his chair. 'She's having a psychotic episode. We're going to have to sedate her.' He sought my assistance and I nodded.

We entered the lab stealthily; thankfully our subject appeared too engrossed in her own suffering to notice us. I moved to one side of the bed, ready to restrain her if required, whilst Castor approached from the other side, holding the gun containing the sedative dart.

As soon as Kali felt the metal implement against her skin, her eyes shot open and Castor, too, was sent flying across the room. She looked at me and I shook my head to let her know she'd better not try the same stunt. There was intense hatred in her wild violet eyes, yet I maintained my defiant glare as I willed the sedative gun into my hand.

Fuck you.

I heard her thought and pre-empted her strike with my own will to restrain her.

Her will impacted on me, but I was only cast off balance a second before I was able to impose my will upon her. As my intent was pure and genuine, it won out — Kali was pinned to her bed.

I placed the device against her shoulder.

'Yes, send me back to him,' she invited as I squeezed the trigger.

'To who?' I asked, too late, for she smiled as the sedative took hold, and then groaned again with pleasure just before she blacked out.

'Goddamn it,' said Levi, 'they really got to her. We should never have let her go her own way.'

I'd forgotten he was in the room. Now that I looked at him closely, I could see that he was traumatised by the change in Kali.

'We didn't *let* her go,' Arcturus argued, picking himself up off the floor. 'Kali *insisted*. We just shouldn't have listened.' I could hear in his voice the tears he was holding back. 'Is the damage permanent?' he asked Castor, helping him to his feet, then giving Mathu a hand up too.

'Even in the most ideal brainwashing conditions, the effects of the process are most often short term,' Castor was pleased to be able to inform us. 'The victim's old identity isn't eradicated by the process, it's just in hiding, and once the "new identity" is no longer reinforced, the person's previous attitudes and beliefs will start to return. We discovered that with Levi.'

'If the Nefilim have imprinted her psyche with negative beliefs about you two, it might be best if you don't see her until she's recovered some of her true self,' Levi suggested. 'You're both negative triggers for her just now,' he explained further when Tamar's father and partner objected strongly. 'Until we can get her to remember otherwise, she's going to see you as evil, which will retrigger the false memories and perpetuate the problem. We're going to have to move her to the top-security holding cell for the time being anyway.'

Arcturus winced; he'd spent some time himself in the gold Orme-reinforced cell. 'Is that really necessary?'

Levi frowned. 'Considering what you've just seen, do you really have to ask?'

Who is the HE she wanted me to send her back to? I wondered quietly. I placed my fingertips to her neck and extracted the answer. *Killian*. 'I thought so,' I said aloud.

'What did you think?' Arcturus asked.

'That Ill is fiendishly clever.'

What better way to foil our plan than to set Kali and Mathu against each other and place Killian right in the middle?

'How long until Tamar starts to remember her old identity?' I asked Castor.

'Levi took the better part of a season to recover, and even then he still had flashbacks.'

'Well,' I said, taking a deep breath, 'we still have eight months up our sleeve. Let's hope it will be enough.'

Mathu was shaking with remorse and anger. 'Our enemies got to her before I did *again*! I have failed her, over and over.'

'Rubbish,' I told him. 'If you hadn't defeated Pintar, she wouldn't be here at all. She will recover, and when she does we will end this war and go home. Understand, Mathu, you have an underdeveloped emotional body and at first it will cause you to doubt yourself.' I placed a hand on his shoulder. 'But you must believe in the power of love; it truly will conquer all.'

'You've been through a huge ordeal yourself,' Castor added. 'You may be a demi-god but that doesn't mean you don't need to rest and recuperate after having your consciousness bounced about through time for aeons.'

Mathu was dumbstruck a moment and slightly discomforted. 'Why do I suddenly feel like a novice among masters?'

I laughed at the role reversal. 'Well, we've been human a hell of a lot longer.'

'And some of us still can't get it right,' Arcturus said, forcing a grin. He couldn't stop his gaze drifting back to his daughter.

'Don't you start believing the negative rubbish Ill put in that girl's head!' I gave my old friend a shake. 'I know you're worried, but have a little faith in your daughter's abilities. She will come through this.'

He nodded and put on a brave face, but I knew deep down he also felt he'd let her down. 'What should I tell Meridan?' he asked.

'She's going to lose her focus if she knows we have problems here,' Castor advised. 'Wait a week or so and see if Tamar's condition improves any, then the news you deliver may not be so bad.'

Arcturus was unsure. 'I think she has the right to know that our daughter now hates us!' His hurt began bubbling to the surface. 'Goddess knows what kind of perverse vision of us the Nefilim have pumped into her head!'

'It doesn't matter.' Levi grabbed hold of Arcturus by the shirtfront to get his full attention. 'It's false!'

I separated the two men, who were glaring at each other, although Levi appeared to have got his point across. 'If you like, I can work with Castor during her recovery and find out exactly what falsehoods Ill has filled her mind with,' I offered.

'That would be wonderful,' Arcturus said gratefully. He knew I rarely used my psychic skill to probe the minds of others, but in this case I thought it justified. 'But won't you experience all that she has?' he went on, concerned.

'I need see only fragments, not enough to be harmful,' I assured him, although inside I was dreading the process. Still, we Dragon Queens had been so focused on getting the grid up and running that we had lost sight of our primary objective — to protect the key to Amenti, Kali. I felt I had much to make amends for and so any pain I might suffer as I tried to right this tragic oversight would be a small price to pay.

CHAPTER 29

THE PEACE PROJECT

MIA DEVERE — MERIDAN

I hadn't walked the streets of New York since my university days at NYU, and it felt strangely surreal to be back in the real world again. We strutted through Central Park, my two Dragon sisters and I, getting hit on by every group of males that passed us. Spring was in the air, the sun shone overhead and the park was abloom with beautiful pink tulips, cherry blossoms and myriad other fragrant flowers. This natural oasis was a world away from the crowded streets of the city that bordered its environs and the atmosphere seemed alive with positive frequency — whatever Killian was doing to the people down here it was certainly working!

'Feel that energy!' Vespera commented, breathing in deeply as we approached the area of the park that the Peace Project had taken over. There were people chanting, singing, meditating, doing yoga and other disciplines involving mind, body and spirit coordination, and yet they were all in harmony with each other.

The man we had come to find, now known as

Chris Molier, was seated on a low-rise stage doing an interview with a famous night-show host.

'This has nothing to do with religion,' Chris was insisting with a cheeky smile. 'This is pure science.'

'That our intention affects everything around us?' The interviewer sounded sceptical.

'Before we say or do *anything*,' Chris explained, 'our intention is already doing the good or the damage that we *intend* to do.'

'And you can prove this?'

'I can.' Chris motioned the interviewer to follow him to another part of the stage where some machinery was set up.

'That looks like a lie detector,' the interviewer said.

'It is,' Chris confirmed, raising his eyebrows a couple of times to heighten the suspense. The crowd laughed.

'Well, I hope you don't plan on hooking me up to that,' the interviewer said, looking alarmed. He'd been privy to more than a few scandals during his career.

'Fear not,' Chris said, playing up the joke, 'this test requires a subject that's a little more innocent.' He called to one of his assistants. 'Sharon, could you bring over the unsuspecting rubber tree, please?'

This brought a great laugh from the crowd and the interviewer.

'You intend to hook that plant up to the lie detector?' he said. 'Is that legal? Could we be sued by the greenies?'

'I want to stress that the plant will not be permanently harmed in any way,' Chris said with mock seriousness.

The interviewer was almost in tears of laughter as Chris went about connecting the electrodes to the plant.

'The waxy insulation between the cells in plants causes an electrical discharge that mimics a human stress reaction,' he explained. 'A polygraph reading offers evidence of those stress levels. I'd like to point out that this wasn't my brilliant discovery, but that of Cleve Backster, this country's greatest expert in lie detectors and a refiner of the polygraph.'

Chris turned the apparatus on and directed the interviewer's attention to the monitor, which was being projected onto a bigger screen so the crowd could also see what was going on. The polygraph pen was swinging very mildly on the paper.

'As you can see, we have mild stress levels at the moment,' Chris said.

'The poor little fellow probably has stage fright,' the interviewer joked.

Chris laughed, agreeing that he was most likely right.

'Now see what happens when I say something nice.' Chris walked over and placed his hands on the leaves of the plant. 'My, but you are the most exquisite rubber tree I have ever seen. You're just gorgeous!'

The crowd applauded as the pen on the polygraph swung lower.

'No, you're not,' Chris said, changing his tune and ruffling the leaves, 'you're hideous! I don't know why you ever bothered germinating! I hate you!'

There wasn't much of a swing in the stress level of the plant at all and everyone looked confused.

'My words and actions didn't make much

difference to the plant's state of being,' Chris said. 'But what happens if I really intend it harm?'

He held out his hands in plain view of everyone, without touching the plant, and closed his eyes. Within seconds the recording pen swung to the top of the polygraph chart and nearly jumped off.

The crowd gasped, as did the reporter. To all appearances, Chris hadn't said or done anything. 'What just happened?' the interviewer asked.

'All I had to do was think about burning one of its leaves with a match,' Chris explained. Everyone was gobsmacked by the implications. 'It wasn't my action but my intention that caused this plant harm. But,' he held up a finger to let everyone know he wasn't done yet, 'what I find even more interesting is this.'

He waved his assistant forward once more and this time she brought with her a piece of slimy pipe, which she handed gingerly to Chris, an expression of disgust on her face.

Chris held the pipe up. 'This is your average piece of old sink pipe, the type you'd find in your own home, filled with years of grime and slimy build-up. In other words, *bacteria*, some of the tiniest living organisms known to man.'

As Chris spoke the polygraph did a little stress jump. 'I haven't done anything yet,' he said to the plant and the crowd giggled.

'My assistant has a jug of boiling water . . .' Again the pen did a little jump. 'Stop that,' he joked and then appealed to the crowd. 'Please don't send me hate mail for harassing plants.'

He certainly hasn't lost any of his charm, I thought; he had the entire crowd hanging on his every word and laughing at all his jokes.

'Now, I'm taking my hot water and my microbe-filled pipe all the way over here, where the plant can't see,' Chris said, causing a riot in the crowd as he moved across the stage to hide the proceedings from the plant.

As soon as the water hit the pipe the polygraph began swinging around wildly.

'The plant sensed you were going to hurt the bacteria,' the interviewer concluded.

'No, the plant felt the bacteria's distress and, being empathetic towards it, became distressed itself,' Chris corrected.

'No wonder plants won't survive in my kitchen,' commented the interviewer as he applauded the display.

'So, having discovered this and much more thanks to quantum science,' Chris said, moving back towards the interviewer but really addressing the crowd, 'I had to ask myself what would happen if we, as human beings of the twenty-first century, knowing what we know now, focused all our good intentions into the more tension-filled areas of our globe. Would it have a real impact on crime, health and well-being within that troubled area — And how could such a movement be organised? That's how the Peace Project came into being, so that through pure science — not hearsay or faith — people could be made aware of the power of their intentions. We all use the excuse that as individuals we can't make a huge difference to the troubles in the world, but I say that one person *can* make a difference. If I can send a plant into deep stress with the thought of a threat, just imagine the harm the sum total of human intention is doing to this planet. This project asks for nothing from anyone besides your best wishes for our continued success. Any involvement anyone wishes to have with us beyond that is entirely up to them.'

'Chris Molier, thank you very much for speaking with us today live from Central Park,' the interviewer said, then went into his closing spiel. Chris waved and left the platform.

'Quite the entertainer,' Talori commented.

'Apparently there are numerous science tents all around showing similar demonstrations,' Vespera enlightened us as she flicked through the program.

I looked around at all the amazed and excited faces. 'He really has created something here.'

My sights came to rest on Killian, caught up in a throng of curious and adoring fans. Fourteen years older than the last time I'd seen him, he was even more handsome: the long hair that had once hung in his eyes had been shorn into a crew cut, and his dress sense was casually classy.

'We may never get to speak with him, however,' I said. 'That crowd is ten people deep.'

'No problem.' Talori put on her large sunglasses, which made her appear even more the wealthy heiress, and strode over to the crowd. As those in the crush saw her coming, they were captivated by her regal air and parted to make way for her. 'Thank you so much,' she repeated graciously as she moved to the front of the line. Once there, she threw her arms wide. 'Chris, darling!'

For a moment our target was stunned by the beauty before him. Talori had to lower her sunglasses before he finally placed her, and then he nearly choked on the shock.

'Oh my goddess, it's you!' He laughed, over the moon to see her. 'What are you doing here?'

'We've come to help you, my love.' She patted his cheek and directed his gaze in our direction. Vespera and I waved.

'Well,' he was so caught off guard he didn't know what to say, 'that's wonderful!' His eyes were fixed on me, and a shy smile crossed his face as he excused himself from the crowd to come and greet us. 'Mia.' He held his hands out to me and kissed both my cheeks — it seemed some of his French mannerisms remained with him. 'I've been anticipating this moment for fourteen years.'

I was flattered by his attention, as I was the envy of every woman present, and painfully aware of the clicking of cameras all around us.

'I thought you'd have forgotten all about me by now.'

'Does anyone forget their greatest inspiration?' he said sweetly.

Feeling my cheeks beginning to flush, I directed his attention away from me. 'You remember Ajalae,' I said, indicating Vespera, whom he greeted warmly. 'And Susan, of course.' I picked names from their past lives; it wasn't wise to use our staff names whilst doing fieldwork.

'Of course,' he said with a delightful grin as Talori allowed him to kiss her hand. 'Well, ladies, would you do me the honour of joining me for lunch? It seems we have much to discuss.'

'I thought you'd never ask,' Talori said, taking hold of one arm. Vespera took the other. I suspected they sensed that the man's adoration made me a little uncomfortable.

I was surprised to see that the paparazzi hung back and respected his space; perhaps Chris Molier hadn't reached the high level of fame I'd imagined and was still a minor celebrity in the eyes of the press.

Over lunch in the park, during which no one bothered us, I asked Killian about the lack of media and fan harassment.

'There are times when I open myself to the attention of others and times when I don't,' he replied. 'The reason I'm not harassed is because I don't wish it . . . this is my reality, after all.'

'Bravo,' Talori said, raising her glass of sparkling water to him.

'Still, I feel your work has made a difference to everybody's consciousness on Earth,' he went on. 'Even the paparazzi aren't as aggressive as they used to be . . . they're much more respectful of the feelings of others. You have all made my job a hell of a lot easier . . . so cheers!' He raised his glass of water and toasted us in return.

All through lunch the conversation centred around Killian's science projects, especially those concerning photo-sonics, biochemistry and microbiology. Some of it was interesting to me, but most of it was very technical and lost me — partly because I was inwardly flustered by Killian's adoring gazes across the table.

'When we're done here, I'll introduce you to the respective heads of the departments you'll be assisting, if you like,' Killian suggested. 'My entire team is here.'

Talori and Vespera were very receptive to the idea, until they realised it would leave me alone with Killian. They both looked at me with pleading faces, requesting permission to abandon me.

'Don't worry about Mia,' he assured them. 'I have something special I want to show her.'

'I look forward to it,' I said with a smile, and in truth I was curious to catch up with all that had transpired in his life between his escape into 2003 and now.

'You know that disappearing act you pulled in Nova Scotia landed me in some hot water,' I said as we strolled through the project to wherever it was Killian was taking me. The smile left his face for the first time since our reunion. 'Until we got back to 2017 and I got patted on the head for letting you go,' I added.

His broad smile returned. 'Did you think I would disappoint you?'

'No,' I said firmly, 'I didn't.'

'But your husband assumed the worst?'

'He's ... protective,' I said.

'With a family such as he has, I can't blame him,' said Killian, bearing Arcturus no malice. 'The truth is, I wanted to make you proud of me,' he went on a little shyly. 'You've become something of a mother figure to me.'

Mother figure! I was so relieved to hear this.

'No offence or anything,' he said, misreading my expression. 'I know that seems a little silly now that I look older than you do —'

'No, no,' I assured him. 'I understand completely.'

'I meant a mother figure in a spiritual sense,' he clarified.

'I realise that ... and I have to say, I am proud of you. You're doing really wonderful work here. Finally, Molier's money is being put to good use.'

Killian laughed at the private joke, for only the staff of Amenti knew about his shift in identity. 'I've invested the entire fortune into the project. Thankfully, others believe in my work too and have brought their own funds and resources to the enterprise. Now it's kind of self-perpetuating; since we've had so much success in lowering crime, sickness and abuse in the cities we've worked in, we're being invited to other cities, all expenses paid! I've trained people to begin Peace Projects in other countries too, so we have affiliate groups working in India, Africa and Bosnia. There are only a few cities left on my list that I'm going to have to do some fancy negotiating to get into.'

'Your list?' I enquired, then became distracted by the sight of an old phone booth in the corner of the large marquee we'd just entered. Its windows were reinforced with blue metal screens.

'Can I get you a cuppa?' Killian motioned to the tea- and coffee-making facilities in the marquee.

'I'm good, thanks.' I approached the oddity, noticing that it even had a light on the top. 'Is this a replica of the Tardis?' I asked. 'I used to watch the *Doctor Who* series as a girl.' I reached out to open the door and the light on the top began flashing and an alarm went off.

After having a brief laugh at my expense, Killian walked over and touched the structure. The alarm went silent and the door clicked open — it sounded more like a bank safe opening than the door of a phone booth. 'Proof that Lugh Lamhfada has a sense of humour — this is his contribution to my cause,' Killian explained as he waved me into the dark space with him.

Once the door closed behind us, the lights came on, illuminating a control centre with huge monitors connected to microcomputers all around the room, all of which were performing different functions.

'This is amazing.' I was more impressed by the structure than its contents. 'This is the kind of thing I'd love to be designing — what an amazing example of etheric engineering.'

'I knew you'd appreciate it.' Killian moved to a control in the centre of the room — it looked a bit like the *Klieo*'s holographic console, although it was operated by a keyboard instead of a telepathic plate. 'As you've already guessed, this is an etheric interior inside a physical shell,' he said. 'The *Artemis* —'

'Greek goddess of light,' I cut in, liking the name.

'I always thought you were rather like Artemis — quick to defend the powerless from unjust treatment,' Killian stated and I had to laugh.

'I wasn't Artemis,' I assured him, 'but I was killed by her brother Heracles once.'

'Mad!' Killian said with a laugh. 'So, as I was saying, the *Artemis* doesn't move through time and space, but she's a wonderfully efficient way of moving my operations base around. She's completely mobile and —'

'— and you leave her sitting in a tent in Central Park?' I couldn't believe he'd risk such a precious thing being stolen.

Killian waved off my concern. 'Mia, you are *so* last dimension. Get with the times! The people in this time line you created are much more trustworthy. Besides, the *Artemis* will only open or move for me.'

'She's attuned to your personal sonic,' I deduced.

'Exactly. Now, you asked about my list.' He punched a few commands into the control panel and a holographic globe of the world appeared before us, its surface overlaid by patches of shadow and light.

'It's monitoring consciousness,' I said as I realised that the brightest patches on the globe were where our Signet stations were located.

'Frequency, yes,' he said. 'My hot list of cities the Peace Project must visit is derived from my prior knowledge of spook world operations and this monitoring system. Some sites are obvious as they've seen so much bloodshed: Jerusalem, Vietnam, Tibet —'

'I would have expected Belfast to be worse,' I commented, noticing that it appeared clear of shadow.

'We've already been through Ireland and closed down the dark vortex there,' he said, grinning triumphantly. 'There were a few surprises in the dark porthole stakes though.' He pointed to a very dark patch over Italy.

'Oh my goddess, I know the Romans did some terrible things there in ancient times, but ...?'

'Illuminati,' he explained. 'One of the primary portholes to Irkalla is located there, beneath the Vatican City.'

When I thought about this, it made sense. Back in her days as Ashlee Granville-Devere, Solarian had had a run-in with a Holy See official from the Church of Rome who had been taken over by one of the Nefilim. And in my own past life experiences I had seen, at the very least, an information alliance between the church and the spook world.

'Jeez,' I whistled at the size of his ambitions, 'that *is* going to require some fancy negotiating skills. Have you been visited by any of your old Underworld associates?'

'Not directly, but I have had death threats and there've been a few assassination attempts. They've had no success though, and it's all been great press for me.'

My gaze wandered off to the other screens around the outer walls of the round chamber — one of which was monitoring the exterior of the *Artemis*. I saw that a woman had entered the tent. She was very good-looking and was dressed all in black leather.

'Killian ... sorry, Chris, I think someone's looking for you?' I pointed to the woman. 'Do you know her?'

'Not yet,' Killian smiled. 'Shall we?' He motioned to the door.

'I think I'll go into security mode.' I vanished from his sight. 'If that's all right by you?'

'Works for me ... after you.' He opened the door and shut the lights off.

I stepped aside once we'd left the *Artemis*. Killian looked at the beautiful stranger, who was obviously seeking him out as the look on her face was one of awe and relief.

'Are you looking for me?' he asked hopefully.

'Killian,' she said, and my heart nearly stopped beating. I was sure his must have skipped a beat or two as well, but he played naive.

'It's me,' she said. She looked around to check no one could see her and transformed into her true Anu self.

'*Ereshkigal!*' Killian was completely delighted for

the second time today, but the woeful look on the Anu woman's face tempered his joy. 'What brings you here?' he asked. 'Is something wrong?'

She resumed her disguise and forced a smile. 'I decided to take you up on that dinner date.'

He wasn't buying her story and raised both eyebrows to appeal for the truth.

'I can't do it any more,' she said in quiet distress. A human would have been sobbing by this point but the Anu rarely shed tears, even under the greatest duress. Nevertheless, her entire body was trembling. 'Ishtar's disappearance has left a lot of bored males in Irkalla. When I only had to deal with Erragal's unwanted attentions, that was one thing, but they've done things to me ...' She couldn't bring herself to expand on this. 'I just can't do it any more, I'm losing myself. Please help me ...'

'It's okay.' Killian hugged her and she melted into his embrace as if she had finally come home. 'We'll take you to Lamhfada.'

'No,' she said quickly, 'not yet. I want to stay with you.' She hugged him tighter. 'I have dreamt of little else for what seems an eternity.' She raised her big soulful eyes to him and kissed him passionately.

This is uncomfortable, I thought. Almost as if he detected my discomfort, Killian brought the steamy moment to an end. 'I've thought about you too, believe me,' he said, 'but now isn't the time —'

She kissed him again, and with such desire that he either forgot or didn't care that I was present.

As they were in the throes of expressing their feelings for each other, I got to wondering: how had Ereshkigal escaped? She couldn't use Dexter's porthole, and she hadn't contacted any of her Anu kin or the staff of Amenti. I glanced back to the star-crossed lovers just in time to see the lady in question activate an Orme spike from her wristband.

I had disarmed the weapon and restrained her in an arm lock before Killian even realised his bliss was over.

'That would explain why they let you out,' I said. 'An *assassination*.'

Killian looked stunned when I showed him the weapon. He detached it from Ereshkigal's wrist and asked her why she'd done it. He was hurt to the core and I was very surprised not to see his dark side surface.

'I told you, they did things to me,' she defended, appearing as horrified as we were by what she had intended to do. 'I knew they'd done something to my mind, but I wanted to get out so I didn't ask any questions. I swear, I never told them we'd met ... not consciously, I swear it! I didn't know you were my target.' She collapsed into tears, trembling violently.

'She's telling the truth,' Killian said, seeming very sure about it. 'I too was sent on assassinations I didn't know about until after the fact. Get her into the *Artemis*.'

'She's too much of a security risk like this,' I said. 'We need to take her to Susan and Ajalae.' I almost tripped over the names, not yet used to my sisters' undercover identities. 'They should be able to straighten her out, or at least assess the risk factor.'

'In that case, let's get her to my hotel,' Killian suggested, and I agreed that was a better idea.

'I'll do it — best you don't attract attention to yourself,' I advised. 'You get Susan and Ajalae and meet us there.' I held out my hand for his room key. 'The Ritz-Carlton?' I said as he handed it over, and raised both brows at him, very much doubting he'd sunk *all* the Molier money into the Peace Project. 'It's a *very* nice reality you've created for yourself.'

'Hey,' he defended, 'that's where they put me. It has great views of the park. Who am I to argue? That would just be rude.' He grinned, then placed a hand on Ereshkigal's head. 'You're safe now,' he told her, and her entire body relaxed as he poured healing energy into her via his palm.

She took a deep breath, then her eyes opened and she smiled beatifically. 'Oh my goddess, that was amazing!' She turned to Killian, seeing him in a whole new light. 'Oh my lord,' she gasped and fell to her knees, 'you are the vessel of the Sanat Kumara. He *is* here, fighting the good fight.'

Both Killian and I attempted to hush her.

'Forgive me, lord, but I feared you would never come back for us. I live only to serve you.' She bowed to the ground, weeping with euphoria.

'Ooops, too much,' Killian said with a grimace.

It was obvious I had to get her out of here. I bent down to whisper in her ear. 'If you wish to be of service, you can pull yourself together and walk out of here as though you never found who you were looking for. Can you do that?'

She breathed deeply to regain her equilibrium and nodded to assure me she could.

'Go,' I instructed Killian, and he left us to fetch my sisters.

'This is an inconvenient development,' Talori commented, looking at the Anu warrior woman now lying sedated on Killian's luxurious king-sized bed. We had stripped her bare and thrown all her clothes into the hot tub, to disable any tracking or surveillance devices that may have been planted in them. Her naked body was now covered by a fine foil blanket, which, Vespera explained, would block any microwave mind-programming signals that might be picked up by devices implanted in her body.

'We really don't need to be babysitting a psychotic double agent right now,' Talori went on, 'especially on the very day that we arrive on the scene!'

'Your compassion is overwhelming,' Killian teased her, having just joined us.

'Do I tell a lie?' she asked us all, and even Killian had to agree. 'Our adversaries must be keeping close track of our timeline movements,' she concluded, 'if they're aware of the day we departed this decade for 2003?'

'They are,' Killian cut in. 'They were tracking the Blue Flame emissions from the *Klieo* when it disappeared in Australia to hook into the Montauk wormholes. Thanks to a piece of Mia's hair in my possession at the time, I was able to follow the whole thing through her eyes.' He made the confession openly, no longer blaming himself for the adverse things he'd been forced to do in order to escape the Montauk Project.

'So why wait until the day we get here to send their assassin?' I posed. 'You'd think they'd try it out before we arrived to complicate things?'

Talori shrugged, and moved to the bed to activate a device that would carry out an X-ray scan on Ereshkigal. She glanced back at Killian. 'Unless you want to be led into temptation, you'd better adjourn to the next room.'

Killian grinned. 'I have to tell you, being a holy channel for the Sanat Kumara really sucks sometimes.'

'Never mind, you'll get your reward in heaven,' I said, ruffling his hair. I accompanied him into the next room, leaving Vespera and Talori to it.

'Now Ereshkigal thinks I'm the Lord of Earth.' Killian threw his arms up in frustration.

I made light of his woes. 'Good, then she won't distract you from what you came here to do.'

'That's what my men told me about Magdalen once,' he said, reminding me that the last saviour of the Earth had also needed companionship.

'This is different, Killian. This girl isn't just from a different bloodline, she's from an entirely different *evolution*. Her soul group and yours are worlds apart! She can't be anything but a beautiful distraction —'

'Oh no!' Killian's eyes were glued to the sky, where several strange glowing orange-red and pink spherical forms were hovering over the park. 'The Nefilim *are* trying to distract me.' He rushed to the door.

'Where are you going?' I asked, following him.

'I've seen these lights before. I have to get down to the park.'

'What do they indicate?'

'Electromagnetic activity, which could result in just a severe storm or a mild earthquake, if we're lucky.' He grimaced, pressing the button for the lift.

'*Just* an earthquake, in New York city!' I emphasised.

'There are far worse things that spook world technology can inflict on an area,' he told me as the lift doors opened and we stepped inside.

'What do you plan to do?'

He shrugged, as if the answer was obvious. 'I plan to stop it.'

CHAPTER 30

COVERT OPERATIONS

ASHLEE GRANVILLE-DEVERE — SOLARIAN

While Kali was under heavy sedation I probed her thoughts for the Nefilim's false memory implants. When I perceived the nightmares and lies they had fed her I was sickened — I had to remove my hands from her being and clear the ill will and fear that pierced my body like daggers. My body temperature plummeted and it took a moment to bring the shivering under control.

Castor, who was monitoring my work through a security system in another room, spoke to me through the intercom system. 'Are you okay, Solarian? Do you need a break?'

I nodded, then shook my head. 'One minute,' I said, and, breathing deeply, I found my stomach. With three more deep breaths, I dispersed the dark perceptions and their crippling side effects. Now I felt on top of my game again. 'Okay, I'm good,' I told Castor.

I looked at the sleeping goddess and my heart filled with compassion and empathy for all she had been through for her people. As my admiration welled, so did the love and goodwill I felt towards her. Half of this soul mind, the human half, had once been my daughter too; the other half of her had always seemed rather alien to me, until now. For Kali was the outsider, working alone and unassisted to free her people from the curse of their mistakes. Even during her past life as my daughter, Charlotte, this had been the case. She had died a horrible death at the hands of the leader of the Dracon after I had departed for service in Amenti. As I had not been there to comfort her in that dire moment, I felt deeply moved to be awarded this chance to heal her now.

I placed one hand on her forehead and one over her heart and channelled into her all the goodwill and compassion that was bursting through my heart centre. After a time, I kissed her forehead and sat back. 'I hope that helps, little one.'

There was no response from my sleeping patient, but she did appear at peace.

'You're glowing,' Castor informed me.

'Really? What colour?' I asked as I approached the interior cell door to be let out.

'Indigo, of course.'

Indigo was the colour frequency my pyramid resonated to. The door's metal barrier retracted and I passed into the middle security chamber, then the door behind me closed before the door ahead of me opened.

Arcturus met me in the corridor. 'Are you all right? You were crying at one point.'

'I'm fine,' I told him.

'Is it bad?'

I couldn't tell a lie. I looked him straight in the eye and nodded. 'It's no wonder she wants nothing to do with you or Mathu,' I said sadly. 'She's not going to appreciate seeing Meridan either.'

He gasped, not wanting to pursue answers and yet morbidly compelled to. 'What filth have they put in her mind about us?' His voice cracked as he asked the question.

I took a deep breath; there was no way I could candy-coat this. 'Abuse, of all kinds.'

'No,' Arcturus squeaked, so horrified he could barely breathe.

'But already the misconceptions are fading,' I said, although I was only going on Castor's advice that they would.

Arcturus's stress levels rose rapidly and, as with most men, he chose to get angry rather than upset. 'They have traumatised my little girl ... those —'

I placed a hand on his shoulder. 'Albray, my old friend, I know you're inconsolable right now, but please don't become part of the problem. You must try and channel your energy into being constructive.'

He curbed his anger, although it took great effort. 'You're right,' he said, breathing through it.

'She's safe now, and she's recovering,' I assured him.

'I should have stayed with her and protected her.' Tears welled in his eyes.

'You couldn't have stayed with her, even if you'd known she was going to fall into such peril,' I told him. 'None of us could have stayed ... we'd all skipped to another dimension!'

'Why?' he appealed, remembering nothing.

'To save you from the same fate!' I blurted out, flustered by the anger he was directing at me.

He was gobsmacked. 'I would gladly have put myself in her place!' he cried, regretting that he'd had no say in the matter.

'They didn't just lead you to believe you went through agony,' I told him, my voice breaking as I recalled how worried I'd been about him, 'they really did torture you.'

Arcturus was immediately remorseful for misdirecting his anger at me. 'I'm so sorry,' he said, and hugged me close. We both wept. 'And after what you've just been through for Tamar ... I must be the most ungrateful bastard on earth,' he said at last.

I laughed and wiped my eyes on his shirt.

A whistle drew our attention to my husband, who was standing with his arms folded watching us. 'I'm not even going to ask,' he said good-humouredly about our embrace. 'Dexter wants to see us pronto. Castor too.'

'Why?' Castor stuck his head out the observation room door. 'What's going on?'

'Lamhfada wants to meet with us ... there's something big going down in Central Park.'

'But that is where Mia is!' Arcturus let me go and set off at a run.

Mathu came out from the observation room. 'Are you all going?' he asked.

'We'll be back soon,' Castor said. 'Will you keep an eye on Kali until then? You know where everything is.'

'I will, but what if my queen awakes and has a fit and I have to go in there?'

'Don't!' I said, having seen the horrible visions of him in her head.

'But I've had an idea about how I might be able to get close to her without —'

'No,' I insisted. 'You are wise, Mathu, and a master of logic, but emotionally speaking you are still a novice and could be prone to misjudgement.

382

So, please, just observe from outside, and tell me about it when I get back.'

'But in the case of an *extreme* emergency ...?' he appealed.

'The doors operate automatically and are programmed not to let Kali out,' Castor assured him and Mathu looked relieved.

'Okay then,' he said with a wave. 'Don't worry about a thing, I'll be fine.'

His abrupt change of manner was a little worrying, but my male colleagues were ushering me along and there was no time to investigate.

Tamar Devere — KALI

I was trapped in my delicious nightmare, seducing Killian with my evil charms and my oiled, naked body.

'I know you want me,' he whispered, his moist breath causing me to tremble as I pressed my naked self against him.

'Yes ... I am yours.' I kissed his mouth and then his forehead.

'My queen,' he whispered, his voice distorting into someone else's, 'my desire.'

I pulled away from him. 'Killian?'

'No,' he shook his head. 'It is I.'

His beautiful body distorted and shredded and the large, blood-soaked, demonic form of Ill towered over me.

My heart swelled in my chest; this was my big opportunity.

'My lord.' I opened myself to him and beckoned him in close. 'I want you ... to go to hell.'

But before I could inflict my evil intent on the demon, a bright beam of indigo light streamed down from the darkness above to encapsulate me in love. The demon faded and I began to float upwards into the beautiful, peaceful, calming indigo glow.

'I hope that helps, little one,' a sympathetic voice stated as I fell into darkness once more; only this time it was not fear I found in the blackness, just peace.

'Tamar?'

A voice called me, and I tried to look around for the source, but there was only darkness.

'Are you waking?' the familiar voice asked, and in my mind I put a face to it as I came to consciousness.

'Emmett.' I was pleased to see him beside me, as I remembered him fondly. 'My friend.'

He nodded and took my hand in his to kiss it. 'I've been so worried about you, Tamar. How are you feeling?'

'I feel . . .' I thought about this a moment — my mind was a blank as to where I was, where I had been, and my emotions were numb as well. 'I don't really feel anything,' I realised.

I tried to sit up and found myself strapped to a bench with metal bonds. Now I felt something: *panic.* 'Why am I bound like this?'

'Please don't be angry or alarmed,' he said calmly. 'Your fellow staff members were concerned that you would hurt someone, as the Nefilim have implanted false memories in your mind. For a time it is going to be difficult for you to tell the difference between fact and fabrication.'

'How do I know you're not one of the Nefilim trying to trick me?' I retorted.

'I guess you don't,' he said, and shrugged with a half-smile.

I tried to look past his physical form to view his aura, but I couldn't. 'My second sight . . . it isn't working!' I tried to move Emmett with my will but that was also ineffective. 'What have you done to my powers?'

'I haven't done anything,' he said. 'While you were held prisoner in Irkalla, you were immersed in a diluted Orme solution which has dulled your conscious control of your powers. The effects will wear off soon they tell me.'

'Then why restrain me?'

'Because, unconsciously, you are still *very* powerful.'

As Emmett smiled down at me, I found it very hard not to trust him.

'So how long do you plan on keeping me restrained?' I asked.

'I'm not in charge so I cannot say. When you are no longer a danger to yourself and others, I expect.'

Danger to others. I associated that premise with only one entity, and suddenly my mind began working again.

'I have to see Killian,' I told Emmett. 'It's very important.'

'Why do you need to see him?'

'Because he has some information I need.'

'Then tell me, and I'll go to him and get the information for you.'

'He won't disclose this information to you,' I told him. 'You don't have the same persuasive skills I have.'

He chuckled at this. 'I'm sure I don't. But Killian is working with the staff of Amenti now —'

'What?' I freaked. 'But he's in league with Ill!'

'Not any more,' Emmett said.

'Yes, he is!' I insisted, but Emmett just told me to calm down.

'You're confused right now. I told you you would be.' He placed his hands on me to calm me, but I continued my futile struggle to break my bonds.

'*I am not confused!*' I yelled. 'If the staff of Amenti are working with Killian, it is they who are confused!'

Emmett rose from the side of my bed and backed away. 'I really didn't want to upset you.'

'I am not *upset*.' I calmed down so as to stop scaring him. 'I just need to speak with one of the other staff members. Can you find one of them for me?'

'None of them are here right now.'

'When will they be back?'

He shook his head. 'I don't know, but I'm sure they'll come to see you the second they return.'

'*If* they return!' I said as he backed towards the exit door. I suddenly realised I was in solitary confinement in the Amenti complex. 'Don't leave me here, Emmett … please!' I appealed as the interior security door retracted and he stepped into the middle chamber.

'I'm not authorised to let you out,' he said apologetically.

'But the staff are in grave danger!' I yelled as the door closed and locked me in the Orme-reinforced cell. I was angry and struggled to free myself, in vain. When I couldn't break my bonds I yelled out my frustration.

Don't be such a baby, my Anunnaki half insisted. *If our powers are only effective in a subconscious state then we must be calm.*

I breathed deeply to comply with my inner voice.

That's it … sleep.

CHAPTER 31

RAINBOW
ROUND TABLE

Ashlee Granville-Devere — SOLARIAN

All the staff of Amenti remaining at the Giza complex met with Lugh Lamhfada in the usual place — the outer chamber that contained three portholes, one of which led to Lugh's realm.

Thank you all for coming, Lugh began. *I am here to deliver a request from our father that you all join him in Central Park, New York, within the next Earth hour.*

'When you say our father, you refer to En Ki?' I clarified.

He gave a graceful nod and opened his arms wide. *The Sanat Kumara.* He brought his hands together again in a gesture of appeal. *He requires your aid to avert a great disaster that is about to befall the city and his Peace Project there. He has used his Chosen One to avert such a disaster before, but the strain on his mortal-angelic body was too great and our lord fears he will not survive a second solo attempt.*

'But Killian is more powerful than any of us,' Castor said.

Lugh nodded to concede this was a valid point, but he knew something that we did not. *But put all twelve of Amenti's staff members together and it is a very different story, for combined you have an extraordinary power; it was designed to aid you to protect the planet from a pole shift when the Sphere of Amenti is finally brought back down into the Earth and we return to the Ranna time flow.*

'What is this power?' Polaris was eager to know.

Because you all resonate to a different vibrational frequency and colour tone, when united you can form what we Anu term a Rainbow Round Table.

'Of course we can!' Dexter said excitedly, as he knew something of photo-sonics from his partner's work. 'And use Killian as the thirteenth pillar!'

The rest of us looked at Dexter without a clue as to what he was talking about.

He attempted to explain. 'The thirteenth pillar is the conductor, as it were, for the Kundaray.' When we still looked blank, he rolled his eyes. 'The theory goes that an RRT during an SAC period can draw down sound current from the Primal Sound Fields in the fifteenth dimension, through the Primal Light Fields of the twelfth dimension, through Gaia in the ninth dimension, Tara in the sixth and into our third-dimensional planetary grid. The current takes the form of a rainbow ray; and, as it contains the original blueprint for creation as intended by the God Source, it restores the natural electromagnetic balance of the planet. So not only should it deflect any disaster, but it will fix any dis-ease done to an area since the Kali rift began!'

'Well, why didn't you say so? Let's do it!' Arcturus was raring to go.

'But to channel that kind of energy would require a Kundaray,' Castor said again. 'An ascended master with an activated DNA strand template of between thirty and forty-eight strands!'

'Phew!' we all whistled. That was beyond the capability of any of us here, even Lugh.

'Not even Killian is that accomplished,' Castor said, looking doubtful.

Lugh raised both brows to assure us. *But the Sanat Kumara is.*

Mia Devere — MERIDAN

Inside the *Artemis*, Killian got comfortable behind one of the monitors. 'In your absence, the Nefilim have stepped up their efforts to extend the reach of their electromagnetic field and radio frequency technologies in regard to both human mind control and the Earth's climate,' he explained. 'HAARP has numerous high-power transmitters operational in the world at this time that we're aware of, including satellites and space stations.'

'We?' I queried.

'Lamhfada and I.'

'So you kept up the friendship.'

'He is the only reason I am still here,' he said.

'But are the powers-that-be in the spook world truly capable of causing an earthquake?' I asked. I hadn't been briefed on the developments in the climate control and frequency fence situation, as it was my male teammates who had been assigned to addressing that little problem.

'They've been capable since the 1960s,' Killian assured me. 'In 1900, Nikola Tesla applied for the

389

patent to transmit electrical energy through natural mediums. He pioneered the technology, and many other revolutionary technologies, until secret government operatives took his work and continued to develop Tesla technologies for covert government uses.' Killian bypassed the keyboard for the telepathic handplate connected to the monitoring system to enter his request for information. 'The activation of the Signet Grid in 2003 cut through their anti-grid and prevented many of their networks from linking up; in other words, you've put big holes in their frequency fence.' Killian glanced at me adoringly, then looked back to the screen. 'So what I'm searching for here is active EM field transmitters in the vicinity, and I bet I can guess where one might be.'

The world map on the monitor zoomed in on a blue dot that was flashing on Long Island.

'I knew it. I've been keeping my eye on my childhood stomping ground, as rumour has it that one of HAARP's major transmitters is no longer in Alaska, but has been moved to Long Island. There's an antenna farm there, in the Westhampton pine barrens, which is protected by Delta Force-type personnel with automatic weapons.'

'That does seem a lot of security for parkland,' I agreed.

'Since Levi destroyed the Montauk subterranean complex, they've made it seem as if the air base is shut down, despite maintaining security levels. Still, there's plenty of room in that underground complex for implementing a particle-beam technology project ... which probably isn't connected to the previous mind control and time-space operations there as Levi reportedly rendered everything useless. Still, the HAARP system would definitely work at Montauk due to the extraordinary characteristics of the major Earth grid power spot and its ability to amplify electromagnetic and radio frequency waves.'

A bunch of blue cracks appeared through the map of New York on the screen.

'These are the fault lines that run under the state,' Killian explained, looking worried as one ran through Long Island and across Central Park. 'They're going to use my project for target practice! Then they'll pin the blame for the earthquake on something we're doing here.'

'The American defence department will hardly be seen to be attacking their own cities,' I said, thinking him paranoid.

'They won't be seen,' he replied, 'they never are. This technology doesn't exist as far as most of the world is concerned, so how are they to be busted for using it? Besides, although the defence department and government-based technology companies of many countries have had a hand in developing the facilities for the spook world agenda, they don't know the full story. Those involved are either Illuminati operatives or they're kept in the dark.'

'But how can they target your project so precisely?'

'The EM technology for creating weather engineering, earthquakes, city-busting explosions or zapping spacecraft and UFOs is basically the same system, all that differs is the amount of energy per micro-second per square metre poured into the target. They can send a blast in our direction via geomagnetic electron flow lines within the Earth, and target us from space to ensure the blast doesn't miss the target.'

He seemed very sure about what was about to happen. 'Okay,' I said, 'so how do you plan to stop this?'

'I can't do anything until the attack is launched.'

'Any idea when that might be?'

'After the lights appear . . . a couple of days at the most.' He shrugged. 'We'll hear it coming, it sounds like —'

'Chris!' The call came through the intercom. We both looked at the monitor that showed the exterior of the *Artemis* and saw Sharon, Killian's personal assistant, waving at the camera. 'Chris,' she called again, 'are you in there?'

'I'll go see what she wants.' Killian slid out the door and closed it behind him.

'Thank God!' Sharon said, glad to have found him. 'You've seen the lights, I take it?'

He nodded, and she gripped his upper arms. 'You're not to try to stop this again,' she insisted. 'I won't let you do it! I thought we'd lost you last time.'

'It's okay,' he assured her. 'I learned a lot from my last encounter.'

She breathed a sigh of relief.

'I'll have some backup this time,' he said and she gasped in fear.

'No,' she pleaded.

'Trust me,' he said sweetly but her frown indicated his charm wasn't working.

'That's what you said last time.'

'I'm not going anywhere before I accomplish all that I intend to do,' he assured her. 'You know the power of intent … I really need you to stay focused on a positive outcome.'

She sniffed back her tears and gave a half-laugh. 'You mean, I shouldn't let a small thing like a pending earthquake distract me,' she joked.

'Certainly not,' Killian said cheerfully.

'How about the prospect of losing my dear friend and mentor?' she said more seriously. 'The project won't have the same momentum without you leading it … I can't do this on my own.'

'You did an excellent job in my absence last time.' He gripped her by both shoulders. 'And besides, there's nothing to fear. I have angels watching over me.' He glanced at the exterior camera on the *Artemis* and gave me a wink.

After hearing Sharon's fears for Killian's safety, I was curious to know more about the previous event they'd mentioned and how he planned to handle this one differently. Then I observed my teammates entering the tent.

'Here's my backup now,' Killian said, and went to welcome them.

I had never seen most of my fellow team members dressed to blend into my era, and it was very amusing for me. After Sharon had excused herself from the tent, I opened the door to the *Artemis* and joined them. 'Fancy seeing you here …' I said with a grin.

'One Rainbow Round Table at your service, madam,' Dexter announced with glee.

'Wonderful!' cried a voice from the tent entrance: Vespera. 'You thought of it already!' And she launched herself into Dexter's arms and kissed him for being so clever.

When their lips parted, Dexter admitted, 'Actually, it was Lugh who thought of it.'

Vespera shrugged off her delightful mistake. 'Oh well, I missed you anyway. The Round Table only just occurred to me when I saw the lights in the sky.'

'You know about the light phenomenon?' Killian asked her.

'Oh yes, it's been associated with earthquakes the world over since the early 1900s,' she replied.

Killian looked at me with a knowing smile. 'The same time the patent to transmit electrical energy through natural mediums was first lodged.'

'Tell me of your last encounter with this phenomenon,' I said, sticking to what was foremost in my mind.

He shrugged. 'It happened when the project was in Baghdad; there was a fireball event.'

'A meteor?'

'No.' He sounded very sure about that. 'This was more yellow-blue-white in colour, it dropped no glowing fragments, and had no long luminous tail or sparks. It travelled parallel to the Earth's curvature in a long arcing trajectory, not the usual high-angle inbound meteor trajectory. The sounds heard before the object arrived were definitely not normal electrophonic sounds — they pulsed with a roaring diesel-engine sound. The fireball's speed was probably similar to a fast jet plane. It was definitely travelling at less than the speed of sound though, as the loud pulsing noises were heard in advance of its arrival.'

'So you called upon the Sanat Kumara to help you avert the disaster?' Denera said. Being Keeper of the Hall of Records and the greater Akashic Record, there weren't many events that happened on Earth that she didn't know about.

'Actually, it was the other way around … the lord called upon me,' Killian said. 'Fortunately, it took place in the early hours of the morning, so there were very few witnesses to see me draw forth the Kundaray, reduce the oncoming fireball into its finest particles and then vanish from the scene.'

'Where did you go?' Polaris was curious to know.

'I turned up in exactly the same place, two months later, as sick as a dog!' Killian said.

'The electromagnetic radiation,' Talori assumed.

Killian shook his head. 'The massively pure frequencies of the Kundaray — even with an ascendant master's aid, the sonic nearly shook my mortal body to pieces.'

Denera was highly impressed. 'That was a very brave feat, Killian.'

'It's nothing when you fear nothing,' he said with a smile, flattered by her attention.

'Two months later,' Polaris picked up the part of Killian's tale that was of concern to him. 'I was wondering about the repercussions of channelling energy from way beyond the constraints of time … we could avert this disaster only to discover that we've missed D-day in December this year and the world has gone to hell!'

'It's just primordial ether really, and so is subject to will,' Dexter said, not too concerned. 'In other words, the Kundaray may not understand time, but we do and can advise it.'

'You hope.' Polaris detected a fair amount of guesswork in Dexter's supposition.

'Well, it's not as if anyone's ever done this before … in this harmonic universe anyway,' Dexter defended.

'I was actually focused on two months ahead at the time my little time shift took place,' Killian said, supporting Dexter's theory. 'I'd just been planning another large event in Pakistan ... which I subsequently missed due to illness.'

'Might be a good idea if we all stay focused on the present,' Levi concluded, and we all agreed.

'We all have superhuman resilience thanks to our time beneath the Blue Flame,' Dexter continued, 'so surely we can shield Killian's mortal form from the Kundaray when he draws it forth.'

'But isn't the Kundaray drawn forth from within?' Vespera asked.

Killian nodded.

'Then how are we to protect you from the frequencies?'

'The Sanat Kumara isn't going to draw the Kundaray through me this time. It will be drawn through the RRT,' Killian announced, and you could have heard a pin drop.

'So how does an RRT work?' I ventured to ask.

Dexter rolled his eyes and motioned for me to step aside the Artemis with him so he could explain. 'Better fetch Talori so we don't have to repeat this again,' he added.

'I'll go,' my husband volunteered and then vanished before our eyes.

'What the ...?' I was stunned. 'I had no idea he was capable of vanishing.'

'Not vanishing,' Polaris corrected, looking perturbed, 'teleporting. Damn it, he's remembered.'

'What do you mean, he's remembered?' Solarian asked her husband.

'It was something he learned by accident during

the Sabine Labontè debacle,' Polaris confessed. 'He was so desperate to enlist me to his cause of finding out what had happened during their private meeting, he accidentally willed himself to me. But then when I went back and changed time, the incident was forgotten.'

'And you never thought to tell him of it?' Denera was surprised by how deep their competitive streak ran.

'He told me not to tell anybody,' Polaris defended, 'as, quite frankly, he didn't have very much control over it.'

Next thing Polaris knew he was being swiped across the back of the head.

'I'm getting the hang of it now, though.' Arcturus grinned as Polaris turned to confront him. Talori, who was with Arcturus, took a step back out of their argument.

'Truce,' Denera demanded. 'It's time for you two to end this annoying vendetta you have against each other.'

'Hear, hear,' all the staff agreed.

They both began to protest, as they rather enjoyed it.

'No buts,' Denera insisted. 'Unless the twelve of us can be a harmonious whole, the RRT won't work. You are supposed to be as brothers.'

The two men looked at each other puzzled.

'We *are* just like brothers,' Arcturus said.

'This is what brothers act like,' Polaris agreed, then looked back to Arcturus. 'They just don't get us,' he said and Arcturus nodded.

'Shhh,' Killian said, suddenly wary. 'Did you hear that?'

We all listened.

'Like a distant pulsing,' Castor said; being shamans, he and his mate had the keenest ears. Talori nodded.

Killian staggered, hit by a dizzy spell. Zalman and Levi, who were the closest to him, each caught him by an arm.

Denera closed the tent flap and rallied us. 'There is no time to waste. Form a circle according to the number of your Signet stations around Killian.'

Zalman helped our unsteady colleague onto a seat in the centre of the circle.

'Sorry I didn't tell you about the teleportation thing,' Polaris quickly said to Arcturus. 'But to my credit, I did save you from Ishtar.'

'Well, I apologise for not delivering the ring as you instructed,' Arcturus replied. 'But I did save it from falling into Nefilim hands.'

They grinned at each other, knowing there was no true ill-will between them.

I took my position between Castor at eleven and Dexter at one, and we each held our partner by the wrist as we formed a circle. 'So how do we do this?' I asked.

'We don't do anything,' Denera instructed from her number four position between Vespera and Talori. 'Just hang onto each other and don't break the circle. Our lord will do everything else.'

All eyes turned to Killian, who was still hunched in his seat, his body twitching violently. He fell backwards, his head flopping over the back of the chair as if he were unconscious.

The roaring, pulsing sound grew louder and the Earth trembled in the distance.

I was growing worried that our lord wasn't going to make an appearance, when Killian's entire body went as stiff as a board and floated up to a standing position. His eyes remained closed, but his head turned about, giving the impression that he was viewing everything perfectly well — the lord must have been utilising Killian's third-eye vision. He turned in the direction of the pulsing. 'The force travels underground,' he said.

His voice and language were not of this Earth, yet we all understood him.

'En Ki,' gasped Solarian, who had met with the lord before.

'Brace yourselves, my children,' he instructed.

As we tightened our grip on each other, En Ki pointed to Dexter, who released the low reverberating note that resonated to the frequency of deep red. Then he pointed to Arcturus who sang the slightly higher note that was the harmonic frequency of orange. In quick resonate succession, the lord conducted the whole circle: Vespera — yellow; Denera — green; Talori — blue; Solarian — indigo; Thana — violet; Levi — gold; Polaris — silver; Zalman — deep sparkling blue; Castor — sparkling silver-black. At last the lord pointed to me and, through no will of my own, I sang the note of crescendo that was the highest sonic frequency of white.

The amazing harmonic drowned out the ominous pulsing. My eyes closed and fluttered as I plunged deep into the liberating serenity of our rainbow synergy. I could feel the vibratory frequency of my body rising, to the point where I buzzed all over with such intensity that I thought I might black out.

Above his cosmic choir, the lord spoke in his native tongue of Anuhazi:

E-Ta'-TA
Um Sha-DI' UR'A'
UN UR'-A-Or'-Nam' OOR
De-a-mir
Mah-Hah-Rah-Tah Bi-Vec'TI
Ah-Ta'Un'ta E'sa
Tra'zd-Jna

Which, roughly translated, meant:

Come forth in being,
All-Embracing Pillar of First Cause Light,
anchor the Divine Sea of Liquid Light in this moment.
Reflect outward through this circle
the Divine Christos blueprint past-present-future.
Let it now be established, always and forever,
in eternal abiding reverent love.

The words caused a rush of consciousness and I was no longer aware of the shaking of the ground beneath me, nor even of my own voice or presence, for my awareness was racing inwards into the tiniest particles of my being. I left my incarnate self in the world of gross physical matter and entered into another harmonic universe, astral in nature. Here in this galaxy, with its solar system containing several binary suns, was an orbiting planet of astounding beauty, where I joined with the entity that was my soul being.

For an instant I was fully aware of being Meridan. This was Tara, my home and life, as physical and more real to me than any other life I had led. I was creating blooms in my garden in celebration of the coming spring, and my work filled me with satisfaction, inspiration and delight. The violet rays of the sun were beginning to ease the winter chill on the breeze, and I was enjoying the challenge of cleaning up outdoors in the wake of the cold season. My concentration was broken by the recurrence of the essence of an experience I'd once had and I experienced a very strong sense of déjà vu. I detected a low and disturbing frequency, one I had not felt since my days on the Amenti Project. Then I remembered: *the Rainbow Round Table*. I looked down upon myself and recalled my experience of this moment, and I was thrilled to be able to advise myself, just as I did then: *Do not be alarmed by what you find upon your return. Your efforts this day have more of an effect than you realise. The answer lies with Kali, she has not betrayed you.*

Again I was drawn inwards to a subatomic level and through the zero-point barrier into an even higher causal universe. I left my soul self and entered into another harmonic universe where galaxies were being created under the guidance of my over-soul self, who was working in a region known as Gaia.

For a moment I was aware of being Elohim, in this realm of pure consciousness, thought and creation. I had been expecting me, for I had set into motion the causes that had brought me here. *The pendulum of time swings both ways. You may occupy each instance of time once . . . any time missed is open as a destination to you.*

My journey sped up as I was drawn inside the smallest particle of the causal world and into liquid-light fields of pre-matter — a vast, breathtaking dance of colour and brilliance. My consciousness expanded to such a state that I felt myself part of this entire realm known as Aramatena. Here I was one with my avatar self, and I saw all of creation laid before me, from its highest potential to its lowest and densest state.

I felt a trembling within me and my exaltation grew as I rushed towards the vibration in the very depths of my being. Here, resonating in all its purity, was the alpha and omega of all life, the divine heart of my Sovereign Integral being, pumping out the wave frequencies into primal sound fields of my creation. The wave frequency was the carrier of cosmic light, and light was the carrier of the blueprints of my creation, which every molecule in the five harmonic universes knew how to read and interpret. But in some of the lowest parts of my creation, my divine plan had gone awry — it had been lost in translation and fallen into shadow, so I was compelled to send forth a note of revision.

I was expelled from my Sovereign Integral, where a wave of inspiration caught me up and I plunged back into the sea of liquid light to ride the slipstream of my divine intent down through my existence on Gaia and Tara.

Back in the realm of gross matter, the divine spark of inspiration that I had carried forth with me from the primal sound fields entered my body through the light particles being emitted from the light centre of my heart. The sonic ascended to my throat centre, where it burst into the world via my larynx, in the form of one long, continuous, perfect note.

Although my eyes remained closed, through my third eye I saw my spiritual father drawing into himself the colours of the spectrum from our circle, which he then redirected down into the Earth below him and the sky directly above him.

There was a great clash of force some distance above and below us, which dissipated before it reached our vicinity.

The Earth ceased its shaking and the Rainbow Choir fell silent.

A blissful moment followed as the peace of the divine energy settled over our gathering, filling us all with a sense of deep love, purpose and well-being.

'It is done,' En Ki announced, still glistening with the Kundaray energy.

A sound like a crack of thunder shattered the silence.

'An aftershock,' En Ki warned, then vanished in a huge blast of blue-white light.

Blinded by the force, I was engulfed by a wave of liquid blackness so violent that I was torn from the strong grip of my teammates and sucked into underwater darkness.

CHAPTER 32

DEFEATING FATE

Tamar Devere — KALI

When I became conscious again, the metal bonds that had restrained me were broken, but I was still trapped within the holding cell in the Amenti complex. For an age I called to be freed — I pleaded, begged, demanded, then screamed for someone to hear me, but no response was forthcoming.

I was beginning to doubt that I would ever see another person again. I felt in my being that there was something seriously amiss. My fellow Amenti staff members, although not overly disposed towards my kind, would not leave me in limbo like this for so long when there was still so much work for me to do.

Now that I had recovered my rational, conscious mind, I had serious doubts about Killian Labontè. Yes, the visions I'd had of him during my psychosis had stirred deep sensual desires in me. But why did Ill want me to find Killian so attractive and not my prince? One thing that had been made painfully obvious to me was that Killian and Ill were in some way connected.

'I think something bad has happened.' Emmett's voice came through the intercom.

At last: another presence. I stood. 'Define bad.'

'The entire staff of Amenti are missing and I don't know what to do.'

'The first thing you should do is let me out of here,' I said pleadingly.

'But I was told not to, under any circumstances.'

I threw my hands up in frustration, then drew a deep breath to calm down. 'How long have they been missing?'

'About twenty-four Earth hours.'

'Shit!' I paced as I asked the next vital question. 'Did Killian have anything to do with their disappearance?'

There was silence.

'You don't know or you won't say?'

'He was with them at the time —'

'I knew it!' Why didn't anyone ever listen to me?

'But I don't know if he had anything to do with their —'

'Oh, he did,' I assured him. 'Whose side are you on anyway? You've always despised Killian.'

'I misunderstood him.'

I had to laugh. 'I think you might have been one of the few people on Earth whose initial instinct about him was correct! Has Arcturus changed his tune about him too?'

'Um ... no.'

I nodded, not surprised. 'Smart man, my father.'

I looked up into the lens of the surveillance mechanism. 'If you won't trust my instincts, then won't you trust his? I have to speak with Killian yesterday! You're a smart lad, Emmett, but you're way out of your depth. You need help. *Please*, let me out.'

There was another long silence and I feared he had left.

'Emmett?'

The doors to the cell opened to expose the exit into the corridor I had been dreaming about. I hurried through the security doors to find Emmett awaiting me.

'Please don't kill me,' he said, cowering.

I grabbed hold of his arm on my way past. 'I'm not going to kill you … at least, not until you've filled me in on all I've missed.'

He didn't look any less frightened by my claim. 'I learned all I know from the Hall of Records.'

I stopped dead in my tracks and turned to face him. 'How do you know about the Hall of Records?'

He shrugged defensively. 'I heard your teammates talk of it, and when no one returned, I went in search of it. I thought it might be able to fill me in on what happened.'

'Well, it was a brilliant thought, but people have been lost forever trying to get through this labyrinth,' I lectured him. 'Not to mention the fact that you need a certain quality of DNA to operate the sacred tool. You should be dead!'

'Really?' He grimaced. 'You know me. I'm a curious guy when it comes to alien technology.'

I had greater concerns right now and I resumed dragging him through the Thoth complex. 'Be more careful in future — you have no idea what you are dealing with.'

On the way to the Hall of Records we passed the chamber known as the Hall of Consciousness. As its title suggested, it housed the arcane equipment used for monitoring Earth's consciousness via the Earth grid. Inside a large crystal ball on a round pedestal in the centre of the chamber stood the scales of consciousness. On one side of the scale was a sphere of darkness and on the other was a sphere of light, and for the first time ever the scales were tipped to the side of the righteous.

'Damn it!' I said.

'What's the matter?' Emmett asked. 'Doesn't this mean the world is now ready to host the Sphere of Amenti?'

'That's exactly what it means,' I said. 'But without the Black Madonna to form the Staff of Power from the ring and the rod, I can't bring down the sphere.'

'And there's the small matter of your prince,' Emmett ventured.

I took a deep breath as I thought about Mathu. 'I'm a bit confused about him at present,' I confessed. 'I have mixed memories of finding him, but I'm not sure if any of them are real. He may still be trapped in Irkalla, or maybe he was never there at all.'

'So you accept that the Nefilim have altered your memories?' Emmett said.

'I do.'

'Then how do you know you're right about Killian being in league with Ill?'

I fobbed off the possibility that I could be wrong about Killian. 'Call it instinct. And considering what's happened, I'd say I'm more likely right than wrong, wouldn't you?'

A large liquid-light screen took up one wall of the room. It depicted a simulation of the SAC alignment taking place up through the harmonic universes, which was on the latter end of its alignment. I glanced up at it.

'There's only one way to find out the truth about Killian. And time is running out.'

'You do know it was Killian who led the Amenti staff into Irkalla to rescue us?' Emmett said.

'And it was also Killian who led us into Irkalla in the first place!' I retorted. *Us*. I dwelt on the sudden realisation that Emmett had entered Irkalla with me.

'True,' he conceded. 'But he could have been under duress.'

My eyes opened wide as I recalled Emmett transforming into Mathu. 'Deceiver!' I accused him, backing away.

'No,' he said.

'Then why are you still masquerading as Emmett Rich?'

'Because Ill implanted false memories of me in you and I didn't want to aggravate the situation.'

He transformed into his true self. I had waited aeons to stand before my love again, but I felt none of the rejoicing in my heart that I had imagined would accompany this defining moment. I doubted his motives and continued to back away from him.

'How do I know it's not you that the Nefilim have reprogrammed? Why would my prince trust Killian Labontè's word over mine?'

'Please, dear goddess, hear me out.' He fell to his knees before me.

I shook my head. 'You're trying to distract me. I must hurry.' And I ran from the room and made haste to the Hall of Records and locked myself in, so I couldn't be swayed by his pleas. It made perfect sense to me that Ill would send the person I cared for most to distract me from addressing the peril of my fellow team members.

But why would an enemy let you out of solitary confinement? I found myself asking as I approached the telekinetic control platform. I stopped dead in my tracks, for I had no answer.

Awful images of Mathu with other women flooded through my mind, sickening and confusing me. Part of me knew they were lies, but the images were so vivid that they cut into my heart like daggers. I could not bring myself even to look upon Mathu at present and resolved that I would be more effective handling Killian alone.

I stepped up onto the plate and viewed the tail end of the incident in Central Park, where Killian and the Amenti team's Rainbow Round Table had averted a huge earthquake. In the wake of the event there was an unusual aftershock, which had left Killian unconscious and caused all those channelling the RRT to vanish.

I asked the Hall of Records to track the whereabouts of the Amenti staff at present, but it informed me that they were no longer within its sphere of detection.

They must be in Irkalla, I thought. Where else could they possibly be if the Hall of Records was unable to detect them? Time to visit my old friend Killian and get some answers.

I stepped down from the control platform and entered the green porthole at one end of the hall, heading for Polaris's station in Nova Scotia. From there it was only a short trip to my desired destination.

The door to Killian's hotel room was opened by none other than the Queen of the Underworld herself. She was disguised as a human, but I could see her true form behind the façade. 'Ereshkigal . . . why am I not surprised to find you here?' I said.

'Kali!' She was shocked to see me, and stood stunned for a moment, unsure of what she should do next.

'I wish to speak with Killian, or is he Ill right now?' I forced a grin.

'You've got it all wrong,' she said and moved to close the door on me, but I prevented it.

'I *am* going to see him,' I assured her, and she gave up the struggle and stepped aside to allow me to enter.

'He's in there.' She motioned to the bedroom.

'I must say, I expected more of a fight from you, Ereshkigal.' I paused to look her over, and saw that although her auric body had some muddy patches, she was one of the Nefilim no longer; she had returned to the ranks of the Anu.

'I have no fight left in me,' she said, her tone defeated and her expression bitter.

'Why are you here?' I asked flatly.

'I believe I have been exposed to the Nefilim for the Anu spy I am,' she said. 'I have been psychologically damaged by our brethren and have become a threat to everyone. Killian has been hiding me, so I have some time to sort my head out.'

'You should have gone straight to Lamhfada,' I lectured.

'But I was programmed to come *here*,' she snapped, 'and *murder* Killian. Praise the goddess that Meridan was present to stop me.'

'What?' This made no sense to me. 'Why would Ill want his future embodiment dead?'

'Because Killian is too much of a threat now. They can't control him any more and he is causing their plan real trouble. *Please*,' she appealed to me, 'you must trust him.'

'Why should I?' I was insulted by the plea.

'Because he is the channel of the Sanat Kumara.'

I was shocked to my core by her claim, but it was delivered with such heartfelt devotion that she obviously believed it.

'Who else but the Lord of the World would have the compassion to hide someone who had intended to murder him?' She began to weep, something the Anu so rarely did, and sank to her knees to implore me. 'Please, *please*, great queen, do not harm him.'

It was quite clear to me that she felt more than a devotee's love for the man, and I took mercy on her for all she had apparently been through in the name of my cause. I placed a healing hand upon her head to calm her.

'If the situation is as you say, then you have nothing to fear. Wait here,' I instructed, and she nodded and raised herself to take a seat by the window. I entered Killian's room alone.

'*Tamar*!' Killian was also surprised to see me, and, although his voice was weak, I could tell that he was unsure if this was a pleasant turn of events or not. 'If you have come seeking answers about the staff, I have only theories,' he said, assuming I wasn't here out of concern for his welfare. 'If I was somehow to blame for the disappearance ...' He winced at the notion as it clearly pained him. 'But I can't tell you what my involvement was.'

As soon as I set eyes on Killian, the passion that I had been programmed to feel for him ignited in me; however, I had enough control to realise I had to ignore my desires. I had been prepared to storm in here and beat the truth out of him, but my suspicions about him dulled in his presence, for he exuded the most heavenly energy. I felt immediately calm and safe — like coming home to the security of my father's house.

I climbed onto the huge, king-sized bed he was resting on and sat facing him. 'Tell me what you think happened,' I said.

'I don't know ... the Sanat Kumara was in control of me at the time so I remember nothing.' He sat up a little straighter against his pillows. 'However, I can tell you what your mother predicts has happened to them.'

I was shocked. 'You've spoken to Meridan since the event?'

'No,' Killian said, confusing me even more.

'My mother foresaw this event then?'

Killian sounded uncertain. 'Not exactly. The truth is, I'm loath to tell you how I know what I do. Circumstances may have changed since my source was put to paper ... although everything else seems to have come to pass pretty much —'

'Hold on.' I had to pull him up as he was rambling. 'You read this somewhere?'

There was a knock on the hotel room door and my body stiffened with alarm.

'Expecting anyone?'

Killian shook his head and I immediately retreated to the lounge room to investigate, suspecting that the Nefilim had come for the rest of us. I hid and instructed Ereshkigal to open the door.

'Oh my lord!' she gasped when she saw the visitors and quickly invited them inside so she could close the door.

It was Mathu, still in the form of Emmett Rich, and Lugh Lamhfada, also wearing a very handsome human male disguise.

Lugh held a hand to Ereshkigal's cheek. 'Greetings and salutations, little one. I hear you have experienced some grief.'

'Where have you been?' I asked the Otherworldly lord, who turned and bowed deeply to me upon hearing my voice.

'Why, Your Majesty, I have been looking into the disappearance of Amenti's staff,' he replied.

'And have you discovered what has become of them?'

'I have not,' he said sadly, 'although I do have a theory.'

'Do tell,' I requested, taking a seat.

'What if the EMP blast that the Amenti staff dispersed with the RRT was more than just your average electromagnetic pulse?' Mathu cut in, impatient. 'What if the Nefilim rebuilt their time-travel technology at Montauk and then combined it with their —'

'— electromagnetic field technologies,' Killian interrupted. He was leaning heavily against the bedroom doorway to keep himself upright.

'My lord, you are not strong enough to be out of bed.' Ereshkigal rushed to support him and Killian did not object.

'That's right ...' he said slowly, as if beginning to remember details rather than confirming the statement, '... that's what that aftershock was.'

'It's a damn shame,' Lugh interjected. 'The RRT's Kundaray cleared far more dis-ease from the grid than even I expected. If the staff of Amenti were still here, it would be game, set and match to us.

The only way for the Nefilim to thwart our victory was to take them out of the equation.'

For the first time since I'd awoken from the spell put on me in Irkalla, I felt as though I was heading down the right track.

'If the Nefilim did intend to get rid of the Amenti team, where would be the best place to send them?' I asked, then voiced my suspicion: 'Irkalla!'

'Where you could rescue them before D-day?' Lugh said. 'No, we need to think like one of the Nefilim.' He paused and then went pale when he figured out the answer. 'They have been sent into the future, beyond the SAC alignment.'

Mathu nearly choked. 'If they have, that means we fail, as Meridan won't be here to unite the rod and ring.'

Lugh nodded. 'There would be no chance of an Anu rescue then, as the failure to bring the sphere down into Earth by the end of the SAC alignment would send the Signet Grid offline, and the physical world and the astral world will again be cut off.'

'And we have no way of telling to what time in the future Amenti's staff have been sent?' I asked.

Lugh shook his head slowly.

'And so it unfolds,' Killian, said, getting paler by the second. 'They have been sent to 2976.'

Mathu gasped, knowing this year all too well. 'The end of the Kali rift; the year of Earth's final destruction.'

'If they are in the future when we have lost and the Signet Grid is offline, then there is no chance they can get back to us!' I began to pace as I pondered how I might rescue the Amenti team. 'And I'll bet my bloodthirsty brethren will be waiting to milk our staff mates of their pure angelic essence, and then it truly will be game over.'

I stopped pacing, having decided on the best course of action. 'As we seem to have lost all our double agents in Irkalla, I volunteer myself for the job.'

Everyone protested at once.

'I will go, and I'll wait until my staff show up,' I insisted.

'That's nearly a thousand years,' Mathu appealed. 'It will be too late to bring down the Sphere of Amenti by then, and all will be lost anyway.'

'The pendulum of time swings both ways,' I reminded him. 'I can come back.'

'How will you do that?' He was desperate for me to reconsider.

'I'll have a millennium to figure that out,' I said, and looked at Killian, who nodded sadly. 'So this event was also prophesied?' I asked him.

Again he nodded, with a look of utter devastation on his face. He waved me closer, and I approached and leaned in close so he could have a quiet word.

'None of this is your fault,' he said, far more emotionally than seemed warranted, but then I suspected there was much that he knew about the future that he wasn't prepared to share. 'I know what I must do and what you must do, and I want you to know that we forgive you.'

I could tell the sentiment was heartfelt and had to wonder what it was that I would do in the future to warrant such a sincere absolution. *We forgive you?* Who else did he mean? Still, as he'd made a point of keeping the information quiet, I didn't question him further; besides, the man was obviously exhausted.

'Keep doing what you have been doing,' I said, forcing a smile, not pretending to understand what he was trying to convey to me. 'If I do succeed eventually, I need to know that the world will be on track to host Amenti no matter when I return.'

I wanted to ask outright if I did succeed, but refrained. Still, as Killian smiled and nodded at me, I felt encouraged.

'I cannot let you go back to Ill,' Mathu said, assuming his true form as if that would add more weight to his statement.

'Listen to him,' Ereshkigal pleaded. She knew full well what the Nefilim were capable of doing to a being's sanity.

'I have but one task to perform on this Earth and one route to follow to achieve it,' I said. I looked to Lamhfada for further argument, but, unfettered as he was by emotion, he offered no objection and thus I knew my reasoning was sound. 'If I don't make it back by the eleventh hour, you will see everyone here safely into your realms,' I requested of him.

'I surely will, Your Majesty,' he pledged.

'Your last stay in Irkalla nearly destroyed us. Imagine what an extended stay will do to your sanity,' Mathu protested, but I hushed him with a finger over his lips.

'If you are to be trapped for all eternity somewhere, I would much rather it be in the Ranna time flow than in the downward spiral of the Kali rift,' I said.

'Not without you,' he insisted.

I decided a more private conversation was in order — and Killian offered his bedroom so that we might speak alone.

'I will return, I promise you,' I told him, gripping his face between both my hands. The confusion of my psychosis was beginning to clear and my heart opened anew to the soul who had endured so much torture in my name. 'But before I go,' I moved closer to him, 'there is something I want you to do for me.'

His eyes met mine and I didn't have to speak the request for he knew what it was I desired.

'Not like this,' he stalled. 'Not with you distrusting me and —'

'Shhh.' I kissed him to silence, and savoured the delight of the act. When our lips parted, Mathu was not so resistant.

'Please, take me now,' I urged him with all my heart. 'My virtue and inexperience will only be a curse where I'm going. I need just one sweet, truthful memory of you that I may cling to in Irkalla.'

'They will make you like them.' He pressed his forehead against mine and his eyes moistened at the thought.

'Not really.' I brushed his soft silver hair from his deep soulful eyes. 'The flame that burns violet in my heart cannot be extinguished, and that flame will always lead me back to you.'

Mathu wanted to argue against my decision, but the more pressing need — to strip me bare and finally consummate an entire evolution's worth of desire — took precedence. Finally, we immersed ourselves in the only truly perfect moment either of us had known in any of our lives.

CHAPTER 33

THE DESCENDING SPIRAL — 2976 AD

MIA DEVERE — MERIDAN

In the liquid blackness there was no way of determining which way was up. I tumbled aimlessly around in a panic until I was finally forced to release my breath and my lungs filled with salty liquid. The water filled and bloated me, and I floated about like a sponge at the mercy of a strong tide. This was surely the depths of darkest density: it was freezing, stifling and oppressive.

It took me some time to determine that I hadn't died. I could still wiggle my cold, water-swollen digits and, although it got me nowhere, sway my limbs. So I floated, wondering if this was to be my fate for all time.

A large, long entity surged past me, and in its wake I spun around furiously, until I finally ebbed to a stop. I had barely recovered my sensibilities when I felt the entity coming up underneath me again. My heart pounded in my chest so hard that I knew this was no dream or even a nightmare; it was very real.

The motion of the entity felt fluid, like a large school of fish, and I wondered if perhaps that was what it was, for as it surged upwards, it divided, separated and circled out around me and I was again set swirling in circles, but more gently this time. Could any living thing truly exist in this place? What was its interest in me? The deep rumbling of the massive body of liquid around me was drowned out by the fast swirling sound produced by the entity, and as it spun faster it began to make a clicking sound — like metal components attaching to one another.

After a time, the clicking stopped and everything went silent. There was a whooshing sound, like a vacuum below me, and my body lowered with the water level to come to rest upon a solid metal grate. As the fluid drained from around me, a bank of lights came on; even though they were quite dim, the glare was blinding. I turned on my side and vomited a massive amount of seawater from my lungs, windpipe and stomach.

Nostrils and throat abraded from the effort of my purge, I pulled myself to a seated position, rubbed my eyes and finally looked around. I was in a small metal pod, just big enough to sit cross-legged in.

Meridan. It spoke to me in my husband's voice.

'Arcturus? What's going —'

Just sit tight, we're bringing you in.

He spoke over me, which led me to believe that either he couldn't hear me or it was a recorded message, meant to set me at ease.

But what if it's a Nefilim trick? I asked myself.

This is not a Nefilim trick, the recorded voice said, and I felt the little pod begin to surge through the water.

This kind of nanotechnology had Nefilim associations, so I feared I was being taken for a ride in more ways than one. I drew a deep breath for courage, and coughed up more seawater. What choice did I really have but to trust in the universe and be thankful to have been retrieved from the cold, dark abyss?

The universe! The resolve stirred recollections of the meetings I'd had with my higher selves. I recalled being Meridan and her ominous warning about the outcome of the RRT: *The answer lies with Kali, she has not betrayed you.* An even higher source had told me: *You can occupy each instance of time only once, but any time missed is open as a destination, as the pendulum of time swings both ways.*

I began to shiver violently. *What has happened to us?* I thought. I had never felt so wretched and betrayed. I knew within my being that during the Rainbow Round Table, under the instruction of the Sanat Kumara, we had channelled something magnificent into the Earth grid; so where had this hell come from?

I felt sure I was frozen solid in my huddled pose by the time my little metal ice-sphere slowed to a standstill. With the sound of interlocking metal latches above, my transport was abruptly hoisted upwards for a long, long way, then stopped. All was still and silent a moment, then a thunderous metal crack startled me. The pod instantaneously dispersed into a swarm of shadows that flew off towards a storage module in the dimly lit loading bay, and I fell a short distance onto a padded landing mat.

'That's the last of them,' said a female voice that

I'd been so sure I would never hear again. Yet here it was, coming from right in front of me!

A pair of fabulous high-heeled Gucci boots rose up and over the knees of the tall warrior woman. The rest of her form was hugged by a dark body suit made of chain mail and leather, rather risqué in design. Her hands rested upon the large buckle of her weapons belt, which was, thankfully, free of devices at present.

'Ishtar?' I said through chattering teeth and she nodded. I was confused. I thought I'd been shot back into the past, but the goddess appeared as one of the Anu. 'I saw you leave for the Hall of Amorea,' I said, puzzled.

'Yes, you did,' she confirmed with a smile. 'Where I sped through my spiritual healing process, thanks to you aiding me to clear my blockages naturally before leaving the physical world. En Ki gave me the green light to return and join Lugh's taskforce here on the Earth plane as a guardian to our lord's staff of Amenti. You didn't really think the Lord of the Earth would allow the enemy to send you hurtling a thousand years into the future without —'

'A thousand years!' I gasped in shock.

'Give or take a few hundred years.' She crouched beside me and placed an arm around me for comfort. 'All the other eleven staff have been retrieved and are recovering here in HC-BS-XXXV. The Sanat Kumara has seen to their safe delivery.'

'Killian,' I said with a smile, believing I had him to thank for saving our lives.

'I'm afraid that Killian is long dead,' Ishtar said sadly.

'And Tamar?'

Isthar's expression soured. 'She is the Queen of the Underworld. She lured Killian to his death. Lugh Lamhfada and Mathu followed her into Irkalla and have not been seen since.'

I found myself gasping again and Ishtar rubbed my back. 'I am not completely sensitive in emotional matters yet. If I could have delivered the news more subtly, I am sorry.'

I shook my head, still processing it all, and shivered uncontrollably. 'What became of Ereshkigal?'

The hatch to the pod bay opened and the being in question stood facing me. 'I became the leader of the resistance,' she said, 'whose sole purpose was to get to you before the Nefilim did and return you to the past. I owe Killian that much,' she added sadly. 'With your deliverance I am halfway to completing that goal.'

I attempted to stand, but as my limbs were numb, Ishtar had to assist me. 'What I hear about Kali can't be true,' I said. 'During the RRT I spoke to my higher self who told me that the answer lies with my daughter and that she has not betrayed us.'

Ereshkigal strode up close and looked straight into my eyes. 'Oh, I can assure you that she has betrayed us, over and over again.'

'But why —'

'Because she has lost her mind!' the warrior-like Ereshkigal hollered at me.

'Ereshkigal, are you trying to confuse the issue?' Arcturus entered through the pod-bay hatch. He was bedraggled from the quantum leap into the future, but to my eyes he'd never appeared more handsome.

'Damn all these emotions,' Ereshkigal said,

stepping away to compose herself. 'However do you control them? I've been attempting to master the emotional bandwidth for centuries now and I still fail miserably. My apologies, Meridan, for I owe you much.'

I hugged and kissed my husband, revelling in his body heat. 'I'd say we're square,' I assured Ereshkigal, for I was deeply thankful for all she had done in order to save us.

'We need to talk.' Arcturus held me at arm's length to assess my well-being. 'And you look like you could use some warming up.'

He rubbed my arms in an attempt to stop me shivering, then put his arm around me and guided me out of the pod bay and into a corridor with large windows along one side that gave a very high-angle view of the world. Sunshine poured into the enclosed walkway and I hurried over to bask in the warmth. After my time in the murky, wet darkness, to be warmed by the sun was quite simply a dream come true. Still, as I observed the dark, stormy planet below that had once been my home, my heart sank.

'We're only a thousand years in the future,' I said. 'I didn't think all this devastation happened until much later in Earth's history?'

'That was before we went back and changed events in 2003,' Arcturus said as he came to stand alongside me. 'Our actions prompted the Nefilim to develop their electromagnetic technologies faster, and events sped up. One of their ionospheric heating experiments went horribly wrong, resulting in a fireball in the ionosphere over the North Pole. The solar furnace melted the icy wasteland in a quantum blink of an eye.'

423

That explained the massive flooding I could see below. I gasped at the thought of what the event must have been like for the unsuspecting souls still living on the surface of the Earth. 'It's Atlantis all over again.'

'They say the glare of the explosion was seen all over world ... and that it was the last light the remaining inhabitants of the Earth ever saw.'

'Was everyone lost?' My heart ached for all those we had failed.

'Many enlightened souls were evacuated to the Inner Earth cities and, in future, they will come to occupy these sub-bases, which have been constructed beneath what is termed a —'

'Terraform island,' I said, realising that Levi had already explained all this to me.

Arcturus was surprised by my knowledge. 'The project was the brainchild of Ereshkigal, or at least she devised an elemental process known as —'

'Hypercording.' I surprised him again.

'Is there anything you don't know?' he said.

'I don't know where the rest of the staff are.'

My Amenti staff suit had dried and repaired itself during my moment in the sun and now I felt ready to do something about correcting this blow the Nefilim had dealt us and the rest of the inhabitants of the Earth.

My husband smiled broadly at my resolve. 'This way.'

The complex was largely unoccupied, as were all the terraform substations at present, for they were still in the primordial stages of their accelerated development. Moving around from substation to substation to check on the progress of the terraforms was what had kept Ereshkigal and her small band of Anu warriors sane during the long wait for the arrival of the staff of Amenti. They were the only beings on surface Earth that had managed to slip under the Nefilim radar.

Arcturus and I entered the boardroom, where the rest of our teammates were listening intently to Denera. We sank quietly into a seat each to listen to the abysmal account of our enemy's accomplishments in our absence.

'The Nefilim and Dracon gained access to the Halls of Amenti, and the breach in security prompted the universal stargate system to shut down,' Denera explained. 'This event effectively sealed off humanity from the protection of all the guardian races. All the evolutions taking place in every harmonic universe above ours have become stifled, for they are unable to fulfil the natural evolutionary process of ascension without the soul minds of their soul group trapped here in the Kali rift. This has always been the core motivation behind the Old World Order's continuing Grail Quest — they believed they needed to possess the Rod and Ring of Power in order to accomplish their objective of claiming Earth and the Amenti stargates.'

I feared I'd missed something. 'But if I'm the only person on Earth capable of forming the key, then how could they have gained access to Amenti?'

'Kali,' Denera said sadly.

Again, I was lost. 'But even she can't —'

'You are the only being on *Earth* with the power to create the key, but even independent of each other the ring and the rod are very powerful,' Denera enlightened me, 'and Kali knew this. Although she couldn't form the key herself, she commanded Lugh Lamhfada to bring the items to her.'

'My daughter is still on our side.' I felt it in my heart.

'Tell that to Killian, Lamhfada and Mathu,' Ereshkigal said, joining our council.

'Why would my higher self lie to me?' I insisted. 'Kali knows that once she has us back, we can use the Staff of Amenti to go back in time and change all of this.'

'She might have known that once upon a time ...' Ereshkigal sounded hesitant to concede even that much. 'But I fear that she forgot her objective and allies centuries ago.'

'Many thought the same of you once,' Dexter commented, but Ereshkigal's opinion was not to be swayed.

'Whether Kali remembers or not is irrelevant. Going back without her is a complete farce. She *must* come back with us,' Denera concluded, putting an end to the speculation.

'Whatever has become of the world is of no consequence if we can get back to the past and change it,' Polaris added.

I was quick to second his proposal. 'You can occupy each instance of time only once, but any time missed is —'

'— open as a destination,' the rest of my teammates chorused, and I smiled. It seemed we'd all got the same message from the Elohim.

'But how to get back, that's the question,' Dexter mused.

I suggested the obvious. 'The *Klieo*?'

'Lost,' Polaris said, looking gutted. 'In the ion fire blaze.'

'Montauk got us in,' Levi suggested. 'Montauk could get us out.'

Ereshkigal put a damper on that idea. 'They destroyed Montauk precisely to ensure that couldn't happen.'

'There is only one way left to us,' Denera concluded, having already assessed all the possibilities. 'The Rod and the Ring of Power.'

'But since the grid was cut off from the Sphere of the Blue Flame, both tools have been rendered useless,' Ereshkigal stated.

All eyes looked my way. 'What?' I said.

'You are the living channel of Blue Flame energy,' Denera reminded me, 'and that doesn't change in the future, in outer space, inner space, nor even in Irkalla.'

It was true, my powers had not been hindered in Irkalla during my last visit.

'That would also mean I can power up the porthole in Dexter's station,' I said.

Denera nodded. 'You can wield the Rod of Power and get us back to the past. In fact, you are the only one among us who can still utilise your psychic powers at all!'

'So basically,' Levi summed up, 'you can complete this mission on your own.'

'I don't know why the Nefilim even bothered disposing of the rest of us really,' Dexter added.

'I am thankful they did,' I told him. Facing this quest alone would have been far more daunting.

'With all of us here, that means there's no one left in the past to advise Kali,' Arcturus said, obviously as alarmed about the damning reports about our daughter as I was. He gripped the edge of the metal table we were sitting at and the metal folded under his grip like paper. 'What the …! Well, craftsmanship just isn't what it used to be,' he added.

Ereshkigal was awestruck. '*Arcturus*, that table's made from a super-alloy containing tungsten. Aside from Orme-reinforced metals, it's the strongest metal known on Earth!'

'Holy cow!' Levi took a closer look at the damage.

'Of course.' Denera could have hit herself. 'The orange flame you carry — it's the standing wave pattern of Earth's morphogenetic field and is composed of the frequencies of dimensions one through to three, which are the basis of the physical world.'

'Meaning I have super-physical strength!' Arcturus concluded.

'Oh no,' muttered Polaris.

'Looks like I'll have help on this quest after all,' I said, and grinned at my husband, who grinned back. 'Well, I guess that only leaves the question of how we get to Signet Station One?'

'I can get you there,' Ereshkigal said. 'But I'm warning you, it won't be the cushy ride you're accustomed to.'

Smiter and Ishkur, salvaged souls from the Nefilim ranks, had also joined Ereshkigal's band, and were pilot and co-pilot of our vessel. This transport wasn't the elegant, clean Ceres technology we were used to — such vessels relied on Blue Flame energy, or solar energy at the very least. Ereshkigal and her crew had been forced to resort to pirating Nefilim technologies, as they were specifically designed to function in a world without light. The ship clunked, rattled and was bone-shatteringly uncomfortable — not to mention being hideously designed.

I had to admire this handful of Anu who had remained trapped here in the Kali rift in a physical form, cut off from their soul group and all the creature comforts of an astral form and lifestyle. I would do all within my power to ensure that their gamble paid off, so they wouldn't be forced to endure this wretched crusade on our behalf in the first place. It was also plain to me — and to everyone else, I suspected — that Ereshkigal bore Killian's demise like a cross; and given my chance to influence the final outcome, I would not let him die again.

I stumbled my way towards Ereshkigal in the cockpit. She was listening to Smiter swear about 'shitty Nefilim machinery' when I entered and requested to speak with her a moment.

'Well, if it isn't my saviouress.' Smiter acknowledged me with a wave. 'To tell you the truth, I'm not too sure which lifestyle was more hellish!'

Still rather scruffy in appearance for one of the Anu, Smiter wore a large smile on his face and it was plain to see that despite the terrible working conditions he truly enjoyed his rebel existence.

'I'm sure there are places we'd all rather be,' I replied, 'and I aim to see that we get there.'

'I've lived in some pretty bad time lines in the past, but any change to this one will be an improvement.' He punched a fist into the air to spur me on.

'I'll do my best,' I assured him, and followed Ereshkigal into a small electronics bay located behind the cockpit. Once there, I apologised for the need to ask her the date she had last seen Killian alive.

'The twentieth of December, 2017,' she replied, looking uncomfortable.

'Morning or evening?'

'Just before nightfall.' She struggled to prevent tears welling in her eyes. 'Killian went after Mathu when he failed to return from a secret meeting with Kali. You must not let him go into Irkalla,' she stressed. 'Ill has more power over him than he realises, and in Irkalla the Sanat Kumara cannot assist him. Once Ill has absorbed Killian's vital fluids, he will possess all of his psychic ability and then the devil will have true power. You *must not* allow Killian to go to Mathu's rescue.'

'I promise,' I said.

'Hey, Ki-gal,' Smiter called from the cockpit, 'we've got a major blizzard down there.'

We'd been flying above the weather, but now had to descend into it to land.

'It's about to get bumpy,' Ereshkigal said, and advised that I go find something to grab onto.

'What do you mean, *about to?*' I jested, feeling that surely the ride couldn't get much worse than it already was without this vessel being shaken apart.

The Nefilim's attempts to speed global warming in order to free their ships trapped at the South Pole had backfired badly. For although the fireball incident at the North Pole had melted the ice cap and flooded the globe, the resulting storms that had plunged the surface of the planet into the utter darkness of a nuclear winter had sped up the freezing process in Antarctica and plunged the lower part of the planet into a mini Ice Age.

Ereshkigal followed me back to the mid-section. 'We'll descend to the ice flats and then drill through to the Signet station,' she advised us all.

We gave her the thumbs up and did our best to get comfortable.

'You may as well kiss goodbye to any feeling in your arse for the next couple of hours,' she added with a grin. 'By the time this is over, any of the hells in Irkalla will seem an attractive proposition.'

CHAPTER 34

SLEEPING BEAUTY

TAMAR DEVERE — KALI

After my return to Irkalla and the ranks of the Nefilim, I resumed dabbling in the genetic research I'd carried out for Lord Ill once before. It hadn't taken me long to pick up where I had left off. With all their brainwashing know-how, the Nefilim allowed me to remember just what I needed in order to aid them. Nevertheless, I suspected there were many aspects of our history that they had blocked from my memory, as the lab itself kept sparking a feeling of something gravely important that I'd forgotten about.

It didn't take much for me to learn to hate with the intensity the Nefilim did, for in order to prove my loyalty I was challenged to betray allies from my past.

The day before the SAC alignment was to end — when I was sure the staff of Amenti were not going to reappear — I arranged for Lugh to bring me the Rod and Ring of Power that Ill so desired. To my bitter sorrow, Mathu accompanied Lugh to the meeting and I was forced to kill them both before my kindred did so much more cruelly and painfully. I also handed over the Amenti stargate system to our enemies — not that the trade served the Nefilim for very long, for as soon as the last moment of the SAC alignment passed, the stargate system shut down. The rod and ring were rendered useless and, cut off from the Earth grid, the Sphere of Amenti returned up the Ark porthole passage towards the Pleiades star system where it had been hidden for aeons before this. Unfortunately, the event also cut off humanity from its soul group and all the guardian races. So although Ill's plan to conquer the universe via the stargates was put on hold, his desires to dominate humanity and build an empire of darkness were consolidated, and I remained in favour.

I was working in my lab the day I began to reawaken from my thousand-year nightmare. The sound of an explosion close by snatched my attention, then there was another. Could today be the day I had waited a millennium for?

'Irkalla is under Dracon attack,' Erragal advised through the intercom.

I gasped as a flash of déjà vu transported me back hundreds of thousands of years to the last time the Dracon had declared war. I had been in my lab, just as I was now. In my memory, the six observation tanks, which contained several dead mutant Nefilimcrossbreeds, transformed into six stasis tanks. I moved closer and was shocked to find they contained six Dracon females.

My eyes widened with the revelation, then Erragal stormed into my lab and snatched my attention back to the present.

'Ill wants to see you,' he ordered, and waited for me to accompany him.

433

He and Namtar led me to Ill's main court; both Nefilim warriors were wearing their hideous true forms today. 'Is it Halloween?' I jeered, hoping they might disclose some information. 'Or are we just trying to look a little scarier for our enemies?'

'Shut up, slut.' Namtar slapped me across the face for speaking out of turn.

I was no longer considered a threat since I'd become Ill's mistress and an Orme addict like the rest of them. I cursed Namtar under my breath, maintaining my shadow self and the delusion that suppressed my true reason for being in Irkalla.

We passed a window that looked down upon the palace courtyard and I was distracted by the sight of Dracon and human warriors fighting it out to the death using all manner of weaponry, modern and old. This was a repeat of the same battle that had prompted Kali to suicide during her first life here on Earth! In this instance, however, the human contingent had been brainwashed to become the same mindless killing machines the Dracon had once been. The Dracon, on the other hand, had evolved enough to know that they were tired of being subordinate to the Nefilim, and so had decided to re-enact their infamous rebellion of the past. But who was leading them?

'Took you long enough!' Ill was slouched on his throne, wearing Killian's form. The Dark Lord often assumed this form since Killian's sad demise in order to hurt me as much as possible.

When Lugh and Mathu did not return from their fatal meeting with me, Killian had come looking for the three of us. Once the SAC alignment ended, he was cut off from all higher dimensions and could not draw on the cosmic support of the Sanat Kumara or the Blue Flame of Amenti to defeat Ill.

Ill did not get the privilege of sucking Killian's soul dry as he'd planned to, however, for Killian was smart enough to take his own life, swearing with his final breath that this wasn't the last Ill would see of him. If Ill had got to Killian whilst he was alive, all his incarnations in every lifetime would have ceased to exist! I had murdered my prince and the legendary Lugh Lamhfada for the same reason: to protect their existence in other lifetimes. Without Mathu I could not bring down the Sphere of Amenti and none of the Amenti team would be able to return to Tara.

Ever since Killian's death and my murder of my prince and Lamhfada, I had hoped and prayed that when I found the staff of Amenti in this the year 2976, I would be able to go back in time and save them all. I realised now what Killian had forgiven me for in his New York hotel room, and his words of forgiveness had been my only comfort since that time. My psychic senses had been dulled by my addiction to Orme, so every time I looked at Ill, I saw only Killian and all the unfulfilled potential of the man I had led to his death.

'I plan to destroy this backwater hole of a planet today,' Ill began casually.

I panicked for a second as the staff of Amenti still had not manifested here in the future as I had expected they would — or had they? I had thought the Dracon uprising was the catalyst for this drastic move, or was there another reason Ill sought to destroy the Earth on this day in particular? I swallowed my panic and said composedly, 'This is sudden, my lord.'

'Not really,' Ill advised. 'I've had this event planned for over a thousand years.'

This seemed to confirm what I suspected. Could I dare to believe that the staff of Amenti had finally returned to Earth? The thought brought relief in waves and my heart filled with joy. Although weakened by the heavy weight of my Orme addiction, the violet flame I harboured within me burned its way through the dense blockages in my being. Even the intense sadness and pain I felt at the loss of my prince and my friends was a blessing compared with the numbness of my past state of being. Nevertheless, I blocked the transformation yearning to take place within me. *Not yet*, I told myself. *It could be a trick*. But in truth, I did not care any more — damned to a state of nothingness would be paradise compared with life in Irkalla.

'Treasonous bitch!' Ill spat at me, but the way he squirmed denoted his fear. 'Your very presence makes me want to hurl. It wouldn't surprise me if you were the mastermind behind this Dracon rebellion!'

I laughed, sincerely amused by his accusation. 'I am flattered that you think me so resourceful and ingenious … but I don't need an army to conquer you, my lord.'

Seduction oozed from my mouth, sweet as honey, and as I walked slowly towards his throne I assumed an Anu form using an auric simulator. (My Orme addiction prevented me from doing this through my own power.) Ill held no feelings for me, but if there was one thing I had learned from our intimate association it was that he still had a thing for his long-ascended queen, Ninlil. He often ordered me to assume her form before we mated.

Ill sat back, appearing unmoved. 'Don't think you can fuck with my heart, Kali. I don't have one, because that *whore,*' he pointed to my Anu guise, 'ripped it out when she chose the Kian way over me!'

'I know you have gone out of your way to rebel ever since then —'

'I just embraced the dark truth, baby. I was sent to this little hellhole in the universe to take charge and I did!'

'You've halted evolution in all five harmonic universes!' I pointed out sarcastically and Ill laughed, flattered.

'Now that's power! I am more powerful than the Sovereign Integral, so why should I settle for its extensively long, harsh, *insignificant* plan for me?' He leered at me. 'I used you, *sweet arse,* and now that you are of no further use to me, I'm going to leave you. I do hope you enjoy the final holocaust we have planned for you this afternoon. Not much point sending you a postcard from the Eye of Ra, but I assure you that I'll destroy the capstone and send every evolution in this universe and the next spiralling into my devolution within the Kali rift.'

I managed to stop my jaw dropping as I learned of the Nefilim's full aspirations. Whether or not they had the resources to back up Ill's claims, it was still a very scary premise.

'So this is goodbye, Kali — you always were a treacherous snake. And don't worry — once I've defrosted my mother ship, I'll finally dispose of your secret little science project. I'm hardly going to risk a repeat performance of today's revolution in the future.'

'I was under the impression you'd disposed of them already,' I said. Ill had screwed with my brain so often I could no longer trust my own memory. Then I noticed the presence I was speaking with beginning to break up. '*Ill*, you coward!' I yelled. This was the second time I had been tricked in this way.

The simulation laughed at how long it had taken me to realise that I was wasting my energy on a relay device. Killian's form waved farewell as it broke down into a swarm of flying nanobots that quickly dispersed through a grate in the wall and were gone.

'I have suffered long and hard for the privilege to uncreate this dark hole in the universe,' I said, under my breath at first, for I was so used to repressing my thoughts and feelings. But then I spoke up loud and proud. 'I will rewrite history,' I announced determinedly, 'and Irkalla will fade into myth where it belongs!'

Overwhelmed by the task of finding the staff of Amenti and the means to return us all to the past, I fell to my knees and allowed myself to weep like I never had, never could. And for the first time in an age, I let myself recall the last few private hours I had spent with Mathu. How I longed to know him again ... how I longed to feel *anything* again. With a mighty howl, my desire to embrace the horror that was my life shattered the casing around my light-body and all my withheld feelings rushed through my light centres like a whirlwind. My entire body went into spasm as the high frequency of the violet flame forced out the dis-ease and purged me of the dark fluid.

The agony was unparalleled, and sparked in me memories of Kali's experience of the same process during her first lifetime as one of the Anunnaki. There had been someone watching over her then, to ensure that she did not kill herself during the seizure — a loyal assistant. I recalled her words.

'Great mistress, it is too dangerous to keep going.'

Kali had implored her to be brave. 'I must do this, Jezabel, for all our sakes.'

I remembered how, in the midst of her delirium, Kali kept her focus on her assistant's concerned face. Jezabel was not Nefilim, nor was she human; she was a rarity never before seen upon the Earth — a female Dracon. This top-secret project had been assigned to Kali by Ill himself, and had been long forgotten by all but a handful of the fallen still left on Earth. If the female Dracon were still in stasis on Ill's mother ship as he claimed, and weren't rescued before Amenti was opened, then these six souls would be left behind.

When my vomiting subsided and I could again draw a deep breath, I hauled myself upright and wiped my soiled face on my clothes. 'This war ends yesterday,' I vowed with renewed conviction.

CHAPTER 35

ICE BREAKING

MIA DEVERE — MERIDAN

The descent to the icy surface had been severe, as expected, but otherwise uneventful. Somehow the craft had held together and, having engaged the large drill head on the nose of our vessel, we were now ploughing our way through a thousand metres of ice under which Signet Station One was buried.

'This isn't so bad,' Dexter yelled over the deafening sound of the drill head. 'How many hours did they say it was going to ...'

The drill shut off and all fell silent.

'... take?' He lowered his voice.

Ereshkigal entered, a stunned expression on her face. 'We have a little surprise development,' she said, opening the hatch door, whereby stairs dropped to ground level. The exterior lights of our craft illuminated a tunnel already drilled through the ice, using a drill head twice the size of our own.

'Well that's rather impressive!' said Polaris, reflecting the sentiments of all. We climbed down and observed the freshly made passage. 'Nefilim obviously.' He looked to Ereshkigal for her opinion.

She nodded.

'I thought the portholes were useless to them?' Dexter was concerned for his station.

Ereshkigal shrugged. 'They are.'

'And why would the Nefilim be interested in this porthole, which can only lead back to Irkalla now?' Dexter looked even more perplexed.

'How shall we proceed?' Ereshkigal asked. 'There's another porthole to Irkalla at Giza — we could try that one.'

Zalman spoke up. 'If this is a trap, they'll have laid another at Giza.'

'Confront them now or confront them later, it's all the same to me,' Arcturus said.

The rest of the staff were of the same mind, so we seconded his suggestion and clambered back on board.

When we reached the much larger cavity in the ice where the Signet station was located, we found a super-sized model of our own vehicle parked there and abandoned. Beyond a field of frozen stalagmites, the Signet station lit up like a Christmas tree then faded into darkness again.

'What the hell is going on?' Dexter raced off into the station.

'Wait, Dex!' Polaris called out, but to no end, so he and Arcturus went after him.

As I was the only one among us with any psychic power, I felt compelled to join the charge.

'Thank you, for everything,' I said to Ereshkigal, and took her hand to convey how heartfelt my sentiments were. 'I shall see you in the past.'

'Take care of Killian,' she instructed.

'We all will,' Talori assured her, and dragged me by the arm into the tunnel.

In the cavern before us an icy path led through the forest of frozen stalagmites to the entrance of Signet Station One. Our steps were more cautious now, and as we reached the control centre we spied a handful of Dracon. All bar one of the reptilian warriors stepped onto the defunct porthole. The remaining warrior held an ankh tool out before him and fired at it with one of Levi's liquid-light guns. The small blast of liquid light was amplified and shot a stream of Blue Flame energy into the porthole — strong enough to light up the entire Signet station for a few moments and send his comrades into Irkalla.

'They must be using the porthole to invade the city,' Dexter whispered to us.

'Exactly right,' said the remaining Dracon, turning in our direction.

Dexter nearly had a heart attack. 'Taejax!' he cried, and went running to greet his old comrade. Polaris and Levi were close behind.

My first acquaintance with our primary Dracon ally had taken place way back when we opened the Hall of Records, before Tamar had even been born! Many of the staff had known and worked with Taejax for centuries longer. Last time we had all seen him, the reptilian warrior had been blown to pieces saving Tamar's life.

'What are you doing here? *How* are you here?' Dexter had never expected to see the Dracon warrior, now turned Anu, back on Earth.

'Waiting for you, of course,' he retorted. 'Been waiting a *long* time.'

'When did you get back?' Polaris gave the reptilian a large slap on the shoulder. 'And why are you back in your Dracon guise?'

'I came back after I heard about the aftershock of the RRT,' he said. 'I figured I owed it to you all to come help you finish up down here.'

Solarian gave the creature a huge hug. 'Good show, old chum.'

'As for my choice of exterior,' Taejax went on, 'since being cut off from all the higher dimensions, we Anu can no longer shape-shift and so I had to choose a form to inhabit for this mission. This one has served my purpose better than any.'

'Where did you get that?' Levi pointed to the liquid-light gun in the reptilian's hand.

'Off the *Klieo*,' replied Taejax and Polaris almost jumped on him.

'When?'

'A few weeks back —'

Polaris gave a whoop of joy, then calmed himself to hear the details. 'How is she?'

'She appears fine, Captain,' Taejax informed him with a grin. 'She just got blown off her mooring. She must have drifted into the tornado region and got spat out south of the equator where she washed up on one of the outermost ice banks of the Antarctic. I picked her up on radar and, after much digging through ice, we found her, hooked her up to our vessel and towed her out of the ice.'

'Where is she now?' Polaris asked eagerly.

Taejax pointed straight up. 'We towed her here to keep an eye on her.'

Polaris gave the reptilian a smacking kiss on the cheek. 'You utter, *utter* legend!' he said. 'That's our ticket out of here … if she'll still start. Do the Nefilim know about her?'

'Ah, no,' Taejax was proud to say. 'I've been keeping them a little occupied lately. A few weeks back the Dracon launched a rebellion, attacking Nefilim centres around the globe. I saved Irkalla for today, which is why our big, ugly friends were far too occupied to try and track down you lot when you materialised here in 2976, despite their full intention to seek and destroy.'

'2976,' Solarian repeated. 'Why does that year ring a bell with me? Something significant happens then — I just can't recall the exact details at present.'

'It's the year that Mathu predicted Ill would finally destroy surface Earth and all who live upon her,' Taejax said. He'd been present at the same gathering that Solarian was beginning to remember.

'That's right,' Polaris said; he had been present at the prediction too, and he looked at Vespera, who also remembered.

'What is left to destroy?' I asked in disbelief.

Taejax motioned around us, referring to the Antarctic region, then pointed up to the star ships frozen in the station's icy ceiling. 'Not even Ill wants to live here any more — he's going to try to simulate the fireball disaster that nearly destroyed the planet, only this time he's aiming at the Antarctic.'

'Tell me they haven't planned the attack for today?' Levi just knew he was asking too much.

'I cannot tell a lie, boss,' Taejax said to his old friend. 'They know you're on Earth now, and even if they can't murder you all personally, they'll want to ensure you're dead before they depart.'

'Then we don't have much time,' I said, and stepped onto the inactive porthole.

Everyone else followed suit, except Polaris.

'I'm no good to you down there,' he said, and glanced back towards the entrance to the Signet station. 'I should go take a look at the *Klieo* and ready her to depart.'

Levi stepped off the porthole to join him. 'You might need some help with that.'

'I can get Kali out of Irkalla on my own,' Taejax assured us all. 'The fewer of us we have to get to the *Klieo* at the last minute, the better.'

'A good point.' Denera stepped off the porthole, as did everyone else not integral to the mission, which left Taejax, Arcturus, Dexter and me.

Arcturus looked at me. 'If they're going to start the ship and test the systems, they'll need power.'

But I wanted to rescue our daughter. 'How will you get back topside without me?' I said.

Taejax raised his light-gun. 'I still have plenty of ammo.' He passed me a small hand-held communications device. 'We'll keep in touch.' Then he guided me back off the porthole and, before I could protest further, shot his ankh with a liquid-light bullet and activated the porthole once again.

'Don't worry,' Arcturus said with a big smile, before he dropped down the funnel into spook world central.

CHAPTER 36

MELTDOWN

TAMAR DEVERE — KALI

I'd led the world into a holocaust and betrayed friend and foe. Today was the day I'd find out if I was to be damned for my actions, or if the universe had understood and supported the method behind my madness.

What to do? I thought as I raced to the main court chamber's door. I feared the door would be electronically locked from the outside, but before I could test it, it slid aside and there was a Dracon in my path.

This was no ordinary Dracon, however, for beyond his brutal exterior I saw the splendid form of an Anu warrior. 'Taejax?' I gasped, recognising him from many of my lives on Earth. I was doubly taken aback to realise my psychic talents had returned. 'I thought you were dead!' I cried.

'Long story.' He grabbed hold of my hand and began dragging me back through the palace.

'Ill plans to melt the South Pole today,' I yelled over the din of the battle.

'Tell me something I don't know,' Taejax said, and continued to pull me along, at the same time fending off the human bodies falling all around us, who, despite their frenzied bloodlust, were dropping like flies under the more seasoned attack of the Dracon.

'But he's going to —'

'It doesn't matter what he's going to do,' Taejax insisted, 'as we are going to undo it.'

We passed through the Dracon front line and into the part of the palace they had already secured.

'We are?' I said hopefully and Taejax nodded.

'Provided we can get you out of here before our exit door gets fried!'

'Tamar!'

I heard my father's voice, and saw him standing up ahead. I pulled free from Taejax's grasp and ran towards him. 'Father!' I cried, wanting to throw myself into his embrace and revel in the comfort and peace of it as I had when I was young. But Arcturus drew his sword in warning and I slowed. 'Father?' I couldn't stop my welling tears from choking my voice.

'Is it true that you lured Lugh, Mathu and Killian to their deaths?' he demanded.

'Yes, it's true,' I spluttered, 'I killed them myself.' I lost my breath at the memory, overwhelmed by grief. Eventually, I managed to continue. 'I had to do it, to get into Irkalla and wait out your return. I thought the Rod and Ring of Power could get us back to the past, but they were rendered useless after the SAC alignment ...' I collapsed to my knees before my father, weeping uncontrollably — there were so many painful memories I had suppressed. 'I killed Lugh and Mathu for nothing!' I sobbed. 'I'd planned to go back and change everything, but now ... you may as well kill me.'

'You know I cannot kill you, I have to take you back with us,' Arcturus said.

'But I've just got through telling you that I have no way to get us back!' I wept.

My father's response was to sheath his sword, and when I ventured to look at him, his smile filled me with joy.

'You've found a way,' I said, and with the realisation I summoned the energy I needed to stand up again. My actions had been supported and to me that was the universe's way of saying 'we were with you all the way'.

'I've missed you, Father,' I said, my voice hoarse with the relief of being in his presence again.

He embraced me and stroked the back of my head. 'I will always believe that your intentions are the best, child, but that's not to say the rest of Amenti's staff will see it that way.'

'I know.'

'The chit-chat can wait,' Taejax said, urging us to keep moving.

As I was still a little unstable, my father swept me off the ground and carried me in his arms. I allowed my weary head to rest upon his shoulder. It was heartening to know that there was still one place on this screwed-up planet where I felt safe.

'I'm so sorry if I've been a worry to you,' I said.

'Sweetheart, you are one of the very few souls on this planet who isn't a worry to me.'

He kissed the top of my head as we stepped into the elevator and descended to the labyrinth of Ereshkigal.

The porthole back to surface Earth was being guarded by Dexter and several Dracon.

'Since when have the righteous had such a large contingent of Dracon?' I asked.

'Since the time of the RRT,' Taejax informed me, 'when I returned to Earth as a Dracon and started enlightening my kindred from within their Underworldly ranks.'

I gasped as I realised something. 'That would have been another contributing factor to the success of the RRT — no one would have expected the excess of high frequency on Earth at that time to be coming from the Dracon quarter.'

'Indeed,' Taejax concurred, 'the Nefilim consider reptilians to be mindless, souless and so unevolved that they have never attempted to bring my species under the influence of their frequency fence.'

The Dracon around him were amused by this, and I was amused to see Dracon laughing. Beneath their harsh exteriors they were Dracon no longer; they were my people — or at least they were Anu who would one day evolve into the Anunnaki. I knew these Dracon from my time in Irkalla — they were all of high rank — and yet I had never seen Taejax in the Underworld until today. Obviously our ally had been operating behind the scenes, where there was less danger of him being recognised, and these highly placed Dracon had been reporting to him. I was so proud of them all for fighting for their right to evolve despite the long, miserable, lonely plight of their race. I had always felt one of Ill's cruellest curses was his decree that all Dracon be male. For the hundreds and thousands of years these warriors had survived on Earth, forced to sustain their existence by the most violent means or to perish as a species, they had never known a loving moment — not the love of a mother, lover or child! What a miracle it was that they could still choose to pursue a path of compassion.

'Thank you.' I placed a hand on Taejax's shoulder to convey my appreciation. 'Thank you all — you will be rewarded for your devotion and bravery.' I looked back at their leader. 'If I were to contact you in the past, Taejax, would you meet with me?'

'But, of course, Your Highness,' he said and bowed. 'I am at your service. However, I had not secured a huge amount of support from among the Dracon before the SAC alignment passed, and it took many hundreds of years to convert so many. I fear —'

'Fear not,' I assured him. 'I have something that should speed the troops to your cause rather more swiftly.'

Taejax looked baffled by my claim. 'I look forward … or should I say, I look *back* to our meeting with great anticipation.'

I smiled, then thought to ask: 'How shall I find you?'

'Lamhfada knows where to find me.'

The name took my breath away. I could hardly wait to get back to the past and find safe and sound all those I had betrayed and mourned so long.

When we returned via the porthole to the control centre of Signet Station One, the station was being rattled by the deep resounding pulses of an imminent electromagnetic blast.

I was all too familiar with the sound, as the last time I had heard it was the last beautiful sunny day on Earth. It was also the last day any being on the planet had known freedom — any being who did not drown, freeze or get burnt to a crisp.

'We're never going to make it back to the surface

before that fireball gets here,' Dexter said, leading the sprint to the exit anyway.

'Run!' I heard the waiting Amenti staff members yelling at the top of their lungs from just beyond the ice forest of the outer station.

My father picked up speed, swept me up on the way past and delivered me to the *Klieo* in seconds flat.

'Oh my God!' I looked at him, stunned, as he put me down.

'Yes, my child,' he replied with a grin, then headed off to see what Polaris was doing about getting us out of here.

'Kali, child, you had us worried.' Denera hugged me tight.

'You certainly did,' Ashlee said, joining our hug, followed by Talori, Thana and Vespera.

'Meridan wanted to go into Irkalla after you again, and she wanted to be here to welcome your safe return,' Denera told me.

'But she's being a battery for the ship —' Talori stopped mid-sentence as the drone of the electromagnetic pulse reached a deafening crescendo.

I looked outside to see Taejax standing alone on the ice, watching our departure.

'Come with us!' I implored him, unable to bear that in a moment he would die a horrid fiery death.

'I am already there,' he replied.

The hatch door closed and bolted itself, and the blue-green weblike light field of our vessel's time-shift function engulfed our surroundings. The force and noise of the fireball explosion that erupted in our wake disappeared as the *Klieo* made a quantum leap that reversed the event on our way back to 2017.

CHAPTER 37

THE ASCENDING SPIRAL — 2017 AD

The Amenti team had made a decision to return to 20 December 2017 rather than exactly the same time we had left. If we could bring the sphere down shortly before the SAC alignment ended, that gave the Nefilim no leeway to go forward in time and change the outcome. This also minimised how long we'd need to keep Killian safe from Ill.

I received a grilling about my future conduct from my fellow staff members, all except my mother, who was still unconscious after powering the *Klieo* back in time a thousand years, and my father, who had been despatched, at my insistence, to fetch Killian to safety. I was also demanding to see Lugh and Mathu.

Denera flatly refused. 'Not until we're convinced you are no longer a threat to them.'

'I have to make contact with Taejax as well,' I told her.

She frowned. 'Why?'

'Because he's the only Dracon I know and trust.' I thought this obvious.

'Yes, I understand that,' Denera was getting frustrated too, 'but why do you need a Dracon at all?'

Ereshkigal entered the conference room in Signet Station Four where I was being questioned. 'Arcturus said to let you know that he has Killian with him.'

'Are they here?' I needed to know that Killian was secure within the Amenti complex.

'It's best that you don't know his whereabouts,' Denera cut in, before Ereshkigal could answer my question. It hurt to think I was no longer a trusted part of the team — if, indeed, I ever really was.

'As long as *you* know where he is,' I insisted. 'The same goes for Lugh and Mathu.'

'Shall I chase them up?' Ereshkigal offered. 'I believe Lugh is in his city of Murias, and Mathu is there also.'

'Let me go with her,' I pleaded as Denera gave her the nod. 'Technically I won't be leaving the Otherworld or your jurisdiction.'

'Give me one good reason why I should let you go,' she challenged.

'I'll give you six good reasons.' I took a deep breath in preparation for all the fast talking I had to do.

It was odd to have a smiling Ereshkigal escorting me to Lugh on this mission, for in the future she hated me and had been something of a nemesis; not that I blamed her for getting the wrong impression.

We gained access to Lugh's city through one of the three portholes in the outer chamber of the Giza complex, and emerged from it into the altogether more vibrant and supple realms of the lower astral world. Everything was spectacular here: sounds were more melodic, colours more vibrant, smells more aromatic, touch was a stronger physical sensation, and taste ... well, if you belonged to the physical world it was best not to eat or drink anything here lest you never leave. This was the heaven that we could have on Earth any day now.

The city was beautiful and tranquil. Nobody rushed, as time meant nothing. Nobody worked — they played, they imagined, they learned, experimented, theorised and thrived on the one thing that was truly important in life: *creation*. Be it the creation of family, fine food, great art, scientific invention or beautiful music, everything here was crafted with the greatest of care — it was the exact opposite to Irkalla. Every long-lost Earth species still survived here, in perfect harmony with the Anu residents and the ascendant masters of the human race. There was nothing required for life here that could not be manifested by will; hence there was no need to fight with another or make war. If only the humans of Earth understood that the same principles of intention and manifestation applied on that plane too. All one needed was a fully functioning emotional body filled with compassion — for compassion generated love and created the will and wisdom to manifest what those on surface Earth considered miracles. Here, in the Otherworld, such miraculous occurrences were everyday life.

In Lugh's palace, however, evidence of the Otherworldly alliance with the humans on surface Earth was more visible: we saw Anu warriors donning battle armour.

'It looks as though they're gearing up for battle,' I said.

Ereshkigal was amused that I hadn't foreseen this. 'They are gearing up for the war to end all wars; the only battle in history that will ever really count.'

I smiled. 'They seem to be expecting a lot of resistance, but they won't get it — not if I can help it.'

The doors to Lugh's council chamber were open, and we slowed as we approached for he was speaking with one of my long-lost ancestors, Ninlil. I was delighted to see her back on Earth.

'I must be able to help in some way,' she was saying to Lugh. 'I feel so responsible.'

'Lady, you do not have the constitution for war,' he told her honestly.

'I can command the elements as well as any.'

'To the detriment of your own family.' He implored her to consider what she was asking of herself.

Ninlil hesitated, frustrated.

'Trust me, everything will be fine,' Lugh told her, and drew her into an embrace to reassure her. As he did, he saw us waiting by the door.

'Your Highness! You are back from Irkalla?' He let go of Ninlil and they both bowed to me. Lugh looked confused. 'Have I lost track of time?'

'Pardon?' I had no idea what he was on about.

'I have the rod and the ring right here,' he said, and moved to fetch them.

'Oh!' I realised that he was preparing to go to the meeting where I would murder him. 'There's been a slight change in plan. I need to find Taejax.'

'Taejax!' Lugh halted in his tracks and turned to me. 'How did you know he was back?'

'He told me in the future where I never made it back from Irkalla,' I said, and his face melted in empathy.

'I am so sorry if I failed you, Your Highness,' he stated with all sincerity and I wanted to cry.

'You certainly did not,' I assured him. 'It was I who failed, and I had to, in order to be here today, so no regrets.'

'It is an honour to be in your service, my queen,' he said, and bowed again, before getting back to the point. 'Taejax is deep undercover at present, but I can get word to him. What is it you require?'

'I need him and some of his faithful to join me on a salvage mission.'

Lugh was stunned. 'Now, Your Majesty? But it is the eleventh hour!'

'I realise that, but this is important. Ask Taejax to meet me in the cavern of Mamer as soon as possible.' Now I had only to convince the Amenti team to allow me to take Dracon into Signet Station One.

'It will be done,' Lugh said, although he still looked perplexed.

'My Lady Sud,' I said to Ninlil, using her true name, not the one Ill had given her.

The lady fell to her knees before me. 'I am so ashamed, Your Majesty. My family have disgraced all the Anu.'

'You did not choose your role in this, Lady Sud, it was thrust upon you,' I told her. It was true: Ill had raped her and impregnated her and, due to his royal lineage, they were encouraged to wed. Another three rapes later, she had given Ill four sons to corrupt, and corrupt them he had. 'You are blameless, and a blessing to this universe because there is no warrior in you. Still, you may yet be of service to the plan, so don't go anywhere.'

'Whatever you wish of me, Your Majesty,' she said, and rose to her feet.

I turned my attention back to Lugh. 'I will be back for the rod and ring presently.'

'Very good, Your Highness.'

As I turned to depart I realised there was someone missing. 'I was advised that Mathu might be with you?'

'I have not seen him recently, Your Highness,' he said with a frown. 'I will send a scout to hunt him out, but I feel sure there is no cause for alarm.'

'Many thanks. I shall feel better knowing he is aware of our return.'

'I shall ensure he knows.' Lugh bowed.

I didn't feel so sure of Mathu's safety; I had a horrid feeling in my gut that something was amiss with him. As I was bound to report back to Denera before pursuing my quest, I would ask her to consult the Hall of Records as to Mathu's current whereabouts.

'Not found,' was the Hall of Records' response.

'Is that because all information about Mathu was hacked out of the system in the past?' I asked Denera, who still stood inside the green light-tube of the control platform.

'No,' she said, surprised. 'Since his reappearance, the Hall of Records has been tracking him fine. Just a moment and I'll request to see his whereabouts the last time he was recorded as present on Earth.'

Mathu's image appeared on the walls of the liquid-light chamber: he was entering the Amenti complex's antechamber from the porthole that led into Lugh's realms, with the Rod and Ring of Power in his possession.

I gasped in delight to see him again; it had been so long that his image had blurred in my memory.

But as I watched him cross the chamber towards the porthole to Irkalla, I began to panic. 'No! What are you doing? Please, no ... I am no longer there!' But I was powerless to prevent him entering the porthole to the Underworld. Tears trickled silently down my face. 'When was this?' I asked Denera.

'This morning,' she advised soberly, for she knew the news would sting.

'Right before we arrived,' I said flatly. 'I must go after him.'

'There is no way I'm going to let you venture into Irkalla again,' Denera said. But I could be insistent too.

'What choice do you have? Who can you send who is more capable or experienced than me?'

Denera shut off the light-tube and stepped down from her control panel; she looked affronted. 'May I remind you that with all your skill and know-how we have had to rescue you twice from the Underworld, and there's too much going on right now for me to allocate resources to retrieve you again!'

I humbled myself, which had always been difficult for me since my reunion with Kali. 'My apologies, great lady. I meant no offence and I realise I owe you all so much more than I will ever be able to repay.'

'You do not owe us anything, child, bar your trust in us to handle this,' she advised more gently. 'You have other pressing concerns to take care of.'

I nodded, for she was right: I was far too emotionally involved to be able to think clearly where Mathu was concerned. Denera promised to keep me updated, and advised that she had summoned Dexter and Polaris to aid me with my quest, which I now needed to make the centre of my focus.

This was difficult, for I knew that back in that other time line it was I who had arranged for Lugh to bring me the rod and ring in Irkalla. I suspected that Mathu had anticipated an ambush and had taken the rod and ring into Irkalla early, to prevent Lugh being captured or injured during the handover. Mathu's heroic, misguided actions were my fault; he was being tortured right now and once again I was the reason.

Denera saw my despondency. 'Trust in the universal will that has brought you this far,' she said. 'We will prevail.'

I wanted to believe her, but after such a long and arduous struggle it was becoming harder and harder to believe that the inter-time war would ever end.

'How can you be so sure?' I asked. 'It seems that every time we take a step forward towards our goal, our adversaries shift time and the goal posts move further away.'

'Not today.' Denera reminded me that I had made extraordinary progress in the past twenty-four hours. 'Today, for the first time ever, the staff of Amenti has a full complement of players, and in this game unity is everything.'

CHAPTER 38

STAR-CROSSED LOVER?

MIA DEVERE — MERIDAN

As consciousness slowly took hold, I felt as though I was emerging from a long, intense nightmare. My first thought was for my daughter: I longed to hold her, speak with her and know how she fared. Instead, an image of Ereshkigal's farewell filled my mind: *Take care of Killian.*

Why am I dreaming? I wondered. *I must wake!*

'Killian!' I said, and my eyes shot open and I sat upright. I was on one of the lounges on the bridge of the *Klieo*.

'Right here,' a male voice said, and I looked over to a lounge against the far wall of the flight deck, where Killian sat next to my husband.

'You blacked out, and I figured Killian was the first person you'd want to see upon waking,' Arcturus said with a shrug, 'so I took the liberty of fetching him for you.'

'Praise the goddess.' I drew a deep breath to quell the momentary fear that I'd slept too long and missed Killian's departure for Irkalla.

'I adore you sometimes,' I told my husband, as he approached and crouched before me. I knew Killian wasn't his favourite person.

'Only sometimes?' he challenged.

'All the time,' I admitted, and gave him a kiss.

'Ditto,' he smiled.

'Where's Tamar? *How* is Tamar?' I asked, and when his smile didn't waver my heart was lightened of worry.

'She has matured,' he began, 'and is more single-bloody-minded than ever.'

'But her emotional state?' That was my real concern.

'She's been hardened by her experiences,' Arcturus admitted, 'but she is strong and not embittered. If anything, she has found her compassion.'

I breathed a little easier; after such a long season in hell, I had expected my daughter's state of mind to be worse.

'She's off on a mission already,' Arcturus continued. 'She says she has a plan to nullify any Dracon resistance we may encounter.'

Polaris suddenly manifested before us. 'Have I been here before?' he asked.

'What?' Arcturus said, confused, and Polaris gave a laugh.

'I can do it in reverse!' he said, looking mighty pleased with himself. 'Thank you, that was incredibly helpful ... I am a *happy* man.'

He walked out, leaving us baffled.

'So he can teleport too?' I said.

Arcturus looked rather put out. 'That's *my* thing.'

'Oh well, at least he can't crush reinforced metal with his bare hands.' I ruffled my husband's hair to console him.

'Hi there.' Polaris strolled in again. 'Good to see you awake,' he commented.

What? I thought. 'Thanks.'

'Don't mind me,' he said, looking rather excited and nervous.

'Is something the matter, Captain?' I enquired.

'I think I may have finally discovered my psychic forté.'

'Better late than never, I guess,' Arcturus jeered. Polaris was the last of us to discover his gift.

'I'm just going to try it out, if that's okay with you guys.' He held up a finger and vanished.

'Does this conversation seem a little arse-about to you?' Killian said, coming over to join us. 'I don't think Polaris needs the *Klieo* to time-travel any more.'

'What!' Arcturus looked shocked, but impressed.

'So does this mean Polaris is coming back, or was the first time he appeared the end of this conversation?' Killian said.

I had to laugh — my life was truly absurd.

Polaris appeared again and startled us all.

'Did I go anywhere?' he said. 'Or did you teleport?' He pointed to Killian, which made me laugh again.

Killian shook his head. 'You moved a few minutes forward in time.'

Polaris clapped his hands together and did a happy dance, then froze. 'Hey, I wonder if I can go backwards too.'

'You can,' Arcturus said, sounding bored.

'I'll give it a go.' Polaris closed his eyes to focus and vanished.

He reappeared almost instantly and pointed to Killian again. 'You're still over here? Ooops, wrong way.'

'Will you please just leave?' Arcturus snapped, losing patience with the exercise.

'Out of here!' Polaris held up both hands in defence and vanished.

'That could become really annoying,' Arcturus grumbled, taking a seat on the lounge beside me.

'No more annoying than having you pop in when I'm finally getting cosy with Ereshkigal,' Killian retorted.

'Very cosy,' Arcturus advised me.

I felt the need to go into lecture mode. 'Killian, that's the one taboo you can't break —'

'I know, I know,' he cut in, sounding frustrated, 'we belong to different soul groups. But if we never have any offspring then what's the problem? We are still evolving!'

'Sweetie …' I rubbed my forehead, wondering how I could break this to him. 'This is the eve of the end of our days here on Earth, so offspring from an illicit affair really isn't your problem. Once the porthole in Amenti is opened, humanity are all going home to Tara via Amenti. The Anu are going home to Sirius B to the rest of their soul group, via the Hall of Amorea. The chances of you and Ereshkigal finding each other in the Ranna time flow are pretty slim.'

'But there are Anunnaki on Tara — that's how this whole mess got started!' Killian said stubbornly.

'Not in Tara's past, which is where you're bound.'

My wording made Killian curious. 'You're not going there? To Tara's past, I mean?'

'No, we Ceres belong to Tara's Otherworldly realms,' I explained. 'You could say we are timeless in nature.'

Killian smiled. 'So I could still find you all, if I tried hard enough?'

'Heaven forbid!' Arcturus rolled his eyes, but I could tell he was starting to warm to Killian.

Killian returned to his lounge and collapsed onto it. 'What a shit about Ereshkigal. But there must be something that can be done! I mean, surely the Lord of the Earth ...'

I shook my head. 'It is beyond the Sanat Kumara's jurisdiction in the cosmic scheme of things. Killian, can't you trust in the plan of the Sovereign Integral, who is infinitely wiser —'

'No!' Killian was on his feet again. 'God got it wrong! Damn it all!' He looked as if he wanted to kick something. 'Why can't I be one of the Anu?' He slumped back onto the sofa to sulk.

'Was the last saviour this moody?' Arcturus said in an aside to me.

'Way worse.' My thoughts turned to how we were going to keep Killian safe. 'We need to take him into the Amenti complex.'

'No,' Arcturus said, for obvious security reasons.

'But he's a sitting duck anywhere else,' I countered.

'Lovely!' Killian didn't appreciate my comment. 'I'm not completely without influence, you know.'

'Denera suggests that we hide him in Murias until after the SAC alignment has passed,' Arcturus said in a lowered voice, but Killian still overheard.

'That's one of Lugh's capitals! A lot of help I'm going to be during the forthcoming crisis locked away inside an Otherworldly palace!'

'You've done your part, Killian,' I implored him.

'You've raised consciousness on Earth way beyond anyone's expectations. But if Ill gets his Orme spike into you, he's going to take all your power, including your ability to braid and unbraid your DNA. That will grant him access to the Halls of Amenti and the Signet Grid ... and then we can kiss goodbye to evolution in all five harmonic universes.'

Killian's jaw dropped. 'You talk about this like it's already happened.'

'It *has* already happened and we're here to change it,' I told him. 'I promised Ereshkigal that I wouldn't let you die again.'

Killian perked up suddenly. 'You did? She mourned me?'

I nodded, and Arcturus nudged me in warning. 'Don't encourage him,' he said. 'And you wonder why the lad is confused!'

My husband was right, but, deep down, I too thought that the Sovereign Integral might have got it wrong in this case.

'So you'll go to Murias?' I asked Killian.

'Will Ereshkigal be there?' His grin broadened.

'Probably,' Arcturus said. 'At least, she accompanied Tamar to go and see Lamhfada.'

Killian felt bound by his Earthly obligations. 'Do you know what I had to go through to get the Peace Project into the Vatican City? We open tonight!'

'Tomorrow we'll end the Kali rift and all the destruction will be undone,' Arcturus said. But when Killian still looked uncertain, he put his foot down. 'I'll let you loose on surface Earth over my dead body, so ...' He shrugged and raised his eyebrows to await a response.

'Murias,' Killian said, not keen on a fistfight with my husband and his recently discovered super-strength. 'Sounds like a plan.'

We delivered Killian to Lugh Lumhfada's palace, then followed the Anu leader back towards the porthole, as he'd been called to an emergency meeting with Amenti's staff in the Hall of Records.

'What's happening?' Killian asked. He wasn't parting company with us until he knew what the emergency was.

'Ill has Mathu,' Lugh said, keeping us moving.

'He wants me, doesn't he?' Killian guessed.

'I don't know what his demands are,' Lugh replied, trying to avoid the subject, but Killian already knew the truth. He threw himself in front of us to block our path.

'Let me handle Ill for you,' he said. 'I'm stronger than he is. I can —'

'No!' we all insisted at once.

'Mathu has taken Ill the Rod and Ring of Power,' Lugh said, 'so no matter how powerful you think you are —'

'What? No! No, no, no, no, no!' Killian grabbed his head with both hands, overwhelmed by grief. 'It's my fault! Mathu wouldn't have known about the ambush if I hadn't told him!'

'What ambush?' Lugh asked, confused, but Arcturus, having been to the future, understood what Killian was talking about.

'I know what he means,' Arcturus said. 'What I would like to know is how Killian knows?'

'Can we sort this out later?' Lugh was getting frustrated by the delay.

'Promise me you'll stay put,' I said to Killian, as I was less likely to get an argument. 'Please.'

I waited to receive a reluctant nod, before I moved through the porthole after the others.

We were halfway through the outer chamber of the Giza complex when I looked back to see that Killian had followed us.

'I know Ill won't destroy the Amenti complex if he believes he can use it,' Killian said, moving towards the porthole that led into Irkalla.

'Where the hell do you think you're going? Take one more step towards that porthole and I'll forget that my lady holds you in such high regard!' Arcturus said, moving to apprehend him.

With a thought, Killian sent him hurtling backwards.

'I'm sorry, Arcturus, but I have to do this — it is written.'

'What are you talking about?' I said. 'Written where?'

Killian shrugged, frustrated and apologetic. 'No time,' he said.

'If Ill gets his hands on you, there will be nothing to stop him from taking not only the Giza complex but the entire Signet Grid!' Lugh warned.

'Sorry again, old friend, but you're wrong. I am the *only* one who can stop him,' Killian said, and we all gasped in horror as he took a flying leap through the porthole into the Underworld.

'Goddess almighty!' Lugh said, horrified.

'Arrogant little pri—'

'Arcturus,' I said, 'try to be constructive. We'll go after Killian. Lugh, you inform the rest of the staff what's happened.'

Lugh gave a nod, although he was curious. 'Have you written a prophecy about these events, Meridan? What did he mean "it is written"?'

I gasped so suddenly that I startled both my companions. 'The third book of my trilogy,' I said, thinking back twenty years to Montauk. 'Erragal took the only copy from my Signet station. Killian must have read it.'

'Then maybe he does know what he's doing?' Lugh said, most intrigued, before hurrying off to report to the Hall of Records.

'I still think he's trouble,' Arcturus said, following me to the porthole.

I was trying to keep an open mind, for I believed Killian thought he was doing the right thing. Whether he could truly defeat Ill, or he was just attempting to satisfy his ego by defeating his childhood demon, remained to be seen.

Before entering the porthole, I turned to my husband and kissed him. 'To hell with us then,' I said, making light of our sudden change of plan.

'At least this time we get to go together.' He grabbed both my hands and pulled me into the Underworld after him.

The portal into Irkalla didn't lead to Ereshkigal's labyrinth, where we had entered before; it led directly to Ill's great courtroom. Arcturus and I were dropped onto a raised lit platform surrounded by an abyss that fell away into darkness. The room itself was formed of dark matter and the porthole that had granted us entry could have been located anywhere within the darkness that surrounded us on three sides. Across the abyss were the thrones of Irkalla. In the largest lolled the biggest, ugliest Nefilim I'd ever seen. Beside him, on what had once been Ereshkigal's throne, sat Mathu. The Nefilim had him in a headlock, and in his free hand he held the Rod of Power with the pouch containing the ring hanging from it.

My heart began to pound with fear.

Killian was at the foot of the stairs that led up to the thrones, on his knees and offering himself in exchange for Mathu. I wondered why the rest of the Nefilim weren't present. Then again, Ill planned to gain a lot of power and glory today through Killian's death, and the Nefilim weren't inclined to share.

'Have you lost your mind?' Mathu forced out through his restricted air passage.

Ill smashed him in the face, then turned back to Killian. 'Your compassion repulses me,' he said, his voice so guttural it was difficult to understand.

'What compassion? I want Ereshkigal,' Killian informed the demon lord. 'As a human I cannot have her, but if I join with you, I can.'

'Join with me, boy, and you can have anything in the five universes that you desire.' Ill stood, forcing Mathu to as well, and pointed to us. 'Why are they here?'

Killian pointed to the Rod of Power.

'In that case ...' Ill began chanting words I did not understand and huge square Orme blocks closed in on us from every side.

'Hop on,' Arcturus said, encouraging me onto his back, and I didn't argue. I climbed on and he backed up as far as he could and took a running jump at the oncoming Orme wall. His feet hit the upper part of the block, which flipped it horizontal just long enough for him to use it as a springboard to land us before the thrones of Irkalla.

'Move your arse, boy!' Ill urged Killian closer, as he punched Mathu again, then dropped him. He grabbed Killian and turned him about to position the Orme spike against the base of his neck.

I longed to prevent the tragedy, but Killian motioned with his hands for me to refrain, then closed his eyes calmly — as if he were about to meditate rather than be obliterated. Didn't he realise it would? That once the demon took him, Killian would cease to exist and his soul would be damned and lost forever! Still, I reasoned, forever in accordance with this evolution may be less than a day away.

Arcturus nudged me. 'Stop him!'

I turned my third-eye vision on Killian and was stunned to see his astral form standing outside of his physical body, which Ill was holding. When Killian realised I could see his spirit, he smiled mischievously and held a finger to his lips.

'He isn't called the Chosen One without good reason,' I whispered to Arcturus.

As I spoke, Ill activated the Orme spike and thrust it up through Killian's neck and into the pineal gland inside his brain.

'Merciful goddess!' Arcturus cried, frozen in painful empathy.

Ill wailed with delight as he absorbed Killian's genetic data through his vital fluids. The demon lord thought he was damning the lad's soul in the process, but Killian's soul mind was very much whole and stood calmly observing his death.

While Ill was distracted, Mathu snuck up behind him and attempted to retrieve the Rod and Ring of

Power from where Ill had set them aside. Ill, still mid-transformation, grabbed Mathu by the scruff of the neck.

'Hard to believe that the runt of the family could cause me so much annoyance,' he growled. He let Killian's drained body drop from his spike and reached around to grab the rod and ring from Mathu.

Arcturus ran towards the dark lord but Ill, now fully transformed into Killian's form, tossed the tools of power to him. 'Give me a reason, because I would just love to kill this annoying little fuck!' he said, shaking Mathu's body like a rag-doll.

Arcturus halted his charge.

'Give the tools to the Black Madonna,' Ill ordered, sounding very smug.

'No!' Mathu yelled, and Ill head-butted him.

'Who is about as far from black as she could be!' Ill added, sounding amused. 'She wouldn't have been my first guess for the Black Madonna; in fact, I would never have found her if not for your obsession with defeating Molier,' he told Arcturus, whose eyes opened wide with horror. 'If you hadn't made her aware of who and what she was, we might still be looking for her.'

'Don't listen to him,' I told my husband, who was starting to seethe. 'If you hadn't made me aware of who I was, I would never have defeated Molier.'

I shot a glance to Killian's ghost, who nodded and urged me to do as Ill requested. My husband tossed me the tools, shaking his head. I was worried too. How deeply did I really trust Killian? Was this the ultimate opportunity or was I being seduced by the devil himself?

I will make you proud, Killian's spirit told me. *Come on, Meridan, this is my destiny — you know it is!*

I took the ruby Ring of Power from the pouch.

Arcturus frowned. 'What are you doing? You're going to use that against him, right?'

'Let Mathu go,' I said as I held the ring against the hilt of the long, sleek double-ended sword that was the Rod of Power.

'Form the staff first,' Ill demanded.

I pushed gently and the ring passed right through the rod. In a blinding golden-red flash of light, the coil fastened into place and hardened around the rod's hilt. The pulsing energy that emanated from each of these objects individually doubled once they were combined, and the effort it took to simply hold the Staff of Amenti felt as though it might shatter even my superhuman atomic structure.

Ill threw Mathu aside and summoned the staff to him, then leapt off the throne platform and used the Orme squares, which now lay flat across the void, like stepping stones.

'Let's go!' Arcturus called to me. He hauled Mathu over his shoulder and set off after the dark lord before his demons could remove the path from beneath our feet.

Ill reached the last stepping stone, launched himself into the darkness and vanished.

We'd built up too much momentum to stop now. Yelling, we launched ourselves into the abyss after him.

CHAPTER 39

THE DRACONESSES

TAMAR DEVERE — KALI

I was ecstatic to see Taejax alive and well; he was my most cherished subject, apart from my prince, for he had given his life to save my own many times.

'My queen.' He bowed low and urged his five new Dracon recruits down alongside him as I approached down the long, narrow earthen bridge that linked one side of this huge underground cavity to the other.

'My dear Taejax, please rise.'

I waited for him to comply, then wrapped my arms about him and gave him a huge squeeze.

'Your Majesty?' He wasn't sure why he was receiving so much affection. 'You honour me.'

'No, Taejax,' I pulled back to assure him sincerely, 'it is you who honour me.'

I looked at his new recruits and recognised in them the seasoned revolutionaries who had saved my life in the future. 'Loyal knights of the Anu,' I addressed them, and they seemed to like the title, 'in a far-flung future you saved my life and that of the entire Amenti team. And should we be successful on the morrow, you will have saved all life on Earth.'

My knights were a little stunned to hear this, especially since they had only recently become secret agents for the cause of the righteous.

'I promised you then that one day you would be rewarded for your bravery, and today is that day,' I told them.

Taejax was a little confused. 'Lugh said something about a salvage mission?'

I nodded. 'That is correct. Recently, I had a cathartic experience during which I recalled a secret genetic project I had been working on for Ill, just prior to the first Dracon uprising.'

'The first?' Taejax frowned. 'There was only one rebellion that I know of.'

I smiled. 'You boys get very busy in the future.' They looked doubly pleased with themselves. 'This secret project was very close to my heart and Ill knew this. When I took my own life rather than work for him any longer, he planned to destroy my greatest work. At the same time, you were taking over the ground-based EM transmitting stations . . .'

The Dracon looked delighted when I reminded them of the event. Prior to the Dracon uprising, the Nefilim had been using this technology to manipulate weather patterns and green certain areas of the Earth. But the technology had been destroyed in the uprising and it had taken until the last few hundred years to redevelop and establish it on Earth.

'What a storm that was,' commented one of the Dracon.

'We brought down three out of four of Ill's ships,' boasted another, 'including his mother ship! Unfortunately, Ill wasn't on it at the time.'

'The Nefilim all escaped on the one ship we didn't freeze out of the sky,' Taejax said, sounding disappointed. 'The three craft we damaged were all remotely operated; there was no one on board.'

'Yes, there was,' I corrected, which startled him. 'And I believe they are still trapped there. Ill and I are the only ones who knew they existed at all, so I fear that if we do not save them before we open Amenti, their souls may be lost forever.'

I looked over at Dexter and Polaris, who were already briefed and committed to my cause.

'We'll take the *Klieo*,' Polaris advised, and he switched off the cloaking device to allow the time-space vessel to become visible in its position beneath the cavern bridge.

'All right!' exclaimed one of the Dracon recruits. 'Hey, I'd have taken the side of the righteous a long time ago if I'd known they had these kind of perks.'

Taejax gave a sentimental sigh. 'I've missed this old girl ... so many grand adventures ...' He shook his head.

Polaris smiled broadly. 'Welcome back. It will be an honour to have you aboard again.'

'The pleasure is all mine, Captain.' Taejax took a running jump and landed on the long run of arced metal panels that joined to form the *Klieo*'s sail. 'It's great to be back ... Whoo-hoo!' He slid down the sail and landed firmly on both feet on the deck.

His recruits looked at each other and, with a unanimous nod, leapt after him. 'Whoo-hoo!' they all yelled.

'I don't think I've ever seen the Dracon having good, clean fun before,' Dexter said, tickled by the sight.

'It's high time,' I replied with a grin.

The Dracon were overawed by Signet Station One, which wasn't half as icy as the last time I'd seen it. There were pools of water forming throughout the outlying stalagmite forest and the sound of dripping came from all around.

'So this is one of the stations that the Nefilim have been trying to get their hands on for all eternity?' said one of the Dracon, Pax.

'Indeed,' replied Dexter. 'And they're doing a superb job of melting this place in order to get to those ships you froze.'

Taejax was the only Dracon who didn't seem overwhelmed, and I asked Dexter about it.

'Taejax is very familiar with this place,' he replied.

'Of course,' I realised, 'he'd have to be familiar with it in order to access it in the future to save us.'

'Exactly.'

'I did that?' Taejax asked, overhearing us.

Dexter winked. 'Total legend.'

'And you saved the *Klieo*,' Polaris added.

'How about that?' said Pax. 'We're all destined for greatness!'

'Well, actually we're changing that history,' Polaris said, and brought them up to speed. They appeared a little deflated.

'Now you're destined for happiness instead,' I cut in.

All the Dracon looked baffled by the concept, but were quickly distracted by the amazing structure and technology of the control centre of the Signet station, not to mention the huge ships frozen in its ice ceiling.

'*Take that*, you Nefilim pussies!' Pax stuck two fingers up at the craft in the ceiling.

Taejax pulled him up. 'Pax, a little respect, please,' and he motioned to me.

'Apologies,' said Pax. 'I'm not used to being around anyone worth respecting.'

'No harm done,' I said with a smile and looked up at the ceiling.

'So how are we going to break through to —'

Before Pax had completed his query I was burning a hole through the ice using the violet flame channelled through my palm. I aimed the beam at the lower hatch door of the mother ship — a craft Kali was very familiar with. A tunnel formed through the dripping ice and the lower hatch was exposed. I silently commanded the door to open, then willed a rope to manifest in my hands. I hung it over my shoulder then with one mighty leap launched myself headlong through the tunnel of ice and into the vessel. Once inside, I straddled my feet each side of the hatch door, secured the rope and dropped it down.

Pax was staring at me in utter amazement. 'So why did Your Majesty need us again?'

'Come on up and I'll show you,' I told him.

This hatch opened into the bowels of the ship, which was very convenient; it would have been hellish trying to access the upper floors of the frozen, blacked-out craft.

'Could anything have survived in here for all that time?' Taejax queried, as he followed the green light of my glowstick.

'There's a good chance,' I replied.

I looked around the icy wreck and remembered how it had looked when I walked its halls during my first lifetime on Earth. I began to recognise features, and suddenly I knew where I was and my pace quickened. I found the door to my lab and, using the violet flame, defrosted the ice around it. When I pushed the door open, my Dracon companions gasped to feel the blast of dry, warm air that came out. They squinted at the light within the chamber, even though their sights adjusted to such changes far more rapidly than a human's did.

I was delighted to find the incubation tanks were still running. 'The ship must have detected the active life support units and transferred all power to this lab when it was going down,' I said.

When Taejax and his recruits saw the occupants of the tanks they could barely believe their eyes. 'They're Dracon,' said Taejax, overawed.

Pax jumped backwards when he saw the large rounded breasts of the subject he was viewing. 'They're female!' he cried, and came closer to look again.

Jinx, another of Taejax's warriors, looked angry. 'The Nefilim had them all along!' he said, but Taejax placed a hand on his shoulder and the Dracon calmed.

'How many are there?' Taejax asked me, as I punched instructions into the system to shut down the incubators.

'Just these six.'

'Only six?' Taejax was immediately concerned for the female Dracon's welfare. 'They will cause a riot!'

'That's where you all come in,' I explained. 'You need to keep them safe until I open Amenti. After that, every Dracon will realise the Anu within and return to Sirius B.'

As the seals on the tanks broke and opened, the Dracon looked unnerved, which amused me.

'Relax, boys, they won't come around right away, they've been asleep for a very long time.'

Pax, the keenest, approached the now open module and gazed upon the female within in total wonder. 'She looks like an angel.'

'Funny about that,' I said. 'Her name's Angelica.'

Pax repeated the name under his breath, and nodded in approval.

'She, like all my Draconesses,' I smiled as I used my pet term for them, and the warriors grinned too, 'is completely peace-loving — opposite to the original cast of the male Dracon in every way. Ill wanted the females to be warlike too, but I was interested to see if the Dracon could have a peaceful nature.'

'And you were successful,' Taejax assumed, his eyes fixed upon Jezabel.

'Too successful,' I said, 'for almost as soon as they came out of incubation as Dracon, they began transforming into Anu, which is why they appear like angels to you,' I said to Pax, who could only grin with happiness. 'That's why Ill demanded I put them into hibernation until he'd decided what to do with them, as they were developing psychic skills and becoming too powerful. I know he planned to kill them, so your revolution most likely saved their lives.'

'All right!' Rattus, another of the Dracon warriors, cheered. 'We're knights in shining armour ...' He looked down at his tarnished uniform. 'Well, armour anyway.'

'These ladies were what led me to suspect that we, Nefilim and Dracon alike, had been lied to by the Pantheon. All of us had souls and we all belonged to the same soul group as the Anunnaki who were lost in the Tara disaster. But because the Nefilim damned the gene pool of the Anu here on Earth, where all the lost Anunnaki souls from Tara were supposed to incarnate, most were forced to enter the bodies of the lizard drones the Nefilim created to do their dirty work. Not even Ill would have realised that he was persecuting his own people.'

'Like he'd care anyway!' Rattus jeered.

Jezabel began to stir, and I moved to greet her upon her return to Earth. I held her semi-Dracon, semi-Anu face between my hands to warm and calm her. 'Jez,' I said softly.

'Mistress!' Her lizard eyes opened, then immediately closed again for the shock of the light was too great. 'Ah!' She raised a long, slender hand to cover her eyes.

'No need to rush your recovery,' I told her. 'I have some gentlemen here who have kindly offered to —'

The entire ship suddenly activated — all the lights came on and the heating too, which immediately began to defrost the interior beyond the lab.

'Oh shit,' said Pax.

'Could have been remotely activated,' Jinx theorised.

'Whether or not the Nefilim are on board, Ill is attempting to break this ship out of the ice, so we need to go.' Taejax picked up Jezabel in his arms. '*Now!*'

Each of his men grabbed an unconscious Draconess and we made haste back to the hatch. With their ladies over their shoulders, the Dracon slid down the rope into the Signet station, where Polaris, Dexter and Ereshkigal waited, urging us to hurry.

I was the last to leave, and as I lined up to jump down the hole the ship jolted and I fell to land with a thud on the cracking ice sheet.

'They're actually going to do it!' I heard Dexter cry out. 'Take cover!'

The next thing I knew I was being dragged across the frozen surface as icicles like daggers dropped from the ceiling. Huge ice chunks crashed down as the ship tore free from its ice capsule and flew off into the sky, leaving a massive hole in the ceiling of Signet Station One.

'Oh great!' grumbled Dexter as he assessed the damage.

'Now that's a security breach, if ever I saw one,' Polaris said. 'We'll get Meridan down here — she'll have it fixed in no time.' He let go of my hands and crouched next to me to see how I fared.

'Too numb to tell,' I said, peeling my battered body off the ice. He helped me to stand.

'Oh dear,' I said as I saw the extent of the damage. With a single powerful thought I raised all the fallen ice back into place. The cracks smoothed out and the ice hardened again into a solid barrier.

'Thanks awfully for that,' Dexter said, although his smile faded as he considered a bigger problem. 'What do you think Ill plans to do with the ship?'

'Attack Giza?' Polaris suggested.

'As long as he doesn't plan to flee in it,' I said, as he still had Mathu.

I turned and headed for the *Klieo*, eager to get back to Giza and help with the extraction of my prince from Ill's realm.

CHAPTER 40

PASSIVE FORCE

By the time the *Klieo* arrived back in the cavern of Mamer, all the female Dracon had awoken and were now excitedly chatting with the Dracon warriors who had saved them from damnation at the hands of Ill. They were intrigued to hear they had been sleeping for the better part of Earth's evolution and delighted to learn about some of what had transpired in the interim.

'Did you ever think of going into matchmaking?' Dexter commented to me as we watched the Dracon from the doorway to the conference room where they were gathered. 'I remember not seeing my love for hundreds of years,' he went on, 'but I cannot imagine how it would feel, never having known a woman, to suddenly be united with the female of your race after hundreds of thousands of years. It must be amazing!'

My thoughts turned to Mathu and I sighed, disappointed that we had yet to be reunited. 'Amazing, indeed.'

Dexter gave me a supportive smile.

Polaris came towards us from the control deck. 'We've got a few problems,' he said. 'Killian went after Mathu, and Arcturus and Meridan went after Killian. And since then there's been no word from anyone.'

He looked at me apologetically and my heart sank in my chest: my lover, my parents and my dearest friend were all in peril.

'I need to get back to Amenti pronto,' I said.

'Ill also has a very powerful EMP weapon aimed at Giza,' Polaris went on.

'His mother ship,' Dexter guessed and Polaris nodded. 'Anything else?' Dexter looked deflated by the new set of challenges facing us.

'Actually, yes.' Polaris drew a very deep breath. 'This cavern is crawling with Dracon.'

He kept his voice low, but the statement still drew the attention of all in the conference room.

'They don't know we're here yet,' he assured everyone, 'but it won't take long before they figure it out. One of the flying Dracon is bound to run into us before long.'

'Damn it, I should have gone directly to Giza from Dexter's station,' I said. Still, I was glad I'd stayed with my Draconesses until they felt comfortable and had been brought up to speed on the situation.

'I could take us to another Signet station,' Polaris suggested.

The problem with that idea was I wouldn't be able to get the Dracon to safety that way, as using any of the Signet stations meant taking them through the Giza complex, where they weren't permitted.

'This is the most direct route to Lugh's realm,' I said. I could see Jezabel and the others safely there, and the route would also give me fastest access to Irkalla.

Jezabel stepped forward. 'You have nothing to fear,' she said, 'we may continue this way.'

Was she naive or did she know something I didn't?

'Honestly,' I told her, 'I can't promise to get all of you to safety through a Dracon mob.'

'They will not harm us.' Jezabel sounded very confident.

'Jez, you've been in incubation all your life,' I pointed out timidly, not wanting to insult her. 'There are horrors in this world that I would rather you never know.'

'I know what you fear, Mistress,' she told me, 'but there is no need.'

'Okay,' Polaris cut in, 'we'll give this passage a whirl. If it doesn't work I can go back in time and change the outcome.'

'How will that work?' I asked, not knowing about the captain's new-found talent.

He skipped the details. 'Trust me, I have a gift.'

'And we have a plan,' Dexter decreed. 'I'll get the weapons.'

'No weapons,' Jezabel requested. 'If you do not have them, you will not use them. Pure intention is always the best weapon, then there can be no misunderstanding.'

'Do you want to tell that to our friends out there?' Dexter retorted. He was all for peace, but I believed he felt his previous experiences with the Dracon made him a greater authority on their true nature than Jezabel.

'I do indeed,' she said, and walked past us into the corridor, followed by the rest of the Dracon entourage.

'She's very wilful,' Taejax said to me on his way past, and smiled. 'I like that.'

'But is she right?' I asked.

'Let's find out.' He invited us after him, as excited as a kid on a sugar high.

The male Dracon, led by Taejax, exited the craft first, which brought a round of cheers from the Dracon mob, because they believed their comrades had captured the now decloaked vessel. When the Amenti staff emerged, however, there was confusion. The reptilian warriors began launching themselves onto the *Klieo* in preparation for an attack.

'I really don't know about this,' Dexter said, keeping an eye on the encroaching hordes as he gave Jezabel a hand out of the hatch.

The instant she emerged, a wave of hushed muttering swept through our enemy. Then the cavern fell deathly silent as the other Draconesses emerged — until one of the mob whistled and a flood of leering began.

One very large Dracon slid down the mainsail to confront our party on the deck.

'Ruffinnic,' Taejax whispered to us, 'a general.'

'What kind of treachery is this?' Ruffinnic demanded of Taejax and his men, whilst observing Jezabel closely.

'No treachery,' Taejax replied. 'These females are as real as you and I. Ill has been hiding their existence from us since our last uprising.'

This news was not well received, which was very much in our favour. But then Ruffinnic turned the tables on us again.

'So when were you planning on telling the rest of us about this?' he said to Taejax. 'Or were you going to keep this little secret all to yourselves?'

The general grabbed Jezabel's arm, and I held Taejax back from jumping to her defence at once.

Jezabel looked deep into the warrior's eyes. The angry expression on his face slowly melted into a soft smile of understanding. He went from demon to teddy bear in a matter of minutes, and allowed Jez to gently remove his hand from her arm.

'This is the beginning of the end of our struggle here on Earth,' she said, and her voice echoed around the silent cavern. 'We will no longer live in the shadows, or be forced to commit atrocities in the name of survival. The meaningful life that has eluded each of you since your cold and lonely birth into this world is now within your reach!'

The mob cheered.

'The Nefilim's rule on Earth can come to an end before midnight —' Jezabel's words were drowned out by applause and catcalls. She paused to smile and then spoke more loudly, 'And all you have to do to facilitate this process is ... *absolutely nothing.*' She let her hands drop to her sides to emphasise her point, and then laughed heartily as her adoring crowd chanted their support.

'And you were worried,' I said, looking at Dexter, who was grinning broadly.

'I never thought I'd see the day when humans and Dracon were on the same page,' he said as the crowd parted to make way for us to pass, Jezabel on General Ruffinnic's arm.

'The situation simply needed a woman's touch,' I replied. 'Now, finally, the Dracon can know what it is to have the goddess in their lives.'

Taejax overheard my comment. 'Thanks to you, I was lucky enough to know the goddess much sooner.'

The comment was so sweet and sincere that I had to give my old friend a hug. Arm in arm, we fell in behind the party making its way towards the portal to Giza.

CHAPTER 41

UNITY

MIA DEVERE — MERIDAN

Arcturus and I landed safely in the outer chamber of the Giza complex, not far behind Ill. The chamber was filled with Anu warriors and all the Amenti staff members not out on other missions. Everyone gasped to see that Ill had managed to take out Killian and now held the Staff of Amenti in his hand.

'Meridan, how could you?' Denera's eyes filled with tears. Beside her stood Ereshkigal with daggers in her eyes.

'I don't understand it either,' Arcturus said to me quietly as he set Mathu's weary form to rest on the chamber floor.

'Now, you all know I have to be nice in order to be here,' Ill said in a girlish, patronising voice. 'So don't force me to clear a path into Amenti.'

Everyone quietly stepped aside as he requested.

As I watched the dark lord enter the holy of holies, I wanted to die. But I would not doubt what my gut instinct had told me. I got to my feet and pursued Ill as fast as I could.

He didn't stop or look back as he entered the corridor containing the forty-nine symbols of Christ consciousness, which led to the passage to the Amenti complex. As Ill neared the end of the corridor, Killian's spirit swept past me and remerged with his old form. I heard my sisters gasp as they followed behind me, and knew I was not the only one to see the apparition.

At the end of the corridor, instead of turning right towards the Amenti complex, Ill turned left and headed into the labyrinth.

'Wait a second!' he protested, not understanding why he was being sidetracked. 'Where am I going?'

He began to squirm in an attempt to resist the force that had taken control of his body, and when he turned and tossed the Staff of Amenti to me, I could have died of happiness.

'What's going on?' Denera demanded.

I smiled at her. 'It's Killian.'

'What do you mean?' Ereshkigal grabbed hold of me.

'He begged us to let this happen,' I tried to explain through tears of relief and excitement. 'Killian said he could do this.'

'Do what?' Denera appealed.

'I don't really know,' I confessed, as much in the dark as everyone else.

'Where could he be taking him?' Ereshkigal asked, unsure if she should be grieving or thrilled to know that Killian was still with us, in spirit at least.

We all gasped again as we saw Ill approach the Hall of Records.

'You can fuck me gently with a chainsaw, but I'm not going in there,' he yelled, and grabbed the doorframe in an attempt to resist entering. But he was no match for Killian and his body was forced inside.

I was shocked when I entered the outer chamber at Giza to find my prince lying on the floor, whilst a crowd of our people cluttered up the route to Amenti.

'Mathu!' I dropped down beside him, my heart breaking as I saw that he looked half dead.

'I'll find out what's going on,' Polaris said, and headed into the crowd, Dexter hot on his heels.

'I'm going to get these ladies to Murias,' Taejax said quietly. He was the only Dracon at this stage evolved enough to withstand passage through Giza's portholes.

'All my best thoughts are with you in your quest this day, Mistress,' Jezabel said, and blew me a kiss.

My other Draconesses did the same as they followed her and Taejax through the porthole to the Otherworld.

'I will see you all on Sirius B, in the not too distant past,' I vowed to them, grateful for their faith in me and their encouragement.

Mathu stirred as I cushioned his head in my lap and kissed his forehead gently. 'Kali?'

'Yes, my love,' I replied, my cheek against his forehead. I was so thankful to be able to hold him in my arms and feel him close.

'You must stop Ill,' he said, and pointed towards the crowd of Anu warriors. 'He has the Staff of Amenti.'

The news passed through me like a shockwave. As I looked towards the entrance to the Giza complex, Polaris came running out to give me a report.

'Ill and Ki are fighting it out in the Hall of Records. It seems Killian finally figured out how to get both sides of his brain to operate at once — he's channelling both the Sanat Kumara and Ill at the same time. Ki is trying to convince Ill that his dream of ruling over a shadow universe will never be. They keep running all the possible scenarios through the Hall of Records, but no matter how many times it predicts Ill's destruction, Ill won't consider the path of light.'

'The Staff of Amenti, however, is back in our possession,' said Solarian, who'd followed her partner.

My father and Levi put in an appearance soon after, looking as if they were on a mission.

'What are you lot up to?' I asked.

'We want to do something nasty to Ill's ship,' my father said. 'But I need to know what the control deck looks like, in order to teleport us there.'

He crouched beside me and I smiled, happy to assist. He placed a hand over my third-eye area and closed his eyes to receive the image of the control deck as Kali remembered it.

'Thank you, sweetheart,' he said, and kissed my forehead. 'We'll be back.'

As my father joined hands with his teammates, he warned Polaris, 'Now be sure to let me do the driving or we'll end up somewhere in World War II.'

Solarian and Levi looked amused, but Polaris wasn't so happy. They vanished before I could catch his retort.

'I fear Ill will never choose the path of light by choice,' Mathu said, sitting up and gazing into my eyes. 'He's never loved anything.'

He leaned close to kiss me, but I jumped up. 'Sud!' I cried. 'We have to go.'

Mathu suppressed his disappointment and dragged his long-suffering body to its feet to accompany me on one last tiny quest.

CHAPTER 42

MICRO-DEATH

ASHLEE GRANVILLE-DEVERE — SOLARIAN

On the control deck of Ill's mother ship we were confronted by half a dozen Nefilim warriors, Erragal and Namtar among them. Although I had never seen the latter in his Nefilim form, I'd heard talk of his golden cape. All three of us began firing liquid-light darts and, with no Dracon to protect them, the Nefilim were sitting ducks.

'Where's Polaris?' I called out to the others. It seemed we had lost my partner en route.

'I told him to let me drive,' Arcturus said drily as he took out the last of the Nefilim.

Erragal was not among the bodies now purging themselves around us, and Namtar had pulled his famous disappearing trick the instant he saw our liquid-light guns.

'Erragal must have escaped into the ship,' Arcturus cursed, needing another man to back him up. 'Where's Polaris?'

'You don't know where he is?' I said, horrified. 'I thought you and he must have planned his absence.'

'I'm going after Erragal,' Levi said, without waiting for our agreement.

Arcturus and I were torn. If Namtar was with Erragal, it would be two against one. If Arcturus left me here, I might have to face Namtar alone.

'Go after him,' I urged Arcturus.

'I won't leave you,' he vowed, as he had many times before. He had spent so many years in my service, protecting me from danger, that he seemed to forget I was now very capable of taking care of myself.

'I don't carry the ringstone any more, so let that damn curse go, can't you?' I said, and pushed him towards the door where he finally relented. 'And don't worry about me,' I added. 'I believe Polaris isn't here because he knew something bad was going to happen —'

And then I felt the spike against my neck and every hair on my body stood on end.

The look on Arcturus's face was one of utter bewilderment and horror.

A shock like a bomb blast shot through my entire being and all my lives flashed before my eyes as the Orme spike pierced my skin and shot into my brain . . .

'Let that damn curse go, can't you?' I said, and pushed Arcturus towards the door where he finally relented. 'And don't worry about me,' I added. 'I believe Polaris isn't here because he knew something bad was going to happen —'

I felt an eerie sense of déjà vu, and knew it meant something, but by the time I remembered, I felt the spike against my neck. *Too late.*

The look of horror on Arcturus's face turned to relief at the soft sound of a light-bullet being fired. I felt the spike scrape a large bloody scratch down my back. *Polaris*. My eyes filled with tears of love.

My foe dropped to the floor and my husband moved into his place behind me, where he kissed my bloodied wound. 'I've always got your back, my love,' he told me with heartfelt relief, and I turned and kissed him passionately.

A whistle distracted us from our momentary indulgence.

'Erragal,' Arcturus prompted, and we stepped over the convulsing Nefilim bodies to venture into the ship after Levi.

When we found him, he had Erragal backed up in a small storage room and was aiming a light-gun at him. Rather than force the disgruntled warrior to convert, however, Levi was giving him the option to come willingly. We sat quietly out of the Nefilim's view, not wanting to disturb their discourse.

'Why won't you give up this dead-end path of darkness and step into your true destiny in the light?' Levi asked.

'You angels are all fucking pussies!' the warrior spat back.

Levi was amused. 'How do you figure that, when we're the ones winning this war?'

Erragal growled, resistant to the truth. 'Wait a second … I remember you,' he said, suddenly intrigued. 'You're the timewalker that blew up Montauk!'

'Aye, that was me,' Levi said, rather proud of the fact.

'How did you do it?' It sounded as if the demon respected the feat.

'I can summon and emit EM pulses,' Levi said, trying not to sound like he was boasting.

'Fuck me!' Erragal forced a laugh and then looked regretful. 'I had true power once.'

'You still have true power,' Levi enlightened him, 'it's just been dammed.'

Erragal slid down the wall and we heard his large form land with a thud on the floor. He invited Levi to shoot him. 'Come on then, let's get it over with.'

'Do you repent of your sins on Earth?' Levi asked before he would fire.

'I don't know.' Erragal sounded agitated, as all Nefilim were when confronted with emotional issues. 'I've had a gutful of living this way — is that the same thing?'

'I guess it's a start.' Levi was looking for any sign of remorse and thought he'd try the oldest trick in psychiatry. 'What about your mother, don't you miss her?'

'No! Treacherous snake!' Erragal spat back.

Levi wasn't convinced. 'That's Ill talking. Try digging a little deeper.'

'I can't,' Erragal protested.

'Why not?'

'Because ... because ...' Erragal strained to get his words out, then choked on his remorse and broke down into tears. 'Because it *hurts*!' he wailed loudly.

'That'll do it.' And Levi pulled the trigger to speed the Nefilim through the painful purge.

'Well done,' I said to Levi as Erragal went into spasm.

He acknowledged my praise with a nod. 'I believe our work here is done,' he said.

Arcturus raised both brows in anticipation. 'Only one more to go.'

CHAPTER 43

MACRO-LIFE

MIA DEVERE — MERIDAN

In the Hall of Records, Killian stood perfectly still inside the light-tube of the control panel. The celestial bodies of En Ki and the Lord of the Underworld were visible on the liquid-light walls on opposing sides of the rounded chamber as they continued their debate, whilst their futuristic scenarios played out in full technicolour on the ceiling. It was like watching the gods play chess with history.

Ill didn't seem any closer to conceding the truth about his dark plans for the universe; if anything he was becoming more determined and more irate.

'You can take your god consciousness and shove it up your arse, brother!' he yelled. 'I will defeat your precious cosmic light if it is the last thing I do!'

'To do so is to defeat your own creation,' En Ki advised, his voice filled with compassion as always, 'and therefore —'

'— it *will be* the last thing you do,' finished a female voice.

We all looked around to see Sud, better known as Ninlil, walk into the middle of the chamber to confront the huge image of Ill being projected, via Killian, onto its wall.

At first Ill looked stunned, then his smug, careless demeanour returned. 'Nice try, Kali, you deceitful moll!' he said, then stumbled on his words as Kali stepped into the chamber and gave him a wave. Mathu, who was with her, waved also.

'Ninlil?' Ill sounded a little panicked.

She nodded and smiled warmly at him. 'It is I. I have come to take you home.'

For a split second I could have sworn I saw joy in Ill's face, but aeons of scepticism were not so easily overcome.

'You abandoned me!' he told her, letting his hatred fly. 'You're a contemptuous whore and I loathe you!'

'Only because I bring out the good in you,' she replied. 'You know that I know the truth about you, and if you cut me off then you'll never have to deal with that part of you that wishes only to be trusted, to be recognised and rewarded as your half-brother was.' She motioned to En Ki. 'You need not fear your father's wrath —'

'I fear nothing!' Ill roared.

Ninlil shook her head. 'If that were true, you would be on the side of the righteous, who truly fear nothing. The truth is, Ill, you fear *everything*, to the extent that you have become fear itself. There is a big difference between inciting fear in others and being fearless.'

'*You left me!*' Ill squeezed out the angry words through gritted teeth.

'Yes, I left,' Ninlil defended herself, 'so that I might find a way to free you. I sought out Lamhfada, and he sent me through the Hall of Amorea, home, to Sirius B!'

'Bullshit,' Ill said. 'The Hall of Amorea is a myth.'

'No, it isn't. And you know it must be true if I can be standing here before you. Queen Kali of the Anunnaki, who rules the race that the Anu will evolve into in the next harmonic universe, arranged with the staff of Amenti to build the Hall of Amorea so that we all — Nefilim, Dracon and Anu — might return to our soul group and no longer suffer for our selfish, impetuous mistakes of the past.'

Ill's sons entered the room, barely recognisable in their glistening Anu forms.

'No,' whimpered Ill, 'not my sons!'

'Mother!' Erragal led the charge to hold her, and within seconds the goddess was lost amid the throng of her four huge Anu sons.

'My boys!' She squeezed each one and kissed them in turn. 'How I have *missed* you. I've been so worried … I thought I was going to lose you all forever!'

'It seems like forever,' Erragal said, hugging her again.

Ill cried out in pain and vanished from the screen, and inside the light-tube Killian began convulsing.

'Help him!' Ereshkigal called out.

'I can't do anything from out here,' Denera told her. 'There's no external override.'

On the screen above us, Ill's dark life and deeds began flashing across the screen. So horrific were the memory transferences that we all turned away to protect ourselves from their potentially harmful frequencies.

Inside the light-tube Killian had changed to Ill's demon form and was spewing black muck everywhere; thankfully the light-tube was containing the mess and holding him in an upright position. It took some time for the beautiful Anu spirit to emerge. When it did, Ill's defunct demon body did not vanish from existence as was usual after the conversion process; he simply floated apart from it. And as he looked at his family breathlessly awaiting him, he smiled for joy.

'I am ready to go home now,' he said.

The light-tube deactivated, spilling black bile all over the floor, and Ill's demon body fell to the ground. His Anu self floated forward to embrace his family.

It was heart-warming to watch. Spying my daughter, I moved to embrace her from behind; I had been so very worried about her.

'I couldn't have done it without you all,' Tamar said, rubbing my arms. 'I can't believe that every last Anu soul has now been found and spared from damnation.'

'I couldn't be more proud,' I said, and kissed her cheek. She was far too tall now for me to kiss her forehead or her crown as I used to.

Amidst all the merriment and excitement I heard someone crying and sought the source. It was Ereshkigal. She'd sunk to a seat by the wall to stare at the dead demon. I knelt before her to explain why I had broken the promise she did not remember I had made her.

'I'm so sorry,' I said. 'Killian told me it was his destiny, and I believe it was.'

'I know,' Ereshkigal said. 'I knew from the moment he touched me that day in Central Park that he was no ordinary human being.'

Then her eyes opened wide in horror as the demon body started to twitch. She pointed, unable to voice her fear that perhaps the demon part of Ill lived on.

Half the people in the room pulled out weapons and took aim at the creature, myself included; but upon activating my third-eye vision I was relieved to see Killian's spirit powering the corpse.

'Help!' he cried, struggling to raise himself from the bile-soaked platform.

Ereshkigal recognised his voice and was with him in a heartbeat. 'Killian! What's happened to you?'

He sat upright, still in the demon form, and scratched his head. 'I'm not too sure.'

He looked up at En Ki's image on the screen, which was smiling down on the happy scene. 'Would my lord care to fill us in?' Killian invited.

'How inspiring it is to me that someone so *ill*-treated as a lad,' En Ki punned, 'could become so selfless that he would give his life for the good of humanity.'

Everyone in the room sighed, but Killian waved the praise aside. 'I had many good teachers,' he said, indicating everyone present. 'But, my lord, you have not answered my question.'

'Well,' said En Ki, 'such a selfless act deserves rewarding, and as you are accomplished enough to shape-shift, I figured this body would serve you as well as any? It's certainly better than no body at all, in which case your soul mind will just have to reincarnate on Tara. Of course, if you choose to keep this body, it will technically make you one of the Anu.'

'No shit!' Killian gasped.

'No, I am not kidding,' the lord said with a smile.

Killian was a little confused. 'But won't that mess with soul groups and evolution and the rest?'

'In the great scheme of things, as long as every soul gets back to source and none are left behind, that's all that counts. We are all one after all,' En Ki was happy to say. 'Unconditional love is the most powerful force; it truly can rearrange universes.'

Those of us who were aware that this was Killian's greatest wish come true let loose squeals of delight, and cheered the couple who were now gazing adorably into each other's eyes.

'Would you please get in touch with your shape-shifting ability?' Ereshkigal requested, not too enamoured by Killian's demon appearance. 'I would really love to kiss you right now.'

'I'm so excited I don't know if I can focus!'

Still, with such incentive, Killian morphed into his own form; only now his features were slightly more Anu-like. His eyes and hair were still dark, however, and his face and most of his body were still covered in bile.

Ereshkigal wiped around his mouth with her sleeve then smiled. 'Better,' she said, and they finally kissed to the cheers of all present.

'Who is ready to go home?' Denera called out, and everyone confirmed their eagerness.

'The Kali rift is over! Blessed be all in the Ranna.'

CHAPTER 44

END OF THE RIFT

It was difficult parting from our Anu allies; we had all endured so much together. But as the end of the SAC alignment was only hours away, we knew our goodbyes would have to be short and sweet.

Arcturus and I were in the process of bidding Killian and Ereshkigal farewell when Polaris interrupted.

'I've just had a thought,' he said. 'I seem to recall that I promised to take you back in time, Meridan, so you could deliver the manuscript of this tale to your publishers.'

I laughed. 'I've been a little too busy of late to do any writing.'

But Killian cut in. 'It's already been done,' he said.

When I looked baffled, he explained further. 'I stole the copy of *The Black Madonna* that Erragal took from your Signet station when I was still undercover with Montauk, and I delivered it to your publisher last week. I thought you'd be pleased,' he said uncertainly, as my baffled expression hadn't altered. 'After all that work you did on it back in the fifth century, I —'

'So that's how you knew about the ambush Kali had set for Lugh,' Arcturus said in an accusing tone. 'And you told Mathu about it in advance, which was why you felt responsible for his actions.'

'You planned to ambush me, Your Highness?' Lugh turned to Tamar with a stunned expression.

She raised both brows in an apologetic gesture. 'Not if I could help it — and I did.'

'Jolly good show,' he said, relieved.

'So you did read the book,' I said to Killian, and smiled at having my suspicions confirmed.

'You knew about this?' Arcturus asked.

'I only really cottoned on today,' I confessed, but it did explain why Killian had always admired me so greatly, way beyond the bond we'd formed over the twenty years we were forced to spend together. I grinned as I recalled how he'd watched me working away on the manuscript and never once hinted at the fact that he was carrying the completed version around in his backpack.

Mathu stepped between Arcturus and the accused. 'Actually, I tricked Killian into revealing what he knew,' he said.

'That's how you knew the year the Amenti team had been sent to.' Kali was having a few realisations of her own about Killian.

'So if you did read the book, you already knew how all this was going to unfold.' Polaris joined the interrogation.

'Which means you weren't being selfless at all,' Arcturus figured; and Killian ducked before Arcturus could reach around Mathu to take a swing at him.

'Read that part too!' Killian called back as he stepped swiftly into the porthole to Lugh's realm and the Hall of Amorea. 'See you in the next universe!'

'Not if we see you first,' Arcturus yelled back, and waved him away.

'Ah well, the point is that the book does get published and I'm saved a trip,' Polaris concluded.

'And not only did we manage to get that little SOB away from my daughter,' Arcturus said, finally finding the silver lining to his Killian cloud, 'but he's expelled from the human race.'

'We rock,' Polaris said, giving Arcturus a high-five.

'Finally, something they agree on,' Solarian said, to the amusement of all.

Tamar Devere — KALI

With everyone evacuated from the Giza complex back to their proper realms within the planetary scheme — humans on the Earth plane, Anu in the astral — the way it was always meant to be, it was time to finally bring the Sphere of Amenti down to Earth. This event would mark the successful conclusion to the project we'd been working on for hundreds of thousands of years — give or take a few centuries we may have skipped here and there. It also meant our time as the staff of Amenti was almost over. The Dragon Queens were more than a little sentimental about this fact.

'Why are you crying?' Dexter asked, as everyone stood in front of the central porthole in the Halls of Amenti chamber. The sphere hovered in the Arc porthole passage, waiting to be safely deposited into the Earth grid. 'We're all going to the *same place*, and a much better place at that!' he added, puzzled.

'We know,' Talori said, 'but we won't be working together any more.'

'You can all do lunch,' Arcturus suggested, 'but not if you don't stop blubbering and form a circle around these two lovely people' — he motioned to Mathu and me, who were already standing atop the indigo porthole, bathed by the light of the sphere above — 'who are waiting to take us home.'

Denera broke up the Dragon Queens' huddle and the six women joined Mathu and me on top of the porthole. 'Dragon hug,' Denera said, and the next thing I knew I was being cuddled from all sides.

'You two have shown us that the Anunnaki are a truly miraculous race of people,' Denera said, speaking for her sisters too. 'You have met your many challenges with grace and honour, and we look forward to a continuing harmonious relationship between our peoples once we return home.'

'As do I,' I told them all honestly. 'I truly feel that you are my sisters.' My emotion began to choke me, and suddenly I was in tears too.

'What is it with women?' Dexter was baffled. 'No matter what race they come from, they can't speak to each other without tears!'

'Can't we just say our goodbyes once we get there?' Polaris said. 'I mean, it's only the end of existence as we know it?' He stuck out his bottom lip and shrugged.

'Just tell them there's a big shopping sale on Tara,' Zalman commented. 'That ought to get them moving.'

The men found this frightfully amusing.

'Very well,' Denera barked, and waved everyone back to their places. 'We're going.'

'Just awaiting your cue, Maestro,' Dexter said to me once they were all in place.

I turned to face my prince. There was so much I wanted to say to him, but I would save most of it for another time, when the entire evolution of the five universes wasn't at stake.

'You exceeded my expectations on this quest, my love,' I told him.

'I will always,' he replied, and placed his hand below my own on the Staff of Amenti, and kissed me briefly.

The Rainbow Round Table began to chant their cosmic scale of sonic frequency.

'Want to take me home?' Mathu queried.

'I surely do,' I replied with zeal, and together we raised the Staff of Power and directed its energy towards the Arc porthole passage.

The porthole shattered and silver light-liquid splattered down upon us like a stardust shower and the huge white, blue-green, violet sphere of light descended.

In the glare of all the energy and light I could barely see Mathu, but I clung to him as I felt the exhilaration of being engulfed by the sphere completely.

I was filled by my experiences here on Earth, filled with hope, knowledge and emotions, which I would take with me to the next universe. Sometimes we need to go backwards in order to go forwards, and I hoped that my new take on creation would make all the difference to ensuring that none of my people would ever again be responsible for a disaster of this magnitude.

My consciousness turned liquid violet and plummeted into the core of the Earth, joining with thirteen other violet streams of light to form a burning star. I shattered into a zillion sparkling pieces that scattered to the four cardinal points of the universe, then I was back into my singular being once more.

I was conscious of being unconscious as I stirred from my sedation. I remembered what I had programmed myself to remember upon awakening.

I am victorious!

I am Kali, Queen of the Anunnaki.

And I am home.

MERIDAN

I awoke in a light-rimmed pod, like those we'd slumbered in beneath the Blue Flame on Earth. I sat up to find that many of the team had awoken before me, and were now chatting amongst themselves.

Arcturus stuck his head into my pod to greet me. 'Way to go, partner,' he said and kissed me. 'We pulled it off!'

'Tara's morphogenetic blueprint is whole again!' Denera said excitedly. 'It's as if the entire Kali rift never happened!'

'Well, that was what we were aiming for,' I said with a wink.

'But seriously,' Denera looked around at us all, 'how many of you actually thought we were ever going to see this room again?'

'I knew we would,' said Thana, ever confident.

I climbed out of my pod and made my way to a window. Our complex was located in Tara's most beautiful Otherworldly region and gave a splendid view over our city. I could see my house from here, with its large garden all around it, and I could hardly wait to get home; it had been one hell of a day at the office.

I wondered if I'd included this part of our tale in the final book of my trilogy, soon to be published back on Earth. I smiled to think that if I had, Killian would have read it and would have known that all would go well with us beyond our parting. I wished I had a book to read that would tell me how his new life, as one of the Anu, turned out.

I thought about what reality back on Earth would be like now.

The sphere had been set in place at the Earth's core, hence the Earth's frequency will have risen to a point where it is back in line with the Ranna time flow. The people of surface Earth will wake in a reality much like that here on Tara. That will be the only reality they remembered: a peaceful, happy, bright and prosperous life, with no horror, no fear, no hate, pain, greed, lust, betrayal — those outdated modes of behaviour will have ceased to exist along with the concept of hell and all its demons.

The people of the Earth, one by one, will awaken to their true selves, like the staff of Amenti, they will feel the pull toward Giza, where they will seek to walk the Halls of Amenti home to Tara, and they will find the doorway home wide open.

GLOSSARY

Ankh — an object or image resembling a cross but with a loop instead of the top arm; used in Ancient Egypt as a symbol of life.

Blue Flame of Amenti — (keylontic dictionary) constitutes Earth's portion of Tara's morphogenetic field stored in the Sphere of Amenti. Visually, this standing wave pattern looks like an electric blue flame with a pale shade of green, about 10 centimetres in height. The souls on Earth can ascend out of this universe through the fifth dimension — blue flame — and continue their evolution through Tara.

Cathars — a religious order that was declared heretical by the Roman Catholic Church, which began the Albigensian Crusade to wipe the Cathars out. The name Cathari means 'pure' in Greek, and it was rumoured that the Cathars were hiding many of the secret treasures pertaining to the Grail legend.

Density — (esoteric) the eighth sphere — the lowest rate of vibration of atoms. Inhabited by souls too new in the evolutionary scale to understand physical life whilst in a physical body; they desire to take an unrighteous path and create their own hell plane to inhabit.

Etheric Double — (esoteric) an invisible electromagnetic field that interpenetrates everything in the universe, from the atom to the great central sun. This field absorbs emanations from everything, forming a pattern for its future existence.

Etheric World — (esoteric) the overall picture of invisible space. The atmosphere that contains all seven levels of energies (seven planes) with their functions and life forms. Also known as the Otherworld.

Eye of Ra — (esoteric) the point where all this universe's ley lines converge.

Fire-Stone — (Grail lore) the organic equivalent of ORME, given to select kings prior to general human use of ORME; essentially, the menstrual blood of the goddesses of the Anunnaki.

Grail (Messianic) bloodline — (Grail lore) in medieval times, this was the line of Messianic descent that was defined by the French word Sangreal, meaning 'royal blood'. This was the bloodline of Judah — the kingly line of David, which progressed through Jesus and his heirs.

Halls of Amenti — (keylontic dictionary) the dimensional passageways one must pass through in order to ascend out of Earth's time matrix, through the blue flame held within the Sphere of Amenti, and home to Tara.

Kali rift — (esoteric) a fracture of 'true time' in our reality; the gap that exists between Earth's true time flow in the Ranna time wave and where the planet currently sits in the continuum.

Light-body or **aura** — (esoteric) an invisible, electromagnetic energy field completely surrounding an entity, which acts as a blueprint for that entity, adjusting the vibrational frequency of the atomic structure in accord to that entity's level of awareness.

Light centres or **chakra system** — (esoteric) an invisible, inter-dimensional system comprising seven concentrated centres of energy located in the light-body between the base of the spine and the tip of the head. These concentrated energy centres are called the root, spleen, solar plexus, heart, throat, third eye and crown chakras, and each is perceived clairvoyantly as a colourful wheel or flower. Light centres convert cosmic energy into body energy and vice versa.

Morphogenetic field — (keylontic dictionary) all matter and forms of consciousness, including planetary bodies and human bodies, are manifested through a morphogenetic (form-holding) imprint, which is composed of specific patterns of frequency. The morphogenetic imprint holds the instructions and design for form-building. The Earth's morphogenetic imprint is held within the blue flame of Amenti. Forms manifest and evolve as patterns of frequency are drawn from a unified field of energy within which the morphogenetic field is placed. This drawing-in to the morphogenetic field of frequency patterns progressively expands and creates an evolution of form through the fifteen-dimensional universe.

Nature elemental or **Nature spirit** — (esoteric/fairy lore) etheric world beings akin to the four elements of nature: Earth, Air, Fire and Water. Ranging from a very high to a low level of intelligence, they keep themselves occupied with the development of the natural world and are, understandably, wary of human beings.

ORME — (alchemy) also known as Ormus, the Philosopher's Stone, the Elixir of Life, the White Powder of Gold, Ma-na or Manna. Is also an acronym for 'Orbitally Rearranged Monatomic Elements' — see David Hudson's research (internet). In Grail lore, ORME is the Highward Fire-Stone, which is also related to Star-Fire, or the Fire-Stone — see Laurence Gardner's books (Bibliography, p. 401).

Prima matra — ancient alchemical term that means prime unviolated first matter.

Ranna time flow — (esoteric) the true flow of time in this universe.

Rainbow Round Table (RRT) — (keylontic dictionary) formed by a group of angelic humans who are commissioned to run the Rainbow Ray or Kundaray (primal sound current from beyond the fifteen-dimensional time matrix) into Earth's planetary shield during an SAC alignment (natural stargate opening cycle). Running the Rainbow Ray during an SAC alignment enables the planet to regain its natural electromagnetic balance to avert pole shift.

Seven Bodies of Man — (esoteric) the Physical body, Astral body, Mental body, Causal body, the Spirit, Monadic essence and God consciousness.

Seven (higher) Planes of Existence — (esoteric) Physical, Astral, Mental, Causal, Spiritual, Monadic and God consciousness.

Signet Grid — (keylontic dictionary) the organic interdimensional core energy systems of a planet, along with the inherent portals, vortexes, ley lines and stargates by which a planet is connected to many other interstellar, interdimensional, space–time systems.

Sphere of Amenti — (keylontic dictionary) morphogenetic field of the human race, created to give the souls fragmented from Tara and lost in the Earth's dimensional fields the pattern of the twelve-strand DNA imprint necessary to re-evolve into their original Turaneusiam form. The Sphere of Amenti serves as a host matrix (surrogate morphogenetic field) through which the lost souls of Tara can evolve and return home.

Star-Fire — (Grail lore) an umbrella term for the Highward Fire-Stone (ORME) and its organic equivalent, Fire-Stone.

Tara — (keylontic dictionary) planet counterpart of Earth located in the harmonic universe above our own.

Telos Aarkhara — the capstone over the universal tear which exposes the Eye of Ra.

Time codes — (keylontic dictionary) also known as 'Veca codes', these are the mathematical programs of manifestation that clear all unnatural seals from the bodies of humans.

Universal tear — a tear that exposes the Eye of Ra, the central node where all energy ley lines of this universe converge.

BIBLIOGRAPHY

Baigent, Michael; Leigh, Richard & Lincoln, Henry, *The Holy Blood and the Holy Grail*, Arrow Books, UK, 1996.

Begich, Nick, *Angels Don't Play this HAARP — Advances in Tesla Technology*, Earthpulse Press, USA, 1995.

Deane, Ashayana, *Voyagers — the Secrets of Amenti*, Wildflower Press, USA, 2002.

Gardner, Laurence, *Lost Secrets of the Sacred Ark*, HarperCollins, London, 2003.

—— *Bloodline of the Holy Grail*, Multimedia Quest International, UK, 2001.

McTaggart, Lynne, *The Intention Experiment*, Harper Element, London, 2007.

INTERNET REFERENCES

The Twelve Pyramids of Thoth:
   www.crystalinks.com/12pyrthothpreface.html

The Keylontic Dictionary:
   www.keylonticdictionary.org

'Hell of Eternal Sleep and Darkness', quoted by H.P. Blavatsky from the work of Carl Richard Lepsius, Egyptologist:
   www.blavatsky.net/magazine/theosophy/ww/
   additional/ListOfCollatedArticles/Inventions
   Christendom.html

www.ingramcontent.com/pod-product-compliance
Lightning Source LLC
Chambersburg PA
CBHW060810120726
47909CB00006B/1857